DU

The
rea

About the Authors

...ol Marinelli recently filled in a form asking for
... job title. Thrilled to be able to put down her answer,
...e put writer. Then it asked what Carol did for
...axation and she put down the truth – writing. The
...ird question asked for her hobbies. Well, not wanting
...look obsessed she crossed the fingers on her hand
...answered swimming but, given that the chlorine in
...ool does terrible things to her highlights – I'm
...you can guess the real answer.

...er McKenzie happily lives in the Canadian
P...ies with her husband and young daughter. She was
...luced to Mills & Boon in Junior High School but
had a...lready decided on a career in medicine. After
com...leting her medical training, she went back to
Mills & Boon and entered So You Think You Can
Write 2012. As the second-place winner her dreams
...e ...ulfilled and she now has it all, two careers and a
... she is very proud of.

...h a background of working in medical laboratories
... ove of the romance genre it's no surprise that
...Mackay writes medical romance stories. She
... e her first story at age eight and hasn't stopped
... . She lives in New Zealand's Marlborough Sounds
... e she indulges her passions for cycling, walking
...kayaking. When she isn't writing she also loves
...ng and entertaining guests with sumptuous meals
...nclude locally caught fish.

4

D0608621

A&E Docs

A&E Docs:
His Emergency
Secret

CAROL MARINELLI

AMBER MCKENZIE

SUE MACKAY

MILLS & BOON

All rights reserved including the right of reproduction in whole or in part in any form. This edition is published by arrangement with Harlequin Books S.A.

This is a work of fiction. Names, characters, places, locations and incidents are purely fictional and bear no relationship to any real life individuals, living or dead, or to any actual places, business establishments, locations, events or incidents. Any resemblance is entirely coincidental.

This book is sold subject to the condition that it shall not, by way of trade or otherwise, be lent, resold, hired out or otherwise circulated without the prior consent of the publisher in any form of binding or cover other than that in which it is published and without a similar condition including this condition being imposed on the subsequent purchaser.

® and TM are trademarks owned and used by the trademark owner and/or its licensee. Trademarks marked with ® are registered with the United Kingdom Patent Office and/or the Office for Harmonisation in the Internal Market and in other countries.

First Published in Great Britain 2021
By Mills & Boon, an imprint of HarperCollins*Publishers* Ltd
1 London Bridge Street, London, SE1 9GF

www.harpercollins.co.uk

HarperCollins*Publishers*
1st Floor, Watermarque Building,
Ringsend Road, Dublin 4, Ireland

A&E DOCS: HIS EMERGENCY SECRET © 2021 Harlequin Books S.A.

The Socialite's Secret © 2016 Carol Marinelli
The Surgeon's Baby Secret © 2015 Amber Whitford-McKenzie
A December to Remember © 2015 Sue MacKay

ISBN: 978-0-263-30025-3

MIX
Paper from
responsible sources
FSC™ C007454

This book is produced from independently certified FSC™ paper to ensure responsible forest management.

For more information visit: www.harpercollins.co.uk/green

Printed and bound in Spain
by CPI, Barcelona

THE SOCIALITE'S SECRET

CAROL MARINELLI

DUDLEY LIBRARIES	
000003093955	
Askews & Holts	15-Jul-2021
AF ROM	£7.99
2DU	

CHAPTER ONE

No news wasn't always good news.

It was just the tiniest of diversions from Luke Edwards's usual morning routine but, having poured a glass of grapefruit juice, Luke turned the television on and listened to the news as he got ready for work.

It was just after 5:00 a.m. on Monday.

There was the usual stuff that should make mankind weep, yet it was immediately followed by the news that Anya's Saturday night performance at the O2, the last in her sell-out world tour, had been amazing and she would be heading back to the States today. The reporter moved to the next piece of celebrity gossip—a football star's wife who was rumoured to have had buttock implants.

He changed channels and found that it was just more of the same.

Luke flicked the television off and, though he still had half an hour to kill, he was restless so he decided to head into work. He went upstairs and selected a tie, which he put in his jacket pocket. As he came back down he grabbed his keys and glanced in the mirror, wondering if he really ought to shave.

No.

His straight dark hair needed a cut too but that could wait for next week.

It was still dark outside as his garage door opened and Luke headed out into a cold and wet November morning. He drove through the practically deserted, sleepy, leafy village, where he lived, towards the heart of London. He had recently been promoted to Consultant in a busy accident and emergency department at a major teaching hospital.

People sometimes said that he was crazy to live so far out but he also had a flat at the hospital for the times when he was on call or held back at work.

Luke liked it that where he lived was between Oxford, where his family were, and London, where he worked. The very distinct separation between his work and home life suited him well. The village was friendly but not overly so. He had been living there for close to a year now and was getting to know the locals at his own pace. Luke knew that, despite what others might think, he had made the right choice.

Or not.

It all depended on today.

It was a long, slow drive but he was more than used to it. Often he listened to music or a lecture he had heard about, but this morning he turned on the radio.

He needed to know if there was any news.

For the last four days Luke had been on edge and hypervigilant while doing all he could not to show it.

The traffic was terrible, he was told.

Thanks for that, Luke thought as he glanced at the time.

There was a huge snarl-up on the M25.

Luke was in the middle of it.

Finally, just before 7:00 a.m., the sun was coming up, the hospital was in sight and a new day had dawned.

He drove towards the underground car park, where he had a spot reserved, and was just about to flick off the radio, as reception was disappearing, when there was a break in a song.

'Unconfirmed reports are starting to come in that Anya...' the newsreader said, and Luke sat, blocking the traffic and listening to the brief report, before he drove into the basement. He parked but, instead of heading straight into work, Luke sat for an essential moment to collect himself.

His instincts had been right.

Today was the day, just not for the reasons he'd hoped.

Luke got out of the car and went up the elevator and made his way through the hospital.

Security guards were starting to race towards the accident and emergency entrance but Luke refused to rush. The only concession that his skills might be immediately required was that, as he walked along the corridor, he put on his tie.

'Morning,' Luke said to Geoff, one of the security guards, as he raced past him.

Not 'good morning'.

They weren't any more.

'Have you heard who's coming in?' Geoff answered by way of response, though he did slow down and fall into step with Luke.

'I have.' Luke nodded. 'It just came on the news. Can you call for backup and start setting up the security screens? How long until she gets here?'

'Ten minutes.'

Luke nodded his thanks and walked into the department.

'Thank God you're here early.' Paul, his registrar, came straight over.

Yes, Paul was very glad that his boss was here. Luke Edwards epitomised the calm that the department would be needing today—Luke never got ruffled and simply dealt with what was. 'Anya is on her way in,' Paul explained. 'She's in full cardiac arrest. The place is going to blow.'

Luke disagreed with Paul's assessment. Yes, drama was about to hit but the place would not blow.

Not while he was in charge.

'What do we know?' Luke asked as they walked into the resuscitation area where the nursing staff were already setting up.

'Just what I told you,' Paul answered.

'Have you called for an anaesthetist?'

'The first on call is in Theatre. The second on is David. He's coming just as soon as he can but he's with a sick child on PICU,' Paul answered, as Luke started checking and labelling the drugs that Barbara, a very experienced senior nurse, was pulling up. 'I was about to see if Switch could do a ring around...'

'It's fine.' Luke shook his head before Paul could suggest otherwise. 'We'll more than manage until David gets here.'

'Do you even know who Anya is?' Paul checked, because Luke looked completely unruffled by the news of who was on their way into the department and the fact that the anaesthetist wasn't there.

'Yes.'

Oh, Luke knew.

Better than most.

Anya had been famous for forty of her fifty years of life and would, after today, be even more so.

Especially if she died.

'You'd better let the director of nursing know,' Luke said.

Paul gave a worried nod. 'I already have.'

'Good. I'll go and make sure the screens are up outside.'

As he went to go out, Heather, the director of nursing, was running down the corridor towards him.

'Do we know what she's taken?' was the first thing that Heather asked when she caught up with Luke.

'We don't know that she's taken anything.' Luke's response was tart and Heather flushed as Luke continued to speak. 'Let's just make sure that the screens are up and no cameras can get a shot of her.'

The media were already starting to gather. He could hear the sound of a helicopter hovering overhead but thankfully the ambulance bay was covered.

Right now it was about affording Anya some privacy.

Whether she would want it or not.

Paul came outside and briefed them further. 'Ambulance Control has just called. It's an unspecified drug overdose...'

'Well, that was never going to happen.' Heather's response was sarcastic.

'If you want to help—' Luke had heard enough innuendo and the patient hadn't even arrived. He turned and faced Heather and made his feelings on the subject very clear. '—then cast judgement aside. If you can't manage that—leave.'

He meant it.

Luke had long ago learnt not to judge and to keep his own feelings very much in check, and it would take everything he had in him to maintain that today.

'I was just—' Heather attempted.

'Well, please don't,' Luke interrupted.

Heather looked over at Paul and they shared a glance. Luke had worked at the Royal for just over two years now. He was never the sunniest of people but he rarely snapped and his mood seemed particularly dark today.

The ambulance arrived and as Luke opened the doors

he saw that Anya was being given cardiac massage by a paramedic and that a sun-tanned man was shouting orders in a strong Californian accent. He informed Luke, only when asked, that his name was Vince and that he was Anya's private physician.

Luke already knew.

And he hated that man more than anyone could possibly imagine.

'What's the story?' Luke asked him, as the paramedics worked skilfully on the unconscious woman while they wheeled her in and Luke pulled on a gown and gloves.

'She must have taken some sleeping tablets,' Vince said.

It was a vague response but, with time of the essence, for now Luke ignored him. Instead, he listened to Albert, one of the paramedics, who relayed far more information than the private physician seemed willing to give.

'She was found unconscious by her daughter at six a.m.,' Albert said, as they moved Anya over to the resuscitation bed.

'Semiconscious,' Vince corrected.

'The daughter, Scarlet, is hysterical,' Albert said. 'It was hard to get any information out of her. Apparently Anya was given an opiate reversal but then vomited and went into respiratory and then cardiac arrest.'

'What has she taken?' Luke asked Vince, but any clear information remained unforthcoming.

'We're not sure.'

Albert gave Luke a wide-eyed look, which he took as meaning that the paramedics had had as much trouble extracting details.

Paul took over the cardiac massage as Albert relayed the rest of what he knew. 'There were no bottles or syringes and she had been intubated before we arrived.'

Oh, so they'd had a little tidy up, Luke thought, and he

looked over to Vince as he listened to Anya's chest. 'What medication is she on?' Luke asked.

Vince gave Luke a short list that consisted of antianxiety medications and some light sleeping tablets.

'So why are there no bottles or packets to be found?' Luke pushed.

'I give Anya her medication,' Vince answered coolly. 'I also have her on a strict regime of nutrients...'

'We'll get to them later,' Luke snapped, as he started delivering vital drugs that might reverse anything Anya could have taken. 'Any opiates?'

'Only when her back injury is exacerbated.'

It would take pliers to extract any useful information from him, Luke was sure. 'Get a toxicology screen,' Luke said to Barbara, who was pulling blood as he listened to Anya's chest.

'Her chest sounds terrible.' Luke was very concerned that the tube might be somewhat blocked. 'I want to replace the tube.' He wasn't happy that the right size had been inserted or that, given Anya had vomited, the tube was clear, so he decided to reintubate her.

'Watch the vocal cords!' Vince warned.

The billion-dollar vocal cords!

Luke did not look up but Heather swallowed as she watched Luke's jaw clamp down as he was delivered an unnecessary order.

Luke did not pause in his treatment plan, he just carried on with the procedure and then secured the tube, but he offered two words in response to a very unwelcome guest in his resuscitation room.

'Get out.'

The celebrity physician did not.

Luke repeated his command, but added a couple of expletives this time, and everyone startled because Luke rarely showed emotion. He never really swore or raised his voice. He didn't need to assert himself angrily. He just chose to now.

No one present could even guess at Luke's true loathing for this man.

Luke listened to Anya's chest again and, happy that the tube was in the correct position and that her air entry was better, he pulled off his stethoscope and asked Vince to repeat whatever it was he had just mumbled.

'I'm not leaving Anya,' he said.

'Oh, but you are,' Luke responded. 'Unless you can tell me, right now, exactly what Anya has taken, and why it took so long for you to get her here, you are to leave my area now.'

Foolishly he did not.

David, the anaesthetist, arrived then and took over the care of Anya's airway. Luke called for more anti-opiate and inserted that into Anya's IV line and then awaited its effect.

'Can we can call for Security?' Luke said.

'Security?' Heather checked, knowing that they were busy outside and wondering why they might be needed in here.

'I want him out,' Luke responded, and as he did so he briefly turned to the unhelpful and unwelcome visitor in his emergency room who was diverting his concentration yet still refused to move.

Luke kicked at a silver metal trolley. It clattered into a wall and the implication was clear—Anya's private physician would be leaving by any method that Luke saw fit to use.

Paul's assessment had been right after all—the place was about to blow, only not for the reasons anyone had been expecting!

What the hell was going on with Luke?

'You make me sick!' Luke shouted, and, wisely perhaps, Vince chose to leave.

Everyone glanced at each other but Luke made no comment. He simply did all he could to focus his attention fully on Anya, who was on the very brink of death.

It was a long and lengthy resuscitation.

The drugs were reversed and her heart started beating but she had aspirated too. It was more than an hour before they had Anya under control. Then it was another fifteen minutes before she started to rouse and began gagging at the tube.

'It's okay, Anya,' Luke said, and then blew out a long breath because for a while there he hadn't thought that it would be. 'You're in hospital.'

Anya was fighting and confused, which were good signs—all her limbs were moving and her terrified eyes briefly met Luke's before David put Anya into an induced coma.

'I want her up on ICU,' David said, and looked over at Heather, who was just returning from a lengthy phone call with Admin. 'Can you call them and ask how long until they're ready and then arrange to clear the corridor?'

Heather nodded. 'I'll get onto it now. Luke, will you speak to the press?'

Luke hated how normal policy seemed to have been thrown out of the window. He was certain, quite certain, without checking, that the department would have seen several drug overdoses overnight. He just loathed how everything had changed simply because of who Anya was.

'I'll speak with Anya's family first,' Luke said in response to her request.

Even Heather had the grace to blush. 'I've put them all in the staffroom.'

'Who?' Luke checked.

'Her manager, the vocal coach, her doctor, her body-guards. Scarlet's in there too.'

'Scarlet's her daughter,' Paul added, because unless it was rugby or medicine, no doubt Luke wouldn't have a clue who she was.

'Okay, I'll speak with her now,' Luke said, as he binned his gloves and gown.

He walked out and although the department had grown busy in the hour or so that he had been working on Anya, all eyes were on Luke as he walked past. Everyone wanted to know what was going on and how Anya was.

Luke didn't stop to enlighten them.

Instead, he walked around to the staffroom and saw that Anya's huge entourage were all there on their phones. As Luke went to go in and speak with the daughter, one of them had the nerve to ask for his ID.

'It's your ID that I need here,' Luke responded, and with that line he warned them how any dealings with him would be.

'How is she?' a frantic woman asked.

'We've been waiting for more than an hour for an up-date,' another person said.

Luke just ignored them and walked into the very full staffroom. 'I'm Luke Edwards, I've been taking care of Anya. I'd like to speak with the immediate family.'

And there, in the midst of it all, she was.

Scarlet.

Still beautiful, Luke thought.

She was sitting, trembling, with her head in her hands. Even her cloud of black ringlets was shaking as her knees bobbed up and down. She seemed oblivious to her sur-roundings but then she suddenly looked up and her already pale face bleached further in recognition.

'Luke?'

'Luke Edwards,' he said, doing all he could to keep them anonymous, to not let everyone present know the agony this was. 'I've been treating your mother. Are there any other relatives?' Luke checked.

Scarlet shook her head and opened her mouth to speak but no words came out so she shook her head again but then managed two words. 'Just me.'

'Then I'd like to speak to you alone.'

'We need to know what's going on,' a woman said. 'I'm Sonia, Anya's manager.'

'I'm speaking now with her next of kin.'

Luke's stance was not one to be argued with. It wasn't just that he was tall and broad—after all, there were far more burly bodyguards than he. More it was his implacable expression and cool disdain that had the manager step back and the path cleared for him to leave.

Scarlet was seriously shaken; her legs felt as if they were made only of liquid.

She was about to be told that her mother was dead, Scarlet was quite sure of that.

'This way,' Luke said, and down another corridor they went, and when she needed him to take her arm, instead he walked on briskly.

Luke opened the door to his office and she could see his grim expression.

She was dead, Scarlet was sure.

Luke was here.

Scarlet was very used to feeling conflicted but it was immeasurable now.

She stepped into his office and the first thing that hit her was that it was so quiet.

So completely quiet and calm that after the chaos of that morning the stillness hit her like a wall.

For the first time since she had found her mother, there was, apart from her own rapid breathing, the sound of silence.

Stepping into her mother's hotel bedroom had been something she would never forget.

'Mom?'

She had crept in quietly and seen her mother lying in her bed, face down.

'Mom?'

She had tried to turn her over but Scarlet was of slight build and she hadn't been able to.

She had screamed for help and after a couple of moments a shocked butler had arrived.

From then on it had been chaos. Hotel staff had started to appear. Vince, her mother's physician, had arrived dressed, wearing trousers and a shirt, and Scarlet couldn't understand why he had taken a moment to get dressed.

She had stood back, sobbing, watching chaos unfold, and finally had picked up her cell phone and dialled the UK emergency number.

She shouldn't have rung it, she had been told.

There was already a private ambulance on the way.

Scarlet opened her mouth to ask the inevitable question—'Is she…?' But her throat had been dry and scratched from screaming and no words had come out.

Luke could see her confusion and anguish.

'Take a seat,' Luke said, and he turned the engaged light on above his door that warned people he was not to be disturbed.

Still Scarlet stood there.

She was going to hell for all that she'd done, Scarlet knew. In fact, she was going to hell twice because, instead of asking how her mother was, instead of begging him to tell her the news, she blurted out what was now at the forefront on her mind.

'I'm sorry…'

'Just take a seat,' Luke said.

She went to take a seat, but the chair seemed a very long way off and Luke's hand went on her shoulder to guide her towards his desk, but then he changed his mind.

His hand slid from the nearest shoulder to the farthest arm and he turned her into him. Luke's arms wrapped around her and he pulled her right into his chest and he held her so tightly that for a moment nothing remained but them.

There was the scent she had missed, the body she had craved and the understanding that Scarlet had never known till him.

It was an embrace she had been absolutely sure she would never, ever feel again.

'I'm so, so sorry,' Scarlet wept.

'It's okay, Scarlet.' That lovely deep, calm voice hushed her. Luke's chest was such a wonderful place to lean. To feel his breath on her cheek and his hand stroke the back of her hair was a solace Scarlet had never thought she might know again. 'I think she's going to be okay,' Luke said.

He was talking about her mother.

While she was sobbing for them, for their beautiful, painful past and all that they had lost.

CHAPTER TWO

CALM, PROFESSIONAL AND DETACHED.

That was how Luke had intended to be with Scarlet as he updated her on her mother's condition. The entire walk from the staffroom, right the way to his office, Luke had been telling himself that he was more than capable of being just that.

Luke had learnt a long time ago to push emotions aside—with patients and their relatives, with his own relatives too.

He had just never quite mastered objectivity when Scarlet was around.

It was something he knew he had better start working on.

Just not today.

Now the very last thing Scarlet needed was calm, professional and detached, but more to the point the impact of actually seeing her again meant that Luke could be none of those things.

Just yet.

As he pulled her into his arms, the embrace was as necessary for Luke as it was for Scarlet. There was so much anger and pain inside both of them. Their traumatic past was perhaps insurmountable but he dealt with the present now.

She was here. Not by the method he would have pre-ferred—Luke had hoped Scarlet would contact him be-fore she'd left for America today—but, yes, she was here, and so Luke held her in his arms and smelt again her hair, fighting not to kiss her salty tears away.

How messed up was that? Luke thought to himself.

He'd had a few months to prepare for the possibility of seeing her again. Since Anya's UK tour had been an-nounced late last year, the thought that their paths might cross had been constantly on his mind. Since Anya and her entourage had touched down in England he had been wondering if Scarlet would call, if their history meant as much to Scarlet as it did to him. And, since seven this morning, when the news had broken that Anya was in an ambulance, being blue-lighted towards the Royal, he had dealt with the knowledge that he'd face Scarlet today.

Every preconceived response to her that he'd had crum-bled.

Yes, there was an awful lot that needed to be discussed but Luke knew that Anya wasn't the only vulnerable, crit-ical casualty that had been bought into his department today. Scarlet was another and, at a very personal level, he cared about her so very much more. Luke didn't want to let her go because, when he did so, back to her world Scarlet would return and so Luke took another moment to hold her.

Scarlet held him too.

She didn't just lean on him, she had slipped her hands into his jacket and wrapped her arms around his solid waist and just breathed in the delicious scent of him. Tangy, musky, male. It was a scent that she had yearned for and never forgotten and one that had been made familiar again now.

How could it be that he felt the same to her hands?

After all that had gone on, how, on this day, could Luke's arms be the ones that were holding her up?

As she was in England she had hoped that they might meet, but she had expected harsh, accusing words to be hurled at her. Words that he had every right to deliver, but instead of that he held her and made the horrible world go away for a moment.

As she had sat in the staffroom, waiting for news, Scarlet had blocked out the sounds of the people around her. Vince had been trying to speak with her, telling her what to say, insisting that her version of events wasn't quite correct. Her mother's manager, Sonia, had demanded to know where Scarlet had got to yesterday and why she hadn't been there to see her mother go on stage.

None of them knew about the row she'd had with her mother in the early hours and Scarlet had sat revisiting that as she'd done the best to block everyone else out.

And then in the midst of the madness she had heard the calm deepness of Luke's voice.

Her frantic heart seemed to have stopped beating for a second.

Oh, she had known that Luke was a doctor but she hadn't known he worked in London. When they had met he had been here for an interview but had been unsure if he'd take the job.

It had never entered her head that Luke might be here in the hospital and be the doctor fighting to save her mother's life.

Yet he was.

When Scarlet had looked up she had felt the very same jolt that had run through her the night he had walked into the club and their worlds had changed for ever.

He'd been wearing a suit that night and he was wearing one now.

It was the little things she noticed and remembered.

The other stuff was way too insurmountable for now.

And, as Luke had the first night they had met, when she clung to him he pulled back.

'Tell me.' Scarlet held him tighter, not ready to let go. If the news was bad, and given the morning's events she expected it to be, it was like this she wanted to hear it.

'She's doing better.'

Scarlet held her breath.

'Your mother briefly opened her eyes,' Luke explained. 'And she was fighting the breathing tube. That's good. For now she's been placed in an induced coma.'

'Is she going to die?' Scarlet asked.

'I don't think so but she came very close.'

'I know,' Scarlet said. 'I called an ambulance.'

'That's good.'

'You told me the number.'

She took a splinter of their time and they both examined it for a moment. A little shard of conversation that, had it come from another, would have been swept away, never to be examined again, but both now recalled that tiny memory with absolute clarity.

Scarlet looked up but not into his eyes.

Never again, Scarlet knew, would she be able to meet that deep, chocolate-brown gaze. There was just too much regret and shame for that. Instead, she looked at that lovely unshaven jaw and the deep red of his mouth that had once delivered paradise.

And Luke, feeling her eyes scan his mouth, despite the circumstance of this meeting, wanted to lower his to meet hers.

It was as simple as that.

But those days were gone and so, because he had to,

he let her go. 'Have a seat,' Luke said in his best doctor's voice.

Calm, professional, detached.

If he was going to do this properly then he could be no other way.

Scarlet remained standing as Luke took off his jacket, threw it onto a chair and then went around the desk and sat down, waiting for her to do the same.

'Tell me what happened.' Luke kicked the interview off.

'I told you,' Scarlet said. 'I called an ambulance. Vince had called for backup but they were taking for ever and—'

'Scarlet,' Luke interrupted, 'we need to start at the beginning. Before this morning when did you last see your mother?'

'Last night,' Scarlet said, and watched as Luke picked up a pen and jotted something down. 'There was a party to celebrate the end of her tour and...' Scarlet shrugged but didn't finish.

'And how was she?' Luke asked.

'I didn't make it to the party,' Scarlet said. 'I saw her back at the hotel.'

'What time was that?'

'About midnight.'

'And how was she?'

'Tired.'

'Who was the last person to see her?'

'Me,' Scarlet said. 'I think.'

'Around midnight?'

'Around one. Can you stop taking notes?' Scarlet asked. 'I can't talk to you when you're writing things down.'

'Scarlet, these details are important,' Luke said, but he did put down his pen.

He'd been using it as a distraction.

Not a word of this conversation would he ever forget.

'You found her?' Luke checked, and Scarlet gave a tense nod.

'What time was that?'

'Just before six.'

'Were the two of you sharing a room?'

'No.' Scarlet frowned.

'Were you staying in the same suite?'

'No.'

'So why were you in your mother's room at six a.m.?'

'I just went in to check on her.'

'Why?' Luke persisted.

'Because I was worried about her.'

'Why?' Luke pushed, but Scarlet did not elaborate. 'Come on, Scarlet. I can't help if you don't tell me.'

'You can't help me.'

'I'm talking about your mother!' Luke's voice rose, just a fraction. It had to if they were going to stay on track. That little pull back served to remind not just Scarlet but himself that this was work. He watched her eyes fill with tears at the slight reprimand but he had to push through. When no further information was forthcoming he chose to be direct.

'Has your mother been depressed lately?'

'No, no.' Scarlet shook her head. 'It's nothing like that. She just took too much.'

'How, when her physician keeps her pills?'

'She keeps some on her,' Scarlet said.

Luke honestly didn't know if Scarlet was covering up for her mother or simply had no idea how serious the problem was.

'Scarlet.' Luke tried to meet her gaze. 'Why did you go in to check on your mum? I'm not going to write anything down. Just tell me.'

'I was worried.'

'More so than usual?' Luke checked, and she nodded. 'I need to know why.'

'We had a row.'

'About?'

'Please don't ask, Dr Edwards.' It was Scarlet now who rebuked him, just a little but enough for him to get what she meant—if there were lines that could not be crossed, if he wanted to keep this professional, then, right now, the answer to that question could not be discussed. 'We had an argument.'

'Okay.'

'They want my mother to be moved to another hospital,' Scarlet said.

Luke had guessed that they might. 'Well, as of now, the only place your mother is being moved to is Intensive Care. Here.'

'They think that she needs to be somewhere more used to dealing with...' Scarlet stopped what she had about been to say. Luke loathed the word 'celebrity'.

'She's in the best place and in no condition to be moved,' Luke said. 'As her daughter, you get to make that call.'

'I don't think so.' Scarlet gave a worried shake of her head.

'I know so,' Luke responded.

'But she has Vince. He deals with all that type of thing.'

'Yes, well, Vince is going to be a bit busy for the foreseeable future. After I've spoken with you, believe me, I'm going to be speaking with him and getting a far more accurate history than the one he gave me earlier. I may also be speaking with the police so trust me when I say that I'll back your call if you want your mother kept here.'

'Luke, please, don't bring the police into this.' Scarlet started to cry and not very quietly.

He sat and watched unmoved. *Those* tears did not move

him and certainly he would not be swayed by hype and celebrity status when he made his decisions.

He just needed more facts but few were forthcoming.

His pager trilled and Luke checked it. Seeing that it was Heather, he made a phone call and rolled his eyes as she told him that the press were becoming more insistent. 'Just say no comment,' Luke responded tartly. 'How hard is it to say that?' He let out a tense breath. 'Unless there is a change in Anya's condition, or you need me for another patient, you're not to disturb me. I'm speaking with a relative now.'

He looked over and saw that in the couple of minutes it had taken to speak with Heather, Scarlet had stopped crying long enough to take out her phone. Luke watched with mounting irritation. They were speaking about her mother's near-death and yet Scarlet was checking the news reports and quickly scrolling through social media!

'What are you doing?' Luke asked.

'It's everywhere!' Scarlet said, but then she really started to cry and they weren't false tears this time. As she put the phone down on the desk, Luke saw an image, and he reached over and picked it up.

The photo that he saw was of Scarlet. She was dressed in a pair of red pyjamas and her feet were bare as she stood on the street beside the ambulance that her mother was being loaded into. Two bodyguards were restraining her from climbing in. Her black hair was a mop of wild curls, her usually pale skin was red from crying and there was a look of sheer terror on her face.

Luke looked up from Scarlet's phone and at the woman who now sat on the other side of his desk—she was the perfectly groomed star in crisis now! Scarlet was wearing tight leather leggings and a tight black top. Over that there was a large silver leather jacket that looked as if it had been thrown on at the last minute. Her black curls were now perfectly tousled. Luke knew, though, from very personal experience, that the photo was a truer portrayal of Scarlet's morning locks.

He pulled away from that memory; instead, he looked back at the phone and the image that had been captured by the press.

It showed a rare moment of reality in a very unrealistic world and this would be the photo that would dominate, Luke was sure.

Scarlet looking less than perfect.

It was the Scarlet he far preferred.

'It's going to be worse than ever now...' Scarlet could not stop crying. Yes, she was terrified for her mother, but she'd had so much hanging on today, so many plans in place. There wasn't a hope of escaping from the press now and, Scarlet knew, now more than ever her mother needed her to be near.

'They're going to make my life hell.'

'Don't feed them, then,' Luke said. Her head was in her hands, her fingers were scrunched in her hair, but she lifted her face and gave him a scornful look as he continued to speak. 'You don't have to respond to the press, just focus on your mother and yourself.'

'What would you know?' Scarlet scoffed.

'Oh, I know,' Luke said. It was pointless to sit and pretend that he could take a comprehensive history from Scarlet and leave the personal aside. 'David, the anaesthetist, will take a more thorough history once your mother has been transferred to ICU.' He handed her back her phone, and as he did so he looked at Scarlet's slender, manicured fingers and remembered hands that were as smooth as a kitten's paws.

No, anger at her spoiled, pampered life didn't now gnaw

at him; instead, it saddened him that that funny, adventurous mind had been locked away for so long.

Yes, the world was supposedly Scarlet's oyster, but Luke knew that since the day she had been born, her life had been magnified by a lens.

'You're handing me over.'

'I'm handing your mother's care over,' Luke said. 'That's normal policy when a patient is moved. I need to get back out there, Scarlet. I have patients to see.'

'What about me?'

Typical, Luke thought, but, though he tried to generate anger, though he did his best to remind himself of the spoiled princess Scarlet was and the absolute diva she could be, he failed.

'What about us?' Scarlet said.

'There's no us,' Luke lied.

He *was* angry now as he recalled all she had done, but instead of standing to leave, he sat there.

And so did she.

They sat in the silence of his office and as the world carried on outside, both went back to a time when things had seemed so different.

When hope had arrived in both their hearts.

Even if it killed them to do so, both remembered.

CHAPTER THREE

'I'VE GOT A HEADACHE.' Anya closed her eyes and massaged her temples. 'I'm going to have to go back to the hotel and see Vince.'

Scarlet frowned in concern and said all the right things to her mother but inside all she felt was relief. All she wanted was to get away from the noise of the club and close her eyes and go to sleep. It was after midnight and Scarlet had been up since seven. She had given interviews and done a shoot at London Bridge, and the rest of the day had been spent propping up her mother, telling her that she could get through the show.

'We'll get you back,' Scarlet said, and nodded to her mother's bodyguard.

'What would I do without you?' Anya asked, and Scarlet felt the knot that had lived in her chest for more than ten years now tighten a notch. And then, because she was Anya, her mother changed her mind about leaving when a young guy came over to their table with a drink and told her how amazing her performance that night had been. 'I'll just stay for one more,' Anya said.

Scarlet moved over to give the young man room to sit next to her mother but then she stood up.

She saw the exit door and started to walk towards it.

Scarlet wanted fresh air.

More than that she wanted to run.

'Hey, Scarlet...' A hand was on her arm and she turned to the face of one of her mother's bodyguards. 'I'll send Troy outside with you.'

She didn't want Troy.

Scarlet didn't want anyone, she just wanted one day, one moment to be allowed out in the world alone.

She didn't want to be here in this club.

And then she looked up and saw a man who looked as if he didn't want to be there either.

He was taller than most and, unlike others, he was wearing a suit. His hair was dark and as he raked a hand through it, it remained a touch messy. He was smart yet dishevelled, present but unimpressed, and there was something about him that had Scarlet intrigued.

'We're all leaving now,' Troy suddenly informed her. 'Your mother's ready to go.'

'I'm going to stay on.'

It was a rare request.

An almost unheard-of request, in fact, and one that did not go down too well.

'I don't need your drama now, Scarlet,' Anya hissed. 'I've been working all night and my head feels as if it's about to explode...'

'Vince will sort that out,' Scarlet said.

It ended the conversation.

Scarlet had known that it would.

Anya could stay and argue for ten minutes with her daughter or head back to Vince.

How Scarlet loathed that man!

And so, as her mother left the building, Scarlet remained.

Not alone, of course. Three bodyguards were still present, but for now at least she was minus Mom.

* * *

Luke, even before they had arrived in the club, had had enough.

It was his younger brother's twenty-first birthday and Luke really didn't want to be here, but up until now he'd had no real choice.

He'd bought dinner and had done the cursory pub crawl and had decided that he'd buy the first round here, stay for a little while and then disappear.

It wasn't a regular nightclub. Marcus's friend knew someone and had got the boisterous group into some very trendy, exclusive basement club.

At twenty-eight years of age, Luke felt old.

He'd always been more sensible than most, more responsible than most, and this place tested that to the limit. Everyone was off their heads and the noise just ate at him.

Still, it was his brother's birthday so Luke had gone along with things till now. He had been down from Oxford anyway, in London for an interview, and at lunchtime he had checked into a hotel.

His interview had been scheduled for four, which should have given him plenty of time to meet his brother and friend at seven. Except the interview had gone really well. So well that not only had he been extensively shown through the department, his potential new boss had asked him to wait back so he could meet a colleague who was in Theatre. Of course Luke had agreed. This was a senior registrar's position with a junior consultancy at the end of it at the London Royal after all.

There hadn't been time to get back to the hotel to change so he had arrived half an hour late to meet his brother and had felt on the back foot ever since. Especially here. Everyone was dressed in far less than a suit and drinking bright cocktails and were high, if not on life, just high.

'Nice to be single again?' Marcus asked, as Luke bought the drinks.

'Actually, yes,' Luke said, though it was wasted here, he thought privately.

Marcus and his friends hit the dance floor, which actually consisted of most of the place, and Luke took a mouthful of his drink and leant against the bar. He thought about the day he'd just had.

He wanted the job.

And that might prove to be a problem.

It hadn't been a difficult break up.

A painless procedure might be the best description.

Luke and Angie had been going out for a couple of years and had been about to move in together. Angie worked at the Royal and had told him about the upcoming role. But within a week of Luke applying, their relationship had finally come undone.

There just wasn't the passion that should be there for a couple who were about to move in together. Added to that was Luke's refusal to, as Angie had annoying called it, share.

Only she hadn't been talking about the last chocolate in the box!

'I know they're in there,' Angie would insist.

'What?'

'Feelings.' Angie's response had been exasperated. 'Emotions.'

'We don't all have to ride the roller-coaster, Angie. Just because I don't…' Luke had bitten his tongue rather than admit that yes, there were hurts there. Angie would have far preferred that he rise to the bait but Luke had consistently refused to. 'I guess I'm not messed up enough for a psychiatrist to date,' Luke had offered.

Luke was straight down the line and dealt with whatever life threw in his path without fuss. He saw no need for prolonged discussions as to how the past had shaped today. He had no wish to come home from a long and difficult shift and to share how it felt to lose a four-year-old or whatever agony the day had brought.

How he felt was his concern, he'd regularly told Angie. Amicably they had agreed that opposites did not attract and had quietly broken up.

There was one thing, though, that Luke needed to do if he was going to take the role at the Royal—and Luke was quite sure that it was his. He needed to be sure, very sure that Angie would be okay having her ex working at the same hospital.

Luke took out his phone and saw that there was a text from Angie, asking how the interview had gone, but it had been sent three hours ago.

It was far too late to return it now.

They were exes after all.

'Well?'

A soft voice, very close to his ear, pulled Luke out of vague introspection and he caught the heady scent of summer in the midst of winter as he turned to the sight of a young woman.

She had long, black, curly hair and huge navy eyes. Her face was incredibly pale but those large navy eyes were alert and smiling. Her lips were full and she wore dark red lipstick and not much else, just a tiny, tight, red dress.

'Well, what?' Luke asked in answer.

'Aren't you going to buy me a drink?'

'No.' Luke shook his head and tried to gauge her age. He was usually good at it but with her it was an impossible ask. Her skin was smoother than any he had seen and yet her eyes were wise. 'Are you even old enough to be drinking?' Luke checked.

'Of course I am.' Scarlet frowned at the odd question. Everyone knew how old she was. A fortnight ago she had turned twenty-three and it had been a massive affair—Anya had bought her onto the stage in Paris and had sung 'Happy Birthday' to her.

'I'm Lucy,' Scarlet said, just to test his reaction and to make sure that this man really didn't know who she was.

'I'm Luke,' he responded. 'And I'm still not going to buy you a drink.' Luke had already decided that he was going back to the hotel.

The bartender came over. 'Hey, Scarlet! Can I get you anything?'

'Scarlet?' Luke frowned and watched a small blush spread up her neck and to her cheeks. 'What happened to Lucy?'

'That's my…' Scarlet didn't finish her sentence. She didn't want to tell him about the alias that she used for hotel bookings and things. There was a heady thrill that Luke really had no idea who she was.

It was unbelievably refreshing.

'I'll have a glass of champagne,' Scarlet said to the bartender, instead of answering Luke's question.

'Put it on mine,' Luke said.

'Thank you.'

'No problem.' Luke drained the last of his drink and turned to sort out the bill. 'See you,' he said.

'You're going?'

'God, yes,' Luke said as the music pumped.

'That's not very polite! You can't buy me a drink and then leave me alone.'

Luke conceded with a small smile. 'Drink fast, then.'

She took the tiniest sip.

'And another,' Luke said, and then he started to laugh

as Lucy—or was it Scarlet?— pretended to take another tiny sip.

They were, it would seem, going to be here for a very long time.

'Who are you here with?' she asked.

'My brother and his friends,' Luke said. 'It's his twenty-first.'

'And why are you wearing a suit?' Scarlet asked, and then took another tiny, tiny sip.

'To ensure that I look like an idiot.'

'Well, I think that you look…' She looked over his body and then up to his pale face. He was clean-shaven but there was a dark shadow on his jaw, and his eyes, when she met them properly, were a very deep shade of brown. So dark that she couldn't see his pupils. 'I think you're beautiful.'

'I don't think I've been called that before,' Luke said, smiling at her Californian accent. 'Though I'm quite sure you've been called it many times.'

Now Luke looked at her properly, in the way he'd been wanting to since he had turned around to her voice.

That dress showed far too much pale skin and the red stilettos she wore looked a little too big for her skinny legs. His eyes moved to her face and she was way more than beautiful. That fluffy hair was at odds with her delicate features and her mouth was very full and red.

A little too full perhaps, Luke thought, wondering if she'd had fillers, but, God, she was surely way too young for all that sort of thing.

He wanted to kiss her.

That in itself was a rather bizarre thought for Luke. While he thought about sex for approximately fifty seconds of every minute, to want to reach over and kiss, simply kiss, a virtual stranger was something he had never felt before.

Luke checked his memory.

Nope, not once.

This was a new feeling indeed.

'So who are you here with?' he asked.

'A few people.' Scarlet shrugged but was saved from elaborating when one of his brother's friends came over. 'Hey, Doc,' he said, and picked up his drink, but then he gave Luke an odd, wide-eyed look and left them.

'Doc?' Scarlet checked.

'Doctor,' Luke said, and told her a little bit more about himself. 'Which is the reason I'm wearing a suit. I was at an interview earlier.'

'Doctor?' Scarlet frowned and, almost imperceptibly, screwed up her nose, as if he had said that he specialised in sewerage and had just dropped in for a drink midshift.

'What do you do?' Luke asked her.

Scarlet looked at the bubbles fizzing up in her still very full glass and it matched her veins because they seemed to be fizzing too with excitement. Luke really didn't know who she was, which meant she could be anything she wanted to be.

Anything at all.

But what?

And then she remembered her time in Africa and a very far-off dream, and she brought it to life but with a little slant.

'I'm an OB nurse,' Scarlet said.

'Where?' Luke asked, rather hoping it was at the Royal! 'Back in LA.'

'You'd be called a midwife here.'

'A midwife?' Scarlet checked. 'A what?'

'A midwife,' Luke said, and watched as she started to laugh.

He didn't get a chance to play with words and, oh, they

wanted to play with words, but his brother was heading over and Luke had no intention of sticking around for a drunken conversation with him. 'I've got to go,' Luke said, and as he moved to his full height from leaning against the bar he realised just how tiny she was because even though she was wearing stilettos he towered over her.

'So,' she asked, 'where are you moving on to?'

'Moving on?' Luke checked, and then realised that she was asking him what club he was off to next. 'Bed.'

'Yum!'

She took another sip of her drink and met his eyes. Luke had never met anyone like her in his life and, leaving aside the flirty offer, he actually wanted to know her some more, but well away from this dive.

'I meant...' Luke said, then gave up trying to correct her. 'Can I *Call the Midwife*?'

Clearly she didn't get his little joke because she frowned at his invitation to get in touch.

'It doesn't matter,' Luke said. She was from another part of the globe after all and, yes, he was going back to the hotel, he decided, as an overly friendly Marcus joined them.

'Can I have a word?' Marcus asked, slapping him on the shoulder.

'Sure,' Luke agreed, knowing full well that Marcus would be asking for some more money to be put behind the bar before Luke left. Marcus was studying medicine and was perpetually broke. It annoyed Luke. He himself had worked all his way through med school but he chose to say nothing tonight as it was Marcus's birthday.

But as they pulled away from Scarlet, and Luke went to get out his wallet, it turned out that Marcus had other things on his mind.

'How did you two get talking?' Marcus asked.

'What?' Luke frowned. 'Do you know her?' he checked, wondering if she was cutting one of Marcus's friend's lunch. 'Is she here with—'

'You don't know who she is, do you?' Marcus grinned. 'Do you ever come out from behind that stethoscope of yours? That's Scarlet.'

'I know that.'

'Anya's daughter.'

'Oh!'

Yes, Luke did know who Anya was. After all, she had been famous before he'd even been born, not that Luke paid much attention to such things, but he had seen Anya and her entourage leave the club. Now that he thought about it, he did recall that Anya had a daughter who went everywhere with her.

He glanced over and saw that Scarlet was trying to get away from some loud, obnoxious guy who was trying to drag her over to dance, and two burly men were moving in.

She was here with her own bodyguards, Luke realised, not the vague friends that she had alluded to. Now he understood Marcus's friend's odd look when he had come over.

Scarlet was a star.

'She seems nice.' Luke shrugged. She had. 'Anyway, I'm heading off. I'll go and settle the bar tab and put some more behind. You have a good night.'

As Luke went to the bar Scarlet came over.

'Dance?' she offered.

'I'm just leaving.'

'Just once dance,' Scarlet persisted, but he shook his head.

'Not with your bodyguards watching.'

'You know who I am now, don't you?'

'Not really,' Luke said. 'I know two of your names and

I've heard of your mother. You're not a midwife, I take it?' She shook her head and Luke glanced down at the bill he had just been given. 'There should be champagne on there,' he said to the bartender.

'It's on the house,' the bartender said, and smiled at Scarlet as it dawned on Luke that she didn't have to pay.

Scarlet's presence in the club was more than enough.

It annoyed Luke.

Not that Scarlet had been playing him along—now that he understood why, it didn't annoy him in the least—but he wanted to have bought her that drink.

'Add it,' Luke said, and handed back the bill.

'Sure.' The bartender shrugged.

He turned around and Scarlet was still there. 'Take me with you,' she said. Her arms went around his neck and Luke went to peel them off but then he heard the desperation in her voice. 'Please.' Scarlet closed her eyes. She was so tired of the noise and no doubt drama would await her when she returned to the hotel. It felt like for ever that she had been trying to escape. She looked up at Luke and he was so calm and so slightly bored with it all, as was she, and she gazed into his beautiful eyes. 'I'll make it worth your while.'

'You don't need to offer sex, Scarlet.'

'I want to spend some time with you.'

'Why don't you ask me to take you for dinner?'

'Dinner?' Scarlet frowned.

'Well, it's nearly one, so I'm not sure where.' Luke smiled but he let her hands remain around his neck and his hands moved to her hips. The urge to kiss her was back.

'I haven't eaten since breakfast,' Scarlet admitted.

It was almost that time again, Luke thought, but then he pushed that aside. Unlike most men, the thought of a one-night stand didn't thrill him—his father's perpetually roving eye meant that he'd lived with the fallout for long enough to learn from James Edwards's mistakes.

'You really want to take me for dinner?'

'I do.'

'I'm sorry I lied to you,' Scarlet said. 'I just wanted to see if you'd like me if I was normal.'

'You are normal,' Luke said.

As was his body's reaction to her.

There was a need, an absolute need to get her away from here, to just talk, to get to know her some more and, yes, to get to that mouth.

'Can you lose your bodyguards?' Luke asked. He couldn't stand the thought of them overseeing things. He wanted Scarlet away from the hype and he knew he would take good care of her. Judging by her previous offer to make it worth his while, they didn't take proper care of her either.

'I can't.' She shook her head. 'You don't get how it is—I can't go anywhere without them.'

Luke didn't play games.

Ever.

'Can you lose your bodyguards?' he asked again, and Scarlet heard the warning. If she said no, he'd be gone.

'They'll dial 911 if I disappear.'

'Well, they shan't get very far if they do,' Luke said, and he told her the UK emergency number. 'I'll take care of you but I'm not buying you dinner with an audience.'

He *wanted* to take her for dinner!

'I could go to the loo and try to…'

'Climb out of the window?' Luke scoffed at her plans. 'Why don't you simply tell them that you're having a night off?' But then he halted as he realised, for the first time, that life in her world wasn't that simple.

'Please take me for dinner,' she said.

'I'll go outside and wait down the back,' Luke offered. 'If you can't get out of the loo there will be an emergency exit. But,' he warned, 'if you tell your bodyguards what you're up to, if I even get a hint that they're around, I'll hand you back over to them. I'm not going to be playing your celebrity game, Scarlet.'

Luke meant it.

CHAPTER FOUR

WHAT THE HELL was he doing? Luke thought as he stood in a cold, dark, basement alley next to bins and looked up at the tiny windows.

She'd never get through them, Luke realised.

Maybe she had changed her mind, Luke decided, because it had surely been ten or so minutes that he had been waiting. He was just about to give in when he saw one red shoe poke out of a very small gap in a window, followed by one skinny, pale leg and then another.

'I've got you,' Luke said, as he guided her legs out and tried not to notice that her dress was bunching up. He moved his hands from her flesh and then held her by the hips and negotiated Scarlet's body out of the small opening. As he dropped her down to the ground he turned her around. She was breathless and Luke could see the exhilaration in her eyes.

Not just that she was free!

Scarlet's dress was ruched up from her rather undignified exit and she could still feel where his hands had made contact with her thighs. Now she faced Luke and, despite his very cool demeanour, Scarlet knew that he was as turned on as she was.

Her hands moved up back around his neck and she

moved into him for warmth and for confirmation of his arousal.

'Oh,' Scarlet said.

An odd remark perhaps but she could feel him on the length of her stomach and those hands on her hips let her rest there a moment. His voice when it came was a bit ragged.

'Come on.'

He got the 'Oh' comment. Luke was feeling it too.

That urge to kiss was there and a whole lot of other urges too but a stinking dark alley wasn't at the top of his wish list and her bodyguards would no doubt realise that she was missing some time very soon. So, rather than kiss her, Luke grabbed her hand and they ran up some metal stairs and out onto a seedy street and then turned into another.

Luke hailed a black cab and, a touch breathless, they both climbed in.

He gave the name of a restaurant that he knew stayed open late, which he had been to with friends a couple of times when he'd been in London. It was nice and low-key with booths where they could tuck themselves away and he could get to know her some more.

Luke wanted that.

He really did, but as the taxi took off, the driver glanced in the rear-view mirror and must have seen just who his fare was.

'Scarlet!' He turned and smiled and it annoyed Luke that Scarlet smiled back and that she and the driver started talking about Anya's performance. Was it possible to have a conversation that didn't include her mother?

'Just drop us here,' Luke said, as they reached a busier street. They walked into a different restaurant from the one he would have chosen but the reaction to her was the same there and they left.

'I told you…' Scarlet said.

It was impossible.

No, it wasn't.

Luke took off his jacket and put it around her and then he went into the pocket, took out a serviette and removed her trademark lipstick.

God, he wanted that mouth.

Luke saw a bus and pulled Scarlet onto it.

Instead of going up with the night riders, they sat downstairs for two stops.

'Someone will recognise me…' Scarlet said as they sat at the front.

'Not with my face over yours…' Luke had it all worked out.

He took her face in his hands and the shiver that went through Scarlet had nothing to do with the fact it had started to rain outside. He made her wait for first contact. She watched as he looked at her mouth and then back to her eyes and then their mouths met. She felt the first nudge of intimate flesh, a tiny precursor, a small tease, and then Scarlet found out that he *had* been holding back on her since they'd met because there was no tentativeness. He led this kiss, taking her lips between his and then parting them, only to expose bliss. It was a kiss of contrasts—his tongue was slow and tender and yet his jaw was rough and his hands kept her head steady, so there was nowhere to go but to taste and feel the bliss of Luke.

It felt like she'd never been properly kissed until now. They breathed together, their tongues mingled and probed and it took all Luke had to pull back as the bus jolted and to remember where they were.

He looked out at the dark, shiny streets and took her

hand and they stood. 'Come on…' As her hand, in his, moved up to ring the bell he halted her. 'Someone's already rung it.'

'I never have though.'

She pushed it and the driver moaned and she went to ring it again but Luke stopped her. The doors hissed open and they stepped out into the rain.

'Where are we?'

They were just a short walk from his hotel. 'We're going for that dinner I promised you!'

'And?'

'That dance we never had,' Luke said.

'And?' Scarlet asked, as she tried to keep up with his long strides, even though Luke wasn't walking particularly fast, but he halted then and turned her to face him.

'Let's see how those two go.'

He really didn't like one-night stands, they left him feeling like a user and he didn't ever want to use her.

Luke was quite sure she'd had enough of that in her life.

Not just with men.

The free drinks for the crowd she pulled, the circus that was her life.

And, perhaps more pointedly, he didn't have any condoms with him.

They walked to his hotel with his arm around her, passing through the foyer, and no one really noticed.

Without that exposed skin and red lips she didn't stand out so much and he had her pulled tight into him.

The elevator was empty and as she went to resume a kiss he pointed a finger and told her to stand back.

'Not here,' Luke said.

He was very confident and a bit bossy and she wasn't used to being refused.

'I like you,' Scarlet said, as she leant back against the elevator wall.

'Good,' Luke responded. 'I like you too.'

Up they went to his suite and as the door closed on them, for Scarlet it felt like home. It just did. There was a suit holder over the chair and an overnight bag on the bed, which was open.

She thought he'd resume their kiss now that they were alone but instead he picked up a menu.

'It's after midnight so it's just the night menu...'

'Are we eating?'

'You said that you were starving.'

'Oh.' Scarlet was very used to being starving.

She was starving all the time, in fact.

He handed her the menu and Scarlet instantly knew what she wanted. She usually stayed away from carbs but this was her night, her great escape. 'I want the club sandwich.' Then she changed her mind. 'Maybe the burger.'

She couldn't choose.

'Both,' Scarlet said, and Luke smiled and picked up the phone and placed their order. 'Twenty minutes.'

'Whatever will we do?' Scarlet smiled and Luke watched as lifted the hem of her dress and went to peel it off.

'Scarlet...' He stopped her. 'I hope we're going to take more than twenty minutes and I don't want interruptions.' Luke watched as she went over to the bed and lay back, sulking. 'They said that we should order breakfast now if we want it delivered in the morning.' He picked up the menu cards that would need to be hung outside the door. 'What?' he said when he saw that she was staring.

'I want a kiss.'

'Let's sort this out first. Tomato, pineapple or grapefruit juice...'

'Grapefruit.' Scarlet sighed, and he pulled a face. 'Don't you like it?'

'Too sharp,' Luke said, and he ticked pineapple for himself.

'Don't you like me?'

'Why do you ask that?' Luke asked. 'I don't need you on your knees within the hour to like you, Scarlet.'

He guessed she wasn't very used to that.

And he did like her and want her.

But it was more than that…

She picked up a wad of paper that was beside his overnight bag. 'What's this?'

'Just notes I made for my interview.'

'Were you nervous?'

'No,' Luke said, and then glanced up to see she was really reading his notes.

'What was it like?'

'It was an interview.' Luke shrugged but then thought about it and realised that, unless it was for the media, Scarlet wouldn't know so he amended his earlier response. 'I wasn't nervous because I was quite sure I wouldn't get the role. Now I am nervous because I want it.'

'Do you think you'll get it?'

'I think so.'

'So why be nervous?'

Luke usually left such conversations where he had first left this one—at a shrug. There was no point discussing it till he knew if the role was his, but Scarlet was curious rather than nosy and he forgot about breakfast for a moment and, to his own surprise, told her something that was on his mind.

'My ex works there,' Luke said. 'We only broke up last month. I need to speak to her about it.'

'Why?' Scarlet asked. 'Do you still fancy her?'

'No.'

'Does she still fancy you?'

'No.' Luke smiled. 'It was a long overdue break up.'

'No problem, then.' It was Scarlet who shrugged this time. 'I don't believe you, though.'

'Sorry?'

'Can you ever unfancy someone?'

'Actually, yes.' Right up to the moment the words left his mouth Luke had believed it, but in that split second he disbelieved it also.

Not when he looked at Scarlet, who had just kicked off her shoes and was still reading through his notes. Her knees were up and she rested on the pillow, holding the paper above her face, rather than sitting up to read. He could see the hollow of her stomach and the jut of her nipples through her dress and then she moved the papers so that she could see him and smiled.

And Luke doubted if he could, as Scarlet put it, ever unfancy her.

'Breakfast,' Luke said, and tried to take care of the morning.

'I don't eat breakfast,' Scarlet said. 'Just a coffee.'

And again, for Luke, everything changed. He wanted dinner over and done with, he wanted to dance, and then he wanted her naked and writhing in the bed.

'You're going to be starving in the morning, Scarlet,' Luke said.

Something in his voice had her throat tighten and she put down the paperwork.

'Then you'd better read me the menu.'

'Cereal, muesli?'

'Muesli.'

'Full cream or—'

'Full cream, I think,' Scarlet interrupted. 'Don't you?'

With each tick they got sexier.

'Toast?' He looked at Scarlet and she shook her head. 'Too many crumbs.'

She came over and stood in front of him and they read it together.

'Ooh, bacon,' Scarlet said. 'That's very forbidden.'

Hurry with that dinner, Luke thought, because he was pressing her bottom into him and his face was in her hair and he wanted to turn her around and have her against the wall.

And she wanted him so badly, in a way she never had. His hand pressed onto her stomach and now his mouth was on her neck and his kiss to her skin was so sexy and gentle.

'I was watching you from the moment you came in,' Scarlet said.

Luke turned her around and looked down at her. 'I wanted you from the moment I turned around.'

There was a knock at the door. He was tempted, so tempted to ignore it, to call to leave it outside, but, no, they should have dinner.

As the trolley was brought in, Scarlet turned on the television and found a music channel.

Luke paid the tip and as soon as the door closed they faced each other. Luke took off his shirt.

Then his shoes. And she watched as he stripped.

What a body.

Muscular, lean and very, very male, given she was used to men more waxed and bald than even she was.

'You have hairy legs.' Scarlet smiled.

'I wouldn't make it off the rugby field alive if I didn't.'

Scarlet peeled off her dress in one easy motion and Luke made no moved to stop her as she took off her tiny knickers and took her seat at the little table.

The burger was fantastic.

Fat, juicy, and when some onion fell on her breast, Luke kindly retrieved it for her with his fingers and they fed each other dinner.

It was the most amazing meal she had ever had because it came from his fingers.

He'd be laughed off the rugby field if they could see him because Scarlet was bringing food to his mouth and he didn't just suck on her fingers, he kissed her palm deeply. When the meal was over, Luke stood.

'Dance?' he said.

With just her shoes on, Scarlet stood.

She went into his arms and he pulled her right in.

Scarlet felt that chest naked against her cheek and her hands moved around his waist; she had never been anywhere nicer in the world. Luke felt her sway against him and inhaled the scent of her hair and then lifted her face so he could again meet her lips, and then they danced like no one was watching.

CHAPTER FIVE

THAT WAS THEN.

And here they were now, sitting in his office, trapped in the fallout of that time.

It was too painful to think about that night with the other there in the room. Or rather it would be impossible to think about what had taken place in the morning and hope to hold a sensible conversation.

And sense was the one thing that he had to maintain today.

'I don't know what to do,' Scarlet said, though the words were said more to herself than to Luke.

Her head was back in her hands as she sat at his desk crying, not for effect, just because she honestly didn't know what to do.

She'd had plans.

Big ones.

She had told her mother some of them.

And now this had happened.

Luke looked again at the picture of her getting into the ambulance and pushed aside the anger he felt. Scarlet had found her mother unconscious and close to death after all.

For all her money and fame she couldn't buy the one thing she required most now. More than ever before, Scarlet not only needed space and peace, she deserved it.

'Why don't you go somewhere else and check in under Lucy…?' She had told him about that secret name when they had fed each other dinner and he had found out more about her life.

How her mother's fame had been declining but then Scarlet had been born and the beautiful baby Anya had worn on her hip had shot her back into stardom.

He had gleaned that Scarlet had been nothing more than a pretty accessory to wear along with her mother's designer gowns and had been far too precious to send to school.

Luke hadn't said that to her at the time, of course. Whatever he felt, he rarely shared.

'Check in under your alias,' Luke suggested.

'And that will buy me a couple of hours before someone tips them off,' Scarlet said. 'And what happens when I want to visit my mom? The press are everywhere, they'll be all over me.'

'Only because you'll arrive at the hospital with your bodyguards in tow,' Luke said. 'You could dress down and come in through the maternity entrance. Nobody would even know that you'd arrived. Security could take you straight up to ICU without anyone noticing. Visiting your mother doesn't have to be a big deal.'

Scarlet just couldn't buy it. 'I need the security now more than ever. The press are more interested these days in me than…' Scarlet stopped speaking then.

She couldn't tell anyone about the jealous row that she'd had with her mother last night.

'Luke, can you help me, please? I need to get away, I need space, peace.'

'We tried that once, remember?' Luke reminded her. 'And you blew it.'

'I won't this time.'

'I don't believe you, Scarlet.' Luke shook his head. 'I

actually don't think you can help yourself. You crave attention...' Luke halted. He didn't want to add to her distress but, two years on, he was still hurting and angry and it was proving hard not to show it.

'I know that it might be a disruption for you if I came to stay...' Scarlet persisted, but Luke swiftly broke in.

'A friend coming to stay shouldn't be a disruption. It's only when that friend brings an entourage along...' He was struggling to hold on to his temper.

'Or is it because your partner wouldn't like it?'

Luke didn't respond. He didn't say he didn't have a partner, that really since two years ago every attempt at a relationship had ended not just because he was cold, arrogant and obsessed with work, but for another reason—guilt. He still thought about their one night together and since then nothing had matched up.

She took his silence the wrong way—that, unlike her, Luke had moved on with his life.

Scarlet stood. 'Can I see my mother?'

'Of course,' Luke said. 'We're just preparing to move her up to Intensive Care.'

'I'd better tell Sonia first.'

'Just have some time with your mother.' He reached for the phone and asked to be put through to the head of security, and Scarlet watched and listened.

'Hi, Geoff. How is it going with clearing the corridor?'

Whatever Geoff said, Luke rolled his eyes.

'I'm going to bring Anya's daughter to see her. Can you please have all her entourage move inside the staffroom and close the door? Tell them Scarlet will be in to speak with them when she's ready to.'

Luke spoke about logistics as she dug one hand into her pocket and her fingers closed on a stone she had picked up on a faraway beach yesterday.

Oh, Scarlet had made plans. She thought about the little cottage she had found, the month she had planned where she might sort out her head space. There was no chance of that now, with her mother's life hanging in the balance.

Luke was right, though not in the way he had meant—she couldn't help herself.

He did his best to prepare her for what she was about to see but he knew that nothing really could.

They walked out of his office and a security guard stood outside the staffroom and gave Luke a nod.

'Thanks, Geoff.'

They walked down the corridor and through the department, past all the nudges and stares. Only Luke noticed them. Scarlet felt sick.

Luke parted the curtains. 'This is Barbara,' Luke said. 'And the anaesthetist, David. And this is Paul, he's a registrar...'

Scarlet didn't hear much else. All she could see was her mother's deathly white face and all the tubes, and all she knew was that this was her fault.

After all, she knew what she had said to her mother last night.

'Can she hear me?' Scarlet turned anguished eyes to the nurse.

'We don't know,' Barbara said. 'Try talking to her.'

Barbara put her arm around Scarlet's waist and Luke was relieved to step back as Barbara did the job she was very good at.

She answered all Scarlet's questions about the machines and why Anya's face was so swollen.

Luke stepped outside.

Scarlet wasn't his problem. If Anya hadn't done what she had, he wouldn't have even seen Scarlet.

He glanced at the time.

She'd have been on her way back to the States by now.

Then, through the curtain, he heard her voice and it tore at his heart.

'I'm sorry, Mom. I should never have said what I did...'

Luke took a breath to the sound of Scarlet completely breaking down and, after a couple of moments spent trying and failing to resist reaching out to her anguish, he stepped back in.

'Paul, could you please go and speak with her manager?' Luke said. 'Give as little information as you can. Just let them know that her condition is critical but stable.'

'They'll want to know more than that.'

'Of course they will,' Luke said. 'And if we let them, the press would be in here, taking photos.'

'Scarlet,' Luke went on, 'can I speak with you outside?'

He nodded to Barbara and David and then he took Scarlet into one of the relative interview rooms.

'Scarlet,' Luke asked, 'what happened last night?'

She couldn't tell him.

'We need to know if this was an accidental overdose or deliberate.'

'It was an accident.'

It had to be, Scarlet thought.

Please, let it be.

'You can tell me.'

She couldn't look at him; she wanted so badly to meet his eyes but she couldn't.

'Tell me,' Luke pushed gently. 'You said you had a row.'

She nodded.

'A big one?'

'I shouldn't have said what I did.'

'Which was?'

Scarlet shook her head. She was scared to go there, especially with Luke.

'Tell me.'

'I said that I wasn't going back to LA with her.'

'Okay.'

He held her hands then and she looked at his lovely long fingers entwined around hers. 'I said some terrible things.'

'Tell me.'

'I can't.'

'You can.'

'I said she was jealous of me…I said…' Scarlet stopped but then she made herself say it. 'I said something about our baby.'

Silence stretched as she voiced it.

Not all of it.

Just the part that rendered them lost or, worse, unsalvageable.

Wreckage that lay too deep for rescue.

It was surely time to pack up the equipment and head for home.

He sat silent for a moment and then dropped her hands and Scarlet sat staring at the floor as Luke got up and walked out.

She had guessed he would.

For two years every day had hurt but some days hurt more than others and that was today.

Scarlet sat in a room where she guessed people found out their loved ones had died and mourned her baby so badly, even if she didn't deserve to.

She had signed the consent form after all—crying and shaking, unlike Vince who had calmly handed her the pen.

It had been the worst day of her life.

Even with her mother lying near death, it still was.

But on that day there had been one saving grace—

a nurse who had sat with her afterwards and let Scarlet speak.

There could be no saving grace today.

She didn't look up as the door opened and Luke came back in.

'You've got two choices,' Luke said, and Scarlet blinked. She'd never had even one. 'I've got a flat here at the hospital you can stay in for a few days, but on several conditions.'

She stared up at his chin again. 'I can stay?'

'As long as you agree to my conditions.'

'Which are?'

'You lose the phone.'

'I need to know how my mother is—'

'I work here,' Luke interrupted. 'I'll be kept updated.'

'But I need to see her, to be with her.'

'She is in a coma,' Luke said. 'There will be plenty people keeping a vigil, I'm sure. I think right now you need some time to take care of yourself.'

'What are the other conditions?'

'This time you don't tell your bodyguards where you are.'

'How?'

His face darkened but, instead of stating the obvious— that she simply didn't tell them—he threw her blue theatre scrubs and a theatre cap, and wrapped up in them were some clogs.

'I'll give you directions…' But even as he said it, Luke knew it was hopeless. In the flat across the hall from him was one of the radiologists known for gossip. There were the domestics who came in and serviced it. So he told her the other choice. 'Or you can go to my home. It will be easier to keep things under wraps there.'

'Your home?'

'It's about an hour's drive from here,' Luke said.

'I can't leave her.'

'That's up to you. But if you do decide to go there, I mean it, Scarlet, if you call in the entourage, there'll be no time to give your excuses because I won't be listening. You'll be out.'

'Why do you hate them so much?'

'How do they protect you, Scarlet?'

'They keep the public back.'

'But when you wanted to make it worth my while when we met, they were fine with that?' Luke checked. 'A quick blow job and they look away?' He watched her cheeks go red. 'That's not protecting you, Scarlet. I can do all that.'

'What if something happens to her and I'm an hour away?' Scarlet asked. 'What if she dies?'

'Then I'll come home and tell you myself.' Luke didn't sugar-coat it and she sat there, absorbing his words.

She would want to hear it from him, Scarlet knew that much.

'You'll take me there?' Scarlet asked.

'No. I have to work. My car is in the underground car park. You go out of here and turn right and then follow the sign for the staff car park. I have a navy Audi. If you press the keys the lights will flash but you'll see it just as you come out the elevator. Can you drive?' Luke asked, but then checked himself. He knew the answer to that one— not very well, given all the little well-publicised prangs she'd had.

Scarlet nodded.

'On the opposite side of the road?' he checked.

Scarlet nodded again.

'What will you do for a car?'

'There are taxis.' He did the best not to sarcastically

remind her of the last time they had got into one. 'I've got friends who can give me a lift too…'

It all sounded alien to her, Luke knew, but she either wanted the real world or she didn't. He wasn't going to handle her with kid gloves, he was way past all that.

'If I need to speak to you I'll ring three times and hang up. Pick up the phone the next time it rings.'

'Can't I call you? Can I page you?'

'No.' Luke shook his head. 'If I'm busy one of the nurses often answers my page. I'll call if I have to but, Scarlet, if I get even a sniff of your bodyguards, or the press find out where you are and it's your doing, you will be on your own.'

'But people will be looking for me.'

'Write a text now, explaining you're safe but you just need some time, and I'll hit Send once I know you're safely gone.'

'What about seeing my mother?'

'We can work out those details later. Right now I need to get back to work.' He handed her one of the large yellow garbage bags. 'Leave your clothes and phone in this.'

'I'll need my clothes to change into when I get there.'

'You'll stand out like a sore thumb where I live, wearing that.'

'Luke, I don't know.'

'Then decide. Go back out there and be with your people or you hit the sat-nav in my car and press Home. It's up to you.'

He refused to make decisions for others unless he was paid to.

'Will you be okay with me being in your home?' Scarlet asked.

Luke chose not to answer that. He was about to; he could

almost feel the sneer of his lips as he went to ask when she had ever taken his feelings into any equation.

But today wasn't the day to row, he told himself.

'It's up to you,' Luke said again. 'You need to speak with David before you leave, though,' he added.

'And tell him what?'

'That you're staying with a friend.' He wrote down his home number and handed it to her. 'Tell him if he needs to reach you to leave a message on the answering machine and that you'll call straight back.'

And then Luke was gone.

David was thorough, going through all that Luke had and more.

'We'll talk again once I've got her settled into ICU,' he said.

'I shan't be here.'

Scarlet met David's solemn gaze.

'I'm going to be staying with a friend.' She waited for him to chide her.

'I think that's wise,' David said. 'Can I have contact details in case of an emergency?'

'Don't let—'

'I shan't.' David nodded and Scarlet handed him the phone number that Luke had given her.

'If you leave a message, I'll call straight back.'

'Of course.'

He left her then and once alone she took off her silver jacket and her leggings and top and her shoes and then slipped on the scrubs and the disgusting clogs Luke had brought her.

Her hair she tucked into a hat.

With shaking hands she wrote a text to her bodyguard but didn't hit Send and then she threw her phone in the bag.

But then she retrieved it.

She needed it. Her mother was desperately ill after all but, recalling his rules and knowing Luke always meant what he said, Scarlet threw it back in the yellow bag.

She walked out and followed his directions and it was slightly dizzying that no one really gave her a second glance.

Past the canteen she went and then she saw a sign for Maternity and beneath that an arrow that pointed to the staff car park elevator.

She stood beside a blonde woman, waited for the doors to open and then stepped in.

'Hi…' The blonde woman nodded to her in the elevator and Scarlet nodded back.

'Are you new?'

'I just started,' Scarlet said.

'Where?'

'I'm an OB…a midwife,' Scarlet replied.

She wished that she was. How she wished this was where she worked and that she had just come from meeting Luke.

Oh, she wanted that to be her life so very, very much.

The woman was waiting for her to give her name, Scarlet knew. 'I'm Lucy.'

'Angie.' She returned her name with a tight smile. 'You're supposed to always wear your ID, Lucy…?'

Scarlet could hear the question mark and the woman's demand for her full name and more information. 'Lucy Edwards.' Scarlet borrowed Luke's surname and gave Angie another smile and then almost folded in relief as the elevator door opened.

She pressed the key and a very dirty navy Audi flashed its lights. Scarlet went to the wrong side of the car, of course, but then remembered and walked to the other side.

She was sweating and breathless, as if she'd been running, and that damn woman was watching her, Scarlet knew. She climbed in, turned on the engine and reversed out, and as she did so she glanced up and saw that Angie was *still* watching.

Angie thought she was an impostor, Scarlet was sure. She just hoped that she didn't call Security.

Any minute now the call that she was missing would go out, Scarlet knew.

And Luke knew it too.

It was already starting.

Scarlet had been gone for too long. Her bodyguards were walking down corridors and knocking on doors. Luke went into the interview room, picked up the yellow bio-hazard bag and walked through the department into his office. He turned on the engaged sign.

Luke opened the bag and took out her phone.

I've gone away with friends for a few days. I just need to get my head around things. Don't look for me.

Luke hit Send.

'I'm busy,' Luke called, when there was a knock at his door.

'It's Angie.'

Luke frowned. Angie rarely stopped by and she was the last person he knew to ignore an engaged sign.

He opened the door. 'What do you want?'

'Are you with someone?'

'No.'

'Then can I come in?'

Luke nodded.

They still got on.

Both had agreed they would never have worked and were now colleagues and very good friends.

'What the hell are you up to, Luke?'

'Nothing.'

'So should I call Security, then? Because a certain famous woman is pretending to be a midwife and driving your car.'

'Angie…'

'What the hell are you doing, getting involved with her again, Luke?'

A few weeks after they had broken up, Angie had seen the change in him and, knowing how lukewarm Luke had been about the break up, she'd been astute enough to know it hadn't been about her. Luke had always been a bit aloof but he was frantic now and had finally told her why.

Angie had held her tongue when she'd heard that he'd had a one-night stand.

That wasn't the Luke she'd known.

And then to find out that the said one-night stand was in LA and pregnant with his child had had her even more confused.

'Are you sure it's yours?'

Luke had always been so-o-o-o careful, it had made no sense.

'Very sure.'

And in the end, reluctantly he had told her, not just about that night but some of the things that had happened afterwards.

'She's trouble,' Angie now pointed out. 'She messed with your head big-time.'

'No,' Luke corrected. 'Scarlet's lifestyle messed with my head. When I was with her she actually cleared it. Anyway, I don't need you with your psychiatrist's hat on.'

'Luke, she had an abortion without even telling you.'

'Do you think I don't know that?' Luke's response was terse.

'Just be careful,' Angie warned.

'Oh, I intend to be.'

CHAPTER SIX

SCARLET COULD BREATHE.

For the first time in the longest time, as the garage door closed behind her, Scarlet sat in Luke's car and dragged in a long breath.

Apart from having taken a couple of bricks out of a very low wall as she had negotiated the narrow driveway to his home, the drive had been an easy one.

She had kept glancing in the mirror, checking that no one was behind. At first she had listened to the radio, but when they hadn't been talking about her mother they had been playing her songs. It had been too much for Scarlet so she had turned it off.

She'd made it, Scarlet thought as she got out of the car.

The garage was small and there was a door that she pushed open, stepping into a utility room and then walking through to the kitchen.

The kitchen was far smaller than any that she was used to.

Scarlet opened the fridge and there wasn't much in there—a loaf of bread, some eggs and bacon. Scarlet thought of the lovely breakfast they had been about to have two years ago but never had.

She couldn't think about that now so she quickly closed the fridge door and sat at the kitchen table, but all she could see was her mother and those awful words from the fight they'd had replaying in her head.

Scarlet was sorry, but not for what she had said but the way those words had been delivered and the effect they had had.

But she had meant them.

It felt odd to be here.

An unwelcome guest.

She walked down the hallway and looked at the phone, and saw that the answering machine was flashing. She hit Play.

'Hi, Luke, it's Emma. Just reminding you about Wednesday.'

Scarlet swallowed. Of course he had a life.

She held her breath as the next message played but it was some man called Trefor to say that training had been moved.

Yes, Luke had a life.

Still, there were no messages for her and that was a good thing so she moved through to the lounge.

There was an open fire and some logs beside it but building a fire wasn't exactly her forte so Scarlet sat shivering on the sofa, still dressed in theatre scrubs. She just stared at the wall and wondered whether, if it hadn't been for her mother, she would have ever seen this place.

Of course not.

He was a very decent man and he was helping her out, that was all.

Even though she was sure he would rather not have had to.

Dusk arrived and apart from a trip to his downstairs bathroom she didn't move, but then Scarlet realised just how hungry she was.

She hadn't eaten all day.

In fact, she'd had nothing since breakfast yesterday.

Yesterday she had driven for miles in a car the hotel had provided, planning her escape, too busy and excited for all that was to come to stop and eat.

There had been a welcome basket at the cottage when she had arrived and in there had been some snacks and local cheese and condiments, but she had been too nervous to do anything other than put them in the fridge.

Scarlet thought about the long walk on a pebbly beach that she had taken and the plans she had started to make that could never happen now.

Anya had made very sure of that.

She wanted the stone she had collected but it was in her jacket back at the hospital.

Scarlet turned on the television and it went straight to the news. Of course her mother was at the top of the hour but, sure enough, they flashed the image of a terrified Scarlet as often as they could.

'Scarlet is holding a vigil at her mother's bedside,' the press release said. *'At this difficult time she asks for your prayers.'*

Scarlet flicked off the news and wandered into the kitchen. She opened the fridge and took out a carton of eggs but then she saw a bottle of grapefruit juice in the door.

It was almost as if it had been left there for her. Scarlet knew, from their one night together, that Luke didn't like it—he had screwed up his face and told her it was too sharp.

The memory of an uncomplicated them made her smile and Scarlet poured a long drink and scrambled some eggs, even if that hadn't been her intention when she had first cracked them.

They were lovely, apart from the bits of shell that she had to crunch through.

Maybe her mother had been right when she'd said last night that Scarlet could never survive without her.

Now, as darkness came, she was ready to check out the house.

The lounge she knew, she'd been in there for a few hours after all, so she pushed open a door and saw a study. There were shelves and shelves of books and on closer examination she saw they were textbooks.

Scarlet pulled one down and opened it at a random page and, rather than being repulsed at the image she saw, it was actually quite fascinating. Still, she didn't have time to read about ligature marks and entrance and exit wounds from bullets so she closed the heavy book and put it back on the shelf.

It was a very masculine house, Scarlet thought as she headed up the stairs. There were no unnecessary pictures or flowers but she'd love to see it in spring, with a huge vase of something pretty in the hallway.

He must have been in the middle of decorating because there were ladders and tins of paint at the top of the stairs. Scarlet found the bathroom but didn't go in. Instead, she went down the hall and pushed open a door and guessed that this was supposed to be her bedroom tonight.

She didn't go in there either. Instead, she hurriedly closed the door and headed back down the hall and into Luke's bedroom.

There were dark green sheets on the bed topped by a dark green duvet, and the bed was all rumpled and unmade. It was a very low bed with low tables at either side. There was a phone on one and some books so she knew that was his side of the bed.

Yes, she was nosy.

Scarlet opened up his bedside drawer and there were some foreign banknotes and cash and a few tickets, and she felt her lips purse when she saw an open packet of condoms, with its contents spilling out.

She counted them.

Scarlet couldn't help herself.

Oh, so he used them now.

Bitterness, anger, jealousy all rose in her chest but she swallowed them down. It was very hard to be bitter about the memory of the love they had made.

It was any woman who had come after her that had Scarlet drop the condoms back into the drawer and slam it closed.

What did she expect? Scarlet asked herself.

That two years on he'd be as stagnant in his life as she was?

Oh, but it hurt, it really, really hurt, the thought of him with another woman.

She left his bedroom and headed back to the one that was presumably hers.

And that hurt even more.

It was why she had so quickly shut the door on it but Scarlet opened it now.

Would this have been their baby's room? she wondered, then answered her own question with the very next thought.

Of course not.

Scarlet would have had her baby back in LA and the baby would have been balanced on her hip and paraded for the cameras and dragged everywhere, just as her mother had done with her.

Luke would never have allowed it, though, and her mother had told her only too clearly the impossible odds she faced if she dared to leave.

'A one-night stand?' Anya had rammed it home again and again.

'It was more than that!'

'Oh, so you're going to be a doctor's wife!' Her mother had gone into peals of laughter and her manager, Sonia, had followed suit. 'I know I told you to dream big, but please…'

Now she stood in the door way and it felt as if her arms were being pulled in two direction as her body was torn apart.

Scarlet had cried so much today that she been quite sure that there were no tears left.

For a moment there were none.

Just a scream of rage that came out so loud and so raw that it had her sinking to her knees on the spare bedroom floor and she sobbed for her baby and, yes, she was going to hell. Not just for the terrible things she had done but right now, right this very minute, Scarlet wished that her mother was dead.

CHAPTER SEVEN

'LUKE?'

It was close to ten and he just wanted home. It had been one of those days that never ended but just as he went to leave, Mary, the night charge nurse, called him back.

'I hate to ask…'

Mary did hate to ask, she could see how exhausted Luke was, but she also knew that he would prefer that she did.

'There's currently a two-hour wait but I've got a man here whose son is on ICU and all he needs is a sleeping tablet.'

Luke nodded.

'And a couple of headache tablets,' Mary added. 'His blood pressure's high and if I get Sahin…'

Sahin, the registrar on tonight, was thorough, extremely so, and he would run a battery of tests, Luke knew.

'Where is he?' Luke asked.

'I put him down in the interview room. If you need a cubicle, I can bring him into one.'

'The interview room is fine.'

Luke knocked on the door and went in. He saw a gentleman pacing and he introduced himself.

Evan Jones was doing everything he could to hold it together, Luke could tell.

'My son's not well.'

'I heard,' Luke said. 'I'm very sorry.'

'We just had some very bad news. The sister in charge suggested that I come down here. I haven't slept for a couple of nights. I really don't want to sleep...'

'You *have* to sleep,' Luke said.

No one really knew why, just that you did, and if you didn't, well, here was living proof that sleep was necessary. Evan's anxiety was through the roof and his blood pressure was high, as was his heart rate.

'Please, don't start suggesting I need to lose weight or investigations,' Evan snapped as Luke removed the blood-pressure cuff.

'I shan't but you do need to sleep,' Luke said. 'Seriously...'

Evan nodded.

'How long have you had the headache for?'

'Since they told me unless they get a liver in the next seventy-two hours that they were taking him off the list.'

'And when was that?'

'Sixty hours ago.'

Luke didn't make small talk and Evan didn't want it. All he needed now was rest and Luke wrote down his findings and wrote up a prescription. He then went and checked the script with Mary then dispensed it himself and went back to the interview room with a small cup of water.

'Take these now for the headache and the same again when you wake up. And here are some sleeping tablets. Take two tonight,' Luke said. 'Good luck with your son. I'm on in the morning. If you're not feeling better...' Luke amended his words. 'If there's no relief from the headache or if you get chest pain or any other symptoms just come straight back down. Mary will make sure you're seen straight away. I'll be on tomorrow—ask for me.'

'Thank you.'

'Are you walking up to ICU now?' Luke checked. 'I'm on my way there now.'

'I might just go and get some air.'

Usually Luke would just go back to the flat on a night like tonight as he was due in at eight tomorrow.

Luke even thought about doing just that.

But Scarlet was at home.

That gave him even more of a reason to stay at the flat, but it would be unfair to her, Luke knew. And so, before calling for a taxi to take him home, Luke headed up to Intensive Care.

There were a couple of waiting rooms outside the unit that he had to walk past. One was taken up entirely by Anya's team, the other contained the rest of the loved ones of patients on ICU.

It was injustice all the way, Luke thought, but then he hesitated for a moment before using his swipe card to get in as he realised he wasn't here for business reasons only.

He was rarely conflicted—he was here for both personal and professional reasons, though he couldn't really tell David that.

Or could he?

For now, Luke chose not to. He wasn't crossing any lines, he was merely here to catch up on a patient.

He would keep it at that, Luke decided, as he walked over to the vast station where various staff sat writing up notes and checking results as well as taking a quick break. All the patients had a nurse at their bedside and he asked Lorna, the ICU charge nurse, if David was still there.

'He's just in with a patient,' Lorna said. 'He shouldn't be too much longer.'

'How's your night been so far?' Luke asked, and Lorna gave an eye-roll.

'Better than it could have been.' Lorna sighed. 'Thankfully the day staff had the foresight to arrange an extra receptionist to cover tonight. We've got one phone ringing hot solely to enquire about Anya, and it's people using any guise…'

'Such as?'

'Her partner, her lover, a close friend, her aunt…' Lorna turned as someone called her name. 'It would seem that it's her daughter now,' Lorna said, and rolled her eyes once more. 'Again.'

Luke was proud of the staff at the hospital and how they guarded their patients' privacy so fiercely. After a brief pause, Lorna was back. 'You'd think they would get someone with a *real* American accent to call and pretend to be Scarlet.' Lorna gave a wry grin. 'Someone who at least knew their mother's real name.'

'Which is?' Luke asked, because he'd never actually got around to that.

'Anne Portland,' Lorna said. 'Are the press still at the entrance?'

'They are.' Luke nodded. 'Hopefully they'll get bored soon and go.'

'Not a chance,' Lorna said. 'They've just got wind that Scarlet isn't here. I don't know how they found out and I don't want to know either. It didn't come from my staff, that's all I can say.' She had seen it all before and on many occasions. 'Anyway, I've got other things on my mind right now.' She nodded out to the unit. 'Ashleigh—an eighteen-year-old waiting for a liver transplant. We're going to have to take him off the list soon.'

'I just saw his father.'

'Poor man. He's been holding it together for his wife but he's starting to lose it. And on the other hand I've got Anya's people moaning about the coffee and the lack of information.' She looked up as David came over. 'How is he?'

'One word or two?' David asked.

'One,' Lorna said.

'Gutted.'

Luke looked over to the young man they were discussing. He didn't need to be told that Ashleigh was in the third bed along. The young man was a sickly yellow colour and completely emaciated and exhausted, yet he managed to smile at his father as Evan walked back onto the unit.

Evan returned the smile.

God, life could be cruel.

'How are you, Luke?' David asked.

'I'm well,' Luke replied. 'I just thought I'd stop by and see how Anya was doing.' He felt as shallow as hell, especially when David rolled his eyes.

'I never thought you'd be one to jump on the bandwagon.'

'I'm just following up on a patient I thought I was going to lose this morning,' Luke answered.

'Sorry.' David gave a brief shake of his head. 'Long day,' he said, 'and it's going to be an even longer night.'

'You're on call?' Luke checked, and David nodded.

'I'm doing a double.' He got back to Anya. 'There's been no real change with her.' He pulled up Anya's notes on the computer and Luke read through the toxicology results that had come through so far. 'She ticks every box…'

'Yep.' Luke read it with a sinking feeling. It really was starting to look less and less like an accidental overdose, especially coupled with the row that she'd had with Scarlet last night.

'There was some discord with the daughter the night before,' Luke said.

'I saw it in your notes,' David said. 'Scarlet didn't mention it to me, just said she was going to stay with a friend.'

Luke said nothing. The fact there had been an argument was pertinent to Anya's care plan and that was the reason he had noted it.

Where Scarlet was staying wasn't pertinent.

'Thanks for that.' Luke stood, though knew he had to ask David for more than he usually would. 'David, can you call me if there is any change in Anya, either way?'

'Where on the list do you want to be?' David sighed as he headed away from the desk and towards another patient and there was a slightly sarcastic edge to his voice. 'Before or after her manager, the DON, the—'

'Can you call me first?' Luke interrupted.

David stopped walking and looked at Luke and frowned for a moment. It was a very unlikely request from a very unstarstruck Luke.

'I'm asking as a friend,' Luke said.

'Okay.'

'Don't ask any more than that,' Luke said.

'I shan't,' David agreed.

'But you will call me?' Luke checked.

'I shall.'

'And will you pass that on to whoever takes over from you in the morning?'

David nodded. 'I'm here on and off for most of the week. I'll be sure to keep you informed.'

'Thank you.'

Luke said goodnight and then he walked out, past the entourage and then down the corridor and there, walking just ahead of him, was Angie. When he called her name she turned around and, Luke thought, she looked just as tired as he felt.

'How come that you're still here?' Luke checked.

'Full moon,' she said. 'Do you need a lift?'

'I'll be fine. Anyway, I live ages away…'

'Which will give us plenty time to talk, and I promise not to lecture. I can listen, though.' Angie gave a wry smile.

Luke never said very much.

'So what are your plans?' Angie asked as they drove out of the car park.

'No plans really,' Luke admitted. 'I think it's just about giving Scarlet some space.'

'You won't get any space if they find out where she is.'

'We'll see.'

They drove in silence for a while.

'Why *do* you live so far away?' Angie asked when they hit the motorway.

'It's just nice to get away,' Luke answered.

That wasn't the full reason, but Luke kept that to himself.

'Have you spoken with her private physician?' Angie asked with a sarcastic edge.

'Not yet.' Luke's response was tart as he thought of Vince. 'He's *unavailable* at the moment.'

'I'll bet.'

They were silent for a while but for Luke it was an angry silence, not at Angie, but because all that had gone on in the past was now firing his mind in all directions.

'Did I tell you that Anya once offered me a job as her private doctor?'

'No.'

It still angered him now. 'That was Scarlet's solution, to put me on her mother's payroll and have me be a part of that circus.'

'I think that sounds more like Anya's solution,' Angie said. 'Anyway, she'd soon have fired you when she realised how tight you are with drugs.' Angie smiled. When she'd had her wisdom teeth out Luke had rationed all the decent stuff, but then she stopped smiling at the memory and was serious. 'The baby would have been a part of the circus too.'

'No.' Luke shook his head.

'Of course it would have, and so would you.'

Luke just stared at the road ahead. He'd thought about it, of course he had. Life as Scarlet's partner or ex, access visits played out with the media looking on.

And even if he could have somehow taken it, which he doubted, what about his own family? They had their own lives, their own secrets, their own issues, and he'd have been exposing them too.

No, he couldn't live that life and neither would he have wanted it for his child.

'I'd never have let it come to that,' Luke said.

'Do you really think you could have shielded Scarlet, a pregnant Scarlet at that, from the press?'

'I'd like to have at least had the chance to try.'

'Is this what this is about?' Angie asked as they pulled up at his home.

'No,' Luke said, but then he looked at his house, which felt very different with the knowledge that Scarlet was in there. 'Maybe. Or maybe I'm just trying to give her a break.'

'God knows, she must need one after twenty-five years of it. Her whole life played out in front of the cameras...'

Luke sat there as Angie spoke.

'Poor kid,' she said. 'She's never known anything different.'

'She wanted to, though.'

It was what he had admired so very much about her.

Scarlet had wanted to escape.

She had told him the morning they had made love.

Luke had always laughed at the very notion of love at first sight.

Not now.

But he could not let himself remember that morning if he wanted to get through tonight so he thanked Angie for the lift, got out of the car and said goodnight.

Scarlet was definitely here. Luke could tell from the missing bricks in the low wall of his driveway, which he guessed the car had clipped. The house was in darkness and he wondered if he'd have to knock but, no, the door opened and he stepped in and locked it behind him.

Her scent was there and there were his car keys on the hall table beside the theatre cap and the clogs he had given her to wear, which had been kicked off.

Luke walked through to the kitchen and, no, Scarlet hadn't done his breakfast dishes, he thought with a wry smile as he saw all the evidence of her scrambled eggs. The shells were on the bench; she hadn't even soaked the pan, though he could forgive that one because he always meant to soak his breakfast bowl but never did.

He poured himself a glass of grapefruit juice and sat there for a long moment before heading upstairs.

Luke walked straight past the spare room. He knew that she wouldn't be in there and he was right.

Luke turned on the lights to his bedroom and there Scarlet was, naked in his bed and asleep, but she stirred as he came in and then yelped as he whipped back the duvet.

'Bed,' he said.

'I'm in it.' Scarlet smiled, not remotely fazed that she was stark naked. 'How's Mom?'

'Same,' Luke said, and scooped her up in his arms and carried her down the hall towards the spare room.

'Luke, I want you...'

'No way,' Luke said.

She was trying to rain kisses on his face as her hands went behind his neck, and recall was instant—he was as hard as anything, feeling her all warm and squirming, but there was no way that he'd be sleeping with her.

'Bed.' He dropped her onto the spare one and wished he'd thought to pull back the sheet first because Scarlet lay naked, her arms above her head and every bit as beautiful as he remembered.

More so even.

She had filled out a little bit and there was a jet of pubic hair that hadn't been there last time.

It was now silky and tempting and taunting Luke in his peripheral vision as he tried to meet her gaze.

Still Scarlet refused to meet his eyes.

'How could you sleep with me when you can't even look at me?' Luke asked.

She didn't know how to answer that and she screwed her eyes closed in shame.

'There's no change with your mother.' Luke tried to keep his voice calm and even as he brought her up to date. He tried to be all professional and detached but with an aching hard-on and closer to tears than she could ever know. 'But she's stable.'

'When will we know more?'

'I'll be called if there's any change. Other than that, I'll check on her first thing in the morning. I'll be leaving early tomorrow. Don't answer the phone unless it's me.'

Scarlet nodded. 'Will you come in and see me before you go to work?'

'Why?'

'Because I don't want to have to wait till tomorrow night to see you again.'

There was so much to say, so many questions, but, no,

he couldn't bear to go there just yet so he gave a brief nod instead.

'I'll pop in and say goodbye.' He could not stay a moment longer. 'Good night.'

'How can it be a good night?' Scarlet asked, as she looked at the man who was walking out the bedroom door.

It was the longest, loneliest night for both of them.

It simply felt wrong to be at opposite ends of the hallway but raw was the hurt that kept them apart.

And the hurt was still there the next morning as Luke had his breakfast then made her a coffee and braced himself to go up the stairs.

'Good morning,' Luke said, as she gave him a just-awake smile.

For both of them it was.

Oh, it was awful still, but better than yesterday's had been, and certainly better than the seven hundred and forty-eight that had come before.

She watched as he put her coffee down but then, suddenly embarrassed by her behaviour last night, she covered herself with the sheet as she sat up. 'I don't get why you're cross that I came on to you.'

'I'm not cross,' Luke said. 'Sex isn't going to fix things, Scarlet.'

'I wasn't intending to fix things, just…' She told him the truth. 'I don't want you to change your mind about me staying here and I thought—'

'I didn't bring you here for sex, Scarlet. Did you sleep?'

'I did!' Scarlett sounded surprised. 'Not at first,' she said.

'Nor me.'

'It's a nice room,' Scarlet said, and even if it wasn't the room she would prefer to be in, she looked around the little spare room, pulled open the curtain by the bed and peered into the dark outside and saw a lamppost and beneath it someone walking a dog.

'I'd love to go for a walk.'

'Then go,' Luke said.

'I haven't got any clothes.'

'I'll sort that out today. I know it's probably a bit boring, being cooped up.'

'Oh, I'm far from bored,' Scarlet said. 'I love your home.'

'Thank you,' Luke said. 'So do I.'

He sat down on the bed and she felt relief that he wasn't dashing off.

'How long have you lived here?'

'Nine months,' Luke said. 'It's a bit far out but I like it.'

'I can see why. It was a nice drive, even if I was terrified I was being followed at first.' She pulled a little face. 'I think I scratched your car. I didn't see the wall on your driveway.'

'That's okay.'

'It's quite a scratch actually,' Scarlet said.

'Yeah, and I'm missing a few bricks from my wall,' Luke said. 'I saw.'

'Sorry.'

'It's not a big deal. I did the same when I first moved in.'

And then, when he should have gotten up and left, Luke did what he had to—as she went to reach for her coffee he halted her.

Not her arm. Instead, his hands went to her face.

Scarlet felt the heat of his palms caress her cheeks and then his mouth soft on hers and he kissed her. Oh, how their mouths needed each other's. It was a soft morning kiss and for it, Scarlet knew, she would float better through the day.

She kissed him back, feeling again the lips she'd missed, and so gentle and unexpected was he that Scarlet felt tears sting in her eyes.

It was just a kiss and neither pushed for more.

'Look at me,' Luke said, still holding her face, yet she still would not meet his eyes.

'I can't.'

'You can.'

But she couldn't.

'Have your coffee,' Luke said, and he let her go and handed her mug to her. 'I'll call once I get into work and I know how she's doing.'

Scarlet nodded and he got up off the bed and walked to the door.

'You'll never be able to forgive me, will you?' Scarlet said, and she waited for his terse response, for angry words, for reproach and to be shamed, but instead he turned around.

'Or you me,' Luke said.

He was Dr Responsible.

Boring, some said, not that he cared what others thought—only what she thought of him and his actions.

In something so basic he had let her down.

'That morning…' He watched the colour rise on her cheeks.

It hadn't been the night.

He had kissed her all over and made love to her with his mouth through the night and Scarlet had done the same to him but it wasn't the night they now remembered.

No, it had been just as dawn had arrived that things had changed and moved in ways he had never thought they would…

Luke couldn't think of that now so he turned and walked off.

She heard him go down the stairs and the closing of

the front door, and Scarlet got out of bed and ran onto the landing, still holding her mug. She wanted to call out for him to come back.

But then came the sound of his car starting up and as he drove down the street Scarlet heard the automatic door to the garage close.

She looked down the hall to his bedroom and stood there, and despite the fact the house was cold, she felt warm as she headed into his bedroom.

Luke had left her alone with the memory of them.

CHAPTER EIGHT

'Thank you for a wonderful night…' Scarlet sat on Luke's stomach and looked down.

That shadow on his jaw was darker now, and his hair was messed up in a way that she liked.

She circled the bruise her mouth had made on his neck and then her fingers moved to the hairs on his chest and she toyed with them. 'It was the best night.'

'It's been great,' Luke agreed.

The lack of condoms hadn't been an issue. They'd found plenty to do without them and now he lay looking up at her as they chatted. 'You don't live in London?' she checked.

'No, I'm just here for an interview.'

'So where do you live?'

'Oxford.'

'With your family?'

'No.' He rolled his eyes at the very thought. 'I was out of there at eighteen.'

'Don't you get on?'

'We do.' He was dismissive and Scarlet frowned.

'Are your parents together?'

Luke nodded.

'How long have they been married?'

'They just had their thirtieth anniversary.'

'Wow!'

He saw her wide eyes as she pictured his perfect life.

'It's not all roses, Scarlet.'

'It sounds it to me.'

And so he let her think that.

Luke let everyone think that.

It wasn't his place to tell.

'So it was your brother's birthday last night?' Scarlet checked.

'Marcus.' Luke nodded. 'He just turned twenty-one.'

'Do you have any other brothers?' Scarlet asked. She wanted to know everything that she could about him.

Luke shook his head. 'I have a younger sister—' Luke started, but Scarlet jumped in.

'I'd love that,' Scarlet admitted. 'I'd give anything to have a sister.'

'It's just you?' Luke checked.

'My mom says we're like sisters.' Now it was she who rolled her eyes.

'Well…' He tried but he couldn't really grasp it. 'I could never see my mum in a nightclub with me.'

'It's embarrassing,' Scarlet admitted, and went a bit pink. 'She gets wasted and the guys chat her up…' She pulled a face that showed her distaste.

Luke thought about his own mother and her love affair with gin. It was bad enough seeing her that way at home— heaven forbid if he had to witness it when out.

'Then she sings,' Scarlet said, and it was the way she said it that had Luke smile.

'Can you sing?'

'Do you really think I'd even try?'

He looked up into shrewd eyes and he wasn't smiling now. This was a young woman who had learnt to never attempt to outshine her mother.

He looked right into her eyes and wondered about all she could be.

'Would you like to sing?' Luke asked.

'No.'

'What would you like to be?'

'To be?' Scarlet frowned. 'Without her, you mean?'

Luke nodded and he watched as the little pink blush that had receded now darkened.

'I've never thought about it,' Scarlet said.

He knew that she was lying and he didn't mind a bit. In fact, he was inordinately pleased that, given her circumstances, Scarlet *had* thought about it, even if she preferred not to reveal her thoughts. And who could blame her? There were secrets in that pretty head, Luke was sure, and no doubt the press would love to know them.

He glimpsed her life again—Scarlet could trust no one, not even the man she was in bed with.

She *could* trust him, Luke thought, even if she didn't know it.

'Do the two of you get on?'

He watched as her eyes narrowed, and he knew she was about to shoot him down, say that of course they did.

'This is just between us,' Luke clarified.

'Of course it is.' Her response was sarcastic and then she met those deep brown eyes and tempered her thoughts. Something about Luke had drawn her to him at the club— his calm disposition at first and then that he'd had no idea who she was had at first been refreshing. Now that he knew, and only wanted her, he made her feel safe.

It would be foolish to let her guard down, Scarlet warned herself. She'd been the victim of pillow talk in the past and yet she could no more imagine Luke selling his story than she could him suddenly sprouting horns.

She might live to regret this, Scarlet thought, but she took a tentative breath and spoke on.

'If I behave we get on.'

'If you don't?'

She shrugged but Luke persisted. 'What happens if you argue?'

'People don't tend to argue with Anya,' Scarlet said.

Luke stayed silent as she prevaricated. It was a survival mechanism, he knew, and it concerned him greatly. He knew she was seriously scarred.

'Ever?'

Scarlet shrugged. 'I choose my battles.' She gave him a smile and moved in for a kiss. 'You're going to be one of them…'

He halted their kiss, wanting to talk some more.

'When you say—'

'You ask too many questions,' Scarlet said. 'We're a one-night stand.'

'Are we?' Luke checked. 'It doesn't have to be.'

'Don't you have a girlfriend?'

Luke frowned. 'I wouldn't be here if I did. I told you we just broke up.'

'When?'

'A month or so ago.'

'That's ages!' Scarlet laughed. 'How long were you together?'

'Two years,' Luke answered. 'What's your longest relationship?'

'Oh, I'm too busy to have a relationship,' Scarlet said. 'Anyway, they only want me to get to my mom.'

'Not true,' he said. 'Scarlet…' He wanted to tell her that was utter lies she'd been fed. He wanted many things, not just for Scarlet but for both of them.

Scarlet's thighs gripped him, but her hands were relaxed to him rather than suggestive. His were the same, running over her slender ribs, positioning her a little bit farther back and just enjoying her as they spoke.

'Why did you break up?' Scarlet asked.

'We just did.'

And he was very glad that they had, or he'd have missed this.

He looked up at her smiling mouth. Her face was flushed and pink and her hair was tousled. Luke's eyes moved down over her body. There was a bruise on her left breast from him and her nipples were darker from his attentions.

He didn't answer her question; instead, he put one hand behind her head to pull her down and, with her body angled over his, he went for the other breast.

'I wish we…' Scarlet panted as he licked her breast and then took it deep in his mouth, but she didn't finish saying she wished they had condoms. He was hard against her thigh and she had never wanted someone inside her so badly.

Luke wanted her badly.

But then he remembered he was the sensible one and dragged her turned-on and wanting body to lay by his side. Scarlet felt as if she were floating, with only his arm pinning her down.

They kissed, a kiss that demanded more from both of them, one that had Luke deciding that soon he'd just get dressed and find an all-night store, but now it was Scarlet that halted them.

'Why *did* you break up?'

'Because,' Luke said.

Because he hadn't want to drag her on a bus and make out with her, because he hadn't had to fight not to pull her down onto his aching hardness.

He wanted all of that with Scarlet.

'When you say this doesn't have to be a one-night stand, does that mean you'll call me?' Scarlet asked.

'Of course.'

'When?'

He reached over and handed her his phone and she tapped in her number and then took a photo of herself lying in his arms. 'Send that to me.'

'Okay.'

He did so and Scarlet heard her phone buzz across the room and smiled.

'Do you want to go out tonight?' Luke asked. He was more than happy to miss checkout and spend the day in bed and then take her out but Scarlet shook her head.

'I can't tonight. Anya's performing.'

'So you can't go out because your mother's working?' Luke checked. 'I don't get it.'

'She needs me there when she goes on and all the build-up beforehand,' Scarlet explained. At first she had said it as fact but, resting her head on his chest, the madness of her world was all the clearer for her short six hours away from it.

'Maybe we *could* go out?' Scarlet said. 'Or we could stay in again.'

'Sounds good.'

She thought of telling her mother that she wouldn't be there today, or tonight, and the hell that would break out. And then she thought of the worst scenario—being there for her.

Again.

And again and again.

Panic was starting to hit and she tried to deny it, to just lie there and keep her breathing calm and not ruin what had been a wonderful night.

Feeling the sudden tension in her, Luke pulled her in.

His hand stroked her arm and that, just that, had Scarlet feeling a little better.

It was the nicest sensation she had ever felt, just these soft yet firm strokes and the thud of his heart, and, despite her best attempts to stem them, silent tears started coming out of her eyes.

'Scarlet?' Luke checked, and lifted her chin. And it was then, for Scarlet, that panic truly hit as she revealed a truth she had never dared to.

'I don't want to go back…'

Tears never usually moved him but hers did. He could almost feel her desperation and she turned in his arms and released herself and lay on her back, panting as if she'd just run a race.

'What do you mean?' He came over her and started kissing her tears, and they were talking in whispers as she revealed her secret.

'I don't want to go back to my life. I've been trying to work out for years how I can get away,' she admitted, and then closed her eyes. 'Sorry, too much…'

'No, no,' Luke said, when usually he'd be thinking, *What the hell?*

'I don't know how to, though,' Scarlet admitted. 'Everyone I speak to is employed by her.'

'What about friends?' Luke asked.'

'All of my friends are hers first.'

She lay there rigid beneath him. His legs were on the outside of hers and Luke was up on his elbows, looking down at her, and a more lonely world he could not imagine.

Oh, his family had their own issues, but nothing like this.

And he had friends that went way back.

There were people he could turn to if he chose to.

That he chose not to was his own issue.

'I've run away before but I never get very far,' Scarlet said.

'What do you want?' Luke asked.

'I want,' Scarlet said, 'this.'

He got it that she wasn't talking about them at that point, just normality, and on a cold, wet morning, in a very warm hotel room, it didn't seem an awful lot to ask.

'We'll make it so, then.'

And then she was more honest than Scarlet had ever dared to be. 'I want you.'

'Good,' Luke said, 'because I want you too.'

Those dark brown eyes looked right into hers.

'It will be okay.'

She believed him.

'It will.' His mouth was on her lips and they tasted of hope and his words were so assured. 'I'm here now.'

His kiss deepened and it was like he had opened a tap in her heart and kept filling it.

She had lain there rigid but now she just moved beneath him. Like curling ribbon, her limbs wrapped around him and her lips were in thrall to kisses that were deeper and edgier than last night.

His skin was rough and she craved it. Her tongue matched his and her breasts, which had already had more than due attention, were needy and sore as his thumb tweaked one so expertly that her hips arched as if he had touched her between her legs.

The covers were too hot and heavy but the weight didn't feel like a burden, it just cocooned them. As her hips arched she felt the thick length of him pressed to her groin and stomach and then he moved back so he was between her thighs and she squeezed them tight and he moved into their vice.

She was damp, he was too, and there was an ache for more that rushed between them and her hands went to his buttocks and dug in.

'I want you.' Scarlet had never heard her own voice in that tone. It was determined, it was assured, it was desperate, though.

He moved and she could feel him thick at her entrance and she felt dizzy at the brief feel of him parting her, but as he pulled back she moaned and pressed her fingers tighter into taut muscle and begged him in.

He entered just a little way and those small thrusts had their breathing halting, because if they dared to take in air they might lose the giddy sensation.

Common sense, where was it? Luke wondered, because he had been overtaken by sheer want. She was swollen and aroused and sore for him and when Scarlet sobbed, 'Please,' he drove in hard.

'Oh…' Scarlet was frenzied. She had never been made love to like this, nowhere even close.

He offered the brief lie that he would stop soon and took her over and over, and it felt as if he were exploring her deep inside because knots of nerves awakened and he addressed each one.

He kissed her cheek and there were no more tears as he moved down from his forearms so more of his weight was on her and he scooped his arms under her. Her body was shaking and taut beneath his and he felt the intimate pull of her—she wanted more.

She was coming and claiming him with her thighs wrapping around his waist, and she sobbed out as he drove in harder and she met each thrust.

It wasn't pretty but it felt divine.

The bed was banging, both could hear it, and Luke, who never lost his head, quite simply did.

The feel of her was intense, the sound of them was volatile, like a drive-by shooting was taking place as they exploded one into the other.

Bang.

Bang.

Bang, bang, bang.

Bang, bang, bang, *bang.*

And Luke, who always held back a part of himself, was moaning and shouting and coming deep into her.

The hotel room rattled to their tune, and they were still going.

She came again, just on the tail end of his, and Luke groaned and shot out a final release, and then they collapsed into a void of silence and breaths and hot kisses and promises that made no sense because they'd been together for just a few hours.

Her hair was wild and damp and it felt as if they'd made love in a sauna.

It was hot, sticky sex with no end in sight because he was still inside her.

He moved to pull out but Scarlet gripped him. She gave him no rest, just a slow kiss to recover, and then a deeper kiss as he started to grow within her. But then came a knock on the door.

'Damn.' Luke laughed. 'Breakfast.'

She had no idea in that moment that the knock on the door heralded the end of them.

Scarlet opened her eyes as if someone had just knocked on the door to Luke's bedroom.

Her face was red in his pillow, her sex still twitching as it had that morning, and still she wondered what would have happened if breakfast hadn't come then.

Sometimes she lost herself to her imaginings of how

their worlds might have been had they not been disturbed, but not today. Instead, she remembered how he had climbed from the warm bed, semihard, and had pulled a towel around his hips.

She'd heard the door open and then, after a moment, it had closed and, suddenly remembering what she had done, Scarlet had closed her eyes in regret.

Scarlet could almost hear the rattle of the tray and Luke's tense breathing as he'd slammed it down on a table.

'Scarlet…' His voice was clipped and she could feel his contained fury. 'There are three security guards outside the door…'

It had been the end of them.

The beginning of a very rapid ending and now, two years later, she lay alone in his room.

Last night, Scarlet had thought she had no more tears left to cry over them.

But of course she did.

CHAPTER NINE

THERE WERE DIVERSION signs in place as Luke drove into the hospital.

'What's going on?' Luke asked, winding down his window and speaking with Geoff.

'One of the news vans broke down at the entrance to the staff car park,' Geoff said. 'At least, that's what they've said has happened. I think they're trying for a view of ICU.'

'Call the police,' Luke said. 'Get them moved.'

Instead of parking in his usual spot underground, Luke took for ever to find a space.

The press were still outside the foyer and security and other staff who were arriving for their shifts were looking very unimpressed with it all.

As was Luke.

Instead of heading straight into A and E, Luke headed up to ICU to catch David before he started handover.

Anya's people were still there but their numbers had thinned down.

In the other waiting room he saw Ashleigh's parents. Evan was sitting with his head in his hands as the mother paced.

When Luke stepped into the unit he found out why.

The space where Ashleigh's bed had been was empty

and Luke walked over to Lorna, who was just coming off the phone.

'Did he get a liver?'

'He did.' Lorna nodded. 'He just went to Theatre.'

He saw that Lorna, who was possibly the toughest of the tough, was on the edge of tears.

'Ashleigh's been in and out of here for the last six months. It's wonderful to see him get this chance.' Lorna shook her head. 'I'm not going to be able to sleep.'

'Well, you need to,' Luke said, 'so you can be back here tonight to look after him.'

'Please, God,' Lorna said.

He glanced over at Anya. 'How has she been?' Luke asked.

'She's had a stable night, apart from a spike in her temperature, but we were anticipating that. David's going to be a while. He took Ashleigh down to Theatre, just to see him put under. He's not staying for the op, though. He should be back soon.'

'That's fine,' Luke said.

He'd call back in on his way home, Luke decided, but for now he made his way down to his own department and worked through his list. But at ten, just before he started the fracture clinic, he called Scarlet.

Luke wasn't sure if she'd be up but he didn't know when he would get a chance to call again so he rang three times and hung up then called again.

Scarlet had spent a long time crying and her eyes were still watery as she lay in his bed and stared at the ringing phone at the bedside.

It rang off on the third ring and then rang again and she picked up the phone.

'Is that you?'

'It is,' Luke said. 'How are you?'

'How's Mom?' Scarlet asked, by way of answer.

'She's stable. There's no real change.'

'Is that good or bad?'

'It's good for now,' Luke said. 'Have you been crying?'

'A bit,' she admitted.

'Well, your mum's doing as well as can be expected and...'

Scarlet listened to his soothing words. She could let Luke think she was crying about her mother.

Later on she might be.

Just not now and she told him so.

'Luke, I wasn't crying about my mom. Seeing you, being in your home, well, it's kind of brought it all back. Not that it ever went away. I'm sorry for what I did—'

'Scarlet,' Luke interrupted. 'Let's not do this over the phone.'

'When, then?'

He didn't answer.

She lay in his bed when she should be sitting by her mother's.

'Do you think I should come in and see her?'

'That's up to you.'

'I know it is, I'm just asking for your take.'

'Okay, then, I think you need some time.' Luke was honest with his answer. He had seen Anya's lab results and it was looking less and less like the accidental overdose the spin doctors were trying to say it had been.

'What if she wakes up and I'm not there?' Scarlet asked.

'Yeah, well, I know how bad that feels,' Luke said, and it was the first real glimpse of his temper weighted against them because he abruptly rang off.

Luke stared at the phone.

He told himself to pick it up and pretend that he'd been cut off.

But as he sat there staring, he was reliving it too.

Not the nice part before, just the hell of afterwards, when he had walked back into the hotel room.

'What are they doing out there?' he'd demanded.

There had been three guys standing right outside the door and he'd recognised a couple of them from the club!

Scarlet hadn't fully understood his anger. 'I texted them to let them know where I was.'

'You. Did. What?'

Each word was an accusation in itself and Scarlet rose in the bed to her own defence. 'I didn't want people worrying.'

'So while we were...' His anger was mounting at the thought that her bodyguards had been standing outside and would have heard the noise they'd made. Worse, that Scarlet thought this completely normal incensed him. 'You told me that you wanted a night away from it all.'

'And I did, but I didn't want to make trouble.'

'You said—'

'You have no idea what my life is like,' Scarlet shouted.

'I'm trying to understand.'

'Well, you can't!' Scarlet could not take it in that he was angry at her. It spun her into a panic and she started crying. There was a knock on the door and then another, and, despite Luke telling her to leave it, Scarlet opened the door to say that she was okay. But, given she was crying, her bodyguards came in.

'What the hell...?' Luke exploded at the intrusion. He was furious at the insult their coming in inferred—as if he might have been about to hurt her.

'So you'll stand outside while she's having sex and then interrupt a discussion?' Luke shouted at the burliest one, and what had him raging was that Scarlet was standing there naked.

'Get back in the bed,' Luke shouted. He wanted her covered, he wanted this audience gone, but she misread his anger and dressed instead and within moments she was gone.

And now, two years later, he sat staring at the phone.

Scarlet couldn't deal with anger or arguments, and no wonder. He could see that now, he just hadn't been able to then.

Today was the second time in their history that he had hung up on her.

He didn't want to discuss the other time but knew that soon they'd have to.

Luke didn't take the easy way out now.

He picked up the phone and called her back.

CHAPTER TEN

THE PHONE RANG again and she didn't wait for three rings but picked it up straight away.

Had he missed her for all of these two years?

Was that what he'd just said?

The brusque tone of his voice gave her no clue.

And if he was angry, why was he calling her back?

'Sorry about that,' Luke said.

'Did you just hang up on me?' Scarlet asked.

'Yep,' he admitted, rather than saying they had been cut off, which was what he would normally have done. Luke had never known anyone like Scarlet, or the feelings she evoked in him. He couldn't remember hanging up the phone on anyone before. He was so obstinate at times that it was usually the other way around. 'I'm back now.'

Scarlet smiled. 'I'm glad.'

'We'll talk properly later,' Luke said. 'I know we have to but not over the phone…'

'I get it,' Scarlet said.

He got back to the subject of her mother. The reason for his call.

'She's not going to be waking up today. They're keeping her under for a day or two more at least and when she does wake up she'll be drowsy,' Luke rather more patiently explained. 'We'll cross that bridge when we come to it.'

'Okay,' Scarlet said, and then she said the nicest thing, Luke thought, when there must be so much on her mind. 'How are you?'

Fine, he was about to say. 'A bit tired,' Luke admitted. 'I'm going to finish up early today.'

'That's good.'

'What are you doing now?' Luke asked.

'I'm still in bed,' Scarlet said. She just omitted to mention whose bed she was in! 'What about you?'

'I'm just about to start a clinic so I have to go. Do you need anything from the shops?'

Indeedy she did!

Luke finished at three and by four-thirty he was in the supermarket to purchase his fugitive's supplies.

Quinoa?

He'd never even walked down the health-food aisle.

Kale?

His mother used to put that in soup! No way.

And she could have button mushrooms, like the rest of the world, Luke decided.

He threw in some eggs but he did make a small concession and got the organic, free-range ones—he'd been meaning to switch to them for a while anyway.

Luke stopped by the meat section but then looked back at the list. Did Scarlet even eat meat?

Yes! Luke remembered the breakfast they had ordered and never eaten but memories like that were too risky to have right now so he moved through to the clothes section.

There wasn't much choice.

He tried to guess her size and guessed she'd be the smallest so he bought some leggings, a couple of baggy tops and a pair of jeans.

And, thinking of the boots she had been wearing, which

weren't really made for walking, he bought some slip-on shoes.

Then he headed over to the underwear section.

Maybe not, Luke thought as he stared at a pack of five-for-the-price-of-three knickers.

He paid and left the supermarket but instead of going to his car he walked down the main street of the village and into a small boutique, which was a first for Luke.

'It's my partner's birthday…'

Trefor's wife smiled.

Trefor was the local policeman and Luke could never remember his wife's name. It was one of those names he should know by now but it was a bit late in the day to ask.

'Oh, well, we'll have to get her something nice, then.'

'Not too nice,' Luke said.

'How have you been, Luke?'

'Very well,' Luke answered, embarrassed that she knew his name.

'What size is your partner?'

'I'm not sure,' Luke said. 'She's very slim.'

'Well, do you know her bust size?'

'Small,' Luke answered, glad that he at least he knew that!

'Do you know, Trefor was just saying the other day that I should put the store online. Apparently men don't like coming in.'

'No,' Luke agreed.

'These are nice,' Trefor's wife said, 'though not *too* nice, and they've got a bit of stretch in them.'

It was very possibly amongst the most uncomfortable twenty minutes of Luke's life but, having made his purchases and thanking her, Luke was just about to head for home when Trefor came through the door.

'Hi, Luke.'

'Hi, Trefor.' Luke was about to head out but then he thought better of it. 'Trefor, I've got a friend staying with me.' He told him who it was. 'I'm hoping—'

'No problem,' Trefor said. 'I'll keep an eye out. Thanks for letting me know.'

Finally he was home.

The house felt nicer with Scarlet there. It wasn't just the warmth from the heater that changed things when Luke came in, it was Scarlet coming out of the lounge, wearing one of his shirts and also a smile.

'I missed you,' Scarlet said.

'Well, I'm here now.'

'How is she?'

'Much the same,' Luke said, and he looked at her worried expression. 'Do you want me to take you in to see her?'

'I don't know,' Scarlet admitted. She could see that Luke was exhausted but that wasn't the real reason she was holding back.

Here she could think.

Beside her mother's bedside she couldn't.

'No rush,' Luke said, sensing her quandary. 'She's stable.'

'I should be there, though.'

He didn't know what to say because his truth was that he didn't want her near that woman, but he held back from saying so.

'I'm going to go and get changed,' Luke said.

He went upstairs and put the underwear he had bought her in his wardrobe, pulled on some jeans and a jumper and then came back downstairs, carrying a mug, and not in the best of moods.

Scarlet had gone and the shopping still stood in the hallway.

'Scarlet!' he called, and she came out of the lounge.

'What?'

'I don't have servants and I've been at work all day.' He gestured to the bags and then held up a mug. 'What's a half-empty mug of coffee doing by my bed?'

'Maybe you were in a rush and didn't finish it?'

'I don't drink coffee.'

'Oh.'

'Were you in my bed this morning?'

It annoyed him that she smiled and nodded. 'It's more comfortable.'

It concerned him that he was fighting not to smile back.

That's what Scarlet did to him, though.

'Don't do that again!' he warned as she picked up the bag that held the lettuce and other heavy goods and carried it through to the kitchen.

'What did you do today?' Luke asked.

'Not much. I read some of your textbooks,' she admitted.

He was putting away the shopping and he held up a bottle of wine and she nodded.

'Do you like your job?' Scarlet asked.

'I love it,' Luke told her. 'I can't imagine my life without it.' He looked over at her. 'Would you like to be a midwife?'

'I just said it that night for something to say.'

'You said it again when you spoke to Angie.'

'Angie?'

'She's a friend.'

'The woman in the elevator!' Scarlet laughed as she remembered the conversation. 'I thought she was about to call Security on me for being an impostor.'

'No, that's Angie just trying to work things out.' He turned and gave her a smile. 'Lucy Edwards.'

Her cheeks went pink and then she told him something. 'I've seen babies being born.'

'When?'

'In Africa,' Scarlet said. 'The first time I went they gave me a private tour of the maternity ward. I didn't want to leave.'

'Really?'

Scarlet nodded.

'I went back again last year.'

'I saw,' Luke said, but without malice. 'Did you visit the maternity ward again?'

'I did, and I saw some babies being born. They'd told me they needed a drug called oxytocin for the women and we brought loads with us.'

'That's good.'

It was good and he turned and smiled.

'Here…' He tossed her a bag of clothes and he started to make dinner as Scarlet went through them.

'I'm not wearing these…'

'I thought the intention was for you to blend in.'

'Supermarket jeans?' Scarlet pulled a disgusted face and then she took out the shoes. 'These are men's shoes.'

'They're not.'

'If I wear these, people will think I'm a lesbian.'

Luke rolled his eyes and carried on chopping as Scarlet brought the subject back to the one they'd been discussing.

'Anyway, I don't think I'd be a very good midwife.'

'Why not?'

'I just don't.'

'Well, there are plenty of other things…' He glanced at her. He could see she was pensive and he could feel the shift in the light-hearted mood and knew she was thinking about their baby.

He loathed it that he carried on with preparing dinner but he did.

That was him.

'I thought you hadn't called me,' Scarlet said, touching on the subject that had to be faced but not yet, Luke thought, not with so much other stuff going on.

'It was only when I tried to ring you. After...' Scarlet sat and looked at his tense back. 'That I realised they'd blocked your number. Till then I thought you hadn't tried to call.'

'Well, I did,' Luke said. 'Over and over and then, when I couldn't get through, I arranged for some time off.'

'I didn't know.'

Luke said nothing. He didn't know what to say so he threw the mushrooms in the wok. Then he glanced up at the kitchen window. It was already dark and he could see her strained features in her reflection.

He was so loath to discuss it, though he knew he had to at least try, and he took the less easy option for the second time that day.

'Why didn't *you* call *me*?' Luke asked, and turned around. 'Why didn't you at least try and call to discuss things with me?'

'Because I was being selfish to land this on you, apparently. Because you had your life planned out and it sure as hell didn't include me.'

'Is that what she said?'

Scarlet didn't immediately answer. 'I was reminded that in two months' time I was going to Africa again. It's my favourite place and I was reminded that I could do a lot more good there...'

'Your mother said that?'

'Everyone said it.'

And by everyone she meant everyone, Luke thought. Every person Scarlet came into contact with was on her mother's payroll. He thought of his own confusion at the time. Everything that had seemed so simple in the bedroom, when it had just been the two of them, had been muddied beyond recognition.

He'd spoken to Angie about the pregnancy and had listened to her objective thoughts, then there had been a long conversation with a friend from rugby he'd gone to school with who had been through similar. He had given somewhat less than objective advice and had suggested that Scarlet was after a meal ticket.

Luke had omitted to mention Scarlet's name and her millions but those words had rattled.

It had been a one-night stand. He'd been aware at the start that they wouldn't last and he'd wondered if he had merely been an escape route.

Luke had looked at his parents' crap marriage, a couple who were together for the children and appearances' sake.

He'd had so many people and life experiences to draw on.

Scarlet had had Anya and her empire.

'Anyway,' Scarlet suddenly said, 'I couldn't do that to my child.'

'What?'

'Give it my life.'

'I wouldn't have let that happen!' Luke responded. 'All you had to do was pick up a phone or get on a plane...' He was trying to keep his voice from rising. Hell, there was a reason he hadn't wanted to discuss this now. It was too raw, and he was exhausted, not just from work but from the impact of having Scarlet back in his life.

He watched her stand.

'Don't walk off!' Luke warned.

'Oh, you can talk!'

'Meaning?'

'It's a shame we're not on the phone. You could just hang up!'

'Scarlet…' He didn't get to finish—the wok was spewing black smoke and he dragged it off the hob, but Scarlet wasn't sticking around to eat, or discuss, charred ruins.

'I don't want dinner,' Scarlet said. 'I'm going to bed.'

Yet there was no relief when she walked out of the room and up the stairs. Words needed to be said.

Dinner was stuffed so he poured a glass of wine and sat there, just staring out at the darkness, until the phone rang.

He took a call from his mother, reminding him about tomorrow and that they'd be there around four but couldn't stay for long.

Good.

He was in no mood for happy families and pretending that thirty-two years of marriage was anything to celebrate when he knew what a sham it was.

Not when he could hear Scarlet crying upstairs.

They were different tears. In fact, he couldn't hear them, just the pad of her feet and the turn of a loo roll and Scarlet blowing her nose once she was back in the spare room.

Luke had learnt to stay back, he'd been told to stay back, to hold in the important stuff and let people live their own lives.

This time he chose not to listen to that ingrained advice and a little while later he made a very long walk and knocked at her door.

'What?' Scarlet lay in bed, surrounded by balls of scrunched-up loo roll.

'I brought you some dinner.'

'I don't want it.'

'Come on,' he said, and then waited till she sat up and put the tray down on her lap. She stared at mushrooms on toast and a glass of wine.

'Aren't you cross?'

'I'm not cross,' Luke said. 'Even if I was, I'm not going to…' He was about to make a joke about withholding food but stopped himself. He could remember her saying that no one won with Anya and he guessed Scarlet flouncing off to her room would have been the only protest she could make.

And he was quite sure they'd leave her there hungry.

'Do you want to talk?' he offered.

'So you can hate me some more?'

'I don't hate you,' Luke said.

'It's okay if you do.' Scarlet gave a tight shrug. 'I hate you too sometimes.'

'Because?'

'Because you've got it all together, because the only mistake you ever made was me.'

'I've made plenty of mistakes, Scarlet, and you weren't one of them.' He came and sat on the bed. 'But, yes, I should have been more careful.'

'Yes, you should have been and so should I,' Scarlet shouted. 'But you're careful now, aren't you?'

'Meaning?'

'How many women since me?'

And he could fudge numbers or say, *Oh, they meant nothing*, or just ride it out, but he answered with the truth. 'Too many,' he admitted, and then he made himself ask the same when usually he would tell himself it was none of his business and back off. 'How about you?'

'Are you serious?'

Very.

He'd seen the smiling photos, the tour of Africa, the red carpet with gleaming plastic men by her side, and he'd tried, God knew, he'd tried to get past the hype, but sometimes, yes, it had felt as if she'd simply carried on without a backward glance.

'You really think I just pulled my knickers back up and carried on...'

'Sometimes,' he admitted, and held his breath, not sure they were strong enough for voicing the truth.

'Well, you're wrong,' Scarlet said. 'You're the one who carried on.' She rose up in the bed and the tray came with her, but she just tossed it to the floor, furious. 'I called you, Luke, and when I told you what I'd done, what did you do, what did you say? Nothing!'

'I didn't want to say the wrong thing.'

'And so you said precisely nothing!' She rose up farther and she pushed on the chest that was so strong but so immovable. 'Believe me, Luke, there was nothing you could have said that I wasn't thinking about myself. I was twenty-three, a woman, I should have been able to know my own mind...'

There were times Luke regretted his inability to speak up, to voice the thoughts in his head or the feelings that ate at him, and one minute ago had been one of those times. Instead, he was glad now that he had held on because the floodgates opened and she beat at him, and raged at him, except it wasn't about him, and Luke knew that.

He had known when he'd walked in the door that her loathing was aimed at herself.

'I listened to them and I shouldn't have.' She raged and raged. 'I'd rather you'd called me a bitch than stay quiet.'

'Really?' Luke took her arms and then he took her chin and still she would not meet his eyes. 'If that's the sort of reaction you were hoping for, Scarlet, then you really are with the wrong guy.' Now she looked at him and she saw those lovely brown eyes she had trusted so much and still did, and she saw tears in them too. 'I didn't know what to think, let alone say,' Luke admitted. 'I was on the way to the airport when you called...'

She started to cry but it was on him this time.

And Luke said nothing, not because he didn't know what to say now but because all she wanted was to cry and be comforted without agenda. And when she'd finished, when there were many more little balls of loo roll added to her pile, it was Scarlet who admitted that she didn't want to talk.

'Fair enough,' Luke said. 'We'll try again when you're ready.'

She looked from his chest to the floor and saw the lovely second dinner he had made dressing the carpet.

'I'll get it,' Luke said.

Scarlet lay back on the pillow when he left quietly and then looked over at the massive wine stain on the carpet and thought about how she'd thrown the tray and shouted. She tried to work out how on earth she could face him tomorrow when there was a knock at the door.

'Third time lucky,' Luke said, and he came in with a tray.

It was completely unexpected and the nicest thing anyone had ever done for her because she really was starving.

No wine this time. Instead, there was a lovely mug of milk and cinnamon and lots of slices of buttery toast smothered in jam.

'Where are the mushrooms?' Scarlet asked.

She'd never ended a row on a smile.

CHAPTER ELEVEN

SOMETHING WAS WRONG.

Scarlet woke and opened the curtain and she looked out at the streetlight and then lay back on the pillow.

The house was cold, even with the heating on. She hadn't felt warm since she'd arrived in England.

She thought of her mother and their row, and whatever had gone on between them, Scarlet wanted to see her.

It wouldn't be fair to ask Luke. He'd had a couple of glasses of wine and was exhausted, she knew that.

She recalled his words—visiting her mother didn't have to be a big deal.

What if she did what he said, went in through the maternity entrance?

The clothes he had bought her really were awful but she put them on and wrote a note and left it on the hall table.

'Gone to see Mom.'

It was an easy drive. There were some roadworks but in less than an hour the hospital came into view. She bypassed the main entrance, indicated for Maternity and parked the car. As she got out Scarlet saw a couple walking towards the door, where they buzzed at the entrance. She walked over quickly.

'Here,' Scarlet said, and held the door open for them as the woman doubled over.

'Thanks.'

She was in.

Her heart was pounding but Scarlet told herself she was doing nothing wrong but then she saw a security guard walking towards her.

'Can I help you?'

'I'm here to see my mother.'

'You can't wander around the hospital at night.'

'The emergency consultant told me if I used the maternity entrance...'

'Scarlet?'

She nodded.

'Geoff.' He gave her a smile. 'Remember?'

Now she did.

'Just wait there,' Geoff said.

He made a phone call and then came back. 'This way.' They chatted as they walked. 'You've saved me a right old drama,' Geoff told her. 'The press have been awful. I've told the ICU staff and they said to bring you up in the theatre lift, which will take you straight onto the unit.'

He went with her but when Scarlet arrived on ICU it was like stepping into a spaceship, but then a woman came over and gave her a smile.

'I'm Lorna.'

'I just wanted some time with her.'

'Of course you do,' Lorna said. 'Did you want to speak with a doctor first?'

'No.' Scarlet shook her head. 'I just want to see her. Is anyone with her?'

'They're all outside,' Lorna said.

It was all very low-key. There were a few other relatives sitting with their loved ones. The curtains weren't drawn as it was break time and the staff were thinner on the ground, Lorna explained.

'I can close them if you need me to. I'll call Ellie back from her break.'

There was no need.

Scarlet sat there and held her mother's hand and was brought a plastic cup of hot chocolate and a packet with two biscuits in.

'Your mum?' a man sitting nearby asked, and Scarlet nodded.

'Who are you here with?'

'My son. He's been in Theatre all day. I've just got in to see him now. I'm Evan.'

'Scarlet.' She smiled.

'I know!' Evan rolled his eyes. 'They're all out there, trying to work out where you are. Good for you!' he said. 'Ashleigh, my son, likes you. He was very fed up that he never got to see you!'

Scarlet laughed.

They chatted.

Not a lot but about how nice the hot chocolate was, how good the staff were.

How scary it was to be here.

'My wife's just gone for a sleep. I had to get some sleeping tablets,' Evan admitted. 'Never taken anything in my life but they did the trick. I thought I was dreaming when I woke up and heard he had a liver.'

'How long has Ashleigh been sick?' Scarlet asked.

'Since he was born,' Evan told her. 'We had a few good years when he turned eleven, but the last year has been the toughest. What about your mum?'

And she was about to make her usual small talk, or smile and say just how wonderful everything was.

Here wasn't the place to, though.

Lies made no difference in the ICU, Scarlet guessed.

It wasn't just the patients who were exposed to serious diagnoses.

'She's been sick for a very long time too,' Scarlet admitted.

'It takes its toll, doesn't it?' Evan said, and she nodded.

'Hot chocolate helps,' Scarlet said. She just sipped on her warm drink and held her mum's hand and then, when the clock nudged three, guessing Luke might need the car early, she stood and gave her mum a kiss on the cheek.

'I love you.'

Scarlet did.

I love you not.

Sometimes.

She just had to love herself more.

'I hope he's improved in the morning,' Scarlet said to Evan.

'Thanks, love.'

And then she offered something stupid, something silly and fun for when Ashleigh woke up, but it made Evan smile.

God knew, he needed it.

The charge nurse called for Geoff to walk her back down and she nodded in the direction of Luke's car.

'I'm fine now,' Scarlet said. 'Thank you.'

'Next time, page the head of security. It's usually me at night,' Geoff said.

'Thanks.'

Scarlet drove home, or rather to Luke's home, feeling better.

Not brilliant but better.

A part of her wanted to turn off the motorway. To simply drive to the cottage that was supposed to have been her haven while she sorted out her head with the luxury of time that had been denied to her now.

How did she tell her mother now that she was still leaving her?

How could she face the impossible conversations that were to come with Luke? And then there were his parents coming later today. Maybe he'd welcome her disappearing?

Scarlet wanted to curl up into a ball and for the world to sort itself out before she came back.

It wasn't going to, though.

The garage door opened as she approached and, hell, England was cold, Scarlet thought. Even the garage was freezing.

The house felt only marginally warmer.

Her note was still there on the table and her midnight adventure had paid off.

She went up to her room and stripped off her clothes then looked at the bed and simply couldn't face getting in. She wanted Luke, not for anything other than who he was and because of where she'd just been.

Scarlet padded down the hall and pushed open the door and there was Luke, deeply asleep. He hadn't even noticed she'd gone, Scarlet knew.

She slipped into the bed and moved straight over to him.

'You're frozen,' Luke said, and pulled her in closer.

Just that.

He stroked her arm as he had once before, and it was as if it was normal that she lie in his arms.

It was.

Luke pulled the covers over her shoulders and went straight back to sleep.

A sleep so deep that Luke even struggled to wake to his alarm. Instead, it blurred into the sound of ambulances or IVs alarming, and then he prised his eyes open and felt Scarlet wrapped around him.

Where it felt she belonged.

CHAPTER TWELVE

HE TURNED OFF the alarm but didn't have the energy to tell her to get back to her own bed, and neither did he want her to get out.

He knew she was awake, he could feel her lashes blinking on his chest.

'Are you okay?' Luke asked.

'No,' Scarlet admitted, and then she said what she'd wanted to when they'd been in the kitchen, as if hours hadn't passed since then. 'I didn't know what to do, Luke.'

Hours might have passed but he knew what was on her mind. 'Tell me.'

'You have to go to work.'

'No.' He did but some things were more important.

'And we can't storm off to bed,' Luke pointed out, 'given we're in it, so maybe we can try and talk.' There were so many details missing, ones he had thought he'd prefer not to know. But that had been when he had thought her callous. 'What was your mother like when you told her?'

'Fine,' Scarlet said from the depths of his chest. 'At first. I had toothache once and she handled it in pretty much the same way—you'll be fine, Vince can take care of that for you. That's when I rang you. I knew we'd ended badly and that I shouldn't have told Troy where I was but—'

'Forget about that now.'

'When you said to come here, that we'd talk and work things out…' She felt stupid explaining it. 'I don't keep my own passport, Sonia does. I didn't know how to get on a plane unless it was my mother's jet. I wanted to, though. I told my mother that I wanted to keep the baby and that I was going to England to speak with you. She went crazy. I didn't get it. I pointed out that she was a single parent and at least I knew who the father was.'

'What did she say to that?'

'She slapped me and told me how ungrateful I was, that, yet again, she had to sort me out. They had a crisis meeting about me. That's when I called you again. She wanted you to come and work for her, alongside Vince.'

'Scarlet, I could never do that.' Luke was honest. 'I wanted to be with you and I wanted us to work out how. I could have accepted some attention and a change to my life but I could never work for your mother.'

'I understand that but when you just dismissed it out of hand…'

'Scarlet, medicine is important to me. I take it very seriously and I could never be paid to prescribe, ever.'

'It seemed like the only way.'

'We'd have worked on finding other ways.'

'And then you didn't call back.'

'I did,' Luke said. 'I was going crazy. I spoke to Angie, and to a friend whose girlfriend, well, his wife now, had got pregnant. I asked my boss if I could take a couple of weeks off. He didn't want to give it to me, given that I'd only been working there for a few days. I told him he could have my notice if he wouldn't give me time off. I was on my way to the airport when you called.'

He'd never forget it.

First there had been relief at hearing her voice when she'd finally called. *I'm on my way,* he had said.

'There's no need, it's been taken care of.'

He'd driven straight into the back of someone.

'I heard the other driver shouting,' Scarlet admitted. 'Then I listened while you moved the car and swapped details and then you came back to the phone.

'Are you still there?' he had asked.

'Still here,' Scarlet had replied, and then had come the agony of him ringing off.

'I'd just got back from the clinic.'

'Did anyone go with you?'

'Mom,' Scarlet said.

So no one helpful, then, Luke thought.

'She was all nice to me afterwards. I was a mess and she had Vince see me and he put me on antidepressants. I didn't take them. I think I was right to be sad.' Scarlet thought back to that very difficult year. 'I knew things had to change and I also knew they were watching me. I picked up a bit when I found out she was going on tour again and that we'd be coming here.'

'Were you going to call?'

She didn't answer straight away. How could she have landed on him not just herself but all her hopes and dreams? How could she have told him about the shiny, poised, together person she had hoped to be when next she saw him?

'I don't know,' Scarlet said instead.

It hurt to hear that. He'd spent the last few months wondering if she would get in touch and to now to hear that she hadn't made up her mind cut deep.

'What would you have done?' Scarlet asked. 'If I'd called?'

'I guess it would have depended how the conversation went,' Luke admitted. 'But...' He couldn't.

She *hadn't* called.

'Tell me.'

'No.' Luke shook his head.

They were nowhere near ready for that. They might never be.

'I hate it that you went through it on your own. I mean, I know you had your mum…' He tried to be polite but Scarlet gave a low mirthless laugh at his effort.

'She didn't come in. Actually, there was a really nice nurse. I thought they'd be horrible,' she admitted. 'I was a bit of a wreck but she really was lovely to me.'

'I would hope so.'

'She was.' Scarlet still sounded surprised. 'I got very upset afterwards. I knew I'd made a mistake and she spoke to me for ages. She said that one day I'd be able to move on and that I didn't have nothing, that I'd learn from it…'

And it killed him to hear her say she'd thought she had nothing and he was very glad of that nurse who had taken the time with her on such a difficult day.

'And I have,' Scarlet said. 'Which is why I blew up the other day at my mother.'

'Can you tell me about the row?' Luke asked, and Scarlet nodded.

'I told her that I was leaving and she laughed and said I wouldn't last five minutes without her.'

His hand was still stroking her hair.

'I said that I had you,' Scarlet admitted, and she started to cry. 'I didn't know if I did, I guessed not, but I was just trying to get away…'

'I know that.'

'And she said you wouldn't want me, given all I'd done, and then I got angry,' Scarlet said. 'Really angry.'

Now his hand was on her arm, the way it had been that morning, stroking her arm gently and firmly, and there was nothing that she couldn't tell him.

'I said that she'd always been jealous of me and that the reason she didn't want me to keep my baby was because she didn't want the spotlight on me and the "Grandma Anya" headline.' Scarlet looked up at him. 'I'm just sorry it took me so long to work that out.'

'I'm amazed that you could work it out,' Luke said. 'Sometimes I think my family is complicated but...'

He stopped.

She was used to it.

Luke always held back.

'It's just as well that we'll never make it.' Scarlet smiled. 'You could hardly have me meet them.'

'They're coming this afternoon.' Luke sighed. 'It's their wedding anniversary so they're stopping by on their way down to London for a long weekend.'

'Do you want me hide in the bedroom?'

'I don't want to hide you, Scarlet,' Luke said. 'Don't you get that?'

She didn't.

CHAPTER THIRTEEN

LUKE WALKED INTO ICU and nodded to Evan and then he looked over to where Anya lay.

On the morning she had come into Emergency it had taken almost everything that Luke had in him to treat her as just another patient.

He wondered if he could do that if she came in now. He hoped so but right now he was so angry that he truly didn't know.

'We're going to try and rouse her later this afternoon.'

It was a different anaesthetist on this morning.

'Did David pass on my message?'

'He did,' Craig said. 'I'll call you with any changes.'

'Thanks.'

'Lorna spoke with daughter last night,' Craig added. 'She's aware of what's going on and—'

'She spoke with the daughter?' Luke was horrified at any leak in information and tried to sort it out. 'How did Lorna know it was her?'

'Because she came in.' Craig gave him a wide-eyed look. 'Lorna wouldn't speak to just anyone.'

'I know that.'

A nurse came past and started laughing. 'Go and ask Evan if you don't believe him.'

'Evan?'

'Over there.'

Luke looked over and there was Evan, doing his crossword. Luke made his way over to him. 'How are you doing?'

'A lot better than I was the last time I spoke to you,' Evan admitted, and he saw Luke go to open his mouth. 'I'll make an appointment with my GP about my blood pressure.'

'Good man,' Luke said. 'I hear that you had a visitor last night.'

'Don't tell that lot.' Evan winked and nodded towards the exit door behind which Anya's entourage sat. He took out his phone. 'Lovely lady...' He glanced at his son, who was asleep. 'Ashleigh laughed when I showed him this morning.'

Luke looked at Evan's phone and for all he hated this type of thing, now it made him smile.

There was Scarlet, looking very unlike Scarlet. Not a scrap of make-up and her hair was wild and she was wearing a very baggy jumper and one of his shirts and smiling with Evan into the camera.

'How long was she here?' Luke asked.

'A couple of hours.' And then he looked over at Anya and he said exactly the same as Angie had. 'Poor kid.'

Luke worked for a couple of hours and then he called home in the familiar style and she answered the phone.

'Sorry,' Scarlet said, peeling her eyes open. 'I was asleep.'

He thought of her driving through the night and then coming back to his bed but he didn't let on that he knew.

'Are you up to going out for a walk?'

'Of course.'

'My parents are dropping by about four. I'll be home before then but I need something...'

'What?'

'Biscuits.'

Scarlet frowned.

'Biscuits?' she checked, because where she was from you ate them for breakfast and with gravy. 'You're going to give them biscuits?'

And then Luke remembered there were so many differences between them.

'Cookies.'

'Why?'

'Because they'll want a cup of tea. We're polite like that,' Luke said with an edge.

'You want me to buy cookies for their anniversary?'

'If you've got time.'

'Ha-ha.'

'Do you have any money?' Luke asked.

'I do.'

'Because there's some in the drawer by my...' Luke hesitated. There were some other things he didn't want her to see in the drawer by his bed. It was too late for that, though.

'I've already found them,' Scarlet said. 'I snooped the first day I was here.'

'Well, beside them is some cash.'

'I'll treat you,' Scarlet said and, suddenly too angry for words, she rang off.

Luke called back.

'Did you just hang up on me?'

'I did.'

'Good for you.'

He liked it that she could argue, that she was starting to find her voice.

'I've got a present for you,' Luke said.

'Really?' Scarlet frowned. 'What?'

'Go and open my wardrobe.'

Scarlet got up and Luke sat there hearing her swear at how cold it was, even thought he'd left the heater on high, and trying not to imagine her streaking naked across his bedroom.

'Where?' she asked.

'There's a bag at the bottom.'

Scarlet peeled it open with delight and pulled out all the lovely knickers and bras. 'Are these for me?'

'Scarlet, if I'm hiding a bag of ladies' underwear in my wardrobe for myself, then we really do have a lot to discuss. Enjoy.'

'Talk to me,' Scarlet said. She was already pulling some knickers on.

'I've got to go, I really am busy.'

A running commentary about underwear with Scarlet he really did not need!

It felt odd to be out in the village. Scarlet had found a scarf and wrapped it around her head. Not so much to hide, but she didn't get why everyone was saying it was mild for November. She'd never felt more frozen in her life.

One thing the English did very well, though, Scarlet decided as she walked through the store, was cookies! Then she saw a recipe card for coffee-and-walnut cake and decided that she'd make that and bought the necessary ingredients. Happy with her purchases, she headed out of the shop but then caught sight of her reflection.

She looked like the Matchstick Girl in the clothes Luke had bought her so she walked into a small boutique and smiled at a woman behind the counter.

'Hi,' Scarlet said.

'Hello!'

She started to look through the racks of clothing. 'Are you looking for something special?' the woman asked.

'I'm looking for something not too special.' Scarlet sighed. 'I'm staying with a friend and I don't have much with me.'

Her name was Margaret and she was lovely and a happy hour was spent trying on various pieces of clothing. Scarlet had soon amassed quite a collection.

'Ooh, I haven't seen this one,' Margaret said, as Scarlet handed over her card to pay.

That card and the money on it was Scarlet's biggest achievement, not that Margaret could know. It had taken a year to get to this point. A year of squirrelling away cash, pretending she wanted to know what it felt like to go into a restaurant and pay. Setting up an account on an auction sight and selling signed photos. Just putting a little away with a dream in mind.

And maybe that dream had been a cottage on the beach to clear her head before she again faced Luke, but that hadn't quite worked out. Still, it felt brilliant to choose and buy her own clothes.

It was a very different house that Luke came home to—the scent of cake hit him as he came in and there was Scarlet looking like a Scarlet he had never seen.

Gone the celebrity, gone too the Matchstick Girl clothes he had inadvertently bought her.

She was wearing a huge chunky nutmeg jumper and thick black stockings and black velvet stilettos and, possibly, a skirt, but the jumper was a bit too big to tell.

'Wow,' Luke said.

'I know.' Scarlet grinned as she spread icing. 'It's my first cake.'

He wasn't talking about the cake but he made the right

noises, even if it did look like she was icing two burnt pancakes.

'How's Mom?'

'They're going to try and take off the ventilator later on today.'

'Should I be there?'

'She's going to be drowsy at first...'

'Luke, please, tell me what to do.'

'Whatever it is that you want to do,' Luke said. 'Scarlet...' He wanted her away from that woman, and to never have to see her again.

But it wasn't his place to say that.

She busied herself icing her cake.

'Coffee and walnut,' Scarlet explained.

They were pecan nuts but he chose not to say anything.

He put a finger in the icing mix and it was butter and not much else.

'It doesn't look like the picture.' Scarlet sighed.

'They never do.'

'I hope they like it.'

'Who?' Luke said, and then realised she had made it for his parents' visit. He'd actually forgotten they were coming. The whole drive home he'd been thinking about Scarlet and her mother, interspersed with Scarlet and what knickers she was wearing.

'Look, I know my being here might make things awkward for you, so if you don't want to have to explain me I can go for a walk.'

'I don't explain myself to my parents,' Luke said. 'The same way they don't have to explain themselves to me.'

'I just don't want to create tension.'

'Oh, there'll be tension,' Luke assured her, 'but I promise it has nothing to do with you. There's no need to be nervous.'

'Easy for you to say. Do they know about us, about…?'

Luke shook his head and gave a tense shrug. 'A bit.'

'How much?'

'Just that I met you a couple of years ago. Marcus wouldn't stop going on about it. They don't know the other stuff.'

'Do they work?'

Luke nodded. 'My father's a professor in cardiology.'

'Your mother?'

'She's a curator.'

He looked at her and could see she was daunted, so he came over and wrapped his arms around her waist. 'Just be yourself.'

'Sure.'

'Scarlet…' He looked right into her navy eyes and, yes, he loathed sharing but he loathed her unease with herself even more, so he said what he could to help her relax. 'My father screws around like you wouldn't believe. He has affair after affair. Some casual, which my mother ignores. Sometimes they get serious and my mother hits the gin when it does.'

Scarlet just looked at Luke as he gave a weary sigh and told her some more.

'Then he stops seeing his mistress, my mother stops drinking, everyone's happy and the cycle repeats itself. It's like living in the laundromat.'

Scarlet laughed. 'How do you know?'

'It's obvious. Well, it is to me but, with that said, Marcus and Emma don't have a clue…'

'Emma?'

'My sister.'

'Oh, I thought she was a lady friend.'

'You're my lady friend,' Luke said, and then he changed tack because his hands were moving southwards. 'Anyway, this weekend they're going to be celebrating thirty-two years of dysfunction, but I'm not allowed to say that.'

She frowned.

'I'll raise a cup of tea and we'll have some walnut cake that you very nicely made and they'll carry on their way. And no doubt by Sunday he'll be out with his latest and my mother will be passed out on the sofa.'

'Why are you telling me this?'

'Because I don't want you to feel intimated.' Luke let out a breath and Scarlet looked at this very deep man.

'Thank you.'

'For?'

'Telling me,' Scarlet said, and then she smiled. 'Some of it.'

He smiled back and then he stopped smiling as tears filled her eyes.

'I'm scared about my mom...'

'I know. Look, I've taken tomorrow off—' Luke started, then groaned when he heard a car in his driveway. 'They're here.'

Oh, they were, and they were also very taken aback to find Scarlet in situ.

Thankfully, though, it would seem they cared less about the famous Anya than they did about their son. His mother ran a very disapproving eye over Scarlet's stockinged legs and the questionable presence of a skirt, and his father simply looked her up and down.

Oh, my God, Scarlet realised, James Edwards was seriously checking her out.

Scarlet actually wanted to laugh as she saw Luke's eyes briefly shutter.

'You made cake!' Rose Edwards spoke as if Scarlet had just come in from the fields and mastered the appliances.

Which she sort of had!

'Not too much,' Rose said, as Scarlet cut a very generous piece.

'So, do you work at the Royal?' James asked her legs as she handed him a plate.

'No.' Scarlet smiled. 'I'm taking a break at the moment.'

'Studying?' Rose checked.

'No.' Scarlet gave Luke a slice. 'I'm just—'

'Scarlet's just taking some time out,' Luke said, and watched his mother pull a noncomprehending face and give a little shrug in a way only Rose could.

'Luke didn't mention anything,' Rose said, and then she frowned. 'Scarlet? Weren't you two...?'

'Scarlet and I go back a couple of years.' Luke gave nothing away with his response. 'She's over from LA and has come to stay for a few days.'

The cake really was amazing! Burnt and unrisen and the butter cream was almost pure butter.

'You're not having any?' Rose said to Scarlet as they all chewed through hell.

'Oh, no.' Scarlet screwed up her nose. 'Full of carbs!'

Luke actually laughed and never had he been more grateful for poor cooking skills because when Scarlet went to offer more, his mother pointed out they had to be in London by seven.

'Can't count on the traffic,' James said.

Scarlet said her goodbyes but stayed in the kitchen because Rose was making frantic eye gestures to Luke to have a word outside.

'Has she moved in?' Rose demanded.

'Temporarily, yes,' Luke replied.

'Luke, she's...' Rose was all pursed lips. 'Just watch yourself.'

Luke stood as they drove off and his father took another brick out of his wall. He walked inside.

'Is that American hussy after your money?' Scarlet was sitting on the kitchen bench and grinned as he walked back into the kitchen.

'It would seem so.'

'Your father!' Scarlet started laughing. 'He spoke to my thighs.'

'I don't know what to say about that.' What could he say? 'Never let him give you a tour of the library.'

'Well, if I ever do get to see your home I'll bear that in mind.'

He came over and she wrapped her arms around his neck, and she could just feel his tension. She just looked at him and smiled.

'Are you adopted?' she teased, only because Luke was a younger version of his father but their personalities could not be more different.

'I wish.'

'Is he like that with all your...?' She hesitated. She wasn't really a girlfriend, she was just the hot mess that had landed at his door.

'Yep,' Luke said. 'So don't take it as a compliment.'

'I shan't.'

He looked at her and usually he found family occasions, particularly if there was a girlfriend present, excruciating, but this one had almost ended with a smile.

His father's actions reflected no more on him with Scarlet than Anya's did on her. Still, he was cross with them.

'I can't stand how she doesn't notice what he's up to, or pretends not to,' Luke said. 'And yet she nitpicks and judges everyone, what they wear, how they talk...'

'How they cook...' Scarlet smiled. 'Poor Luke, having to eat that awful cake!'

'I like it,' Luke said.

'Good, because it's dinner.'

Now she did make him smile. What he had said before about Scarlet clearing his head was true. It was as if the rest of the world was crazy when it was just the two of them.

'You look beautiful,' Luke said.

'I went shopping.'

'I can see.'

'And I *love* my presents.'

'I want to see.' He ran a hand over her bottom as she sat on the bench and they kissed. A kiss that both had been waiting for. Her hands pressed into his hair and Luke moved in between her thighs and she wrapped them around his waist.

His kiss deepened, as if making up for two years of none. A slow, deep kiss that she didn't want to end but it did.

Luke remembered how upset she had been just before his parents had arrived.

He didn't want this to be about distraction. Both knew that at any moment the phone would go and there would be news about her mother. And, though he wanted more than anything to take her up to bed, or even on the kitchen table, there was so much to sort out first.

'Do you want to go and visit your mum?'

'You don't want to drive all that way again…'

'Do you want to go in?' he offered again.

'I don't know.'

'That's an answer,' Luke said. 'It's okay not to know.'

They went through to the lounge and it was like waiting for a bomb to go off. Scarlet sat cross-legged, tapping one foot, and then came over and lay on the coach, in her favourite spot—her head on his lap.

'I can take you in tomorrow and I can stay with you while you speak with her.'

'There's no need for that.' Scarlet shook her head. 'I know you think she's awful but she's not all bad...'

'No one is,' Luke said. 'It would be so much easier if that were the case.'

'She can be so nice. I don't know how to tell her I'm leaving after she's been so ill.'

'Leaving's hard,' Luke said. 'Even when there's no real reason to. Especially when there's no real reason.' And he told her a bit about the demise of his relationships prior to her. 'It's hard to admit something's not working when there's nothing really wrong, but sometimes...'

'What?'

'Well, you should *want* to stay,' Luke offered, not just to Scarlet but to himself as he thought of the demise of too many okay-ish relationships. 'Not have to come up with reasons to.'

He picked up his phone to glance at the time and Scarlet took it as a sign he was about to get up so she turned in his lap. 'Don't go...' She ran a hand over him and her lips did the same. Luke took her hand as she went for his zipper.

'I wasn't going anywhere,' Luke said.

'Just making sure...'

'Scarlet, I don't need a blow job to stay on the couch with you.'

He watched her face redden and tears fill her eyes, but he wasn't shaming her, more those who had taught her that was the way to make someone stay.

'You don't want me.'

'I want *you*.'

'And I want you to hold me.'

Finally!

He lay down beside her and showed her how nice it was to be held for no reason other than that.

'You're hard,' Scarlet said a little while later.

'It'll pass.' Luke grinned. He was as turned on as hell but there was a reason he wasn't tearing her clothes off now and he stopped smiling. 'Is that how you get your affection, Scarlet?'

He'd guessed as much but it hurt when she nodded.

They needed to start from the beginning, and that was why they lay there, half talking then dozing, and he wished they could stay there, but time moved quickly when you didn't want it to and just as Scarlet dozed off he heard the buzz of his phone.

He took the phone call and then sat there quietly for a moment and looked down at Scarlet. He did not want to invade her peace.

But he had to.

'Scarlet…'

'Mmm…'

'That was Craig, the anaesthetist working this evening. It's okay…' He felt her tense. 'Your mum's doing better.'

'Is she asking for me?'

'Yes.'

He could feel her rapid breathing.

'It wasn't an accident…'

'It was,' Scarlet said. 'She just took too much.'

'No.'

'It was.' She started to cry and Luke just sat there, thinking that her intense pain would stop soon because very soon it would be made to.

An accident.

Whoops.

But that just dulled the pain, it wouldn't take it away.

'I need to see her.'

'She's very angry and upset,' he warned, but Scarlet was already pulling on her shoes and he had this awful feeling that back to her world she was going. Especially when she went upstairs and started filling her bag with her flats and the scarf she had pinched from him.

He stood in the doorway, watching her, and told himself that they had, from the moment they had met, been temporary.

'Can I have my clothes,' Scarlet said, 'and my phone?'

'Are you coming back here?' Luke asked.

She just looked at him. 'I don't know!'

Her honest answer felt like she'd thrown a knife.

Luke's eyes felt as if he'd been swimming underwater as he drove back in to work.

People were right—he should live closer.

Except, as he looked over at Scarlet, he wouldn't change where he lived for the world. At least she'd had some time away. He just wished he could have given some more.

He had called ahead before he'd left and had spoken with Lorna, who was back for her night shift.

'David should be in soon,' Lorna said.

'It's not David I'm ringing for,' Luke said. 'Lorna, I'm bringing Anya's daughter in. Could we use the direct theatre lift?'

There was a very long pause as Lorna resisted asking any questions. 'Of course,' she said. 'Do you know the code?'

'I do.'

'I'll see you shortly, then.'

His filthy Audi moved unnoticed into the car park and they took the elevator up to the ground floor, where they headed straight to the central column.

There they took the service lift straight up to Theatre and then another up to ICU. Instead of arriving in the corridor, as the other elevators did, they stepped straight onto the ward.

To their credit, the staff there gave him no more than a slight wide-eyed look as Luke came over to the desk with Scarlet.

'Hi, Scarlet.' Lorna smiled. 'Your mom's been asking after you.'

'I know.'

'Why don't we go somewhere a little more private?' Lorna suggested, and glanced over at David, who nodded.

'I'll be there in a moment.'

'Do you want me to come with you?' Luke offered, but Scarlet shook her head so he stood there as Scarlet and Lorna headed off.

'I'm not sure what's going on between you two,' David said, 'and I don't need to know.'

'Thanks.

'You need to know this, though,' David said. 'She's about to walk into the lion's den.'

'I know she is.

Scarlet sat and listened to Lorna, who explained that her mother was doing a lot better but was insisting that she be moved elsewhere. 'She's not being very cooperative,' Lorna explained gently. 'And she's also extremely angry.'

'With me?'

'With everyone,' David said as he walked in, and Lorna looked up and smiled. 'I want her to stay here and I've told her that but she wants to be moved. I've told her that can't happen yet.' He was honest with Scarlet. 'I've dragged out a couple of procedures and told her it wasn't possible till late tomorrow but I can't force her to stay.'

Scarlet nodded. 'I know.'

'She's very insistent that she leaves.'

'Anya can be exceptionally difficult,' Scarlet said. 'I'm very sorry—'

'Scarlet,' David interrupted, 'you have nothing to apologise for.'

And she took a breath because she knew he wasn't just telling her that she didn't need to apologise for her mother's behaviour tonight.

This wasn't her fault.

Scarlet told herself that as she stepped behind the curtains and saw her mother lying there.

Lorna stayed with her but it wasn't pretty.

It was her fault apparently, and basically Anya told her that if at first she didn't succeed then she would try and try and try again because she could not live without her daughter by her side.

Luke had always thought that he was the strong one.

It had been an assumption of his that was summarily squashed when, after a few minutes of Anya's ranting, he heard Scarlet's clear voice.

'I'm going to go now, Mom. I love you. Please, get well.'

Scarlet walked out and straight to the elevator then she turned as if she'd forgotten something and thanked David. 'And can you thank Lorna?'

'Of course,' David said. 'Are you happy for me to call Luke with any change?'

'Please,' Scarlet said.

And that was it.

They stood in the elevator and made their way back to the underground car park, and Scarlet felt as if she might jump out of her skin.

'Can I drive?' Scarlet said suddenly.

'Of course.' Luke handed her the keys and Scarlet climbed into the driver's seat.

'She blames you,' Scarlet said, 'well, when she's not blaming me.'

'I heard,' Luke said. He didn't really know what to say here but he tried. 'I'm sorry if I've caused a rift…'

'A rift?' She gave him a very wide-eyed look that told him he was a master of understatement and then turned her head to look over her shoulder as she reversed out. 'And do you really think any of this is your fault?'

Wisely he said nothing.

'What?' Scarlet challenged the silence. 'Why do you have to be responsible?'

'I'm not.'

'Why do I?'

'You're not.'

'No,' Scarlet said, and she briefly looked at him as they waited for the barrier to lift. 'I was always going to leave, Luke or no Luke.'

'It's left here,' Luke said, as she missed the exit.

'Not tonight it isn't.'

She drove out of the hospital as if they were being chased by the paparazzi and then he found out that, despite several prangs in her past, Scarlet could actually drive, and rather fast!

There was somewhere she needed to be. Scarlet had known it the very second Luke had broken the news to her.

It had been the place she'd intended to run to that awful morning and it was the place she was taking him now.

'Am I being kidnapped?' Luke grinned.

He didn't blame her in the least for wanting a drive.

'Yep.' She looked over at him. 'So go to sleep. I don't want to talk.'

CHAPTER FOURTEEN

IT WAS A long drive, a very long drive through the night and she liked it that he didn't question her about where they were going and that after a while he slept.

God knew, he hadn't all week, Scarlet realised.

She read the signs, and the roads were very narrow and hilly, more so than she remembered. The hedges and stone walls loomed close but finally they had arrived and she pulled into a small deserted lookout and stared out at a waning moon and an angry black ocean.

The water looked a lot like she felt, cold and churned up and too dangerous to explore, but she wanted the man who was stretching out beside her to know her some more.

And so badly she wanted to know what went on in his head too.

Luke was so closed off and it had taken meeting his parents to realise that his guarded nature didn't just apply to her.

'Where the hell…?' Luke asked as he opened his eyes. The wipers were going full pelt but were still battling against the rain and the windscreen was fogging up.

'Devon,' Scarlet said.

Luke looked at the dashboard clock. It was five in the morning and pitch-black. The wind was howling, the sea was rolling black and white.

'I've dreamt about being here for a very long time.'

'Was it warm and sunny when you did?' Luke asked.

Scarlet shook her head. 'Nope.' It really was the place of her dreams but she had never dared to hope that she would ever be here with Luke.

They got out and Scarlet went into her bag and put on the horrible flat shoes he had bought her and then she put the giant bag over her shoulder. 'Leave it in the car,' Luke suggested, but Scarlet shook her head.

They didn't walk down to the beach, more the wind blew them onto it, and they ran hand in hand along the pebbly shore beside the roaring water.

Scarlet was angry, more angry and upset and terrified for her mother than she knew how to be, and Luke got that. He had heard her mother's cruel words and had seen Scarlet's calm exit but knew she was bleeding on the inside.

'I hate her. I love her but I hate her,' Scarlet said.

'Did you tell her that the other night?'

Scarlet nodded.

'You are allowed to say how you feel. What she did with that information was her choice.'

'You're allowed to say how you feel too,' Scarlet said, 'but you don't.'

'I know.' He pulled her right into his jacket and held her.

'What if she dies because I don't go back?'

And there was the reason that, in this, he didn't offer his thoughts, because one day that might well happen and he did not want to have influenced her choice.

He did not want, years from now, for there to be another reason for deep regret that came between them.

'If you do go back, will it change things?'

It was all he could offer and Scarlet tried to picture herself back home in LA and her mother well, simply because she was there by her side.

It hadn't worked so far.

For twenty-five years, being by her side hadn't worked.

'Do you know,' Luke said, and with his words he offered her no easy solution but acknowledged the hell her decision must be, 'with this wind, if you scream and face out to the water, no one will hear you?'

'Oh, they would,' Scarlet said, because the scream that she held inside was so loud it might split the channel they stared out at.

Luke shook his head. 'They won't.'

And so she did. Scarlet screamed and swore and kicked at the stones, and she was like the witches that she'd read flew over these parts, and it helped.

It really did.

And when her throat was as dry and as sore as it had been the morning she'd found her mother, the morning she had found Luke again, he took her in his arms and he held her.

They swayed to the sound of the waves and moved to their own tune, and against his chest the world felt better. With her in his arms, despite the darkness, the world seemed brighter.

And so they danced, and cared not if anyone was watching.

CHAPTER FIFTEEN

'LET'S GET BACK to the car,' Luke suggested.

Neither were dressed for the weather and both were frozen but Scarlet had other ideas and she took his hand and, shivering wet, gulping in cold air, she started walking along the beach.

With purpose.

They came to a small track and walked up it, arriving at a dark cottage. Luke frowned as she went into her bag and took out some keys. 'Scarlet?'

'I'm not breaking in.' Scarlet smiled through chattering lips. 'I want to show you something.' She pushed open the door and turned on a light, and Luke looked around and there, by the sofa, was a large bag.

'This is why I didn't get to see my mother go on stage that night.'

'What are you telling me, Scarlet?' Luke asked. 'Or, rather, what aren't you telling me?'

'A lot.'

There was a fire in the grate and she went to light a log with the matches provided, which didn't work, so he took some paper and scrunched it up beneath and kept feeding it till the log took.

And, because it was Scarlet, she stripped off, right down to her knickers, and Luke rolled his eyes but also stripped down. He couldn't be bothered to spread his clothes out so he threw them, suit and all, to shrink in the dryer and put a towel round his hips.

He didn't even bother to bring one for Scarlet.

She'd warmed some milk and made drinks and now sat by the fire. He went and sat beside her.

Luke was very used to asking patients their pain score from one to ten.

If there was such a thing as a want score, he'd be demanding knockout drugs now, because for all the times and opportunities they'd had to evade things with sex, this was the biggest challenge he'd met. But tomorrow her mother left and Scarlet might not be with her and he was here in the space she had fought for, in her terribly complex world.

She needed help, not his want.

'How long have you had this place?' Luke asked.

'I booked it a few weeks ago. I've been trying to leave for years,' Scarlet admitted. 'Since I was about fourteen. I just never knew how. I ran away when I was sixteen and I got as far as a bar.' She looked at him. 'I didn't know how to start, who to turn to,' Scarlet admitted. 'Then we had that night together and as terrible as things turned out I knew then that I had to do it. I started looking into ways when Mom said she was going back on tour. I've been squirrelling money away for this place. I've got it for a month. That's why I missed being there when she went on stage. I took a car the hotel provided and brought my stuff here.'

'Did your mum know?

'I told her that I wasn't going to be returning to America with her.'

'You could have got in touch with me, Scarlet. I'd have helped.'

'I know that you would have. I actually told Mom that

I would be looking you up, I thought it might be a bit of a false lead…'

That hurt but, Luke conceded, not as much as she was hurting right now so he let it slide.

'Even though I know what might happen to her, I'm not going back with Mom,' Scarlet said. 'I'm not cutting her out of my life for ever, but…'

She'd made her decision and had made it by herself, and instead of it hurting that she didn't need him, he was proud of the strongest woman he knew.

'I can't live like it any more. I've got this knot in my chest that I thought was normal until the night I spent with you. I honestly thought that was how life felt. I'm twenty-five, Luke. It shouldn't be called running away but that's what I feel like I'm doing to her…'

And he'd always held back. Luke had known she had to come to her own decision but he knew what a difficult one it must be for a woman who had never known anything other than the twisted love she'd been shown.

'You're not responsible for…' he attempted, and by reflex he felt her shoulders stiffen beneath his fingers. 'I've never run away,' Luke said. 'But I did skip school once.'

'Rebel,' Scarlet said, and her eye-roll suggested, what would he know?

'It was for me.' Luke smiled at her sulky expression. 'We took a train to London and went to the movies.'

'Did you get caught?'

'Sort of,' Luke said. 'Well, I ended up telling my mother…'

'You confessed!' Scarlet grinned. 'You are so damn…' And then she stopped because he just looked at her and he had told her something very few knew.

Not his brother or sister.

Nor his friends.

And certainly not girlfriends, because Luke's parents had warned him about sharing the truth.

'On the train back we were all fooling around and I looked over and I saw my father with a woman, getting off...'

Scarlet frowned.

They spoke the same language but it was so open to miscommunication that even Luke smiled. 'Not getting off the train, getting off with each other. Making out.'

'Did they see you?'

'No.' Luke shook his head. 'I went to another carriage and my friends followed. They never knew why I moved. I said I thought I'd seen an aunt.'

'You never said anything?' Scarlet checked, but then she knew she had said the wrong thing.

'Not at first. The next weekend I told my father that I'd seen him and that if he didn't tell my mother, I would.'

'And did he?'

Luke nodded.

'There were some terrible rows and after a couple of days he moved out. Marcus was about seven and Emma was five so they didn't really see it, but in the evenings my mother fell apart. She hit the bottle, cried her eyes out. One night I told her that she needed to go to bed. Do you know what she said?'

Scarlet just looked.

'This is all your fault.'

'For making your father tell her?' Scarlet checked, and Luke nodded.

'I realised then she hadn't wanted to know. I thought I was doing the right thing. I'd want to know, wouldn't you?'

'Oh, I'd know!' Scarlet said.

'She blamed it all on me. He did too. If I'd just shut up, none of that would have happened. After that I just stayed back. People can blow up their lives, do what they want. I'll fix them as much as they want to be fixed but I don't give unsolicited advice. Never again.'

She trusted him.

For the first time ever, she absolutely trusted another person.

Not more than she trusted herself, though.

He wasn't her safety net but it made the tightrope that she walked just a touch more steady.

'Can I ask you what you think I should do?'

Luke had held back for all the right reasons and for much better reasons he stepped in now.

'It isn't your fault. No matter what she says. It isn't. Change what you can,' Luke said, 'nurture the things that make you feel better. Follow your dreams and if that means you head to Africa…' He watched the reddening of her cheeks as he had one very special morning, and he'd been right—there were secrets in that pretty head. 'For what it's worth, I think you would be a brilliant midwife.'

It was worth so much.

'How can I be?'

She didn't feel she deserved it, Luke realised.

'Do you remember that nurse who was there for you? Was she perfect? I'll bet she didn't just sit with you, Scarlet. She brought some of her life, her experience to the bedside, and you've got a whole load of that.'

'Is that what you do?' She didn't get it, she just couldn't imagine Luke talking with someone and spilling out his life.

'In my own way,' Luke said. 'I don't jump in, I don't judge. It doesn't suit all my patients but for the ones that it does, they'll wait to see me.'

'I'd wait to see you.' Scarlet smiled. 'I used to think you were all like Vince.'

'Is that why you screwed your nose up when I said I was a doctor?'

Scarlet nodded. 'I hate that man so much. I was so happy when I found out that he'd only come on board when I was three. I used to worry that he was my father.'

'Do you know who your father is?'

'No idea,' Scarlet said. 'Nor does she.'

'Does it hurt, not knowing?'

'It used to,' Scarlet said. 'I had this notion that one day he'd come looking for me. By the time I got a bit older I'd worked out that, given my mother had no idea who it was…'

'I'm over casual sex,' Luke said, and he looked at her.

They were naked by a fire, the scene was set, he could have her now, but then again, Luke knew, she'd been so starved of affection that a burger could have got him there with Scarlet.

Not now.

She gave him a smile, she sat naked and looked at the most beautiful man on earth and she felt on the edge of something, that love really was worth holding out for.

'And me.'

CHAPTER SIXTEEN

'I DON'T KNOW if I should try and speak with her one more time,' Scarlet said

Luke was driving, and they were near the turn off that decided if they headed for home or the hospital.

He was honest.

'I think you have to,' Luke said. Even if just for Scarlet's sake, maybe it was better that she try again, but Scarlet shook her head.

She knew just how poisonous her mother could be.

It had taken the time away to see it.

'I can speak with her if you want.'

'You?'

'Well, she did ask me to be her doctor once.'

'I thought you stayed back?'

'Not in this.'

There were press everywhere. News of Anya's impending transfer had leaked, but not by the staff at the hospital, Luke knew that.

He nodded to Geoff, who gave him the most bored shrug as he gestured Luke's car to turn to the right. And Luke would thank him later for not letting on that a valuable photo was sitting with her heavy head leaning against the window of his car.

He parked and, at Scarlet's request, he left her in the car. On his way to ICU he called Angie.

He gave sparse details. It was for Angie to make her own judgements and he did all he could not to cloud them.

'If you could be there when I speak with Anya…'

'What if she agrees that I take her on?' Angie checked. 'I'm serious, Luke. If she's my patient…'

'I'll never ask,' Luke said. 'And I'm not just talking professionally, I'd never jeopardise our friendship.'

Absolutely he knew the value of a real friend who wasn't paid for, one who didn't simply say the right thing because it might be easier to hear a lie than the truth.

'Well, make sure you don't,' Angie said. 'I'll meet you up there.'

'Anya's about to be transferred,' David said when Luke came into the ICU.

'To?' Luke checked, and was informed that Anya was being transferred to a very swish private hospital for a couple of days and then would be heading for home.

'She wants her daughter.' David rolled his eyes. 'And she's not used to not getting what she wants.' He glanced over at the close curtains. 'She's furious that she isn't in a private room. She has no concept of ICU.'

'Can I speak to her?'

'You know you can.' David nodded. 'Though I have to say I don't think a lecture from the doctor who resuscitated her is going to do much. Still, it's worth a try.'

'Oh, no.' Luke was honest. 'I'm not here for that. I was invited to be her private doctor once.'

'You!' David frowned and then grinned. 'You?' he checked again.

'Yep, me,' Luke said. 'And, as you've probably guessed, her daughter is staying with me.'

'We had kind of worked that out, long before you brought her up here.'

'How?' Luke asked, not worried that they had, just curious to know.

'Well, the car Scarlet arrived in, Geoff kind of recognised, so we checked her emergency contact phone number and it matched yours.' David grinned. 'Talk about a dark horse…' As Angie came over and joined them, David stopped smiling and shook his head. 'I can tell you now, Angie, that she's certainly not going to speak with you.'

'Well, let's just give Anya that choice,' Angie said, and Luke watched as his friend and ex-lover put her psychiatrist's hat on firmly.

'Are you going to come in?' Luke asked David. 'I'd prefer you to hear what's said.'

'Sure.'

They all walked over and Luke took a breath and then parted the curtain.

'Anya…' He gave her a thin smile. 'I'm Luke Edwards…'

Anya just stared.

'I was the consultant on duty in Emergency when you came in.'

'And I want to thank you.' Anya said.

'There's no need.'

'Oh, but there is.' She reached for his hands and, Luke thought, for all the agony she had caused her daughter, she didn't even remember his name.

'You invited me to be your private doctor a couple of years ago…'

'Excuse me?'

'Your daughter was pregnant and you wanted to put me on your payroll,' Luke said, and he watched as Anya blinked. 'But I refused.'

'I don't want to talk about that time.'

'It's a very painful topic, I agree,' Luke said, 'and as difficult as it might be to do so, it's better that it's discussed.'

'Have you got my daughter?'

'*Got* your daughter?' Luke checked. 'Yes, Scarlet has been staying with me, and before you press that call bell, I want you to listen to me.'

'Well, I don't want to.'

'I'm going to say what I've come to and then I'm going to go.' He introduced Angie and said that she was a psychiatrist who specialised in addiction.

'Oh, please…' Anya said. 'Is this an intervention?'

'Minus the cameras.' Luke nodded. 'Anya, we're extremely concerned. You attempted to take your life and very nearly succeeded…'

'I told the nurse this morning that I was confused when I said that last night. It was an accident.'

'Anya.' Luke held out her drug screen but she refused to take it. 'I cannot see how this could be an accident but if it somehow was, then how that happened needs to be addressed.'

'Which is why I'm being transferred,' Anya said. 'Where's Scarlet?' she demanded, and started shouting for her daughter. 'You're to bring her to me.'

'I'm going to take care of your daughter for as long as she wants me to,' Luke said. 'Me. No bodyguards, no cameras, and if you tell your crew where she is, or it comes out, you are to tell them that they are not to come. If I see another car in the street or someone at my door, I'll move on with Scarlet for as long as she wants to. I will never live your life.'

'You regret it,' Anya sneered. 'If you'd been my doctor…'

'Oh, no,' Luke said. 'I look back on that time and, looking at your toxicology screen, I know for sure I could never have been your doctor. This woman should be,' Luke said, and Angie stepped forward. 'Stay here and work on yourself or go back to the world you've come from.'

'If she can leave her own mother,' Anya said, 'do you really think she's going to stick around with you and play the doctor's wife? She's using you.'

An escape route.

He'd thought about his friend's words at times.

And Scarlet had said herself that she'd used him as a false lead.

But his love was real.

And if that meant he was an escape route, Luke could live with that.

Scarlet's future was worth it.

'We're different people, Anya.' He looked down at her. 'I believe that when you love someone, their happiness becomes a priority. I don't want Scarlet trapped and miserable. She's not some toy for me to keep locked away in the hope she won't leave.' And once, just once, calm, professional and detached he could not be because he sneered at her. 'As you've found out, it doesn't work.' He headed for the curtain and then he turned around. 'There is one thing you don't have to worry about, though—whatever she needs, I'll always be there for Scarlet.'

CHAPTER SEVENTEEN

'WHAT DID SHE SAY?'

Luke sat in the car beside Scarlet and even as he'd climbed in, it felt as if her mother's shadow had got in with him.

'Not much,' Luke said. 'Angie's in with her now.'

She looked at him. 'I don't believe you,' Scarlet said, and saw the set of his jaw. 'Tell me what she said.'

'Just…' Anya's words buzzed in his head. They were a touch too close to home but he did his best to ignore them. 'She was never just going to lie back and let you go. It doesn't matter what she said.'

Scarlet sat there and was glad that Luke didn't turn on the engine but just let her sit with her thoughts.

'I can't just leave her.'

'Scarlet,' Luke said. 'I think that even if you go back with your mother, nothing will change. I don't think anything you do can alter that fact.'

'I know that.'

'But if you feel you have to go back, I get that.'

'What about us?'

It wasn't a selfish question and it was one Luke pondered for a moment before answering. They had been together again for only four days and before that it had been just one night.

'You've still got my phone number?' Luke checked.
Scarlet nodded.

'We're thirty-fifteen on hanging up on each other. It's your turn next.'

'We'll talk?'

'Every morning and every night, just as much as you want to,' Luke said. He hadn't been lying to Anya. He would be there for Scarlet for as long she needed him to be. 'And I've got leave I can take so I can get on a plane and so can you.'

'Are we just friends?'

'In this,' Luke answered carefully, 'I'm your *best* friend. I promise you that, Scarlet. You do what you have to do.'

He gave her the one thing she'd never had—options.

Precious, rare options that came with no strings attached.

No want, or need, to drag her back, no promise of all he could do for her, no safety net, yet he made her able to fly.

'I'm going to go and speak to her,' Scarlet said. Luke was right, for that she *needed* a friend. 'Can you come up with me?'

'Of course.'

Luke walked with her right up to the unit and then he saw Angie coming out from behind the curtains.

'Hi, Midwife Lucy.' Angie smiled and then, when Scarlet felt she might break, Angie gave her a hug. 'It's okay.' Angie gave Luke a smile and then dismissed him. 'I'm going to speak with Scarlet.'

Scarlet sat in another interview room, where she guessed that people were told their loved ones had died. But then she thought about Evan, finding out that his son had a stab at life, and this was a bittersweet room she found herself in, Scarlet decided as Angie went through things with her.

It was just more of the same.

'Your mum insists on leaving here tonight,' Angie concluded. 'She's coherent, she knows what she wants…'

'So do I,' Scarlet said. She did now. 'Can I see her?'

'Of course you can.' Angie nodded.

She had choices and so did her mom.

'Please, take the help that's being offered,' Scarlet said as she sat at her mother's bedside.

'I don't need their help. It was an accident.'

And back to lying and blackmailing Anya went. 'I was thinking, in a few weeks you could go to Africa. I know you love going there and maybe—'

'I'm not coming back with you, Mom.'

'You're going with him,' Anya sneered. 'Believe me, Scarlet, you're only as good as your last—'

'Don't you dare!' Scarlet stood. She just stood up then and she thought of a man who had said no to her frequent offers, and if it had confused her at times it all made beautiful sense now. She could look her mother in the eye and know absolutely that what she said was right. 'I count for so much more than that with him.'

'Please,' Anya sneered. 'Is that what he told you?'

'That's what he *showed* me,' Scarlet said, and tears filled her eyes because over and over, every step of the way, Luke had. 'You need help, Mom.'

'I don't need help.'

'Well, I do,' Scarlet said. 'I need friends, I need support and I need space. I want a career, Mom. You've got one…'

It was almost pointless, but not quite. She was allowed to have hope that one day her mum would be well.

Not yet, though.

She kissed her mum goodbye, even if it wasn't returned, and then walked out and said thanks to Angie, who was sitting at the desk with Luke.

'This way,' Scarlet said to him, and instead of leaving via the internal lift they headed towards the main exit.

There were many reasons to be proud of her, Luke thought, because as they passed Ashleigh's bed, where he lay with his headphones on, Ashleigh gave his father a nudge as Scarlet walked past.

'Not now,' Evan said to his son. Curtains were thin and he'd heard what had just gone on.

Yes, now, Scarlet thought.

And Luke saw first-hand the absolute star that Scarlet was.

'Hey!' Scarlet smiled at Ashleigh and went over. 'Wow! You are looking so much better.'

'I'm feeling it,' Ashleigh admitted. 'I'm going to a regular ward tomorrow.'

'That's brilliant.' Scarlet smiled. 'Do you want a photo of the two of us?'

'Are you sure?'

'Of course I am.'

They snapped a photo, one that caught Scarlet kissing him on the cheek, and Ashleigh grinned as he looked at it. 'I won't share it.'

'Go for it.' Scarlet smiled. 'Show the world how much better you're doing and that they need to watch out.'

She was speaking for both of them!

They didn't leave by the lifts; instead, they walked out the regular exit and Scarlet asked, in no uncertain terms, for Sonia to hand over her passport.

'It's back at the hotel.'

'Then go and fetch it,' Scarlet said, and took a seat. 'I'll wait.'

'Actually…'

Surprise, surprise, Sonia had it in her bag.

And that was it, she was free.

They drove home in silence at first and Scarlet rested her head on the window.

'Thank you,' Scarlet said.

'For what?'

For being the true friend she'd never had. 'All that you've done for me. I've completely messed up your week.'

Luke swallowed. She hadn't messed up his week, she had changed his entire life, but that might not be what she needed to hear now.

'Do you know what you want to do?'

'Do?' Scarlet frowned. 'I don't know. Maybe…' she took a breath '…go to the cottage perhaps, do what I planned to and get my head together.' She took a breath. 'You'll get sick of me soon…'

Luke frowned.

'Tired of my dramas.'

'That's what she said,' Luke pointed out, because, yes, curtains were thin.

Luke looked at the road ahead.

Ten minutes in that woman's company and Anya had watered the weeds of doubt in both of them.

He had never admired Scarlet more—she'd had a lifetime of it but instead of weeds the flowers had somehow thrived.

And the lunatics were not running the asylum, Luke decided.

He was.

If what he had to reveal to Scarlet was too much, too soon, and not what she needed or wanted, then so be it, he wouldn't crowd her.

But something told him that what he felt inside was right. That his words were something that Scarlet, who had never properly been loved, maybe needed to hear.

Whatever she did with that knowledge was fine with Luke but she deserved to know just how very loved she was.

It was time to do what he avoided.

Tell another person just how he felt.

CHAPTER EIGHTEEN

THEY DIDN'T PULL into his house; instead, they pulled up outside the pub.

'What are we doing?'

'Well, I don't feel like cooking, do you?'

'No!' Scarlet admitted.

'So let's have dinner here.'

They walked in together and Scarlet was more nervous than she'd been when she'd stepped on stage in Paris and had had her mother sing to her, but Luke was calm and relaxed.

'Hi, Luke,' Von, the landlady, said.

As they sat down a young couple did a double take and when one of them picked up their phone and started to walk over, Trefor, who was in with his wife, stopped them and reminded them that her mother was terribly ill.

They sat back down and the phone went back on the table.

Scarlet gave them a wave. 'Hi, Margaret.'

'It's lovely to see you, Scarlet.'

They took a seat and Luke grinned.

'What?' Scarlet checked.

'She bought me a casserole the day I moved in. I was so taken aback I forgot her name and for months I've been trying to find it out, without admitting I don't know.'

'Margaret,' Scarlet said. 'The shop's not doing too well, she's thinking of making a web page.'

'You chatted?'

'She helped me choose my outfit,' Scarlet explained.

'And she chose your knickers too,' Luke pointed out.

'I thought you chose them.' Scarlet smiled but she was frowning a little because that little comment was so open to one of her more usual responses, and Luke didn't generally offer such openings.

'I thought it safer to leave it to her,' Luke admitted.

'Safer?' Scarlet checked.

'That you were dressed by Margaret.'

She wanted to be undressed by Luke, though.

'You're in an odd mood,' Scarlet commented.

'Doesn't feel odd to me,' Luke said, and she looked at him, grateful that now she could do just that.

He smiled at her, not a grin or a happy smile, just a knowing one that had her toes curl in her shoes because she wanted to reach over and tell him she was wearing the purple knickers.

She restrained herself.

The shadow that had followed them since they had been to the hospital had lifted but the clearer air between them slightly dizzied her.

She was nervous to provoke, worried she was misreading the edge they were on.

God! Scarlet just sat there and went bright red with recall at some of the offers she'd made so readily, assuming that was what it took to be a guest in his home.

Luke gestured to a chalkboard. 'What do you want to eat?'

Scarlet screwed up her noise as she read the choices.

'The steak and kidney pie is good here,' Luke suggested.

She made a gagging face.

'Really good,' Luke said, unimpressed.

'Fine, then,' Scarlet said, and looked around for someone to take their order. 'Where are you going?'

'To order.' Luke disappeared and she sat there as he did so.

And still she sat there as he went over and had a quick word with Margaret and Trefor and then after a while he came back with two little bottles and two glasses.

'What are these?'

'Grapefruit juice for you,' Luke said, as he poured them. 'And pineapple juice for me.'

And she went a bit pink and then asked a question. 'Why do you have grapefruit juice in your fridge when you don't like it?'

She was so clever, so astute, Luke thought, and he wondered about all she could be.

'I have it in my fridge because I drink it every morning and think of you for a couple of minutes.'

'Oh, so you drink something you don't like and think of me…'

'I love it now,' Luke said. 'That time in the morning that I spend thinking of you is both the worst and best part of my day.'

She just looked at him, into those beautiful eyes, and love hurt so much more than she had ever thought it might.

'You think about me every day?'

'All day,' Luke said.

'And the trouble I make?'

'I think about so much more than that.' He took a breath. 'You know that there have been others—'

'Luke,' Scarlet interrupted. 'I don't want to hear about them. I know we need to talk but I can't take it today.'

'Yes, you can,' Luke said. 'I want to tell you something, I want you to know that, while there might have been others, I've never had sex in the morning since you. And do you know what else? I don't even have breakfast in bed any more, and if I'm in a hotel I go down and eat at the buffet.'

'Why?'

'I want to have that breakfast in bed with you.'

He just stared at her and she said nothing and then their plates came and she picked out all the kidney and tackled the rest of the pie.

'It's yum,' she conceded, glad of the diversion because talking today was surely too hard. She tried to keep it light as she turned her attention to the pastry.

Once she had finished her pie, she reached out to pick at his. 'You see, Luke, we really shouldn't be together because I'd be the size—'

'And I'd still want you,' Luke said, 'and if you stopped putting that stuff in your lips I'd want you even more.'

Scarlet looked at him. 'You say that now.' Her head was all jumbled and rather than look at him Scarlet had a piece of the kidney she'd picked out.

It was nice.

So nice that she had another piece.

And then she had another because if she didn't then she might open her mouth and tell him how much she loved him and beg him not to send her away now that her mum had gone.

Scarlet knew that she needed to get her head together; she wanted to be so suave and calm when she told him how she felt. 'I want to go to the cottage,' Scarlet said suddenly.

'I'll take you.'

'I want a few weeks to get my head together and then...' He didn't rush in so she took a breath and told him what she'd been planning. 'I might call you once things are calmer. If that's okay?'

'Of course.'

'See how you're feeling about me then,' Scarlet said.

'It won't have changed,' Luke said. 'It hasn't in the two years that I've been hoping you might call.'

'You hoped I'd call?'

'Every day, and knowing you were in the country and hadn't...' Luke stopped, not wanting to lay a guilt trip on her. 'I can't see my feelings for you going away any time soon. At least, not in this lifetime. And if that's too much for you to handle, I get that...'

'Too much?' Scarlet checked. 'I thought you were just...'

'Just what?'

'Tolerating me.'

'I don't tolerate you, Scarlet, I love you.'

'What sort of love?' Scarlet checked. 'Like a sister?'

'I certainly hope not.'

'A fancy?'

'Much more than that,' Luke said. 'How about a real love, which, yes, I guess means I can tolerate anything if it helps you to get where you want to be. And if that means holing yourself up in a cottage, or flying off to Africa, or even going back to LA...'

'So long as there are no bodyguards?' Scarlet huffed.

'Scarlet, if you want to carry on as a celebrity, I'll work my way around it. I won't be giving tell-all interviews, though...' He smiled as she laughed at the very thought. 'And don't try sorting out my career for me again...'

'You'd come to LA?' Scarlet frowned. 'For me?'

'For us,' Luke corrected. 'You asked how the conversation would have been had you called, well...' He didn't finish; it still hurt that she hadn't.

It was Scarlet that spoke. 'I was going to call. I knew I'd made a mess of things last time and so I was going to try and work things out at the cottage. I wanted it all to be sorted and for me to be all...' She saw his smile. 'Well, a rather more sophisticated and together version of me was going to give you a call in a few weeks' time.'

She *had* been planning to call.

Their stars would have collided, Luke found out then, and he was no fool rushing in, this *was* love, he knew that now.

All the naysayers, all the doubters could leave now, please, Luke thought, because when it was just the two of them, all was right in the world.

He could tell her everything now.

'Come on,' Luke said.

As they walked out they stopped and chatted to *Margaret* and Trefor.

'I've got some new stock coming in next week,' Margaret said to Scarlet. 'You should come and have a look.'

'I shall,' Scarlet said.

As they walked out of the pub, Scarlet, a little distracted, holding Luke's words in her head and going over and over them, just so they wouldn't disappear, bumped into someone and turned.

And when she saw who it was Scarlet gaped.

'Come on, Scarlet,' Luke said, and grabbed her by the hand as she craned her neck for another look. 'It's rude to stare.'

'But isn't that…?' Oh, my God, she knew that couple—the whole world did.

'Yes,' Luke said. 'They're even more famous than you.'

They walked out of the pub and there was his car.

'I can take you to the cottage now,' Luke said, dangling his keys. 'You can go and get yourself all suave and sophisticated if you want to…' he offered, and she poked out her tongue.

'I can't leave yet.' Scarlet shook her head and they walked hand in hand towards his home. 'I said I'd go and help Margaret get her store online on Monday. Apparently men feel very awkward when they come in to buy things.'

'I don't think so.'

'And they're not very knowledgeable,' Scarlet said. 'I'm not a size *small*, Luke,' Scarlet said and she told him her size. 'Just for future reference.'

Their future was referenced and that made them both smile.

But then Scarlet stopped smiling and she thought of all that had been lost, all the damage done.

'Can we ever get past it?' Scarlet said, and they stopped walking and faced each other.

'We have to get through it,' Luke said. 'And we *can* get through it together.'

They shared a soft kiss that tasted of regret mingled with love as they shared the hurt and what could have been and what had been lost.

They would work through it together.

He smelt her hair and she just leant against him. It was gone.

Her shame.

His acceptance of her, good, bad and the middle bits, would not allow shame to reside in her.

They walked to the house that had a few missing bricks in the driveway wall and she waited for Luke to open the door.

'You've got a key,' Luke said. 'Scarlet, this is your home.'

'Mine.' She laughed at the very notion but then she found out just how much he loved her.

'This village is why I live so far from work. There are couples here who are just as high profile as you are, more so, and they get to live a very normal life on their days off. They might have to work at it, but when they do...'

'You chose this house with me in mind?'

'Everything has been with you in mind. And if that's too much…'

'Too much? No. Never.'

She could never get enough of his love.

'So open up and let us in,' Luke said.

Scarlet did. She turned the key to her home and they both stepped in, and they would keep opening up and keep letting the other in every day of their lives, both swore.

She stood in the hall and resisted the urge to snap a photo and post it and share her joy with the world, but she was very easily distracted by Luke.

'What are you doing?' Scarlet asked. He began to strip off her clothes. 'Luke…'

'What I've been wanting to do all along.'

CHAPTER NINETEEN

'I LOVE YOU.' Luke told her the truth and it came from the very bottom of his heart. 'I have loved you from the moment I saw you.'

It made perfect sense now.

Love had led them to now.

'I love you back,' Scarlet said, and she wasn't afraid to admit it now. Furthermore, there was no hope of being sophisticated and level-headed when Luke was close and holding her the way he was.

Two years after they'd found out that they did, they got to say it and could believe it now.

And this time when he carried her wriggling in his arms and she rained kisses on his face, he didn't deposit her on the spare bed but again Luke didn't pull back the sheets.

Deliberately this time.

He stared down at her as he undressed her in a way that had Scarlet squirm.

Off came that chunky jumper to reveal the very small purple bra. His hands went to unhook it and he removed it without a word.

Off came her shoes and that tiny, tiny skirt came down with her stockings.

'Luke…' Her hands reached out for him but he flicked them away.

He had waited, now so could she.

Scarlet lay as he peeled off her knickers so slowly that her breathing kept catching in her throat as she fought the temptation for haste. Then Luke stood and undressed himself and revealed that delicious male body again, though his eyes did not meet hers. He looked at that jet of hair that he'd tried so hard not to and his gaze burnt so much so that she just lay there and parted her legs.

Still he made her wait because he flipped her over onto her stomach and took her hands out from where they needed to be and placed them palms down beside her head.

He kissed her all over, from the nape of her neck to the soles of her feet. He kissed the small of her back and he kissed the cheek of her bottom so deeply that she started to sob with want. Then he turned her around and kissed her stomach with the same lavish attention. Her spine curved so that her hips lifted but Luke hadn't finished yet.

His fingers were inside her and stroking her as his mouth met her breast and tasted her again, and sucked and nipped till she was frenzied. When she could take it no more, he very abruptly removed his fingers, parted her legs and kissed inside her thighs, not tenderly but deep, bruising kisses that made her remember that a gentle lover he was not.

He tried to be.

But Luke forgot the gentleman he usually remembered to be when her scent hit him.

The silky black hair had not been there last time and Scarlet closed her eyes as his teeth nipped and tugged, and then came the heat his mouth delivered.

Every tear she had cried, all the pain of the days, the months and years dissolved as Luke probed her with his tongue. His hands parted her thighs farther when they tried to close in on his head. He completely exposed her, laved her, tasted her; he drew out musk, he tasted her deep and when she came he held her down and tasted her more, so she screamed.

As she tried to catch her breath he didn't allow her to; instead, Luke pulled her limp body up so she knelt and leant on his chest to recover. Very soon she did, stroking his thickness, feeling him again in her hands, wanting him, as she always had.

She left the safe haven of his chest and found his neck, and she bruised him now with her mouth as she raised herself, wanting him to gather her, yet he reached for the drawer.

'I want your babies…' Scarlet begged, not wanting to stop or wanting to part for a second.

'Not yet,' Luke said.

His love was older and wiser now and they would wait till they could cope with their love before adding to something so big, so precious and so worth protecting.

He opened the drawer and took out a condom and she took it from him and knelt back on her heels, stroking him with one hand and cupping his balls in the other until it was Luke who was now impatient.

'Scarlet…'

With aching slowness, she slid it on.

Luke pulled her in and they kissed, a sexy kiss, and she felt his tongue still and the holding of his breath as she slid down his length.

He moved her legs and they wrapped around him, and the feel of him filling her, moving in her while kissing her was sublime. Her lips closed and tightened and he forced them apart, and when his teeth gritted she felt him swell that final time and they gave up with mouths and just locked in eye contact for that final second before they were lost to each other.

His body mocked the times she had thought he might not want her as he thrust into her, so deep, and ground her down so hard that it could never now be questioned.

And one would hope there were no bodyguards outside the door, because she didn't hold back from sobbing or shouting, and as she came, tight around him, all his restraint was rewarded as he shot hard and released deep inside her.

And then they were back to the other, with eyes that stared right to the very bottom of the other's soul.

'What are you thinking?' Scarlet said.

'You don't want to know.'

'I do,' she persisted. 'Tell me.'

'That was an amazing come. I want to go again.'

'Just that?'

'Yep.'

'What else?' Scarlet smiled.

'I think I'm ready to go again.'

Still rivers did not run deeper when she was hot in his arms.

Scarlet laughed as they lay upside down in his bed. She then climbed up onto his stomach and sat there, playing with the hairs on his chest and loving that she was back where she belonged.

That they could talk now.

And for ever.

Luke loved it too. He looked up at her and she was lost to her thoughts. There were secrets inside that pretty head, he knew. 'What are you thinking?'

'Lots of things.'

'Like?'

'Have you really loved me all that time?'

She knew that he had, it was just hard to take in.

He reached out and opened the drawer, reaching not

for a condom this time but for a receipt, which he handed to her.

It was faded, a long bar bill, and on the end of it was a glass of champagne.

'I never keep mementos,' Luke said, 'but I just couldn't throw it out.'

And there was the hotel bill too and a serviette with faded lipstick, and he had loved her since then, absolutely she knew that.

'What else are you thinking?' Luke asked.

With his love, there were so many things to think about. 'All the things I can do.'

'Like?' He watched the blush on her cheeks.

'What you said about me being a midwife, did you mean it?'

'Absolutely,' Luke said. 'What else are you thinking?'

'That I want to get married.'

Both smiled.

'I would have got round to that,' Luke said.

'We'll be family then,' Scarlet said.

'You're my family now,' Luke told her, but he got her insecurity. 'We'll get married as quickly as I can arrange it.'

'I want a big ring,' Scarlet warned. 'I think it has to be a ruby, but a massive one.'

Luke rolled his eyes.

'And I want a church with bells and hymns and flowers...' Scarlet held nothing back with her demands. 'And I'm going to wear red and...' Then she looked at the most patient man in the world. 'I just want us there, though.'

'Oh, I think we can manage all that.' Luke smiled.

'Maybe Trefor and Margaret can be witnesses,' Scarlet mused.

'Perhaps a little drink back at the pub afterwards?' Luke suggested.

'And we could maybe have a teeny party there?' Scarlet checked. 'Just an impromptu one.'

'No wedding cake, then?' Luke checked.

'Oh, yes, I want cake.'

'You can have cake,' Luke said, 'just as long as you don't make it.'

'And I want wedding presents too.'

Ooh, it was going to take a lot of organising for their impromptu wedding!

His hands slid up from her waist to her breasts and she felt him nudging against the small of her back. She knew exactly what Luke was thinking now and it wasn't about weddings.

'I thought there was no hope for us,' Scarlet admitted.

'There's always hope.'

He believed that—all those years in Emergency had taught him.

Even when it seemed as if there was none.

It was almost impossible to fathom.

As she had been making her plans to escape, Luke had been creating a world she could run to.

And here she was.

In his bed, making love, planning weddings, getting on with their precious world.

That was love.

EPILOGUE

One year and eight months later

THIS WAS THE third birth she had witnessed as a student midwife.

Scarlet knew that she should, as the doctor had yesterday advised, be at home, putting her feet up, but she really wanted to finish this semester.

It was her second one and finally, after all these months of study, for two weeks she had been allowed in the maternity ward and these last two days had been spent in the delivery room.

'I can't do this,' Hannah said, and shook her head.

Hannah was eighteen and alone and terrified, and when she should really be down at the action end, instead Scarlet put her arms around the young woman's shoulders.

'You already are doing this,' Scarlet said.

They had a bond.

Scarlet's first day observing in the antenatal clinic had been Hannah's first visit some four months ago.

Hannah had asked loads of questions and Scarlet had admitted that it was her first day with a real patient and that soon the real midwife would be in and would answer those questions.

'Aren't you…?' Hannah had asked when she had read Scarlet's name tag.

It still happened.

The other day someone had said, 'Didn't you used to be Scarlet?'

'I'm still Scarlet…' she had smiled '…but, yes.'

And now here Hannah was, about to give birth.

Scarlet had arrived on the delivery ward that morning at eight.

A niggling back pain had woken her and had not relented as Luke had driven them into work.

By eight fifteen she had been about to make her excuses—her back had been killing her, the baby had felt as if it was between her thighs and she had known she was in labour. Scarlet had been about to go and find Luke when Hannah had said it.

'I want my mum.'

'I know that you do,' Scarlet said.

Sometimes, so too did Scarlet.

Yes, there had been terrible times but there had been happier ones too, and, as Luke had said, leaving was always hard.

Anya hadn't been able to make their not-very-low-key wedding.

It had been an amazing day. Luke's family had, of course, been invited, as well as David and Angie, who felt like her friends too.

And she had, of course, asked her mother.

Anya had said that she would come but had changed her mind at the last moment. She had called two days before the wedding and said that she was in the middle of recording and had people relying on her.

Scarlet had learnt not to.

Luke had tried to come up with a solution and had suggested that someone else give Scarlet away.

Only Scarlet didn't need anyone else.

'Who giveth this woman to marry this man?' the vicar had asked.

'I do,' Scarlet had said.

And on the day she had found out she was pregnant, she had sat on Luke's lap and cried both happy then sad tears. After a lot of thought she had decided not to call her mother just yet.

They had told no one for quite a while. Her pregnancy had been something that she and Luke had chosen not to share for as long as they had been able to keep it quiet.

They had held in their lovely secret and just taken their time to get their heads around it themselves.

Finally they would be parents.

Scarlet would soon be a mum, or a 'mom', as she called it.

Yes, sometimes you needed a mum or a mom but sometimes you had to make do, and for Hannah today that person was Scarlet.

'Don't leave me,' Hannah begged.

'I'm not going anywhere,' Scarlet replied.

'I can't do this,' Hannah said again.

'Yes, you can,' Scarlet promised, because when she looked down there was a head about to be delivered. 'Put your hands down,' Scarlet said, and guided them to the baby that was about to be born.

Scarlet was, as it turned out, very, very good with women at their most difficult and tumultuous times.

She'd had twenty-five years' experience with the most difficult of the lot, Scarlet had said when Beth, her mentor, had praised her on her ability to connect.

'One day it will be your turn,' Hannah shouted as she went to push again. 'Then you'll know how hard it is!'

Scarlet just held her shoulders and watched as Hannah's baby was delivered onto her stomach and all was quiet with the world except for the noise of a newborn's cries.

A beautiful little boy, who was actually a very big boy, Scarlet thought as she put a little name band on his fat wrists.

And then another contraction came.

Hannah was right. Soon *she* would know.

Very soon, Scarlet thought as her stomach tightened for what seemed a very long time. And, no, these were definitely not imaginary pains and neither were they going away.

'Are you okay, Scarlet?' Beth checked, after they had helped Hannah into a fresh bed and had settled her in.

'I'm bit tired,' Scarlet lied. 'I probably shouldn't have come in but I really wanted to finish up the placement.'

'Go home,' Beth said, and signed off her card. 'Do you have any questions?'

'No,' Scarlet said, when usually she had about a hundred and twenty of them. They could wait, her baby was refusing to. She really wanted to go and find Luke. 'I might go home actually, if that's okay.'

Beth nodded and Scarlet didn't bother to grab her bag, she just left the maternity unit to take the elevator to the ground floor, and as she got in there was Angie.

'Hi, Lucy Edwards.' Angie smiled.

It was a joke they shared now and then.

'Hi.' Scarlet smiled back.

'Where are you off to?'

'Coffee break,' Scarlet said. 'I am starving.'

She lied and Beth knew that she lied. The canteen wasn't that way!

But there were some things she didn't want to discuss with Angie, or Beth, or anyone else, except the man who was, Scarlet soon found out, elbow deep in something in Resus.

'Can you tell Luke I'm free for a coffee?' Scarlet said to Barbara, who was dashing back into Resus.

'He's a bit busy at the moment,' Barbara said, then she saw Scarlet's lips press together. 'I'll let him know you're here.'

Barbara went into Resus, where Luke was observing Sahin put in a chest drain. 'Scarlet's here,' Barbara said.

'Tell her to go for her break without me, I'm going to be a while.'

'Sure.' Barbara headed back outside. 'He said go ahead without him.' Barbara smiled.

'It's fine,' Scarlet said. 'I'll wait. I might go round to his office if that's okay?'

'Sure.' Barbara frowned and watched as Scarlet walked off.

At first Scarlet had been a bit of a shadow, coming down for lunch or coffee, but not lately, though.

She was tiny. From the back she didn't even look pregnant but then she stopped walking for long enough for Barbara to guess the real reason that Scarlet wanted to see Luke.

She went back into Resus. 'Scarlet said that she's going to wait in your office.'

'Fine.'

'Luke,' Barbara said, and Luke looked at her and into the eyes of a very experienced nurse.

'Yes?'

'I'm saying nothing,' Barbara said. 'Except that I think Sahin can take over from here.'

Sahin could. There was just the drain to be sutured in so

Sahin nodded and Luke stripped off his gown and gloves, washed his hands and headed through the department.

There were a few people staring. They'd seen Scarlet waddle around to his office and now a usually unruffled Luke was walking briskly.

He didn't stop to enlighten them!

Luke walked into his office and Scarlet stood there. As he had done many months ago, he saw her fear and turned on the engaged sign and never, ever would she take for granted the luxury of his arms and leaning against this chest and the bliss of the silence that he gave her when she needed it most.

Neither would Luke ever readily dismiss the scent of her hair and the knowledge that even as they stood still life was changing for ever.

Their baby kicked and Scarlet let go of the sob of fear that she'd been holding in for the last hour, just as Hannah had decided that she'd wanted Scarlet to stay close.

Luke felt her stomach tighten and his hand moved between them and he was surprised at the lack of noise from Scarlet because this was a long, deep contraction.

'How often are you getting them?'

'They're getting closer,' Scarlet said. 'I thought it took ages.'

'It might still,' Luke said, and he held her for a long moment but then changed his mind as she moaned into him and tried to bend at her knees. They weren't even two minutes apart!

'Do they know upstairs that you're in labour?' Luke checked.

'No.' Scarlet shook her head. Just as she had wanted to hear it from him if it had been bad news about her mother, she wanted to tell him when it was good.

'Isn't it too soon?'

She knew thirty-six weeks was a bit early but that the baby should be okay. However, she wanted to hear it from him.

'Scarlet, the baby will be just fine.'

He was always so calm.

'I'll call the labour ward and we can head up,' Luke suggested, reaching for the phone.

'I think I might need a chair.'

She had walked, almost run the whole way down to Emergency, holding her secret within her, but the thought of heading up that corridor now was daunting. Luke was, not that he'd show it, also feeling a bit daunted. Scarlet had her hands on his desk and her knees were bending again and she looked as if, at any second, she might squat.

'Barbara!' Luke buzzed around to the department and a few moments later Barbara came with a chair and a blanket.

'Can you call them again and tell them that I want an epidural?' Scarlet said rather urgently to Luke as she clung to the sides of the wheelchair, because it was starting to hurt seriously.

'I'll do that,' Barbara said, and shared a look with Luke. 'Maybe take Scarlet up now.'

'You will call ahead?' Scarlet checked, and thanked Barbara, who put the blanket over her knees.

It was the last time Scarlet remembered to be polite!

On the way to Maternity her waters broke and Scarlet had never been more grateful for the blanket, but by the time the lift got to Maternity she didn't even care about that any more.

'Scarlet!' Beth wasn't surprised to see her, Barbara had called ahead after all, but she was very surprised to see that Scarlet's toes were curling and that she was gripping the arms of the chair. 'Straight through,' Beth said.

'I want my epidural.'

'David's been held up,' Beth told her, rather than telling her that that they were way past that window.

'I don't want to hear it!'

Luke undressed her as Beth gave up trying to attach her to a monitor as Scarlet screamed out her demands.

'You will pull strings,' Scarlet demanded of Luke. 'You will call in favours…'

Scarlet was in full diva mode.

But today she was allowed to be.

'I'm not wearing that.' She just tossed the gown to the floor. 'Where's my epidural?'

'It's too late for that,' Beth soothed.

It didn't work.

'This is barbaric!' Scarlet screamed.

'I know, baby…' Luke too attempted to soothe her but he was quickly shot down.

'Don't tell me you know!'

'You're doing a fantastic job, Scarlet,' Beth said.

Oh, she was swaying, she was shouting, she was sucking on the green whistle, and she really was doing a fantastic job!

'I need to go to the restroom,' Scarlet begged.

'Scarlet,' Beth said patiently, 'you don't. That's your baby…'

And then Scarlet found out there was something she was very, very good at.

Pushing.

She just crouched down and grunted, and instinctively she knew what she needed to do.

'Okay…' David rushed in. 'I'm sorry it took so long to get here. Scarlet…?'

'Get out,' she shouted, and then got back to closing her eyes.

'I want to get on my knees,' she said.

'You can,' Beth said and massaged her back.

Luke knelt down and faced her.

'This is the worst…' Scarlet started to say, but then she stopped and they smiled because this was nowhere close to the worst. She looked right into his eyes and found herself lost there for the sweetest moment. She was exactly where she wanted to be. 'This is the best,' Scarlet said.

'You're the best,' Luke said, because staff were coming for a very rapid progression.

'Go, go, go…' Scarlet said to him, because her baby was coming, and Luke went around and out came a head. He watched it turn.

He saw the dark, cloudy hair and then two eyes opened and he knew even before she was out that he was a father to a little girl. Just as he acknowledged that fact, she was born into his hands.

He passed the baby up to her mother and she sat there, holding her and crying and kissing her little girl.

And there was another thing that Scarlet took easily to—breastfeeding.

She just sat on the cold floor and held and fed her little girl as the cord was cut and the placenta was delivered.

Even as they got her into bed, Scarlet could not let her go. They didn't have a name for her yet, so she was tagged Baby Edwards.

'I'm being selfish,' Scarlet said, because she knew she should let Luke hold her, but her naked skin was keeping the baby warm and Beth put a blanket over them.

'Be as selfish as you like,' Luke said.

He had made them wait for this moment. He had kept

that promise and even though they were rock solid he had insisted that they did not rush into parenthood.

Scarlet had wanted a career, she had just wanted a stab at the world, and he'd encouraged that. They'd celebrated when she'd been accepted to study midwifery and their lives had been happy and busy, but her want for a baby had remained.

And now, finally, their daughter was here.

He watched as the baby stopped feeding.

'She's a bit small,' Beth said, 'so she'll tire quickly.' Scarlet knew that she might need some top-up feeds and she looked at the warmer waiting for their baby, who might need a little bit of help too to regulate her temperature for the next few days. Scarlet rested back on the pillow, looking down at their tiny baby, and then she handed their daughter to Luke.

He lifted the tiny scrap that was lighter than he could comprehend, and weighted his heart with happiness to hold her.

She watched him look into his daughter's eyes and hold her tiny fingers, and for the second time ever she saw tears in his eyes.

They were happy ones now.

'She's beautiful.'

Absolutely she was. A shock of dark hair and navy eyes that might stay the same colour or turn to chocolate brown, and she had lips that were as perfect as Scarlet's now that she'd given up on fillers.

He pulled back the blanket and looked at slender pink feet and then wrapped them back up in the rug. Beth came and put a little yellow hat on her and he knew soon he would have to put her down.

'She's perfect,' Luke said. 'Like her mum.'

Scarlet was going to be an amazing mother, Luke knew,

and in turn he would give his daughter the childhood that her mother had never had.

They'd got this, Luke thought, and then he handed her back to Scarlet.

'She needs to go under the warmer,' Beth said. 'Don't worry, she can stay beside you.' They watched as she slept and her perfect little mouth slipped into what looked like a sleepy smile as Beth got on with the paperwork.

'Have you thought of a name?' Beth checked.

Scarlet looked at Luke and he nodded.

'Emily,' Scarlet said. 'Emily Edwards.'

There would be a couple of hooks at school with the same name, no doubt, and that suited them both just fine.

'I'm starving,' Scarlet said, as, on the maternity ward, she climbed into bed and Beth plugged in the warmer so that Emily could stay with them.

Scarlet had walked round to the ward, rather than be wheeled there. Had he not seen her just give birth, he wouldn't have known she had.

Every day she surprised Luke more and more. Scarlet was so much tougher than she looked.

'I'm seriously starving,' Scarlet said, and looked at Luke. 'Can you get me a muffin?'

They were her favourite thing from the vending machine.

'You've earned more than a muffin,' Beth said. 'It's a bit early for the lunches to come round so I'll go and see if there are any breakfasts left.'

There were.

Toast, scrambled eggs, bacon and mushrooms.

No grapefruit juice, though.

Scarlet pouted.

'It's still pretty perfect,' Luke said, and got up on the bed by her side.

Oh, it was.
Breakfast in bed, with their baby by their side.
It was a very good morning.
They all were now!

* * * * *

THE SURGEON'S
BABY SECRET

AMBER MCKENZIE

To all my female physician friends. Heather, Kate, Jaclyn, KP, Erin, Allison, Rebecca and Kristen it has been amazing being your friend and colleague. Thank you for sharing your lives and friendship with me. You are all both talented and beautiful, like the perfect romance novel heroine.

CHAPTER ONE

WAS SHE RUNNING away from her problems? Yes—and who could blame her? Erin thought as she ventured farther up the hills that comprised Arthur's Seat. Was it working? No. Her trip across the Atlantic to Edinburgh had done nothing to change her circumstances or block the thoughts and feelings that had been tormenting her. The message that had awaited her at hotel check-in had confirmed that.

She looked around her at the lush greenery of the hills, the blue of the sky and the distant sparkle of the ocean. It was breathtaking, even with the signs warning of the dangers of severe wind gusts. She wished everything in life could come with such warnings. Then maybe she would have seen the hidden danger that had been disguised as her dreams coming true.

Erin stopped to catch her breath and smiled ruefully to herself. She felt as if she spent every day running from one delivery to another as an obstetrics resident, but maybe she wasn't as fit as she'd thought, as she took in another deep breath. She looked up the path and saw a bench and made her way toward it. Maybe this hadn't been her best idea. She hadn't even dressed for a hike, her gray blazer and heeled boots a poor choice for any athletic pursuit. But this hadn't been her plan. Nothing had been her plan. But another message from her now ex-husband had pushed her into the open air before she had even set sight on her hotel room.

She felt another wave of anger pass through her just as another gust of cold wind hit. She wanted to still be angry with him. Anger, indignation, hurt, she had felt them all when the truth had first come out, but now all those emotions she had once felt toward Kevin Dufour, her newly ex-husband, had long ago burnt out and had been replaced by disappointment in herself.

She reached back into the pocket of her blazer and pulled out the printed message that had interrupted her attempt at escape.

Erin—Divorce finalized. I think we can agree that you don't belong at Boston General. Kevin

Was he right? Was it worth having to deal with the aftermath of Kevin to stay where she loved to work? Damn, she was doing it again, letting someone else make her doubt herself. Why was she so weak? How had she been so naive?

She felt the gust as she watched the note slip from her hands and tumble down the slope. Instinctively she lunged for it, not wanting Kevin's cruel words to sully the beauty of the landscape surrounding her.

He watched, as if in slow motion, as the woman jumped from the steep hilltop over the edge. For a split second he froze before he sprinted to the spot where he'd last seen her. In the short time before he got there he prepared himself for what he might find and felt relief at the sight of her holding onto the last small outcropping of rock before the hill's cliff. He couldn't make out much of her face as she hugged her body close to the almost vertical ground beneath it, but he saw her tremble with fear. "Don't move," he yelled down to her.

But she did move, her head tilted only slightly to look back up at him, and once again he felt shock at what he was seeing. She was both young and beautiful. Her shoulder-length dark blond hair was being flung around her face as the wind continued to battle with her. Through the wisps of hair he could make out the beautiful large eyes that stood out even more against the pallor of her complexion. He was sure that he would never forget the way this woman was looking at him right now, at this moment.

"Stay still," he reminded her, not wanting to be a distraction to her.

"I'm scared," a small voice came back to him.

He wasn't surprised. Even though he had watched her willingly throw herself from the hilltop it was normal to have last-minute regrets. He needed to keep her calm and establish trust between them. "I know. I'm going to get you out of there. What's your name?"

"Erin."

"Okay, Erin. My name is Ryan and I'm going to help you."

How could he appear so calm and confident? She was literally on a ledge, facing death. Just as she had been reaching for the message a large gust of wind had blown it—and her—over the cliff. If she had thought she had hit rock bottom before, she had been wrong. This was truly it. She had let Kevin's words literally drive her over the edge, and for what? What did it matter? What did he matter? Nothing that had come before this moment mattered except she had never wanted a second chance more than she wanted one now.

She looked up again toward the reassuring voice from above. The sun was shining brightly and she was too afraid to move any further, so all she could take in was the man's muscular silhouetted outline. It immediately instilled confidence in her and she felt some of her fear dissipate. If anyone could help her it was this man.

She watched as he lowered himself to the ground, lying prone, hanging his head and shoulders over the cliff's edge. He extended one long muscular arm toward her. "Erin, when you are ready I want you to reach up and take my hand."

"I can't." The idea of letting go of any of her grip on the limited ground beneath her was impossible.

"Yes, you can, Erin. Trust me."

It was an even more impossible request. She didn't trust anyone, not even herself. "I can't."

"You can't stay where you are forever. Reach up and take my hand."

He was right. She had no options. Still, she couldn't help but marvel at the complete lack of frustration in his voice. When was the last time someone had been patient with her? Or even acknowledged her feelings? Trust? She had sworn against that. But right now she had little more to lose so she took a deep breath and reached out her hand. The moment her arm was fully extended she felt his hand pass hers and grip strongly around her wrist; instinctively she did the same. Then, as if she weighed nothing, she was being lifted until he could grasp her under her shoulders and they both went tumbling toward the ground.

But instead of the ground, she landed on him and felt herself being raised and lowered with his breath, her body lax against his firmness. She was too dazed to move as she took in everything that had just happened. He had saved her, this man, Ryan. Ryan, who appeared to have Herculean strength. Ryan, who smelled like a combination of sunshine and sweat. Ryan, whose whole body she was in contact with.

She rolled herself to his side and for the first time got a good look at the man who had saved her. He was more impressive up close. He was tall and there was no muscle on his body that wasn't defined. His black tech running shirt and blue shorts showed off the golden bronze of his skin. His hair was a light brown and he had a scar that extended from above his deep blue eyes toward his thick cropped hair. She could see at least one tattoo revealing itself from the short sleeve of his left arm.

"Are you okay?" His voice cut through her mental inventory of his assets.

Was she? No, but that wasn't what she wanted to say and likely not what her hero wanted to hear. "Yes."

"Are you disappointed?" he asked, his voice softer than before.

Disappointed? Had he sensed her evaluation? Truth be told, he was the first man she had felt attracted to in over a year and his raw sex appeal and heroism left little room for disappointment.

"No," she answered, embarrassed.

"Good," he replied, appearing relieved. He deftly sprang to his feet and then reached out a hand, which she took, and he helped her do the same. He was tall, her head coming up only to the top of his shoulders as she had to tilt upward to look at him.

"Thank you. I don't know what I would have done if you hadn't saved me." She heard her voice tremble at the end, the direness of her previous circumstance even more apparent now that she was out of it.

"I'm just happy you wanted to be saved. Now, let's get out of here before the wind picks up."

She was shocked when he reached out to take her hand. So shocked that she didn't pull away, not that she could have even if she had wanted to. His grip was as tight as it had been when he had pulled her up. It was as if he was locking her beside him and didn't want her to get away. She should have felt fear. This man, Ryan, was a stranger, but instead she felt taken care of. It was a feeling she hadn't felt in a very long time and she was in no hurry to lose it. So instead she followed his lead and walked with him toward the base of the hillside.

"You're American." He finally broke their silence after several minutes.

"Yes." And she realized from his accent that he must be, too.

"What brings you to Scotland?"

"I'm running away from the disaster my life has become. You?" She almost gasped as she realized the answer that had run through her mind at high speed had also escaped from her mouth.

"Work." He answered as though her response had been completely normal and she welcomed his tact.

"What do you do?"

"I'm in the military."

"That explains it." She covered her mouth with her free hand. What was wrong with her? What was it about this man that made her lose her ability to filter? She turned her focus from the path ahead to look at him and was met with a similar appraisal.

"Explains what?" He had stopped and she felt his blue eyes question her more strongly than his words had.

"I just meant that…" Was it that he was the only man with scars and a tattoo that she had ever found sexy? Or that his bravery and strength in saving her had seemed so effortless it wasn't surprising he was a professional hero?

"It's okay, you don't need to explain yourself." He began walking again and she followed, still linked with him. Time went by as they made their way toward the hill's base and she marveled at how comfortable the silence was between them.

"It's a beautiful country." His words finally broke through.

"Yes, it is," she agreed, more comfortable with the neutral territory their conversation had achieved.

"Have you ever been here before?"

"No, but I feel like I have. My father grew up here and when I was little he would tell me stories from his childhood or sometimes just about this faraway country with princess castles and green grass and blue ocean as far as the eye could see."

"I'm not sure the Scottish would take well to having a strong part of their heritage referred to as 'princess castles.'" She looked back toward him and he was smiling. If she had thought he was handsome before, now he was devastating. She was shocked by the powerful wave of attraction his smile evoked and had to check herself against those feelings. Fortunately they had reached the end of the path, a natural place to say goodbye. She let go of his hand and was surprised by the feeling of loss. All the more reason to get away now before she let her attraction make her life more complicated.

"Thank you again."

"I'll walk you back to your hotel."

She wanted him to, but knew better. "Thanks. But I'm okay from here. I can find my way."

She knew he was going to argue with her so she didn't give him the chance. Instead she turned and headed toward her hotel and never looked back at the kindest, most handsome man she had talked to in years.

She looked nothing like Sabrina but she reminded him of her nonetheless. Both women were beautiful, but that wasn't the similarity that was troubling him. It was the look in her eyes that brought back familiar haunting memories. At first those large round eyes that he'd later learned were a deep blue had just seemed scared, but after she had been returned to safety their depth of emotion had changed from fear to sadness. A sadness he had seen in his sister Sabrina's eyes years ago and which had set off warning bells in his head—not that she hadn't already rung those bells hard by leaping off the hill's edge. What would she have done if he hadn't been there? Would she have followed through with her intention and let go?

He physically recoiled at the thought of losing her and stopped in his tracks. How could he already feel a connection to this woman he barely knew? Most people would blame the dramatic nature of their encounter, but truthfully, to him, that drama had been minor. He was a military trained physician and for the past five years had had a decorated career as a trauma specialist. Pulling a beautiful woman to safety was a nice day at the office compared to the horrors he had witnessed.

It must be the emotional resemblance to Sabrina. The first time he'd seen that look in Sabrina he had missed it. He had been away for too long and hadn't noticed the sadness in his little sister's eyes. His role as a big brother had circumvented his role as a physician and he'd missed all the warning signs of depression his sister had been experiencing. She had been thinner than he'd remembered, with dark rings of fatigue under her eyes. She had rarely smiled and when he had tried to arrange activities to cheer her up, she had gotten no pleasure out of things that had previously made her happy.

Classic depression, and he, her big brother, the physician, had missed it and had just thought she'd been heartbroken and would get over it. That she had been better off. But in the end that hadn't mattered. Instead, Sabrina had suffered for over a year before she'd hit rock bottom and he had never stopped blaming himself. He should have been there for her. He should have recognized the signs and gotten help for her earlier. He had failed her. He hadn't protected her from the man who had broken her heart and he hadn't realized how badly she'd needed help to be put back together.

The thought monologue snapped him back to Erin. She had thanked him for saving her. He wished that it was enough to reassure him. Hadn't Sabrina always smiled politely through her pain? The one thing he was certain of was that this was not their last encounter. Was it a sense of responsibility he felt to her? Intrigue at the cause of her sadness? Or the fact that she smelled of wildflowers and had felt soft and right pressed against him. At this point it didn't matter, his mind was made up. This was not the end of their story, it was merely the beginning.

CHAPTER TWO

ERIN SPOONED ANOTHER morsel of the warm decadent bread pudding into her mouth and let both the food and the ambiance overwhelm her senses. The local pub she had ventured to for dinner had been everything she'd been looking for; the noise and activity were a perfect distraction from the constant replay of her own thoughts. She had almost died today. She might have died had Ryan not saved her. The worst part was it would have been a stupid reason to die.

She needed to take responsibility for inadvertent actions. For her constant ability to let people, mainly her now ex-husband, manipulate her. But today it stopped. When she'd got back to her hotel room, she had torn up the new messages that awaited her and instead lounged in a hot bath and thought about what she wanted in life. She wanted to make a difference to the lives of others, just as Ryan had done for her today. The best way to do that was through her work as an obstetrician-gynecologist. So there was no way she was going to leave her training at Boston General, no matter what demands her ex made.

"Is this seat taken?" A deep voice interrupted her repetition of the earlier inner pep talk. She looked up and saw Ryan. He had changed from his running clothes and was flawless in a button-down navy collared shirt and charcoal-gray dark denim. How was it possible in a city of five hundred thousand people she would run into Ryan again? Attraction followed by fear coursed through her. She wanted to say yes and protect herself from once again being swayed by a handsome man, but how could she? Ryan had saved her life. The least she could do was agree to let him join her table.

"No, go ahead," she agreed, gesturing to the single chair opposite her.

"Are you staying nearby?"

"Yes. You?"

"At the Glasshouse." She felt her eyebrows rise and her eyes widen as he named her hotel. It felt as if they were being drawn together and that was a tough feeling to reconcile in the face of her newfound decision to take charge of her own life.

"How long are you going to be in Edinburgh?" Maybe he would be gone before she had to worry about her feelings toward him.

"A few days. You?"

"The same." Of course, she thought to herself. She took a long sip of the local rhubarb cider she had nursed throughout her meal.

"So you are not running away from your life permanently?"

She looked up to meet his eyes, surprised that he had raised her impulsive comment. "No, I'm afraid that is not an option."

"Glad to hear it." The waitress arrived at their table and took Ryan's order. She was a gorgeous Scottish redhead, tall with a body as luxurious as her hair. She waited for Ryan to notice but he was polite and otherwise unconcerned with the other woman. "I hope you don't mind sticking around for a bit. It's been a long time since I've had good company."

"How do you know I'll be good company?"

"Because you're beautiful to look at and you speak your mind, making you interesting to talk to. It's a rare but highly sought-after combination."

He thought she was beautiful. When had she last heard that? She tucked a lock of her hair behind her ear before finally looking up to meet his eyes. "I don't know what to say to that."

"You don't have to say anything, Erin. That's the benefit of having dinner with a stranger. You don't owe me anything."

"I think I owe you a lot," she acknowledged.

"So tell me something about yourself and we'll call it even."

She thought of all the things she could tell him. She was a physician. She worked at the same hospital as her stepfather and ex-husband. She was recently divorced from the only man she had ever been in a serious relationship with. None of those topics she wanted to discuss. "I was born in Scotland."

"You don't sound Scottish." He was smiling at her and she couldn't help but feel a sense of warmth from him.

"We moved when I was one. This is my first time back."

"Your father never brought you here when you were growing up?"

"No. My father died when I was ten."

He reached across the table and rested his hand on hers. "I'm sorry."

This was where she normally said "That's okay" as casually as she could muster, but something about Ryan changed her response. "Thank you."

His hand lingered on hers until the waitress returned with his dark draft beer. "So tell me something about yourself," she said, genuinely interested in the man before her.

"What do you want to know?"

"Am I the first woman you have ever pulled off a hillside?"

"First, and hopefully last. What else?" He leaned back in his chair and looked completely relaxed with opening his life up to her questions.

"Where are you stationed?"

"I've been mainly in combat zones in the Middle East for the past five years."

"Do you like it?"

"Combat?"

"Being in the military."

"Yes. I originally joined to help pay for school but found myself drawn to the hard work ethic and structure. When I finished school I decided to stay for the challenge."

"You like a challenge?" She was surprised to hear her own voice almost coy, teasing him.

"I've found that everything in life worth having you have to work for." The smile that followed was enough to make her heart begin to race. Was he flirting with her? A second later a horrible thought flashed through her mind and in a moment it also left her mouth.

"Are you married?" She alternated her gaze between the look in his eyes during his response and an examination of his left hand, looking for any hint of an outline of a ring.

"No, never have been." It seemed as if he was telling the truth, but would she know if he wasn't? He didn't seem at all disturbed by her question. "Are you?"

She thought about her new label, hating the way it made her relive all her mistakes every time the label was used. She took another sip of her cider and rested the glass back on the table before answering. "Divorced."

"That bothers you."

"You're observant," she acknowledged.

"I've built my career around paying attention to the subtle clues people give me."

"Then you're lucky. I'm so naive that I miss even the most obvious of signs people give me."

"You don't strike me as naive."

"I'm not anymore." Or that was her new resolve anyway. She still needed to prove it to herself.

"I get the feeling there is a story behind that."

He was more than observant, he was perceptive and he was right. There was a long story behind the loss of her innocence, but not one that she felt like sharing—especially with Ryan. It had been years since she had been a stranger to anyone and she enjoyed the freedom of talking to someone who wasn't privy to the backstory of her life. "Are you always this inquisitive with women you have barely met?"

"No. But considering how we met I think we're already beyond the superficial, don't you?"

It wasn't his words that implied an intimacy between them. It was the way he was looking at her. She again took in the man sitting before her. He was as handsome as he was confident and, as silly as it felt, it felt as if he was on her side. She wasn't sure which feature she found most attractive but attraction was definitely coursing through her body.

"Yes," she answered. "What exactly are we doing here, Ryan?"

She was direct. He'd known that already but he still wasn't prepared for her question, because he didn't know the answer. He had thought about little other than her since they had last parted. Relief had been just one of the emotions he had felt when he'd seen her tonight. If it had only been relief he would have just been happy to see that she was all right and left her alone, but more than relief he felt a complete fascination with the woman he had spotted the moment he'd entered the restaurant.

She looked more mature and somehow more desirable than she had on the hillside. Gone was the young frightened girl and instead, walking past him, was a confident woman. Her blond hair appeared freshly washed and accented perfectly against the blue silk of her shirt. She once again wore heeled boots to add to her height and they clung to her legs in the same fashion as her flesh-hugging gray denim.

Once in the pub he waited for over an hour before he ventured to her table and now he was being asked point-blank about his intentions. Intentions he still didn't even know or understand.

"I'm getting to know a person who has captured my attention and I hope you're doing the same."

He watched as her flush spread from the valley between her breasts that her shirt exposed upward toward her face. She reached this time for her iced water and he watched her bide her time before answering.

"You have definitely captured my attention. But I'm not sure about why we're bothering to get to know each other."

"You really know how to flatter a man." If he'd thought she'd turned red earlier, she had darkened two shades with his last comment.

"What I meant was that neither of us lives here. We may never even see each other again after tonight."

"Do you want to see me again?"

Another long pause before he heard the small sigh escape her lips before she answered. "I've learned the hard way it doesn't matter what I want."

"It matters to me." And it did. He hated seeing the look of defeat in her eyes and felt as if he would do anything to make it go away.

"And if I did want to see you again?"

"Then we would want the same thing."

He waited for her response, or more so her verbal response. He didn't miss the way her pupils dilated or the slight tremble in her response to him. "I want to see you again. I just don't know if it is a good idea."

"Why wouldn't it be?"

"Because things I thought were right for me in the past have been anything but."

"You don't think you can trust me?"

She wasn't ready for this. She wasn't ready for Ryan. Why now? Except she couldn't really begrudge his arrival in her life, because without him there was the possibility she wouldn't be alive. Could she trust him? Her instincts said yes, but she had been so wrong before that the person she really couldn't trust was herself.

"I don't know what to think about any of this."

"What does your gut tell you?"

Her gut told her that she wanted more. More of Ryan and more of the feelings he was bringing out in her. That even talking to him felt so different from her beginnings with Kevin. She didn't feel that sense of being charmed and swept off her feet, which ironically felt better. Ryan made her feel as if this was less about him and more about her and him liking what he saw in her. What would be the harm in spending more time together? To indulge in the feelings he brought out in her? Her first fling and in less than a week they would go their separate ways, and at best he would become a beautiful memory to carry with her as she carved out her new life. At worst, well, really, what couldn't she face after everything she had already been through?

"It's getting late and it's pretty dark out. Would you mind walking me back to the hotel?"

"I think I can do that."

He signaled to the waitress and paid their bill, silencing her objections to his generosity. She also wasn't able to slip past his gallantry as he helped her put on her jacket and held the door for her as they ventured into the slightly cooled night air.

"It is beautiful here, both day and night," she remarked, feeling relaxation take hold of her for the first time since arriving earlier that day. A yawn escaped her as the jet lag she had been waiting for did the same.

"Careful, these roads are charming but a bit uneven." His words were followed by his arm brushing past hers to take hold of her hand. It was the second time she had felt held to him and she allowed herself to enjoy it.

They walked the few blocks toward the hotel and her mind began to quiet as she enjoyed the evening and her time with Ryan. "It's nice to have someone to look out for me," she thought and said simultaneously.

The hand that had so strongly held hers pulled her toward him as they stopped still in the darkness a few meters from the hotel's entrance. "I wish I could say that all I want to do is look out for you." His voice, sounding slightly anguished, made the short voyage to her ears.

"What do you want to do with me?" she asked, surprised, with no essence of the "come-hither" that question would normally hold.

"This," he answered, as his hands moved even closer to hold her against him as his lips descended on hers. His lips were hard yet so soft against her own and she welcomed the contact. She reached up, letting her hands rest against his chest, loving the feel of his firm chest as much as she enjoyed the pressure of his kiss. She felt his desire for more and she wanted the same, opening her mouth to his for him to explore. She wasn't sure how long they stood like that, in the night, kissing, but she was certain that she had never been kissed like that before.

When they finally broke apart she felt breathless

and dizzy, both in a very good way. "Thank you," she murmured against him.

"Thank you?" he said, puzzled.

"I needed to be kissed like that."

"I'd be happy to do it again."

She laughed and she enjoyed the sound echoing through the night.

"Really, Erin. I have full intentions of kissing you again," he stated outright, and she had no doubt of his plans.

"Can you meet me tomorrow?" she asked with a little hesitancy, hoping for the response she realized she desperately wanted.

"Yes."

"Then I have no doubt you will make good on your promise. Good night. I'll see you in the morning." This time she initiated the kiss as she closed the gap between them once again and softly pressed her lips to his, before breaking away and moving through the hotel courtyard to the entrance. He didn't follow her, which was good as she wasn't sure she would be able to resist any further advances.

Ryan walked onto the balcony of his suite, which in the daytime gave him both a clear view of old Edinburgh and the sea. He sipped from a short glass of Scotch and tried to organize his thoughts and motivations.

He could no longer pretend that he was spending time with Erin to protect her from herself. Did she have a hint of sadness to her—yes. But after tonight he couldn't make the argument that she was depressed and needed saving from herself. Maybe he had misinterpreted what had happened on Arthur's Seat. What he hadn't misinterpreted was his attraction to her. Tonight in the restaurant with every word that had come from her perfectly formed lips and every small move of her body toward him he'd felt a pull toward her. He had meant what he'd said to her—she was beautiful and she said what she meant, and he valued both qualities equally. So much so that he had kissed her and now wanted more.

He looked out into the night and had to blink before he believed what his eyes were showing him. On the balcony a few rooms away he saw Erin. She had changed into a dark-colored nightshirt that seemed to come just to the tops of her bare legs. It was loose on her but between the V-shaped cut of the neckline, its short length and the way a mild wind was pressing it against her he thought it was the sexiest bedtime apparel he had ever seen on a woman. He watched her, half mesmerized by her appearance and half concerned about her choice of location. What was she doing on the balcony? He exhaled a sigh of relief as she reached for a large blanket and wrapped her body in it before taking a seat in one of the balcony chairs, where she stayed staring out into the night.

Ryan, Erin thought, was she ready for Ryan? She had only said goodbye to him a few minutes ago and she already missed him, a man she just met. It was hard to reconcile all the feelings she was experiencing. One of the emotions she had felt during her divorce had been fear. Fear that outside her relationship with Kevin she had no experience with other men. Would another man find her attractive one day? And would she ever trust another man enough? And even if he did and she did, would she ever want the man she loved to suffer the same cruel fate she had been dealt? No.

But Ryan. Did she trust Ryan—yes. But were they ever going to be in a relationship—no. This was a brief and fleeting opportunity and one she didn't feel she could turn away. Because she liked Ryan and the way he made her feel and because she was not going to let Kevin take one more thing from her.

Kevin had been a mistake from the beginning. She had just been too young and naive to see it. She had been a medical student on her first clinical rotation in Orthopedics when she'd met him. She had been nervous and excited, wearing her white clinical jacket for the first time and being called student intern. Everyone had seemed more important than her—the nurses, the residents, the staff physicians—and all she had wanted to do was to impress.

Then she'd met Kevin, or Dr. Dufour, her supervising resident, and he had seemed godlike in comparison to her lowly medical student ranking. He would single her out from her colleagues, giving her more opportunities and one-on-one time than any of the other students on the rotation. At first she had been flattered and had done her best to impress him, going that extra mile to stay late and check bloodwork or making food runs to bring to him in the operating room in between cases. Looking back on it, she had been more his slave than his student, but she had been so in awe of everything he'd represented.

Then his attention had become more personal than professional. Subtle touches, comments on her appearance, and she'd continued to be flattered. She had never been involved with anyone older than her and the attention of an older accomplished man had been absorbing. And he'd been a charmer, a snake charmer, really. It hadn't been long before she'd fallen for him and he'd been making late-night appearances at her apartment. She had been in love with the man she'd thought he was and he had been willing to take advantage.

Until—until she'd become pregnant. And until he'd realized that while her last name was the same as her birth father's, Madden, her stepfather was Dr. Williamson, the hospital's chief of staff. That had been when she'd started getting glimpses of the man he really was, but she had been so overwhelmed with concern over her own life and how the pregnancy was going to affect her career that she'd pushed them to the back of her mind.

The same was done with her hesitancy over getting married. Her parents had made it clear that she had already disappointed them and it had been crushing knowledge, so she'd gone along with their demands, thinking that once Kevin got used to the idea of their upcoming family he would settle into their life together.

She had been so wrong. Once they'd married he'd become resentful and disinterested and she'd become trapped and alone. He hadn't even been there when she'd almost died from complications from her miscarriage. To him it had been the final nail in the coffin that was his marriage. He'd felt unable to leave her now, not if he wanted his career. So he'd stayed. She had tried to make him happy. Tried to regain what they had lost, spending months—years—trying to conceive again, but she couldn't.

Then had come the women. She'd met his first girlfriend shortly after they'd married, learning that he had been involved with the other woman at the same time as her up until their wedding. When she'd confronted him he'd told her what she'd wanted to hear and had promised his fidelity. Soon she had been too caught up in her own pain from her pregnancy loss to care whether he was telling the truth.

But as she had risen from her grief and begun to face her reality, she couldn't hide the signs. By then she had graduated medical school and was now the resident at Boston General and Kevin was a staff orthopedic surgeon. When she walked the halls she would notice people taking more notice of her than was normal. When she entered the emergency department she would see nurses turn and speak quietly to one another. Then finally after three years of marriage she received a written note in her locker from "a friend" who wanted her to know that her husband was sleeping with one of the hospital pharmacists.

He didn't even deny it. Instead he blamed his infidelity on her inadequacies as a wife. In some ways Kevin still won in their divorce. She filed for divorce citing irreconcilable differences, too embarrassed to have her husband's cheating and her deficiencies aired publically. His professional reputation remained intact and he was able to carry on at Boston General as if nothing had happened. Meanwhile, she was struggling to gain her own reputation outside her infamous failed marriage and position as the chief of staff's stepdaughter.

Kevin wanted her gone, completely, and communicated more with her postdivorce with his badgering than he had in the year prior to their ultimate divorce. And it would be easier for her just to leave and start over somewhere new with all her baggage left behind, but there was something about Boston General that felt like home and she wasn't ready to give up anything else in her life.

The wind picked up again and she felt the corners of the blanket lift. It was time to try to sleep, to force herself onto Scottish time. She rose from her chair and peered into the night, instinctively turning to her right, looking away from the ocean and at one of the neighboring balconies. She recognized Ryan. The backlighting of his suite and the darkness of the balcony created the same effect as when she had first seen him and the image of masculine perfection was unchanged. They were too far apart for words, so instead she pressed her hand to her lips and extended it toward him before walking back into her suite and closing the balcony door.

CHAPTER THREE

NERVOUS ANTICIPATION FILLED her as Erin dressed for the unknown in the day ahead. Somehow in the heat of her moment with Ryan they had not made true plans for today, she had just asked him to meet her. When? Where? She had no idea, but she had complete faith that she would see him.

She ran her fingers through her hair, deciding to leave it down, and took a look at her appearance in the mirror. It had felt great that morning, getting ready and knowing that there was someone waiting for her who would be appreciative of her effort. Her cream tunic top had a crocheted design that while it covered her it also revealed her shape beneath. The same went for her gray slim-fit summer pants that ended a few inches above her ankles. She had small slip-on shoes that matched and would be perfect for exploring Edinburgh. She hoped she would see Ryan sooner rather than later.

He was waiting in the hotel lobby when the elevator doors opened. He looked up and smiled, sipping from a takeaway cup of coffee. He looked as good as when she had twice previously seen him. He was freshly washed and shaved and the V-neck of his red polo shirt revealed the hint of another tattoo on his chest. She walked toward him and he rose to greet her, and before she could wish him good morning his lips were against hers. The kiss was brief but no less exciting. "I've been waiting to do that."

"I hope I haven't kept you waiting too long."

"You're worth waiting for. I brought you a coffee. I hope you drink coffee."

"I live on it, thanks."

"So what is your plan for the day?" he asked.

"My plan?" Her only plan had been to be with Ryan.

"Well, my plan was to be with you, which I have now accomplished, so now we move on to your plan."

She knew she was smiling like a fool, but still couldn't change the way she felt. "Ah. Okay, then. Today is my only free day and my plan was to explore Edinburgh. I would be very pleased if you joined me."

"Lead on."

With a genuine smile she led them back outside the hotel, where Ryan took her hand. "Let me guess, we're going to the princess castle."

"Of course," she replied, and felt by the time the day was done her whole face was going to hurt from the happiness Ryan seemed to be able to bring out in her. "But don't worry, the princess castle also contains the military museum, which should appease you."

They made their way through the irregular streets toward the Edinburgh Castle entrance. She knew not to object as Ryan paid their entrance fee and they passed through the castle gate. "Look up," he instructed.

Above them was a spiked portcullis designed to

protect the castle against siege. "Not exactly a fairy-tale castle feature," he added.

"I don't believe in fairy tales."

"Another thing we have in common, because neither do I."

Ryan held her hand as they passed in and out of the buildings that made up Edinburgh Castle. She had always enjoyed history and was happy that Ryan also seemed fascinated by the depth of history within the castle walls. They took their time exploring the National War Museum and she was impressed with his knowledge as he took the time to explain to her the nuances of past wars. At the end of the museum was a new exhibit dedicated to war veterans with amputations and the use of prosthetics.

"Amazing, isn't it?" Ryan remarked, as they examined the cabinet filled with examples of modern bionic limbs.

"It is."

"I should have been an orthopedic surgeon," he remarked, not knowing the effect his words would have on her.

"No, you shouldn't have been," she blurted, not able to censor herself yet again.

"Why not?" he asked, confused by the shift in her demeanor.

"Because I like you just the way you are," she answered, trying to cover the real meaning behind her remark.

"Why do I feel like there is something you are not saying?"

She sighed, realizing that her deflection hadn't

worked and she was going to have to bring her past into what was already the best day she'd had in years.

"Because there is. My ex-husband is an orthopedic surgeon and I would like to think that you have nothing in common."

"Ah. So you have a thing against doctors?" She could tell he was testing her and she hoped she didn't sound like a bitter, scorned woman.

"That would make my life very hard, considering I am one. I've just learned the hard way about the dangers of mixing personal and professional lives and would never risk that again." She watched him, waiting for his reaction, and didn't miss the conflict in his face. Was he so surprised that she was a physician or was he just as bothered as she was that her ex had entered into their time together. She wanted to go back and take away her comment. "Besides, the only type of man I could now ever imagine being attracted to is one in the military."

She smiled, and her smile only grew as he smiled back at her.

"Is that so?"

"Absolutely and completely."

"So doctors are not your type?"

"Nope, I only have eyes for ruggedly handsome soldiers who save my life and come with no strings attached." As the words left her lips even she didn't doubt her sincerity. Ryan was the complete opposite of Kevin and the possibility of something between them felt more and more right with every moment they spent together. He was what she needed, a couple of days of abandon to restore everything her failed marriage had taken away from her.

The way he looked at her she had no doubt he was feeling the same attraction she was. "Well, Dr. Erin, I think we are both fortunate that you have equally opened my eyes to the appeal of female physicians. So I take it you are not in orthopedics. What do you do?"

"Obstetrics and gynecology."

"That would be the opposite of orthopedics," he remarked, and she appreciated that he, too, was trying to lighten the mood.

"It's less complicated than taking care of men." She laughed.

"Ouch." He feigned injury.

"It is actually amazing helping women and being there for one of the most special times in their lives."

"Did you know that Mary Queen of Scots gave birth in this castle?"

"No, I didn't."

"Then let's go check out the birth chamber of James VI." He once again connected his hand with hers and she marveled at how the same action brought even more excitement each time he touched her.

She had been right. Her face hurt from smiling. As they toured the entire castle she felt completely at peace and in her element, learning about Scottish history and with a man she respected and whose company she enjoyed. Not to mention an attraction that was growing exponentially. Every time he reached for her hand it felt as if they were connecting and throughout the day she was holding her breath, waiting for the moment when he would kiss her again.

She felt the first drop hit her shoulder as they once again passed through the castle gates. Then the

second, then the third. Within seconds the sky had
opened and rain was pouring down on both of them.
She felt a tug on her hand as he pulled her into the
protection of a narrow corridor between the old brick
buildings. The small space necessitated being pressed
together and any thoughts she had of being cold immediately vanished. Ryan's hand swept her wet bangs
from her forehead before his lips came down on hers.

Finally, she thought as she met him with equal passion. His lips were wet with the rain and added to the
freshness of his taste. She opened her mouth to him,
wanting more, and was rewarded by his response.
His tongue met hers until she didn't know where he
ended and she began. At the same time his hands
trailed from his initial position on her face along the
sides of her body until she felt them on her bare back
underneath the dampness of her shirt. Another point
of heat between them.

She wanted more. Wanted him to move his hands
over her and caress her aching breasts. Wanted to feel
the ultimate fulfillment that the rigidity pressed into
her abdomen promised.

"Not here," he murmured into her ear, when they
finally broke apart.

She looked into the pouring rain. "Want to make
a run for it?"

"Yes," he agreed with the same smile she had become accustomed to.

She kissed him once more, pressing her lips to his
with the firm passion that had ignited inside her, before they broke apart and made their start on the sprint
back to the hotel. It took them ten minutes but on

arrival in the hotel's lobby she was completely soaked through and panting from the exertion of their run.

She followed Ryan's lead and they said nothing to each other, the understanding already present between them as they entered the elevator and Ryan pressed the button for his floor. As soon as the door closed they were once again wrapped around each other. His lips were on hers. His hands were covering her body. And she was burning up despite the cold, wet clothing covering them both.

As the doors opened they broke apart and with one mutual look their sprint continued hand in hand. One swipe of Ryan's key and they were tumbling into his room. They reunited in their embrace, but this time there were no restrictions from being in a public place to hold them back. She watched as he pulled away from their kiss and peeled his soaked shirt from his body. It felt like an unveiling as she got to see first-hand what lay beneath.

Nothing disappointed. Every muscle on his body was defined. The tattoo she had seen hints of on his chest was a serpent entwined on a single rod along his right pectoral muscle. It reminded her of the caduceus, the symbol she recognized for medicine, but it was slightly different. Encircling his right biceps was another design. Either way she had never considered tattoos attractive but on Ryan they were explosive.

Before she could enjoy him any further she felt herself being stripped of her drenched top. She had previously been shy about her body, but not with Ryan. The minute she was exposed she wasn't because he pressed back against her. His mouth rejoined hers but it wasn't long before he was trailing his lips down her neck to her shoulder. She threaded her fingers through his wet hair and felt her body melting into his.

His hands skimmed her back before she felt the clasp of her bra release and the weight of her breasts released from their confines. Yes, she thought, this was what she wanted. He stepped back from her and she was rewarded by the look in his eye and the knowledge that he was every bit as enthralled as she was. With painstaking precision he eased the garment from her shoulders, down her arms and completely off, before he skimmed her breasts with the back of his hand. It was seduction at its finest. Then without pause he was against her, lifting her, his hands cupping her bottom before resting her on the dresser's edge. The move had made up for their foot difference in height and she felt even closer to him.

She was finally rewarded with the feel of both of his hands, each cupping a breast and causing electric shocks of want to course through her body to her core. His hands gently caressed her as his mouth returned to her neck, his thumbs occasionally brushing against the peaks of her rigid nipples. She loved every touch, welcomed it as she felt the anticipation of what was still to come.

He paused his tactile exploration and she opened her eyes to see why he'd stopped. His hand was able to completely cover her own tattoo, a small willow tree on her lower left hip. She blinked hard, thinking about what it represented, not wanting to explain its significance, especially now.

"You're beautiful."

And she believed him. "Thank you."

* * *

A weeping willow, he thought to himself, and instantly the memory of her vulnerability on the hillside played in his mind. What was he doing? He thought to himself. He wanted her, desperately, but was this fair to her? When he knew she was vulnerable? No, it wasn't fair to her, and from what he had learned about her so far she both needed, and deserved, someone to be on her side.

"I think we should slow down." The words were torn from him because it was what his rational thought wanted but not what his body wanted.

"What?" she said. Her eyes dilated in both passion and disbelief.

He couldn't repeat himself so instead he reached into one of the nearby dressers and pulled out a T-shirt, which he proceeded to cover her with. He needed to cover the temptation she represented—it didn't work. She still turned him on and now she looked hurt and that was the last thing he wanted.

"I don't want us to do anything you are going to regret."

"Why would I regret this?"

He wanted to be as honest as she had been. Because he was a physician and she didn't know. Because maybe her deeply hidden sadness was making her vulnerable to him. "Because I'm worried I'm taking advantage of you."

He watched as her arms crossed protectively across her chest and she ran a hand through her hair, which had become wild as it dried from the rain. "In what way?"

"In that I saved your life and maybe you feel indebted to me."

"I don't. I'm grateful, but I don't."

"Okay, but what about the fact that you admitted you were running away from a disaster in your life?"

"I think that's for me to worry about."

"Not just you, Erin."

"I think I should go."

He instinctively lifted her down from the dresser he had perched her on and backed away. He watched as she looked at the wet heap that was her shirt and bra on the floor before deciding to leave it and making her way to the door.

She shut the door of her room and collapsed against the back of it before sinking down on the floor. He hadn't stopped her and he hadn't followed her, and how she had wanted him to. The worst part was that she believed him and understood why he had stopped.

Ryan saw her as fragile and he didn't want to take advantage of her. Where had he been three years ago? And how she wished he had been wrong, but the truth was she was still vulnerable. And maybe she would always have that vulnerability that had been born from being broken.

Was she making a good decision with Ryan? She knew she wanted him and wished he hadn't stopped what had been the most sensual encounter she had ever experienced. But she also couldn't deny that she wasn't in a good position emotionally to be making major life choices. But was Ryan that? She had convinced herself last night that he was a holiday indulgence to be enjoyed but after today he felt like more. And what was worse, she actually respected and trusted him more for turning her away. So where did that leave them now?

CHAPTER FOUR

A KNOCK AT HER hotel room door roused her from the late-afternoon nap she had been indulging in. After she had lifted herself from the room's floor and showered the chill from her body she curled up in the hotel-provided terry-toweling robe, thinking of all the questions she had no answers for.

She fastened the robe's sash tightly and then made her way to the door. She opened the door slightly to see Ryan, who also looked drier than the last time she had seen him. She opened the door wider and stepped aside to allow him inside. Both her eyes and her nose spotted the bag of food he was carrying.

"I thought I would bring dinner to you."

She glanced at the room's clock and realized that her late-afternoon nap had spread well into the evening and it was past eight.

"Thank you," she said cautiously, not knowing where they stood. "How did you know which room I was in?"

"I saw you last night on your balcony and you're welcome." He went ahead and set up his offering on the round table adjacent to the glass balcony doors and she took the seat intended for her.

"Smells delicious," she remarked, trying to keep their conversation neutral but realizing she was more than happy at his reappearance.

"It's nice to see you smile. I was worried I had ruined things between us."

His confession brought out an instant relaxation in her and the awkwardness of the aftermath of the previous encounter dissolved.

"You haven't."

"I hope you like traditional Scottish fare. It was what the restaurant recommended and it seemed fitting. Plus they had the bread pudding that you seemed very fond of last night." He was smiling to accompany the gentle familiarity of his teasing.

"You know what they say about holidays—it's the time to indulge."

"Yes." His voice had changed and contained a masculine huskiness as she realized the other meanings of her words. It was clear that, whatever had happened between them, he still wanted her, too.

"So what are your plans?" she asked, trying to shift the focus from their almost sexual encounter.

He choked on the glass of water he had been sipping from. "Excuse me?"

"For the rest of your time in Scotland," she amended, realizing he'd thought she had been asking about his plans for her.

"I have a commitment the day after tomorrow and then I have to return to the base. What are your plans, Erin?"

"Today was my last free day."

"I refuse to accept that."

"I'm afraid it's true. I have two days of meetings then I'm flying back to the States the next morning."

"But your nights are free?"

"That depends. Why did you stop earlier?" She needed to know. She wasn't prepared to spend more time torturing herself by being with Ryan and wondering how he felt about her and what his intentions were.

"I thought we had covered that."

"What if I wanted to readdress it?"

"Your tattoo."

"What?" She didn't understand his comment.

"Your tattoo."

"Considering your own ink, I'm surprised you have a problem with a woman having a tattoo."

"I don't. I actually think it's beautiful. You can tell that you had it placed for only you to see."

"I did." How did this man read her so well?

"It's a weeping willow, and it reminded me that the one thing I don't want to do is hurt you."

"So don't." She was rewarded with his smile. "Did you know weeping willows are known for their tenacious roots that continue life, but the trees themselves are also a symbol of compassion? My tattoo symbolizes tenacity and compassion, both qualities of the weeping willow and both qualities I strive to possess."

"You don't think you already do?"

"I think, to be the person I want to be and the physician I want to be, I need to work on both."

"I like you the way you are."

It was what she needed to hear after years of being not enough for a husband who hadn't valued or loved her. Ryan's words empowered her. "Thank you. I feel the same way about you. What if I told you you were what I needed? Would that change your mind?"

"Explain." She saw him shifting in his chair and knew she had gotten through to him.

"Maybe what I need is time with a man I respect and who actually renews my faith in men and maybe myself."

"I'm a soldier, first and foremost. I couldn't promise you anything."

"I don't want you to promise me anything. I've been promised the world by a man and it didn't work out. So you don't need to worry about not giving me a promise for forever because even if you did I wouldn't accept it."

"Are you sure?"

"Yes."

He stood from his chair opposite her and she took a deep breath of anticipation until he started walking away from her. "If you are still sure tomorrow then I'll pick you up at seven tomorrow night. If you change your mind, please just stand me up so that I don't try to change it back."

She watched mutely as he walked away and then was surprised when he suddenly turned back. She felt him lift her from her chair and gather her in his arms before his lips made contact with hers. It was hot, it was hard and it was every bit as passionate as she wanted. When he broke away she was gasping for air but still not wanting it to have ended.

"Just in case you needed a reminder. Good night, sleep tight."

How was she ever going to make it until seven tonight? A restless night, thinking of the possibilities, had left her completely devoid of sleep. Added to that, she seemed to have forgotten the skill of being able to sit through hours of seminars and she had no ability to focus on the lectures being presented. The International Society of Obstetrics and Gynecology conference had been her original reason for the trip to Scotland but now it was the furthest thing from her mind.

She had been elected to sit on a discussion panel throughout the conference to provide a perspective on both the American experience and the experience of the younger generation of obstetricians and gynecologists. At the time it had been an honor, but now all she could think of was Ryan.

"Dr. Dufour." A voice cut into her thoughts and she instantly recoiled inwardly. She had registered for the conference before her name had legally returned to her maiden name of Madden.

"Yes," she answered reluctantly.

"What has been your experience in the States with single embryo transfers to reduce the rates of multiple births in infertile couples?"

She did her best to shift her focus away from the nervous anticipation of the upcoming night and back to her original purpose for being in Scotland. She needed to focus on her work, particularly as infertility was her area of interest and she was looking for a fellowship in that area after graduation.

She straightened her navy blazer and took a sip of water before turning on the power to the microphone in front of her. "The single embryo transfer program is a much better option for women whose treatment cycles are funded through government insurance programs. In the United States women still pay out of their own pockets for their cycles, most of the time taking on significant debt for the chance at a baby. Given those circumstances, it is hard to convince them to transfer just one embryo."

"What about the ability to reduce the rate of multiple births?"

She thought back to the aftermath of her miscarriage and the months, years, she'd spent trying for another baby. If she had naturally become pregnant with twins she would have cried with joy. It would have felt as if she was being compensated for the baby she'd lost and the suffering she had endured. Instead nothing, every month nothing, and instead she had felt punished. Punished for unwittingly being the other woman. She should never have been with Kevin. She didn't deserve a baby.

"As obstetricians we have firsthand knowledge of the risks of twins and most of us would not want to roll the dice with the risks of extreme prematurity and the resulting possibility of lifelong complications. Women with infertility feel very differently. They would take any risk for the chance at a child and no amount of counseling from us on the risk of multiple births is going to change that."

She tried her best to actively follow the panel discussion and not fall back into her own thoughts. But she was speaking from personal experience. She knew the risks of twins and still she would have happily rolled the dice for a baby. Babies. It had taken a long time before she had accepted that the life-threatening infection she had experienced after her miscarriage had permanently damaged her so that she would never have a child.

Acceptance of that harsh reality had been one of the reasons she had finally gathered the courage up to leave Kevin. She had realized that one of the reasons she had looked the other way from her suspicions of his infidelity was because she'd seen him as her way to have a baby. When her dreams of being a mother had been lost, she'd no longer had any need to pretend, even to herself, that she was happy in her marriage.

"I'd like to thank the panel for their experience and participation in today's discussion. We will resume tomorrow morning with our special guest speaker and headline symposium 'Postpartum Hemorrhage—Tales from the Battlefield,'" the moderator announced.

Erin snapped back to the present and glanced at her watch. It was four-thirty. That left two and a half hours until Ryan met her. How was she going to make it till then without going crazy?

She left the conference center and made her way to a nearby café. The sun was setting and the streets of Edinburgh appeared enchanting before her, as if they had a promise of something to offer. She ordered a latte, hoping the caffeine would help ground her, before settling into a corner table and dialing.

"Hey, Erin," the voice on the other end of the phone welcomed her warmly, and she instantly felt her nerves settle. It was hard to be infamous and make friends. Most of her fellow residents were intimidated by the fact that she was the chief of staff's stepdaughter. The others were too busy enjoying the gossip her dysfunctional marriage had created to get to know her. But Chloe Darcy was different. She was unthreatened by all Erin's baggage and instead Erin felt as if she had really gained a true friend.

"Hi, Chloe."

"I'd like to think you are calling just to chat and tell me how wonderful Scotland is, but I have a feeling there's something more."

"I met a guy," Erin confessed.

"Um, not what I was expecting to hear, but I'm absolutely thrilled!" Erin could tell she was being genuine. "So who is he?"

"His name is Ryan, he's in the military and he saved my life."

"Are you being literal or figurative?"

"Literal. I was walking on a hillside known as Arthur's Seat when the wind blew me right off. Ryan found me clinging to the hill's edge and pulled me to safety."

"But you are okay now?"

"Yes."

"Wow, that's scary and also incredibly romantic. So, aside from being a hero, what is he like?"

"Honest, kind and interested in me and not himself."

"Sounds perfect."

"It's not forever."

"He sounds perfect. Why don't you just see how things go and not worry about forever?"

"Because not worrying has previously been my downfall."

"I'm not going to disagree with that one. I'm actually not sure you could have picked a more horrible man to marry."

"Has he been hitting on you again?" Erin asked.

Chloe was easily one of the most beautiful women Erin had ever met and was often on the receiving end of unwanted attention. Erin knew that Kevin had made passes at her even before they'd separated.

"Don't worry about it. It's nothing I can't handle. So what is the plan with hero Ryan?"

"He's coming to my hotel room tonight."

"And?"

"And anything beyond that is my decision. He's afraid of taking advantage of me, and quite frankly I'm worried I'm not ready. I might get hurt."

"But you don't want forever and this guy makes you feel happy and valued, right?"

"Yes."

"Are you wanting me to tell you what to do?"

"Yes."

"Well, then, that's easy! Go for it. If you didn't want to you never would have called me. I'm your enabler friend."

Erin smiled and felt herself nodding in agreement, even though Chloe couldn't see her. Maybe her life was coming around. In Chloe she had a friend she needed and now she was on the verge of a romantic liaison with a man who enthralled her.

"Thanks, you're a great friend."

"So are you. Do what feels right and if you want to talk I'm always only a phone call away."

Erin said her goodbyes, hung up the call and finished her latte, then made her way back to her room. Once inside she slipped into the bathroom and drew herself a hot bath, which she soaked in for another hour. Once the water had cooled considerably she forced herself to get out, and proceeded through all her typical rituals, drawing them out as much as she could. She applied lotion to her entire body. She dried her hair in sections, curling the ends under with her round brush. For makeup she decided to keep it neutral and applied only a layer of mascara to her eyelashes and a gloss to her lips. When she looked up in the mirror she liked what she saw.

She moved toward the closet and examined her options. She had packed for a conference, not for this, whatever this was going to be. She selected some of the clothes she had brought for travel. A pair of black footless tights over which she layered two tank tops, black with blue over top. Given her short stature, both ended over her hips. She had a long string of silver beads, which completed the outfit, and Erin was pleased when she saw her reflection. She glanced at her watch. Six fifty-eight.

Two minutes passed slowly, but it was only two minutes, because exactly at seven a knock sounded on the door. She took a deep breath before slowly making her way to the door. Ryan stood there, his white dress shirt layered with a black cable sweater. There were leather patches on the elbows and he had an overall look of sophistication, which she appreciated.

"Hi," she opened hesitantly.

He walked toward her, placing his hands on her arms and his lips on hers. He tasted of mint and felt like heaven. The kiss was romantic and passionate, true bliss. If this was how they would spend their night together, even this would be enough.

"I'm glad you're here."

"It's my room. Where else would I be?"

"You could have gotten cold feet."

"That was you, not me." She watched as he understood her meaning.

"Yes, but you need to know it won't happen again." He was giving her one last warning. One last chance to back out.

"Glad to hear it," she whispered, as this time she leaned toward him and pressed her lips against his. What she meant as sweet acceptance quickly changed. He matched the pressure she had exerted and her mouth opened to his instinctively. He tasted her and she reveled in his exploration. She ran her hand down his slightly raspy cheek and his hands slipped around her, pinning her to him and settling on her lower back. She was shocked when she heard herself purring against him and felt the smile that came to his lips.

"This wasn't my plan," he murmured against her.

"It wasn't?" She couldn't keep the disappointment from her voice.

"Well, it was, but later in the evening after I'd had the opportunity to wine and dine you."

"Then wine and dine away, as long as you and I are both clear on how this is all going to end tonight." She wasn't sure who was more surprised at her words, him or her. Gone was the shy, inexperienced girl she had been a few years ago. Ryan made her feel like a mature, confident woman and it was a feeling she found herself very much enjoying.

"Wow" was all Ryan could think. The small part of him that was still warning him that Erin was more vulnerable than she was letting on was being slowly eroded by the confident, sexual woman before him.

When had been the last time he had been this enthralled by a woman? The answer was never. Everything about her—her honesty, her beauty, her open sexuality—was causing havoc with his cautious conscience.

"You are doing your best to ruin my good intentions." In more ways than one, he thought to himself.

"Good," she purred.

He had to force himself to take his hand from her back and instead grab her hand as he quickly guided her out of her hotel room and away from temptation.

They fell into a comfortable silence as they strolled through the night's dusky streets toward the restaurant he had chosen. Once inside the warmth of the dining room he dismissed the restaurant's host for the pleasure of slipping Erin's light trench coat from her shoulders and pulling out her chair himself.

They both read through the menus but, to be honest, he could have ordered dirt and not noticed tonight. "You pick."

"Me?" she asked, looking at him, puzzled.

"You. I want to get to know your tastes."

"I would have thought they were obvious by now. I like men in the military with tattoos and sexy scars on their foreheads."

He instinctively touched the thin silver line that ran on his forehead. "You noticed my scar?"

"It's part of the appeal." She beamed back at him. "How did you get it?"

It was a question he had been asked multiple times and he knew what response she was anticipating. Like everyone else, she probably assumed it was a combat-related injury.

"I was involved in an altercation," he started.

Erin leaned toward him and he could tell she was waiting for the excitement of a battle story. He could see her almost holding her breath as the gentle rise and fall of her breasts ceased.

"With my little sister when I was seven."

Her face froze and then broke into a larger smile as she burst out laughing. She didn't seem at all disappointed by the truth.

"What happened?" she asked.

"I was teasing her and she had enough."

"And…"

"And she threw a solid plastic castle at me. I needed twelve stitches."

He was rewarded again with Erin's laugh, which sounded like soft musical notes. "The worst part was she took it harder than I did and cried for hours."

"Are you close with your sister?"

"Yes, one of the hardest parts of being in the military is the time away from my family. Do you have any brothers or sisters?"

"No. I'm an only child."

"Do you like it?"

He saw the slight change in her as her shoulder fell and her head tilted downward. She took a sip from the water glass in front of her before she answered. "No, it's hard to have all your parents' expectations fall on you."

"But you're a successful physician." And so much more, Ryan thought to himself. How could anyone not be proud of Erin?

"I'm a divorced obstetrician-gynecologist." She

said it as if it made perfect sense but nothing about her words seemed condemning.

"So?"

"My parents are Catholic and don't believe in divorce."

"And?" He could tell there was more she didn't want to say.

"And my stepfather is an orthopedic surgeon and the chief of staff at the hospital where I'm completing my residency."

"In the same department as your ex-husband."

"Yes. And as you pointed out yesterday, orthopedics and obstetrics are about as polar opposite as you can get. I think I disappointed them both with my choice in husband and in my choice of career."

There it was again, that vulnerability. A need for approval. Part of him was pulling back, wanting to be cautious, but the majority of him wanted to help make her see everything he saw in her. "But you have no regrets?"

"About my marriage? Yes. About my career? Never."

"Well, in the end, it sounds to me like you made two very good decisions, since both of them have brought us together."

CHAPTER FIVE

SHE'D NEVER THOUGHT she would ever smile when it came to talking about her marriage, but Ryan had the ability to make her feel differently about her past. His praise was much needed and valued. It didn't feel like pointless flattery. It was obvious respect from a man she felt the same way about.

The waiter came to their table and looked at Ryan expectantly. He gestured toward Erin and she ordered for them both.

"Perfect," Ryan commented, and she felt even more relaxed in his presence.

She spent the rest of the meal conflicted between never wanting it to end and wanting it to end so they could be alone together. Her sense of nervous anticipation only returned as Ryan signed the check and she once again felt her jacket being slipped over her shoulders.

They left the restaurant and she started walking but Ryan, whose hand she was holding, didn't move. She stopped and turned back to look at him, not missing the serious look on his face. "I'm leaving the day after tomorrow."

"I know," she admitted. She found herself not

looking forward to the end of their brief romance but wasn't going to dwell on it.

"I just needed to remind you."

"I know." She knew the type of man Ryan was. Everything he was he put out for the world to see. She closed the distance between them and kissed him, reveling in his response. She didn't know how long they stayed that way, kissing in the moonlight. It was wonderful and only the desire for a different kind of more had her break away.

He seemed to read her mind. "Let's go."

She wasn't sure she even exhaled during the short walk back to the hotel. As they rode up the elevator and hurried down the hall where both their rooms were located, she glanced fleetingly at her hotel room door as they passed it without slowing. Finally the door to Ryan's room was closing and she felt herself let go of the breath she had been holding.

Within seconds she was gasping for air for a different reason as she found herself pressed against the wall, every inch of her body covered with Ryan's. She opened her mouth to his, once again entangling her fingers in his hair as his mouth sealed with hers. As his lips finally left hers and started kissing down the column of her neck he whispered against her skin, "Last chance, Erin."

She reached down under the hem of his sweater, pulling it away from him to allow her hands access to the dress shirt below. She spread her fingers to feel his tight muscles and the radiating heat of his body beneath her hands. "I'm staying."

"Thank God, because there is nothing I want more right now than you."

His comment made her feel bold and she wrenched the sweater over his head and moved her hands to the small shirt buttons. Slowly she started working them open. The most arousing part was Ryan watching her, his pupils dilated, tracking her every movement. The instant she was done he returned the favor, stripping her of her layered tank tops.

His hands tangled in her hair, lifting it and exposing her bare neck. His mouth returned to her neck and she pressed so hard into his body she didn't know where he began and she ended. She felt the tips of his fingers brush upward just below her breasts. Her breasts ached in desperation for his touch. The clasp of her bra opened and she felt just the slightest release of her breasts before Ryan's hands replaced what the white lace had been poorly concealing.

His cupped hands allowed his thumbs to slowly graze her nipples. His lips brushed against her collarbone before she felt her breast being lifted, his lips gentle against the raised mound.

"Perfect." She felt his word vibrate against her sensitized skin. Before she could respond she felt herself being lifted, with Ryan's hands strong against the backs of her thighs as he carried her across the room. The hard wall that had been pressed against her back was replaced with the softness of the linen-covered king-size bed. But she didn't lack for firmness for long as Ryan drew over her.

His attention returned to her as he once again kissed her softly parted lips, drawing her into him.

As much as she hungered for the intense escalation of their passion, she also felt her entire body liquefy with the slow pace that Ryan was setting. His mouth was close to her breasts and as soon as she thought she might die if he didn't, his mouth closed over one nipple as his fingers rolled its companion.

She arched her back in pleasure and she could feel Ryan's upturned smile against her skin. Her nipple felt cold as his mouth left her but her other one was then treated to the same pleasure as he switched sides to give both breasts equal consideration. When she felt as if she could bear no more she reached for his hand and placed it where she wanted him most. She could feel the heat and moisture at the heart of her and hoped he got the message she was desperately, and not so subtly, trying to send.

He did. He pulled away and his hands gathered in her tights, peeling them away until she lay bare before him, aside from the small white lace bikini briefs that matched the previously discarded bra. She pushed herself up on her elbows to watch him undress, the act accomplished in mere seconds as he shed every article of remaining clothing until he stood naked before her.

"Wow." The word left her mouth before she could filter her feelings. It sounded naive even to her ears but she'd had no idea a man could look like that.

"That's what I was thinking about you."

Instantly her embarrassment at her momentary gaucheness fled and her connection to Ryan intensified. He kneeled on the bed before her and without breaking eye contact pulled at the lace of her panties until she was as bare as he was. He braced himself on one arm as his hand laced through her hair and began its gentle caress down her body. His hand was rough against the softness of her neck, the side of her breast, her abdomen, her hip, as it moved inward toward her thigh. She parted her legs, waiting and wanting. With the softest touch she felt him, his fingers first gently parting her and then a gentle stroke.

"Oh," she gasped, not ready for the wave of electricity that passed through her. He responded by reclaiming her mouth and kissing her deeply. Then she felt it again, the wave of pleasure that came as he stroked her, this time in an unending circle. She felt herself wriggling against him but not wanting to get away. A strange tingling intensity was building inside her and she wasn't sure she could bear it. She cried into his mouth until finally every nerve ending from her core exploded outward and she felt beautifully broken. Finally she realized what she had been missing.

"You're beautiful."

"Thank you, but we're so not done here."

"No, we are just getting started."

She watched as he reached into the nightstand and retrieved a small foil packet. "May I?" she asked.

His eyebrows rose, but he agreed by passing her the condom. She carefully opened the packet but before she sheathed him she took hold of him in her hand, wanting to feel what she was visually devouring. He felt hot and hard against her and she squeezed lightly and he hardened further in her hand. "You need to hurry."

She looked at him and felt every bit the temptress. She gently rolled the condom along his length, looking forward to the moment when she could feel him more intimately. As soon as she reached his base she felt herself being pushed back against the blankets, Ryan's hand pulling her leg around him before he surged into her.

It felt like a completely new experience, an experience that was all pleasure. It was as if he had the ability to stretch and mold her into the most perfect state of arousal. She wrapped her other leg around him as he began to move back and forth within her, each time pushing her to a further level of bliss. Then that intense feeling came back, every stroke setting off a chain of sparks that was building a fire at her core. An all-encompassing need for more grew ever stronger within her until she thought she would die if he stopped. But he didn't. He pushed her harder and further until she burst into flames, screaming his name, not even aware of the marks she simultaneously scored down his back.

He cried out against her and she knew it was a cry of pleasure and not of pain as he collapsed against her, his breath rapid and hot on her neck. He appeared as shattered as she was and she ran her fingers more gently up and down his back in a soothing rhythm.

"You're more than perfect, you're amazing," he whispered in her ear.

"I...I..." But she couldn't think.

He kissed her fumbling lips and she closed her eyes in happiness.

She felt him pull away from her and was hoping

and waiting for him to return to hold her. What would it feel like to be held in the aftermath of such bliss?

"Erin, we have a problem." Ryan's voice was as grave as his words and her eyes opened wide. He looked stricken, staring back at her.

"The condom broke," he explained, and she exhaled with a sense of relief.

"It's okay," she tried to assure him.

"No, it's not okay. As much as I care for you, this isn't forever."

It wasn't just what he was saying about the temporary nature of their relationship that burst her bliss bubble, it was the private information that she didn't want to think of and now had to share.

"I can't have children."

"What?" It was now his turn to be taken aback. How she didn't want to talk about this, but she also knew she needed to put his mind at rest so their night together could return to where it had been.

"I had a miscarriage during my marriage. Afterward I developed a severe infection that scarred my Fallopian tubes and uterus. I can't have children."

"Are you sure?" It was a natural question. One she had asked herself over and over again until she had accepted her fate.

"Yes. I wanted a baby very badly and have spent the past two years trying to get pregnant. It's never going to happen. I've accepted that. So you don't need to worry about the condom breaking."

"I'm sorry." It was exactly what she didn't want to hear. She didn't want tonight to be about her past or what she would never have in the future. She just wanted it to be about them and their night together.

She moved herself from the bed and started looking for her clothes.

"What are you doing?"

"I'm…" *Running from a painful truth and your pity.*

"You're not leaving me, not now, not when both you and I know what we can be together."

She looked back at him, looking for any traces of pity left on his face, but she saw none. All she saw was want and so she stayed.

Ryan reached out an arm and was met with air. He opened his eyes and searched for her, but it was clear she wasn't there. He had planned on telling her more about himself and why he was in Edinburgh, but the moment had never presented itself.

Between making love and holding her as they'd rested between bouts of rapture he had let the night slip away. When he had awoken that morning she was gone and all that remained was a note.

> Ryan, thought you deserved the rest. Please come and find me tonight for a last night together—Erin.

Now he had no choice, he glanced at the clock and knew he wouldn't have time to talk to her privately in person. Still, after their night together he had no doubt that nothing could break the bond and trust they had formed.

Erin couldn't recall when she had last felt this happy. She had slipped from her lover's bed in the early hours of the morning and had hopes of returning to it as soon as she completed her work.

She straightened the black blazer that overlaid a cream lace camisole and her favorite strand of pearls. She had one more symposium before she knew Ryan would find her. She had never felt this free before. A feeling of wild recklessness filled her as she glanced nervously around the room. She hadn't prepared for today's session. Every thought and action had been about Ryan last night and she had forgone any thought of reading through the presentation or even the speaker's background information she had been provided with. She took her seat on the stage, sipping from a glass of the iced water before her to chill the heated thoughts Ryan provoked.

"Ladies and gentlemen, thank you for joining us for our final session, 'Postpartum Hemorrhage—Tales from the Battleground.' Our special guest speaker today is Dr. Ryan Callum. Dr. Callum is a medical officer in the American military. Having served on front lines for the past twelve years, he has developed firsthand experience in the management of massive bleeding and transfusion. This knowledge is becoming more and more relevant to the field of obstetrics, where acuity is forever increasing and particularly our management of postpartum hemorrhage, which, despite our best efforts, we have not been able to decrease the incidence of. Today Dr. Callum is going to shift our attention beyond prevention to optimum management to ensure patient well-being. Everyone, please welcome Dr. Ryan Callum."

All of a sudden the moderator had her absolute attention as she replayed everything he had just said.

His name was Ryan, he was in the military… She watched the entrance, desperately hoping to see someone other than her Ryan. But as the door opened her sense of dread ballooned into extreme hurt as her Ryan walked through the doors. Dr. Ryan Callum was just that, a doctor. Why hadn't he told her? How could he have held something back when she had bared her soul and innermost pain to him?

Had he just told her what she'd wanted to hear, just as Kevin had? He had to have known the conference was why she was in Edinburgh and that she would find out that he was also a physician. Why wouldn't he have told her instead of the public humiliation of learning who your lover really was in front of hundreds of people? It didn't bother her that he was a physician; it bothered her that she felt she had been lied to, even if by omission. The trust that had built between them vanished in an instant and her heart, body and mind felt instantly on guard against this man whom she had briefly let in. She had been a fool, again.

Ryan took his place at the podium and she could feel his eyes on her, but she couldn't turn to look at him.

"Dr. Callum," the moderator continued, "allow me to introduce your panel. Dr. Nicholas Richter. Dr. Richter is the head of Maternal Fetal Medicine at St. Bishop's Hospital in London. Dr. Mary Ellison. Dr. Ellison is a community obstetrician-gynecologist from Canada and also has an extensive background in global obstetrics and gynecology, spearheading multiple international projects around the world. And Dr. Erin Dufour. Dr. Dufour is a resident in obstetrics and gynecology from Boston, Massachusetts. She has been kind enough to provide us with insight both from the American and the younger generation's experience."

At this point she could no longer stare ahead and forced herself to turn her eyes to his. She saw something she had never seen before in his eyes—anger. Confusion and an equal anger set in. What did Ryan have to be angry about? He was the liar. He was the one who had betrayed her trust.

It was the longest ninety minutes of her life. As Ryan talked she had the utmost difficulty focusing on his words. She was aware the panel had started talking and any minute she could be called on to comment.

"Dr. Dufour, do you think there is a need in American centers to adopt the massive transfusion protocol Dr. Callum has discussed today?"

She wanted to refuse to have anything more to do with anything related to Dr. Callum but she managed to swallow her personal feelings and focus on being professional. "As we heard from the outset of today's lecture, we have not been able to reduce the incidence of postpartum hemorrhage in the past ten years. Even when we know the risks are present, all we can do is hope that it doesn't happen to our patients. Having more options for treatment is something every obstetrician would embrace in order to decrease the morbidity we often feel helpless to prevent."

A discussion continued on optimal implementation and the availability of resources in smaller centers. Erin was thinking of her own words. Had she known she could get hurt becoming involved with Ryan? Yes, and no. Yes, it was always a possibility in any relationship, but she had never considered it to be a real possibility, not with Ryan. He had seemed so honest, so genuine in his interest in her best interests. And the things she had told him, everything about her marriage, her infertility, what had he told her in return? Hardly anything. And definitely not the entire truth in what little he had revealed.

An ache settled at the center of her chest. She had told herself he was just a fling, but last night had felt like more and it made the hurt and betrayal all the harder to endure.

Applause broke out as she felt a merciful end to the continued strain of keeping up appearances. She watched as numerous physicians approached Ryan, no doubt congratulating him on a job well done. Perfect, she thought. She had no need to hear any more lies. She gathered her bag and made her way to the door. She had just entered the corridor when she felt herself being pulled into another room. Before she could think she was staring at an empty conference room, empty aside from Ryan.

"Your last name is Dufour?" he demanded more than asked.

She was too taken aback to do anything but answer. "Dufour was my married name."

"Is your ex-husband Kevin Dufour?"

She felt as if she'd been slapped and recoiled. Just hearing Kevin's name on Ryan's lips meshed two realities that she never wanted joined. How did he know Kevin? And what on earth gave him the right to be this angry?

"Yes," she answered defiantly. She wasn't at all proud of that fact but she still was not deserving of whatever was summoning Ryan's anger.

"So you're the one." Ryan ran his fingers through his hair and she had the feeling that he was as disturbed by this conversation as she was. It made no sense to her but she wasn't going to let him continue to attack her.

"I'm the one? The one who lied? No, that would be you."

"I didn't lie to you."

"I consider significant omissions lies, Ryan. Unfortunately I am used to being lied to. I'm just sorry I didn't realize the type of man you were earlier."

His eyes blazed at her as he stepped one step closer to her. "Don't compare him to me."

"Why not?" The realization that Ryan was very familiar with her ex had dawned and she had no problem comparing them in her anger, even when deep down she still sensed that they were very different men. "You are both liars who say what a woman wants to hear, no matter what the truth really is."

"People who live in glass houses shouldn't throw stones."

"What is that supposed to mean?"

"It means I don't believe your victim act. I know the truth."

"The truth about what? What is the truth, Ryan? Do you even know the meaning of the word?"

"I know you had no problem destroying the life of an innocent woman to get what you wanted. You got what you deserved."

She rapidly processed everything he'd just said. *You got what you deserved.* Wasn't that what she had thought when she'd lost her baby? When she couldn't conceive again? It had taken a lot of healing to accept that that wasn't how life worked. She had taken care of enough other infertile women to know that being infertile wasn't the fate of the unworthy.

She was on the verge of leaving this conversation and him before she suffered any more abuse when the rest of his words came through to her: *destroying the life of an innocent woman to get what you wanted.* She thought back to the confrontation she'd had with Kevin's girlfriend after their marriage. She could see the woman perfectly in her mind and the connection became clear. The nose, the eyes, they were the feminine form of Ryan's. "Sabrina…"

"Sabrina Callum, my sister."

Had he known? Had he always known who she was? Was this some sort of revenge for the pain she had caused his sister? Had he seduced her just to hurt her because she had hurt his sister? She blinked hard but when she opened her eyes it was still Ryan and he still looked at her as though she was nothing.

She thought back to her conversation with Sabrina and the pain she had felt on learning for the first time of Kevin's infidelity. To think a part of her had still clung to hope for her marriage. In the end she had been the loser in the love triangle because as much as Sabrina had been hurt by Kevin's betrayal, at least she hadn't had to endure the continual infidelity and emotional abuse Erin had over the years of their marriage.

"She was lucky." She spoke her mind, not meaning to anger him further but also not holding back.

"Lucky?" He seemed stunned.

"Yes, lucky."

"Do you know what you did to her? What it was like for her to one day have the man she loved and had been with for years, the man she was engaged to marry, drop her completely and marry another woman within weeks?"

He was yelling at her now but she couldn't respond. Had she thought about Sabrina—yes, but only after she and Kevin had married because that had been when she'd learned of her. But to be honest she hadn't agonized over the other woman's pain because she had been deep in her own, first learning that her husband had not been faithful and had cast her in the role of the other woman, then struggling with the pain and complications from her miscarriage.

Erin looked up at Ryan and realized there was no point. Nothing was as it seemed. He was no longer a fresh start, an honest man who would renew her faith in men. She honestly didn't know which was worse—the fact that he was a liar or that maybe he had seduced her intentionally to avenge his sister. Either way, it didn't matter. There was no point in arguing further. She didn't care to explain herself to him and there was nothing he could say to her to regain her trust.

"Goodbye, Ryan."

He watched as she walked away from him and tried not to notice that she held her head up. He was still reeling from the sight of her sitting on that panel and the introduction that had been made. As she had been introduced his mind had sparked from one connection to another until the final unfortunate conclusion. Her last name was Dufour, her ex-husband was an orthopedic surgeon and she was from Boston. She was the other woman.

He thought of the glimpses of Sabrina he had seen over the months she had been sick. Serving away, he hadn't been a continuous presence in her life, but even from a distance he had learned enough about the unsavory details of her breakup with Kevin. How he had been entranced and seduced by a woman named Erin, who had then trapped him with a pregnancy, giving him no choice but to leave Sabrina to marry her. Now, having met Erin, he felt torn. Part of him wanted to believe what he had learned of her over their two days together. But the other part of him knew the wickedness of her past actions and worried that she had conned him, as well.

Was he that transparent that she had managed to morph herself into exactly what he wanted? He felt his heart begin to pound at the other possibility. She had trapped one man into marriage, was that her plan again? The sadness she had expressed when she'd told him of her infertility had been so believable he hadn't bothered with a condom again. He was the only kind of fool. Never had he ever trusted a woman when it came to contraception and now there was the possibility of significant consequences for his first lapse in judgment. Time will tell, he thought to himself. He had no doubt that if Erin was pregnant she would make him pay for his mistake.

CHAPTER SIX

Two years later...

"PUSH," SHE ENCOURAGED the woman, whose mind and body spoke of true exhaustion. Erin glanced at the monitor displaying the baby's heart rate.

"Push, Allison. I know you can do this." She kept all sense of panic from her voice as she mentally formulated her backup plan if Allison did not have her baby in the next five minutes.

Another set of pushes and Erin finally saw the progress she had been hoping for. "Perfect, Allison, that's perfect," she encouraged softly.

She would never get tired of this. The experience of watching a couple who at that moment were as close as two people could be welcoming a child into their lives.

"I can't." A small plea escaped from the head of the bed.

"Yes, you can, Allison, and you are. Just a little bit longer and you will get to meet your baby. Now push."

She alternated her attention between the baby's head and the monitor. One-twenty, one hundred, ninety, eighty... The number and the graph descended below normal range.

"Allison." Her eyes were closed and her head tipped back. "Next contraction you need to have the baby."

The woman's eyes opened wide and Erin knew she had gotten through to her. "It's coming," Allison declared.

"Okay, let it build, take a deep breath in, hold it and push."

And a minute later Erin was holding a small, perfect person for just a brief moment before she put him on his mother's chest, gently rubbing him with a towel to stimulate breathing.

She exhaled when a small cry filled the room, followed by his mother's tears of happiness. "Congratulations, momma, you did it."

She finished everything she needed to do and completed her final checks in silence, not wanting to interfere with the couple's moment. After carefully disposing of sharp instruments and counting the sponges, she was ready to leave to complete the required paperwork.

"Congratulations again," she wished them both.

"Thank you so much, Dr. Madden, we couldn't have done it without you."

"Yes, you could have, but thank you for including me." She gave Allison a gentle squeeze on her foot before grabbing the chart.

Erin walked behind the desk on Labor and Delivery and began her charting. She glanced at her watch. It was almost midnight, but it had been worth it. She had followed Allison through her fertility treatments and her pregnancy, and now she had a son. Her pager blared through her peace. She glanced at the number. It was the emergency department.

Instantly her heart began to race, as it always did when she saw those numbers, and she had to concentrate on breathing. She didn't know why she was being paged. She wasn't on call tonight; she had come in on her own time for Allison.

She took a deep breath and let professionalism take precedence over her fear. She dialed the numbers and waited until the call was answered. "It's Erin Madden."

"Dr. Madden, we need you in the emergency department now," the unit clerk relayed to her.

There was nothing normal about the request. Usually she would speak directly with the consulting physician and hear the details of the patient consultation. Never had she been almost ordered to appear.

"What's going on?" She could hear chaos in the background.

"I don't know. Dr. Callum just yelled out that I needed to get you here as soon as possible."

The sense of dread she had been carrying around for the past two years solidified within her. The minute she had seen the announcement welcoming him to Boston General she had been waiting for this moment, but she had almost convinced herself she was going to be able to avoid it indefinitely. As chief resident, she made the schedule and before she assigned herself shifts she always looked at the emergency department schedule to ensure their shifts never aligned. Tonight she wasn't supposed to be here but she was and so was he and he was calling for her.

"Did he say why?" she asked quietly, wondering if Ryan having the unit clerk make the call was his way of making sure she didn't avoid him.

"No, he's tied up trying to stabilize Dr. Darcy."

Erin did a double take as she replayed the clerk's words in her head. "Do you mean work with Dr. Darcy?"

"No. Dr. Darcy was found unconscious in the women's change room. He's with her now."

"I'm on my way."

Erin ran. She rarely ran, but today she ran from the maternity unit to the waiting bank of central elevators. As she frantically pushed the button she tried to control her panic. Chloe. Something was wrong with Chloe and she needed her, and in order to do that she was going to have to see Ryan again.

The minute the doors opened she ran through the halls to the emergency department, going first to the trauma bays, where she feared she would find her. She came to an abrupt halt at the sight before her. Chloe lay on a stretcher, pale and barely conscious of the commotion around her. She was already hooked up to the monitors and Erin glanced at the screen. Her pulse was high at one hundred and fifty. Her blood pressure was low at eighty over forty. She was in shock.

"Where are we at?" she asked the group, needing an answer.

"She's received four units of packed red blood cells and two units of fresh frozen plasma from the rapid transfuser." The voice came from behind her and she didn't need to turn to recognize its owner.

"Can I speak to you alone for a moment, Dr. Madden?"

She could do this, she told herself. She had already been through so much that she could do this, too. She had no choice but to turn and confront the man she had been successfully avoiding until now. "Yes, Dr. Callum."

She watched as recognition flared in his eyes and for a moment he was stunned into silence.

"Dr. Callum, what's wrong with Chloe?" she asked, doing everything possible to bring him back to the professionalism Chloe needed.

"She was found unconscious in the women's change room. A bedside rapid ultrasound of her abdomen reveals a significant amount of free fluid and her beta HCG has returned positive."

She looked away from him back at Chloe. The presentation was classic for one thing, a ruptured ectopic pregnancy, which meant that Chloe was in serious danger and needed her entire focus.

"I need to call the operating room and have them get ready. Make sure she is prepped and ready to go in the next five minutes." She walked away from Ryan toward the nursing desk and one of the phones.

"This is Erin Madden. I have a ruptured ectopic in the emergency department. We need to come now. Set up for an attempted laparoscopic removal and possible laparotomy."

She moved from the phone back to Chloe's side, lifting the hospital gown and feeling her abdomen herself. It was distended and rigid beneath her touch. She pushed down just slightly and heard Chloe moan in response. "It's okay, Chloe. I'm going to take good care of you," she murmured as reassuringly as she could, when inside she was scared to death.

Ectopic pregnancies were still among the highest killers of women in pregnancy. Often they were caught early since women now had more access to ultrasounds in pregnancy and were able to be treated medically. But occasionally they presented without the woman noticing any warning signs and a perfectly healthy woman like Chloe could in an instant be on the brink of death.

She worked through her plan in her head, reminding herself she needed not to do anything differently just because it was her friend. She needed to use the same common surgical sense she would with any other patient. She walked back to the phone and called her supervising staff.

"Hello, it's Thomas."

"Dr. Thomas, it's Erin Madden. I got called to the emergency department for an unstable, probably ruptured ectopic pregnancy that I've just booked for the operating room."

"Erin, you're not on call tonight." The voice was questioning, but not with any misgivings.

"The patient is Dr. Chloe Darcy, the chief resident from Emergency. They called me directly."

"Say no more. I'll meet you in the operating room."

She made two more calls, first to the blood bank to arrange for more blood products to be dropped off directly to the operating room and second to the resident on call to assist. Out of the corner of her eye she saw Chloe being wheeled down the hall toward the elevators for the operating room.

She still needed to change into fresh scrubs, give handover to the awaiting anesthetist and check to make sure the right equipment had been picked, so she took off running. This time she took the single flight of stairs to the second floor, focused only on the task ahead of her. She had half pulled off her scrub top before even entering the change room and quickly completed the task before arriving ready in theater seven.

The anesthetist was at the head of the bed, preparing for Chloe's arrival. "What do you have, Erin?"

"A previously healthy thirty-year-old female with a probable ruptured ectopic pregnancy. She was hypotensive and tachycardic in the emergency department. She has two central large-bore intravenous, each in an antecubital fossa on her arms. She has received four units of packed red blood cells and two of fresh frozen plasma. No repeat CBC has been done yet. I've arranged for another four and two units to be delivered directly to the operating room. I'd like to start laparoscopically."

"Are you sure?"

It was the question she had been asking herself for the past ten minutes. No, she wasn't sure. Starting with the less invasive method might help Chloe in the long run but it also might not work or prolong her time to treatment. Would she be considering this if Chloe were any other patient?

"Yes."

The nursing team brought Chloe into the room and Erin helped transfer her off the bed to the operating table. She watched as the anesthetist did his assessment and felt a small sense of fear grow within her when he called for a second anesthetist to assist him. Erin sat on a stool by Chloe's side, holding the cold hand that lay splayed on the arm board as she was anesthetized, and then it was back to work. Erin positioned Chloe for the planned less invasive surgery before turning to leave the room to complete her surgical scrub in the outside scrub sink. She saw Ryan through the threaded glass windows of the operating-room doors.

She pushed through the doors and he took a few steps back from her. "You need to leave," she stated without anger but with significant conviction.

She understood why he was there. Chloe was loved by everyone and she knew from conversations with her friend that Ryan had become a mentor to her in the emergency department, but still that didn't make a difference to her right now. "Ryan, I can't have any distractions right now. I have a job to do. Think of Chloe."

He seemed to understand. She almost wished she had a minute to look into his eyes and try to figure out what he was thinking, what he was feeling, but she didn't. She checked the ties on her surgical mask and hat before opening the sterile scrub packet and methodically rubbing the sponge up and down each exposed axis of her hands.

When she turned from the sink Ryan was no longer there and she felt a sense of relief, which she knew would only be temporary.

She gowned, gloved and draped Chloe, which made things easier. It helped her separate her fear for her friend from the job she had to do.

"You can start," the anesthetist confirmed.

"Knife." And she held out her hand in anticipation.

Chloe's abdomen was flawless until the moment she made the five-millimeter incision into the base of her belly button. A minute later she had a camera inserted and was staring at the monitor across from her. Chloe's abdomen was a sea of red. She couldn't see anything; particularly she couldn't see where the ectopic was bleeding.

"Can I have her more head down, please?" she asked the anesthetist, hoping that tipping her would move some of the blood away.

"No, I can't move her from where she is now. Her pressure won't tolerate it."

"Okay." She took a deep breath and said the words she didn't want to say. "We are going to convert. Open the laparotomy set."

The nurses in the room scrambled to change the instruments as Erin sterilely repositioned Chloe. "Knife," she called again.

This time her incision was more than five millimeters. She grimaced as she drew the ten-centimeter line just above Chloe's pubic bone, but didn't stop. She worked quickly until she accessed Chloe's abdomen and started removing the blood. She was constantly aware of the amount present as the nurses and anesthetist updated her on the number of canisters she filled and sponges she soaked through. She needed to hurry to stop the bleeding. "Can we make sure that the second four units are on their way?" she directed.

Then she saw it, the continuous pouring from the frayed edges of the ruptured tube. She closed a clamp over it and the bleeding stopped. She felt as if she took her first breath.

"Okay, let's take a moment and finish evacuating all the blood then we'll reassess the tube."

She was buying time. A few minutes later she had to refocus on the Fallopian tube. With the clamp still on she carefully removed the pregnancy from the tube, nothing visible aside from placental tissue and blood clot. Every time she removed a piece the bleeding increased. She struggled in vain to be gentle and not injure the tube further. She tried cautery to burn the edges, but more bleeding ensued. Then she asked for a fine suture for a tension stitch, but the tube was too shredded from the rupture.

"Erin," she heard Dr. Thomas's voice break through her concentration.

"Yes," she answered, already knowing what he was going to say.

"You know what to do." She did. She'd been thinking it for the past five minutes. She nodded in agreement.

"Curved roger." She held her hand out, waiting for the larger clamp. Two steps later she held the Fallopian tube in her hand and felt sick. She hadn't rendered Chloe infertile as she still had her other tube, but still she felt awful about the possibility that Chloe might have difficulty having children in the future.

She looked around again, cleaning things up, until she was aware of a shift in the room. "Do you need help?" It was the voice of Dr. Tate Reed, one of the hospital's most prominent surgeons.

Erin had no idea why Tate was there, but the one thing she was certain of was that she was in control and the only other thing she could do for Chloe was protect her privacy. "You need to leave, Dr. Reed."

"Dr. Thomas?" He was going over her head and Erin held her breath, praying that Dr. Thomas would back her decision.

"Dr. Madden is right. This is not a vascular case, Tate. We are going to have to ask you to leave."

"Okay," Erin heard him concede, but she was also

very aware that he did not venture farther than the operating-theater doors and was watching her every move.

"What is her hemocrit?" she asked, wanting to know if Chloe needed more blood.

She waited as the anesthetist drew a sample and put it in the machine. "Sixty."

"Please give her the next four units and the two fresh frozen plasma."

"If we do, we'll have to keep her warmed and intubated in the intensive care unit."

"She needs the blood. Once she redistributes the rest of her fluid her hemoglobin is going to be much lower than that."

She stared again at where the tube had once been, wanting to be sure Chloe was absolutely dry before she started to close her. The operating-room doors pushed open again. This time she didn't feel any tension at the sight of Chloe's best friend and her friend, Dr. Kate Spence.

"Hi, Kate." Erin acknowledged her presence but didn't change her focus from the surgical pedicles.

"She's going to be okay. We have evacuated the hemoperitoneum and have stopped the bleeding. We are going to be closing in the next few minutes and then she will be going to Recovery, followed by a short stay in the intensive care unit in case she runs into any massive transfusion complications."

"Uh-huh." Kate seemed as stunned as she had been when she'd first got the call. Still, Erin was friends with both women and knew that Chloe was protective of Kate and would want her comforted.

"I'm sorry we had to open her. We tried with the

laparoscope but she had too much blood in her abdomen and was too unstable to tolerate it." She felt self-conscious about her choice, knowing that Kate was a general surgeon with excellent laparoscopic skills.

"But the bleeding has been stopped? Kate asked.

"Yes."

"What happened?" Kate finally asked.

She couldn't answer that. Her job right now was as Chloe's doctor, not Kate's friend. "That's not for me to disclose to you. Chloe will be able to tell you herself later, if she chooses to. I think you should go now and take Dr. Reed with you. She is stable and we'll take good care of her. You can see her in the intensive care unit in a couple of hours, once she's settled in."

"Okay," Kate said, resigned. "Thank you."

Ryan paced the halls of the operating rooms, waiting. His mind flashed with images of the night. Chloe lying lifeless on the change-room floor and all the ways he had seen Erin. First it had been when she had turned around in the emergency department. He hadn't known she'd still been there. Before he had agreed to take a position in the emergency department he had checked the resident listing for the department of obstetrics and gynecology. There were no Dufours listed, or even Erins, for that matter. He had assumed she had left following her divorce and he had taken the job pleased with the knowledge that she was a complication he could avoid.

Then as Chloe had been transferred to the operating room he had assisted and followed her to ensure

her well-being. He had seen Erin again, rushing into
the change room, her shirt half pulled off before the
doors had closed, and that had been when he could no
longer have doubts about who he was dealing with.
For a moment he had forgotten everything except for
the memories of the last time he had shared that intimate a view.

Now he had no choice but to trust Erin with the
care of one of his closest friends and he felt absolutely
gutted by everything that was happening around him.
From the moment he had heard the nurse screaming
for help, to holding Chloe unconscious in his arms,
realizing that the person he needed to make this right
was Erin Dufour, he'd had no control. A career in the
military had prepared him for a lack of control, but
tonight every coping mechanism had abandoned him.
He had already run into Tate Reed in the hallway and
lost his temper, something he never did.

The sound of the operating-room doors swinging
open got his attention and he looked at Chloe, who
was being wheeled out, still intubated, the anesthetist intermittently squeezing oxygen into her. Erin
was at the foot of the bed, assisting with the transfer.
Her blue eyes met his and she nodded slightly and he
knew that Chloe was going to be okay.

After they passed he stood undecided in the hallway until he could resist no longer. He walked into
the recovery room and to the desk where Erin sat.

"You're not on the resident list."

Her eyes flashed back at him and he watched as
she pulled a blue flowered scrub hat from her head,
running her fingers through her hair, which was a

darker blond and longer than when he had first met her. "Yes, I am."

"No, you're not. I checked before I came to work here."

She sighed, pulling her nametag from her pocket and laying it before him to read.

"Alexandra Erin Madden," he read aloud.

"My mother's name is Alexandra. I've always gone by Erin."

"And Madden?" he asked, still wondering how he could have not known.

"My maiden name. Sorry to disappoint you." It was a throwaway comment and he knew by both her reaction tonight and the conversation they were having that she was not surprised to see him.

"You knew I was here?"

"Yes," she confirmed.

He thought about all the time he had been at the hospital and realized that he had never seen her. Through his role as an emergency-room attending physician he knew most of the residents across all the programs, which meant one thing. Erin had gone out of her way to avoid him. He had no idea why that angered him, but it did. "You've been avoiding me?"

She stood from her seat and even though she barely cleared his shoulders the effect was still there. "No different than your attempt to avoid me. I was just more successful. If you want to you can pretend you never saw me tonight."

He didn't stop her as she walked away.

Her heart was pounding. She had made it so far and now with less than three months left before her departure from Boston General she had come face-to-face with the one person in the world she had never wanted to see again. She remembered the feeling of betrayal she had felt in Edinburgh and felt uneasy, not knowing who she was dealing with. For the rest of the night she found herself looking over her shoulder, waiting for another encounter with Ryan. She would be a fool to think it wasn't going to happen again. It was just a question of when.

She returned to Labor and Delivery and checked on Allison and then looked at her watch. She had a desperate need to go home and had enough time to do so before Chloe was conscious and ready to talk.

CHAPTER SEVEN

ERIN STOOD OVER the crib and marveled at the miracle it contained. Not one trace of blanket covered the sleeping baby inside. She reached down and pulled the blanket over her again, knowing the action was futile, but it gave her the maternal reassurance she needed right now.

She had thought that seeing Jennie would stem the panic that had started the minute she had seen Ryan, but it had only made it worse. Everyone who had met her little girl had always exclaimed how much she looked like Erin, but only Erin, who was privy to more intimate information, knew how much Jennie actually looked like her father.

She brushed the wisps of brown hair gently, not wanting to disturb the baby but also needing to touch her. If she had woken up, Erin would have had to face Ryan's eyes staring back at her and she wasn't ready to face that reality. How long would it be before he found out about her baby?

She should have left Boston the minute she had heard of Ryan being hired. Certainly the misery of being in the same hospital as Kevin, a torment that had only increased when she'd become pregnant, had been reason enough to leave. But she had needed help. There had been no way she could be a single mother and continue her training in a specialty as demanding as obstetrics and gynecology without the help of her family and friends, so she had stayed.

She hadn't concealed her pregnancy. At the time there had been no reason to, and it was common knowledge she was a single mother. Most people assumed it was her ex-husband's child and that he just regarded the child the same way he had his marriage—with indifference. As much as she didn't like the connection, she had never bothered to correct the assumption. Jennie was the love of her life and she would do anything to protect her miracle.

After some lengthy time had passed, she forced herself to move away from the crib and out of the nursery. It wouldn't be long before her eighteen-month-old daughter would be out of the crib and Erin wanted to hold on to these moments as long as possible.

It had taken her ten positive pregnancy tests even to consider the possibility that she might be pregnant. Stress, she had thought to herself as her cycle had stopped, nausea had begun to rule her life and her abdomen had become uncharacteristically bloated. She'd even thought she might be going crazy, developing symptoms of a phantom pregnancy that she desperately wanted but was never going to have. So she had taken the test to force her unconscious self to face reality and had been completely unprepared for the positive result that had appeared.

She had never heard of a false-positive pregnancy test, so she'd bought another, and another. Then absolute fear had set in when she'd considered the possibility of having a hormone-secreting cancer that had been making the tests positive. It had taken another two weeks of positive tests before she'd forced herself into action and had asked for help from Dr. Thomas, one of her favorite staff obstetricians.

He had been very gentle and kind when he had broken the news of her pregnancy to her. It had been almost laughable that as an obstetrics resident she hadn't diagnosed the obvious, but it had taken so long to accept that she would never have a child that she hadn't allowed herself to even consider the possibility. Even after he'd convinced her that she'd been having a healthy, normal pregnancy she hadn't let herself really believe it.

Every milestone, every change in pregnancy had both amazed and terrified her. Despite the growing contour of her abdomen she'd still had trouble with the reality that she was going to be a mother. It had felt as though if she believed it, it would hurt more if it all went away.

Then one morning she'd gone into labor and as the hours had passed she'd become ever closer to becoming a mother. She had delivered Jennie with her mother by her side and amid the tremendous joy that had flooded her she couldn't help but feel a small amount of sadness that she hadn't had "that moment." The moment that she loved most when delivering babies. The moment when a man looked at the woman he loved, amazed at what she had done and more in love with her than he had ever been. Instead, while holding Jennie, the moment with her baby's father had been a memory of how she had misplaced her trust yet again and the anger and disdain Ryan felt for her.

The moral part of her had thought about finding him, letting him know they had a daughter. But the protective mother in her had said no. She couldn't say she knew Ryan, not after he had made it clear how he felt about her. She'd known enough to know he wouldn't just thank her for the news and move on. He would want Jennie; who wouldn't? And given the feelings he had for her and his view of her as a person there had been the chance that maybe he would even feel that he was the better parent and try to take full custody. That risk was one she had decided she was not willing to take.

Now that question was reopened. It wasn't a secret that she had a daughter. How long could she last before he put together the puzzle?

Her pager buzzed against her hip and she recognized the number as being that of the intensive care unit. Chloe must be awake. She moved back into the nursery, gently pressed her lips to her hand and onto Jennie's cheek before leaving quietly.

Ryan walked to the bank of computer screens and stared at the images. Black-and-white images filled the screens and he searched for the fracture. He knew it was there. There was no way the cyclist's wrist and arm was that swollen and tender without a fracture, but why couldn't he see it? Because he was distracted. Thinking about Erin. His stubborn pride kept him from simply waiting for the radiologist's report and finally after several minutes the subtle thin line became apparent.

He walked back to the nursing desk. "Who's on for Orthopedics?"

"Dufour."

Perfect, thought Ryan, clenching his jaw to keep his teeth from gritting. He hadn't avoided Kevin since coming to Boston but he also hadn't gone out of his way to make contact with him, either. He had never been close with the other man. When Kevin had been engaged to Sabrina he had seen him socially on one or two occasions when he'd had leave from the military. Each time he had seemed charming and the perfect match for his sister. When Sabrina had talked about him it had been nothing but praise and happiness.

Even when their relationship had ended Sabrina had placed minimal blame on Kevin. He had been lured away. Enticed and trapped by another woman. Now he knew that woman was Erin. He had blamed Kevin more, seen him as weak. But that had been before he, too, had fallen for her charms.

After Edinburgh he had struggled for months to reconcile how he felt about Erin. He would replay all of the time they'd spent together, trying to find the crack, the hairline clue that she had been pretending to be something she wasn't. Trying to appeal to everything he wanted in a woman. Had she intentionally thrown herself from the hillside, knowing he would save her? It seemed ridiculous but he felt as if he couldn't put anything past her. Unlike the fracture today, he had never found that crack, and that frustration he'd felt toward her had only increased because of it.

The confrontation after he'd discovered her true identity had been enough, though. Just hearing her acknowledge his sister, what she had done to her and calling her lucky had been enough to make Ryan want to turn his back on her and walk away forever. Now he no longer had that luxury. She was in Boston, at Boston General Hospital, and the past was simply not going to be able to remain just that.

"Please page him," he told the nurse.

A few minutes later she handed him the phone.

"This is Dufour."

"This is Ryan Callum. I have a wrist fracture in Emergency I would like you to see."

"Page my resident." The reply was both arrogant and irritating. If Kevin had any memory of Ryan it wasn't apparent by his tone.

"Your resident is three consultations behind and seeing them between operative cases. We need to clear the backlog in the emergency department."

"That's not my problem," Kevin dismissed.

"I'm making it your problem." It was a tone he didn't use often, but he wasn't in any frame of mind to take any condescension from Kevin Dufour.

"Who is this?"

"Dr. Ryan Callum, staff emergency physician. We've met."

There was no response on the other end of the line. It was almost as if Dufour was searching his memory for when he had met Ryan. "So are you coming to see the patient or should I call another orthopedic surgeon?"

"Be my guest."

"I will. I hear Dr. Williamson is interested in keeping his hand in clinical practice." The conversation could not have gotten more antagonistic. He had known exactly what he was doing, bringing up the chief of staff and Dufour's former father-in-law. The phone clicked and a few seconds later he heard the empty dial tone.

"Is he coming?" the nurse beside him asked. He could tell that by the small uplift of the corner of her mouth that she had heard and approved of his handling of the conversation.

"I think so."

Ryan continued his charting, sure in his assumption. Dufour would come, not immediately but he would come. Thirty minutes later he saw the other man, striding arrogantly toward him. He took in his appearance, which hadn't changed much since their last meeting, his all-American pretty-boy good looks still at their finest.

"Just exactly who do you think you are?" Apparently their conversation was not over.

"At this moment I'm the senior staff physician responsible for the emergency department."

"Let me make something clear—you don't tell me what to do."

Ryan smirked slightly. It was almost comical watching Dufour make an attempt to intimidate him. He had spent over a decade in the military, including combat experience, surrounded by superiors who had been the essence of intimidation and fellow soldiers who had all been volleying for promotion. Dufour's obvious peacocking was nothing to him, except that it once again challenged his past perceptions of the other man. He was nothing like the charmer Ryan had once met. And with his attempt at dominance neither was he the weak man he had envisioned being seduced by Erin.

Erin. Despite the fact that he couldn't claim to

know her, not really given what he knew about her past and the facade she had presented in Edinburgh, he still couldn't picture her with this man. Never mind be married to him.

"The patient is in exam six." And he walked away, having heard enough from Dufour. He came to a dead stop when the idea in his mind penetrated his thoughts. Sabrina was lucky not to have married him. He thought of her life now. She had since married, had a son and settled down for a quiet life in the suburbs that she loved. Discomfort tore through him when he realized he was thinking exactly what Erin had said to him. When she'd said it he had been furious. But, still, even if that was the case, Erin hadn't known that back then. Not when she'd been seducing another woman's fiancé. But after a few moments with Kevin he was certain that Sabrina had had a lucky escape. But had Erin gotten what she'd deserved?

Erin felt exhausted as she finished her clinic day. Infertility work was 10 percent happiness and 90 percent emotionally draining. Talking to couples about their options, none of which had any guarantee, was a hard conversation. Then there was Chloe.

She had followed up on her twice daily in hospital. Their first conversation had been very hard. Telling her friend that she had been pregnant and had then lost the pregnancy had brought back old memories of the feelings she'd had when she had been in Chloe's position. That feeling of "Why me" and all the possible answers to that question. She had done her best to be Chloe's friend but also remain professional, when truthfully all she'd wanted to do had been to cry along with her.

Now she was busy juggling the demands of her regular work, taking care of Chloe and living with the constant threat of Ryan discovering her secret.

She drew in her breath as she saw him. She wasn't surprised to see him—she'd known it was inevitable. There was no way she could turn around and walk away; she didn't want him to think she had anything to hide. Besides, other than their daughter, she had nothing to hide from him and nothing to be ashamed of. He had accused her of immoral behavior when she had been nothing but honest about her life and past with him. She hadn't even lied by omission, not then, because she'd had no idea Ryan was connected with her past. Now she had no choice. She would lie. She was going to do everything she needed to do to protect her family.

They met outside Chloe's door at the same time.

"Ryan."

"Erin. You're here to see Chloe?"

"She's my patient," she replied, hating that she felt a need to defend herself against such a simple question.

"She's my friend."

"Mine, too."

"Chloe never mentioned you." He was staring at her with suspicion in his eyes.

"Why would she?" She knew he was getting at something and felt a need to emotionally brace herself.

"Did you tell her?"

"About?"

"Scotland."

Chloe had asked about Erin's romantic Scottish

love affair when she had returned home and without giving any details Erin had been firm about not wanting to discuss it and Chloe had been gracious enough to not ask anything further. As far as Erin knew, she had never put together that the Ryan Callum in the emergency department was the same military Ryan Erin had met in Scotland.

"No, I didn't. Enough of my mistakes are public knowledge. I didn't think my latest poor choice in men was worth mentioning." She knew she shouldn't antagonize him, but now, outside the life-and-death scenario Chloe had presented, all of the hurt she had felt as a result of Ryan had come flooding back.

"It probably would have been difficult to explain that you passed yourself off as something you were not and then the truth came out."

"Are you talking about me or you?" She pushed past him and into Chloe's room. She didn't make it far. Chloe's room was filled with their friend Kate and Dr. Tate Reed. She remembered how she'd had to be firm with Tate in the operating room and had asked him to leave. She hoped he realized she had done what had been best for Chloe and wasn't angry with her, because she didn't need another confrontation right now.

"I just came to see if you needed anything," Erin said, deciding to focus on the only person who mattered in the room—her patient.

"I'm good, thank you." She still looked tired and wary but, considering how she had looked a few days earlier, Erin would take it.

"When do you think Chloe will be discharged?" Tate asked, his entire attention focused on her. She quickly glanced at Chloe, who didn't object to Tate's question and appeared to be waiting for the answer.

"She can be discharged tomorrow if she feels well enough to go. But she can't stay alone for the first few weeks."

"She can stay with me," Kate volunteered.

Erin had assumed that was what would happen so hadn't addressed discharge planning with Chloe prior to this conversation. She was shocked when Chloe declined the offer. She was about to offer her own home when Ryan interrupted her.

"Chloe, you are welcome to stay with me." His offer rang with confidence. Erin looked back at him, stunned by his offer. Chloe had never mentioned anything beyond a professional mentor-mentee relationship between them. She knew they were close professionally but not personally. Their lack of personal relationship outside the hospital had provided comfort to Erin, knowing there wasn't a possibility she see Ryan socially through her friendship with Chloe.

"I don't think that's a good idea," Tate replied, before anyone else could interject. Erin was forced to look at both men and the same feeling she had gotten the other night from Tate returned. He obviously cared very much about Chloe and she felt a small twinge of pain at what she didn't have.

She was lost in her own thoughts so that it wasn't until she heard Kate's and Chloe's simultaneous gasps that she realized the conversation had escalated and it felt as though Tate and Ryan could come to blows at any moment.

"I agree with Tate," Erin interrupted the men's discussion. She wasn't sure exactly what had been said, but she knew from personal experience that staying with Ryan was not in Chloe's best interests. All eyes turned to her.

"I don't think *you* are the right person to comment on propriety," Ryan rebuked.

She heard the gasps again, and she would have gasped, too, if she'd had any higher expectations of Ryan's opinion of her, but she didn't. If anything, it reinforced her decision to keep the knowledge of Jennie to herself.

"*Enough.* I appreciate everyone's concern, but I am an adult, capable of making my own decisions and deciding what is in my own best interests. Erin, are you sure I can't go back to my apartment as long as I don't overdo it?" Thank goodness for Chloe. Erin did her best to let go of Ryan's barb before turning back to her patient.

"Yes, I'm sure. With your low hemoglobin and naturally low blood pressure I think you are at high risk for dizziness and fainting and you shouldn't be alone." There, she had done what she had come to do, take care of Chloe. It was decided that Chloe would go and stay at Tate's and, to be honest, Erin was pleased. Tate was a good man. He cared for her, and maybe, just maybe, her recovery would bring them both together. Just because she was unlucky in love, it didn't mean that her friend couldn't find happiness.

She casually said her goodbyes and left the room, trying to make her escape without it being obvious.

"Erin."

She heard Ryan call out her name before she had made it a few feet from the door. She knew she had no choice but to stop for fear that their pending conversation became even more public than it was about to be.

"Ryan," she acknowledged, as she turned and watched as he quickly made up the distance between them.

"What did you think you were doing in there?" It wasn't hard to read the anger in his voice.

"Being insulted in front of my patient and my friends," she replied, before she could stop herself. What was it about Ryan that made her speak her mind and her feelings so freely?

Her words seemed to penetrate through him and the tension between them lowered. "I'm sorry."

At that moment she was more shocked than she had been in Chloe's room. She had been expecting an attack, anger, not the return of the Ryan she thought she'd once known, albeit briefly. "Thank you." She accepted his apology as best she could. "It wasn't about you. I think Chloe would be better off with Tate personally and professionally. It would hurt her professional reputation if she moved in with one of her staff physicians, no matter what the reason. Tate has nothing to do with her career."

She hoped he accepted her explanation and they were done talking. It hurt more than she would have liked it to—to be reminded of how perfect she had thought he was in Edinburgh.

"I talked with your ex-husband this morning." She was acutely aware of him waiting for her reaction to his statement.

"And…"

"And what?"

"There is something you are either waiting to say

or are not saying. Either way, I have nothing to do with Kevin and am not responsible for his behavior, past or present. Are we done here?"

He paused and she could feel his visual assessment of her. The black pencil skirt and turquoise blouse she had chosen now felt more revealing than it had looked in the mirror that morning. She tucked her hair behind her ear before looking him in the eye with raised brows.

"You were right about Sabrina being lucky," he confessed.

Before she could respond to what had almost sounded like an apology, he walked away from her.

CHAPTER EIGHT

ERIN WALKED THROUGH the emergency department with her normal sense of unease heightened. She hadn't had time to check who the attending emergency physician was. She was still counting the days until she was done at Boston General and holding her breath that her secret would remain hidden from Ryan.

As the chief resident, Erin ran her own clinic, filled with patients she took primary responsibility for. Tara, an infertility patient, had called that morning with all the classic symptoms of hyperstimulation syndrome, a condition in which as a result of fertility treatments, overstimulated ovaries caused excess fluid all over the body. Normally she would see all her patients in clinic, well away from Ryan in the emergency department, but Tara had sounded sick on the phone and Erin was worried she was going to need to be more closely monitored.

That morning she had chosen a fitted, knee-length yellow dress with a boat neck, which she had paired with her favorite string of black beads and black slingback low-rise heels. It was perfect for clinic, but she looked and felt out of place in the emergency department.

"Has Tara Compton arrived yet?" she asked the main unit clerk.

"Yes, Dr. Madden, she's in treatment room four."

Erin's assessment had been right. If Tara's symptoms had been mild she would have been placed in one of the lesser acuity rooms. She shook her head. She shouldn't have triggered her ovaries and done the retrieval. She had known throughout Tara's treatment cycle that this was a risk. Her ovaries had responded too well to the medication she'd received and had swelled beyond normal size. But Tara had begged her. Her husband had severe infertility problems and in vitro fertilization had been their only hope of pregnancy. They had saved for five years and this cycle was their only shot at a family. So Erin had persisted and performed the egg retrieval earlier in the week, doing everything she could to lower the risk, but it hadn't been enough.

She walked into the room and struggled to keep her feelings inside. Tara looked very unwell, sitting upright in bed and leaning forward as she struggled to catch her breath. Her abdomen was visibly swollen, so much so that she already looked six months pregnant. Erin glanced at the monitor screen displaying her patient's vitals. Tara's blood pressure was low and her respiratory and heart rates were both above normal.

"Hi, Tara," she greeted her, trying to keep any sense of alarm from her voice.

"Dr. Madden, I don't feel well." Erin noticed that she sounded breathless trying to complete the simple sentence.

"I know," Erin empathized. She already knew Tara

and her history well, so she directed her attention to the immediate problem. "When did this start?"

"Yesterday."

"What is bothering you most?"

"I can't seem to catch my breath and my stomach is hard and swollen."

Erin listened to her chest, noting the decreased breath sound at her lung bases. She tapped her fingers on the base of the lung fields, noting the fullness. With the help of Tara's husband she lowered her onto her back. "I won't keep you here long," she reassured her, aware of the panic in her patient's eyes.

She placed her hands on Tara's abdomen. Uncovered, it looked worse, and Erin estimated there were at least five liters of fluid present. She was able to feel the shift of fluid against her hand as she pushed on one side. With care she helped Tara up again, trying to ease her labored breathing.

She peeked out of the room's curtain and got the attention of one of the nurses assigned to the treatment area. "We need to get some bloodwork and a chest X-ray, stat."

"What would you like, Dr. Madden?"

"Complete blood count, electrolytes, creatinine, prothombin time, prolonged prothombin time, liver enzymes and three views of the chest. Once the blood is drawn and X-ray is done, we are going to set up for an abdominal paracentesis and bedside ultrasound." She held her breath for a moment. "Who is the attending physician in Emergency today?"

"Dr. Callum is on until four this afternoon."

It wasn't what she wanted to hear, but she had few other options.

"Thank you."

She went back into the treatment room to explain the plan to Tara and her husband and then went in search of Ryan. She didn't have to look for long before she found him. He was standing at the physicians' desk, charting.

"Dr. Callum," she addressed him, her only goal to keep this conversation professional.

She saw the muscles in his back and shoulders tense before he turned to meet her eye. She couldn't help but notice how the dark navy of his hospital scrubs complemented his eyes.

"Erin, you can call me Ryan."

"I need your help with a patient."

"What do you have?"

"A twenty-eight-year-old woman with severe ovarian hyperstimulation syndrome She has significant ascites and I need help with a paracentesis."

"What do you need me for?"

"I can't do the procedure blind. I can't risk accidentally puncturing one of the ovaries. I need another physician to do a simultaneous bedside ultrasound so that I can see where I'm going."

"Okay, call me when you're set up and ready."

Thirty minutes later she reviewed all the results and made plans to admit Tara to hospital. She had ordered supplemental oxygen and intravenous fluids to make up for the fluids that were accumulating in her abdomen. She had all the supplies ready and she asked the nurse to get Ryan.

He walked into the room and took his place on the opposite side of the bed from her. "Hi, I'm Dr. Callum. I'm going to be assisting Dr. Madden with the procedure."

Erin wasn't sure why, but the anxiety reaction she had felt for the past two years with regard to Ryan didn't reappear. In fact, the trepidation she had over the upcoming procedure was dissipating. "Okay, Tara, I'm just going to wash your abdomen with this sterile solution. It's really important you keep your hands by your sides and not touch any of the drapes I'm going to cover you with."

She performed the described actions and then looked at Ryan, who nodded his understanding. With the ultrasound probe sterilely draped, he scanned her abdomen. Erin interpreted the black-and-white images on the screen for both Ryan's and Tara's benefit. She could see the black of the accumulated fluid and the outlines of the enlarged ovaries.

"Can you measure the ovarian cysts, please?"

She watched as he did what she asked. "The left side is twelve centimeters and the right side is ten centimeters."

"Thank you."

"Is that big?" Tara asked, an obvious look of fear present in her eyes.

"It meets the criteria for severe," Erin answered. "Now you are going to feel the small burn of the freezing before I do the poke to drain the fluid. Dr. Callum, can you stay centered on the pocket on the left?"

"Yes."

With a precise and quick motion she inserted the needle into Tara's abdomen, quickly enough to limit the discomfort but slowly enough that she could see the opacity of the tip of the needle as it appeared on the screen. As soon as she confirmed placement she removed the sharp tip, leaving the thin plastic catheter that had overlain the needle, and set up the tubing to the suction canisters. She was rewarded as straw-colored fluid began to drain. Then all there was to do was to sit at the bedside and wait.

"Dr. Madden," Tara's voice interrupted her thoughts.

"Yes?"

"Are we still going to be able to do the transfer?" Tara asked, though her tone made Erin believe she already suspected the answer to the question.

"No, we can't. You are pretty sick right now. If we put your fertilized embryos back, it is only going to worsen your condition."

Tears filled the other woman's eyes and began to fall down her face. "I don't care about me. I want a baby." It was an explanation Erin understood perfectly.

Holding the catheter, she contaminated her other hand by taking Tara's. "You will have a baby. It's just going to take a little more time. We'll freeze these embryos and when you are better and ready we'll transfer them back. The most important person to a baby is its mama, and we need to think of you first."

"Are you sure?"

"Yes, I'm one hundred percent sure."

It took twenty minutes, but eventually Erin had removed the bulk of the fluid. Afterward Tara was able to breathe more easily and appeared much more comfortable. She still needed to remain in hospital, but with supportive care was on her way to recovery.

"Thank you, Dr. Callum," Erin said to Ryan, as she pulled the catheter. He nodded at her and left.

She stayed with Tara for a while longer, reviewing her plan for her hospitalization and also her future fertility treatments.

"You were good in there." Ryan's voice met her as she left the room.

"Thank you."

"I think we need to talk."

"I thought you had said everything you needed to say to me in Scotland." She needed him to know that he had hurt her and she wasn't prepared to let it happen again.

"Meet me at five in the lobby?"

She felt lost for words to respond to his request and he took her silence as acceptance as he walked away from her and back to work.

She couldn't believe it herself as she strolled into the lobby of Boston General. She had tried to talk herself out of meeting Ryan but hadn't been able to do it. She felt as though she owed him something, her guilt over keeping Jennie a secret from him growing with every kind word and reminder of the man she had once thought he was. But she still couldn't get past the way they had ended in Scotland. The one-hundred-and-eighty-degree turn from the man he had been had left her lost for how to feel about him. She had memories of the time they had spent together before the symposium, but everything that was happy in her mind had been colored by what had come after.

She saw him sitting in a chair by the large glass wall that defined the atrium's entrance. He had changed and for the first time since she had seen him the night of Chloe's collapse he was not in scrubs.

She stopped halfway to him and let her mind process the effect, and at that moment he turned and it was completed. It was the same man she had been with in Scotland and she had to mentally give herself a shake to remind her that he actually wasn't. She couldn't move from her spot as she watched him come to her.

"Let's get out of here."

She needed time to sort herself out so she mutely followed him.

Ten minutes later she slid into a booth at a wine bar a few blocks from the hospital. It wasn't the Irish pub frequented by most of the hospital staff and Erin was grateful for the privacy. They both ordered from the server and again Erin was reminded of their night in Edinburgh and she couldn't help but feel the difference at the jarring discomfort she was feeling at that moment from the ease of that long-ago night.

"I thought we should say what we need to say to each other, as it seems we are going to be working together," Ryan opened.

"You have more you want to say?" Erin asked, still feeling intensely defensive from his previous attack on her.

He drew in his breath and seemed to put her comment aside. "I was surprised to learn who you were in Edinburgh. I didn't handle it well."

"How should you have handled it?" Why was she waiting for a certain response?

"I should have just walked away. I shouldn't have waged a personal attack on you."

So he hadn't known who she was. A sense of relief passed through her but she still couldn't get past his words. It felt like the classic feedback you got in medical school, a good comment mixed with the bad. Funny how, despite the good, she always focused on the negative part. "But you still would have walked away?"

"Yes." There was no hesitation in his response.

"Why?" It was the question she had asked herself after her anger toward him had left enough room for other emotions.

"I can't be with a woman like you."

"Like me?" She knew she was prying words out of his mouth that he didn't want to say, but she hadn't opened this door, he had.

He took a sip from his beer before he looked her in the eye. "A woman who is willing to be the other woman."

Part of her wanted to tell him her side. That she'd had no knowledge of his sister until she'd already been trapped on a path she had never intended. But it bothered her both that she wanted him to think better of her and that she had to defend herself. In the end what had happened between them hadn't all been about her. "You were not entirely honest with me."

"Yes. I'm sorry"

"Why?"

"At the time I had no idea how important it would be."

She wanted to tell him how much she valued honesty. How it was the most important thing to her, but she couldn't take that stand now when she knew she was prepared to lie about their daughter. "You are walking on a slippery slope."

"I know. That's my punishment."

"I don't see how that is a punishment."

"You're making it hard to stand my ground. Even now, just sitting here talking to you, I have to constantly remind myself of the pain you caused my sister."

"And if you don't?"

"If I don't all I see is the woman I met in Scotland who seemed so perfect and with whom I spent the best night of my adult life."

She felt heat rise through her body and she pulled at the neck of her dress before stopping the telling movement and instead reaching for a large sip from her chilled white wine. Ryan felt the same way about that night as she did. What would happen if she did explain her past with Kevin?

When she looked up he was staring at her and she felt lost in the blue of his eyes. As if it were a different time, he reached out, his hand covering hers. "But it is a different time and we are different people, Erin. No woman, no matter how tempting, would ever lead me to betray my sister."

And just like that his hand was gone and she felt the loss as intensely as she had in Scotland. The thoughts of telling him the truth about her past and the truth about her present evaporated. He had just told her that, no matter what, she would never have a place in his life, his family, and she wasn't prepared to take the risk of her daughter being taken to a family she would be excluded from.

"You don't have to worry for long. Temptation has less than two months left at Boston General and then I'm moving for a fellowship in California with no plans to return."

"You don't have to move because of me."

How could he not understand? "I have to move precisely because of people like you. I'm not going to let the mistake of my marriage to Kevin ruin the rest of my life. Thank you for the drink."

She rose from the booth and left the restaurant, not wanting to hear any more. She was a few meters from the restaurant's door when she heard him call her name and she stopped. She felt his hand on her shoulder and she turned toward him. She didn't even recognize his intention before his mouth was on hers and her face was being cradled between his hands. While the kiss started hard and passionate, it progressed to a tender touch before his lips left hers.

"I'm not sure what we were, but I still felt we deserved a proper goodbye."

She looked up at him, wondering if it was worth the risk, hoping they had another outcome, but then panicked. No man was more important than her daughter. "Goodbye," she said, and with strength she hadn't known she had she walked away from him.

CHAPTER NINE

"Dr. Callum."

Ryan looked up from the chart he had been completing. Amanda, the triage nurse for the evening shift, was standing in front of him.

"Emergency Medical Services has just brought in an eleven-year-old girl with ten out of ten abdominal pain. She's tachycardic, but stable, but overall looks really distressed. I've put her in treatment room two and I was hoping you could see her as soon as possible yourself."

It wasn't often he got requests like these. He normally gave the medical student or resident he was working with the opportunity to see the patient first then review his or her findings. He could tell, though, that Amanda was really worried, and he knew that she didn't worry often.

"I'll see her right now."

He walked the short distance to the treatment area and to room two. He opened the door to find what Amanda had described: an eleven-year-old girl, crying, her whole body rigid in an attempt not to move.

"Hello, I'm Dr. Ryan Callum, the staff emergency

physician on this evening." He introduced himself as he shook hands with each of the girl's worried parents.

"What's your name?" he asked the girl.

"Lauren."

He could tell she was trying to be grown-up and answer his questions.

"Okay, Lauren, when did your stomach start to hurt?"

"At gymnastics," she answered.

He had already come to that conclusion judging by the leotard she was wearing.

"Did you have any pain before gymnastics?"

"No, it came on all of a sudden when I dismounted from the balance beam."

"Okay," he tried to soothe her, "have you ever had pain like this before?"

"No, but it hurts so bad." She started to sob and the minute the cry racked her body she sobbed harder with the movement, perpetuating a painful cycle.

"Does she have any allergies?" he asked her parents.

"No," they both answered.

"How much does she weigh?"

"She's about seventy-five pounds," her mother responded immediately.

"I'll be right back." Ryan walked to the drug room, using his security card to log in to the automated system. He selected Lauren from the list of registered patients and then typed in her weight, as she was a pediatric patient who required all her medication adjusted for her size. He selected the painkiller and waited as the correct drawer was unlocked before withdrawing the medication.

"Okay, Lauren, I'm going to give you some medication to help make you feel better." He waited to see her reaction and was worried when she didn't question the needle he was holding. Most children wouldn't agree to a needle for anything, so the fact that she was ambivalent was a sign of just how much pain the young girl was in. He injected the medication slowly through her intravenous line so she wouldn't have to feel any discomfort with the injection. He waited until he saw her face relax to know the medication had taken effect.

"Lauren, does it hurt more to move or to stay still?"

"Move."

"Can you point to me where you feel the most pain?"

With the most careful movement he had ever seen she moved her hand, not disturbing the rest of her body, and pointed to her lower left side. "I think I'm going to be sick." With a grimace of pain spreading across her face, she rolled to her side. He managed to move quickly for a plastic basin before she vomited.

He helped support her weight and when she was done gently rolled her onto her back, leaving her to rest before redirecting his attention on her parents.

"Does she have any medical problems?"

"No," her mother answered quickly, clearly alarmed by the state of her daughter.

"Any surgeries in the past? Does she take any medications?"

"No, she's always been a very healthy little girl." He could see tears of fear starting to well up in her eyes.

He nodded in acknowledgment and carefully uncovered the girl's abdomen. He touched the upper right half, as far from the spot she had indicated as he could. Her stomach was as rigid as her posture, and she flinched when he palpated gently, but jumped and cried out when he let go.

"It's going to be okay, Mrs. Connor. Lauren is right where she needs to be. I'm going to order a few tests, including an ultrasound, and we will keep on top of her pain and nausea medication so that we can get her as comfortable as possible. Please don't give her anything to eat or drink until I tell you it's okay."

He walked out of the room and found the attending nurse. He glanced at the clock before picking up the phone and dialing the hospital switchboard. "It's Dr. Callum from Emergency. Can you please page the chief resident from General Surgery urgently for me."

"Yes, Dr. Callum. Do you want to stay on the line?"

"Yes."

Two minutes later. "This is Dr. Kate Spence."

"Kate, it's Ryan Callum from Emergency. I have a healthy eleven-year-old girl with a surgical abdomen following sudden onset left lower quadrant pain. She's stable and we are starting with investigations now, but I wanted you to know before you went home for the evening."

"Thanks for the heads-up. I'll be down shortly."

Ryan paced the emergency department, checking on his active patients and waiting for Lauren's results to come in. Kate Spence had come and gone. She agreed with his assessment but wanted to wait for more information before rushing to the operating room.

"Ryan." Erin's voice cut through his thoughts of the girl and started a new one—how was it possible that she had avoided him for so long when now it felt as if their careers were throwing them together at every chance it got? She was wearing scrubs, her hair pulled back and covered by a scrub hat made with purple fabric.

"Kate called me. All pediatric consultations go direct to the chief resident. The scan of Lauren Connor's abdomen shows classic signs of ovarian torsion. She has a left-sided eight-centimeter cyst that has twisted on itself, cutting off blood supply to the ovary and causing it to swell. I'm going to go and talk to her parents and get consent for the operating room. I thought you should know."

"I'll come with you."

She didn't object and he followed her toward Lauren's room. Both parents stood as they entered. Lauren was still lying still, her eyes closed, with occasional moans of pain.

"Mr. and Mrs. Connor, I'm Dr. Madden, the chief resident from Gynecology. The CT scan of your daughter's abdomen shows that her left ovary has become twisted on itself, cutting off its blood supply. She's having pain because it can't drain or receive fresh blood. We need to take her to the operating room and fix it."

"Are you going to take out her ovary?" Mrs. Connor asked, her horror at the idea obvious.

"No. In a child Lauren's age we often untwist it and hope that it heals. If possible we can try to tack the ovary to reduce her risk of it happening again, but we won't proceed with anything that may compromise the health of the ovary."

Ryan alternated his gaze between Lauren, her parents and Erin. He found her words reassuring and his worry for Lauren dissipated. He knew that Erin would do everything she could to save the ovary, the same way she had struggled to save Chloe's Fallopian tube.

"What are we looking at for her recovery?" Mr. Connor asked.

"Hopefully two days in hospital and then a couple of weeks. We are going to try to get her surgery done using a camera and a few incisions that are all less than one centimeter. It will make her postoperative pain a lot less and she will have barely noticeable scars."

"Are you doing it?" the mother asked.

"Yes," Erin answered definitively.

"Good."

Erin crossed the room toward the head of Lauren's bed. "Lauren, I'm not sure how much you heard of what your parents and I just talked about. You're going to come with me and have a nap and while you're sleeping I'm going to take away the pain and make you feel better." She gently reached out and rested her hand on the girl's shoulder for a few moments before walking away.

"She'll be going to the operating room within the hour. There's a family waiting room outside the operating room and she'll go to the pediatric area of the recovery room so that you both can come in and see her as soon as possible."

"Are you a mother, Dr. Madden?" Ryan's attention rocketed to Erin. It was an innocent question. He was often asked if he was a parent when he was treating children, but he knew that for Erin it was a painful one. He looked over at her and she looked absolutely stricken by the question, her pallor evident against the dark blue of her scrubs, her eyes wide.

"Dr. Madden is an excellent surgeon. You're lucky to have her involved in Lauren's care. Dr. Madden, I'll help get Lauren ready for the operation if you want to go upstairs and organize the operating room."

He wasn't expecting a look of gratitude, but Erin just stared at him questioningly before she returned to her planned course of action.

"I'll see you both soon." And she left the room.

Erin exhaled for what felt like the first time since she'd met Lauren Connor. The young girl was slowly waking in the recovery room and the surgery had been a success. She had untwisted the dark swollen ovary and had waited patiently until she'd seen some evidence that the blood vessels feeding it were going to be able to restore it. Before the case she had called home to talk to Jennie's nanny and if she hurried she would still be able to give Jennie her bath and put her to bed.

"How did it go?" She turned and saw Ryan on the other side of the counter she was sitting at. His deflection of Mrs. Connor's question had taken her aback, both by his gallantry and by the guilt that had overcome her when her lie to him had come too close to the surface.

"Great. We did everything laparoscopically and I think the ovary will heal normally. We left the cyst and will follow her closely until it resolves. She's resting comfortably in the pediatric area if you want to see her." She hoped he would as she didn't feel she could face him much longer, knowing her secret.

"You would have been a good mother."

Her mouth felt completely dry as she watched Ryan walk away toward Lauren. She didn't like deceiving him and her doubts in herself were growing by the minute. It was easier when he was judging her, declaring her a lesser and immoral person. Now he was supportive and still attracted to her, she was at a complete loss at how to deal with all the feelings she had toward him. Was she still attracted to him? Yes. The kiss outside the restaurant had left no room for doubt. She also respected him—it was hard not to, knowing his professional reputation and having watched him take care of Chloe and his other patients. But above everything else she was still hurt by him. Hurt that he couldn't see the truth about who she was and that he thought the worst of her. Was she so hurt that she was keeping Jennie from him to hurt him, too? No, she had told herself and reminded herself again.

Erin looked down at her pager and dialed the number.

"Erin, it's Dr. Thomas. If you have a minute I'd like you to come see your friend Chloe in follow-up."

"Is everything okay?" It didn't make sense to her that she would be called for what should be a routine follow-up.

"Just come."

She headed directly to the hospital's outpatient clinic space. Dr. Thomas simply handed her the chart with Chloe's most recent bloodwork on the front page. "It would be a great case for your upcoming board exams. She's in exam room three. Why don't you go see her and do a bedside ultrasound and let me know?"

She nodded in agreement, still not believing what she was reading. She needed to calm herself before she panicked Chloe. She knocked on the door and waited a minute before letting herself in.

"Hey, Chloe. Dr. Thomas paged me to let me know you were in for your follow-up and asked me to come see you. It's hard to believe it has already been six weeks. How are you feeling?"

Chloe was sitting on the exam table, the paper drape drawn over her lap, looking tired but still considerably better than the last time Erin had seen her.

"Okay. Good days and bad days, I guess. I went back to work this week and that has helped. But I haven't been studying nearly as much as I planned and will be more than happy when this exam is done. I'm surprised to see you still at work. I would have thought you would have been off studying, too."

"You know what they say about the best intentions."

"Well, I'm here, aren't I?" She heard the sadness in Chloe's voice and recognized it as the same she had felt after her own miscarriage.

"How are you feeling *really*?" Erin asked, pulling the stool from the end of the bed so she could sit and talk to her friend.

"Disappointed, frustrated—take your pick. It's hard to admit that I made such a mistake, both in getting pregnant and then not even having the medical sense to realize it. I want to be able to move past it, but I can't seem to get back to normal. I still feel tired, nauseated, and I have no control over my emotions, which just leads to more frustration."

Erin looked down again at the bloodwork results. "You may be being slightly hard on yourself."

"I know."

"Chloe, would it be okay if I examined your abdomen and we did a quick bedside ultrasound?" She tried to be reassuring but knew that Chloe knew enough to know that this was not routine.

"Of course. What are you not saying, Erin?"

Erin couldn't answer. Instead she was trying to convince herself that she wasn't feeling what she was feeling. The elevation of Chloe's uterus two centimeters above her pubic bone was consistent with a fourteen-week pregnancy.

"Your bloodwork from this morning shows a persistently elevated beta HCG."

"What does that mean?" Chloe was as confused as Erin had been when she had seen the result.

"It shouldn't still be elevated. If we had performed a salpingostomy and removed only the ectopic pregnancy then some residual placenta might be present in the Fallopian tube, leading to the elevated hormone level, but…"

"But?"

"But your tube had ruptured and we were unable to control the bleeding from the rupture site, so we performed an open right salpingectomy, removing the entire Fallopian tube. The pathology report confirmed the presence of the pregnancy. So your beta HCG shouldn't still be elevated, unless…" She couldn't believe she was about to say this.

"Unless what?"

"Chloe, you may not be able to move on. I think you are still pregnant."

"I don't understand."

"I think your pregnancy was a heterotopic pregnancy. One inside the Fallopian tube and one in the uterus. It's a rare condition, occurring in only one in every five to thirty thousand pregnancies." She wasn't sure who was in more shock, her or Chloe.

"How do we find out for sure?" Chloe asked.

"We look."

And without further discussion Erin squeezed warmed jelly onto Chloe's abdomen and placed the ultrasound probe against her. She saw everything instantly. The uterus filled with amniotic fluid and inside a baby.

"A baby…" Chloe stated with awe.

"Your baby," Erin confirmed. "I'm just going to do some measurements to date the pregnancy."

"There is only one date possible."

Erin smiled as she went along her routine, measuring the baby's head, abdomen and thigh to estimate the gestational age.

"Which makes you about fourteen weeks along."

"Does everything look okay?" Chloe asked.

Erin thought through the complexity of Chloe's case, the heterotopic pregnancy and the complications and medications involved in her initial surgery. Dr. Thomas was right, she was like a hard board exam question. Still, her job wasn't to get lost in the academics; she needed to focus on supporting Chloe.

"As much as I can see right now, everything looks okay, but we're going to need to do some investigations. You received a lot of blood products that they initially didn't have time to match against your own blood screen. You also received some medication we don't recommend in pregnancy, but right now you have a baby."

"A baby…"

"How do you feel about that, Chloe?"

They both turned to watch the monitor and the baby's activity. Erin remembered when she had first seen Jennie and how special it had been to hear her heartbeat for the first time. She moved the ultrasound cursor over the baby's heartbeat and the rapid sound filled the room.

"Wonderful."

"Okay, so we will just go from here. I am going to give you a requisition for prenatal bloodwork and another ultrasound in four weeks' time so we can look at the rest of the baby's anatomy."

"Erin, is it weird that I am excited and terrified at the same time?"

Erin thought back to when she had finally realized she was pregnant with Jennie.

"No, I remember that feeling well. You're going to be a wonderful mother, Chloe. Congratulations."

CHAPTER TEN

A WEEK OF sleepless nights had done nothing to strengthen Ryan's resolve. He hadn't seen Erin since she had taken care of Lauren Connor, but she still filled his waking thoughts and his dreams. He struggled with his feelings toward her.

Watching her take care of the young girl had shown another side of her he had never seen. Amid her professional behavior she had also managed to show her maternal side. It was one more part of her he found disarming. If everything he knew about her was true, it was as though her pros and cons were balancing on a scale and he was worried that any minute the scale might tip to the positive side and he would be forced to choose between Erin and his sister.

If he had never learned about her past with Kevin he would be doing everything in his power to make her his, forever. But he couldn't live life based on what-ifs. It had almost been a relief to hear that she was leaving Boston, enough that he had let his resolve slip and had kissed her again, knowing the temptation she represented would soon be gone forever.

He knocked at Chloe's door and waited. He had promised Chloe that he would help her study for her upcoming board exams and had agreed to come to her while she was still recovering. At first that had been at Tate's and after she had moved home last week they had decided it was easier to keep meeting at her home.

"Hi," she greeted him, as she led him into the living room.

"How are you feeling?" he asked, as he watched her make her way slowly across the room and ease herself back onto the couch. It was hard to dismiss the clinician in him and just be Chloe's friend.

"I have good days and bad days, but Erin says that is normal."

Erin. He had almost convinced himself that he was here just to help Chloe but the moment she spoke Erin's name he knew he had deeper motives. "Have you already seen Erin in follow-up?"

"Yes, last week, and she calls at least once a day to check in on me. Can I get you something to drink?"

"Water, please." He should change the subject. He had already resigned himself to the fact that Erin was not suitable in his life and he should have nothing more to do with her.

"I didn't realize you two were close friends." Damn, guilt washed over him as he realized he was using Chloe to get information on Erin, but he couldn't resist. Erin was still an enigma to him and he needed to know more. Maybe then he would be able to reconcile the past and move on with his life.

"Erin is a pretty private person. I would be, too, if I had gone through everything she has."

"You mean her marriage to Kevin Dufour?"

"I'm not sure I would call that a marriage."

"What do you mean?"

"I mean Kevin Dufour never for one day acted like he was married. I moved to Boston after they were married and the fact that he had a wife never once kept him from making advances on me or any other woman who walked by him."

Ryan inhaled and exhaled slowly as he processed Chloe's words. Did the fact that Kevin was a serial philanderer change things? Certainly it questioned the theory that he had been lured away from a happily committed relationship, as Sabrina had suggested. "Did Erin know?"

Chloe stopped, her facial expression changing, and all of sudden he felt as if he was the one being evaluated. What had started as casual conversation between friends had definitely changed. She paused before she finally answered him. "Eventually, but she didn't see it for a long time. I was with her the day she found a note in her locker anonymously telling her of her husband's affair with the hospital pharmacist."

He winced, both at Chloe's words and at once again wishing he could take back the words he had spoken in anger in Scotland. *You got what you deserved.* If he'd known then what he knew now he never would have spoken them. He murmured under his breath to himself, *"Callous bastard..."* That was how he had behaved.

"There are a lot more words I would use to describe Kevin Dufour, but I don't waste my time and neither does Erin. I'm friends with her because I admire her, Ryan. She walked away from her marriage with her head held high and is an incredible mother to Jennie."

Water lodged in his windpipe and he coughed violently in response. Erin? A mother? Had he heard

Chloe correctly? Confusion coursed through him and he felt as if his chest was being crushed with a vise.

"Erin's a mother?"

"Yes, she has a one-year-old daughter named Jennie. She's beautiful."

One. Erin's daughter was one. His mind flashed back to their night together and the broken condom and Erin's confession. He would have sworn on his life that her infertility had been the thing she hadn't deceived him about. "Did she adopt?"

If he hadn't gotten Chloe's attention before he definitely had it now and he had shown his hand, revealing his knowledge of her infertility. "I didn't realize you knew Erin."

"I know of her from her marriage to Kevin." As much as he didn't like lying to Chloe, he also knew that if Erin hadn't told Chloe about the two of them she would not appreciate Ryan being the one to do so.

"But you knew about her infertility?" Chloe asked skeptically.

"Yes." He wasn't prepared to fabricate a story so instead he acknowledged the truth.

Chloe was silent for a long time before she finally began speaking. "No, she got pregnant around the same time as her divorce became final. Not surprisingly, Kevin has taken no responsibility for the baby, so Erin is a single mother and she's wonderful at it. Jennie is the happiest, most loved baby I have ever seen."

Ryan felt his mind and heart race. Kevin had taken no responsibility for the baby. Was there a reason for that beyond his obvious selfish character flaws? He needed to know more, and he needed to know more now. He looked up at Chloe and knew that she had no more answers for him. There was also no way he was going to be able to sit and focus on helping her study for the next hour. He needed answers now and to get them he needed to talk to Erin.

"Chloe, I just realized there is something I need to tie up back at the hospital urgently. Can I give you a rain check on today and we can try again later on in the week?"

"Sure," she answered, still looking puzzled but not questioning him further.

"Don't worry about getting up. I'll let myself out." He walked back to the large door and looked back at Chloe once more, wondering if she had just been the one to tell him he had a daughter.

Erin led afternoon rounds, her team of junior residents and medical students gathered in the ward's conference room giving verbal updates on the patients.

"How is Mrs. Campbell?" she asked one of the medical students who had just returned from seeing the patient. It was routine to allow the junior residents and medical students independent learning with the patients but she always laid her eyes on every single patient before leaving for the day.

"She's doing better. She was able to walk around the ward this afternoon and tolerated the introduction of food this afternoon."

"Great. Mrs. Gregg?"

"She'll be ready and wanting to be discharged by tomorrow morning," her junior resident responded.

The door to the conference room swung open and the discussion stopped as Ryan entered, walking directly toward her. He wasn't in scrubs but was dressed in a taupe fitted T-shirt and designer denim. He obviously wasn't working.

"I need to talk to you." She wasn't sure if it was clear to the others in the room but it was clear to her that this need did not stem from anything regarding a patient. She looked at her team and tried to figure out how to handle this, instantly worried about what Ryan wanted and his obvious sense of urgency.

"We're just finishing afternoon rounds. I can talk to you in about thirty minutes."

He didn't take her up on her offer. Instead he leaned closer, his voice quieter but no less insistent. "It needs to be now, and I think we should probably talk alone."

She looked out again at their audience, knowing she was powerless to stop this conversation from happening. The least she could do was have it privately.

"Ruth, please finish afternoon rounds while I speak with Dr. Callum. If you have any concerns, please let the on-call resident for the evening know."

She walked from the room, aware that Ryan was following her. She heard him inhale, about to begin their conversation, but she stopped him. "Not here."

She walked farther down the hall until she reached an empty patient room, waiting for him to enter and then closing the door behind her. When she turned back to look at him she knew he knew.

"Tell me about Jennie."

Blood rushed to her ears and she could hear each part of her heart beat as if in slow motion, though she knew it was racing. It didn't even matter how he knew—he knew and all her plans and her life changed now.

"Jennie is my daughter."

"I think you know there is a lot more that I am asking."

She wiped her palms against fitted black slacks before looking up at him. She knew he wasn't going to let this go. She had to make a decision now. How she handled things from here would make all the difference.

"Do you want a paternity test?" It wasn't what he had been expecting. But it was the only way she could buy some time until he found out the truth.

Ryan went from standing to sitting on the empty bed, his hand running through his hair. "So there is the possibility she's mine?"

"Yes." More than a possibility, she couldn't be anyone else's.

"And you didn't tell me?"

"You'd already told me you can't be with a woman like me."

"That has no bearing on whether or not you have been lying and keeping my daughter from me, Erin."

She knew he was angry and didn't want to antagonize him. After she had condemned him in Scotland for lying by omission, she had no ground to stand on.

"Jennie and I are a package deal, Ryan." He needed to know that. That she would never be separated from her daughter.

"You're not going to California."

"What?" She was shocked by the abrupt change in focus.

"You heard me. If Jennie is my daughter you are not taking her across the country away from me."

She wasn't surprised. Hadn't she known that if

Ryan knew about Jennie he would want to be involved? Wasn't that one of the reasons she hadn't told him in the first place? She thought of her fellowship and how long and hard she had worked to earn it. She was amazed that she wasn't going to fight him; Jennie was the most important thing in the world to her and her career was a distant second. From this minute on she needed to do everything possible to prove to Ryan that she wasn't the immoral other woman he believed her to be. She needed him to see who she really was then maybe he wouldn't try to take Jennie away.

"Okay."

She could tell he was ready to argue with her and was not expecting her acquiescence.

"I want to meet her."

"Now?" she asked. "Do you want to wait for the test results instead?"

"No. If she is mine, I don't want to waste another minute apart."

This time she nodded her agreement. She knew she couldn't object because she knew the test results were going to reveal just that. From this moment on everything hinged on him seeing her for the person she was. Maybe even seeing her with Jennie would make him think twice about possible custody demands.

"I need to check on a few of my patients and then we can go."

"I'll wait for you."

She did her afternoon rounds in a daze, hoping that her team had done a good job because she felt as if today she could miss something. Would Ryan see what she saw when she looked at Jennie? His own smaller, feminine reflection looking back at him? It was a chance she was going to have to take.

She finished up in twenty minutes and met him outside the ward's doors. They walked in silence down the hospital corridor toward the parking garage. "You'll need my address. I live at 90 Winchester Avenue."

"I'll follow you there."

Boston traffic was typically heavy, but she wasn't surprised when he didn't lose her tail on the way home. She motioned toward visitors' parking and waited for him at her building's elevator.

"You live in an apartment?"

She found herself bristling at his question but reminded herself she needed to keep her cool. "Yes, I decided that it was better to live closer to the hospital so that I could spend more time with Jennie rather than commuting. The building has a lovely children's play park that Jennie goes to daily."

"Who watches her while you're working?"

"Her nanny, Carolyn. She's been with us since Jennie was three months old and is wonderful with her."

He didn't ask her any more questions as they rode up in the elevator together. She walked to the end of the hallway and unlocked the door to her three-bedroom apartment. From the entry she walked to the combined open dining, kitchen and living room. She saw Jennie playing with her wooden puzzle on her play mat in the living room and, as always, the best part of her day was watching her daughter's face light up when she saw her. "Mum, mum, mum, mum," Jennie repeated, as she pushed herself onto her pudgy legs and with her usual unsteady walk made her way to Erin. Her arms extended upward the moment she ran into Erin's legs.

"Hello, my sweetheart." She brushed her daughter's brown hair back and kissed her cheek.

Carolyn emerged from the kitchen, pausing only slightly at the sight of Ryan. Erin had never before brought a man home and she was impressed that Carolyn was handling the surprise so well.

"How was she today?" Erin asked.

"Great. She had her normal naps and we spent most of the afternoon at the park. Supper is ready in the kitchen for you both. I'll see you in the morning."

"Thanks, Carolyn."

The other woman let herself out and Erin turned back to Ryan, but his attention was entirely on Jennie, who seemed equally transfixed by the new person in her life. Watching them together made Erin's heart cry and question every decision she had made since the moment she'd found out she was pregnant.

She shifted Jennie onto her hip. "This is mummy's friend Ryan."

His eyes broke from Jennie's and he looked up at her. She couldn't introduce him as her father, not yet. "Do you want to show Ryan your puzzle?"

She watched as Jennie evaluated Ryan and then nodded in agreement. She walked with Jennie over to the play mat, sitting them both on the floor and waiting for Ryan to do the same. He did, but he still seemed overwhelmed so Erin took the lead. "Show Ryan where the sun goes." And she handed Jennie the piece.

It was Jennie's favorite puzzle and she took no time

to place the piece near its slot and then with the awk-wardness of a toddler wiggled it in. She looked up at Ryan expectantly.

"You're a smart girl. Do you want to show me where the balloon goes?" He handed her the red, round puzzle piece. She reached out her little hand and took it from him, placing it in the same fashion as the previous piece and then looking back at him. "Good job."

Erin stayed silent as the two worked together to complete the rest of the puzzle. When they were finished two pairs of identical eyes looked up at her. "Would you like to stay for dinner?"

"Yes."

She lifted Jennie from the floor and carried her toward the eat-in kitchen, securing her in the high chair. Carolyn had prepared a large Cobb salad and Erin picked out small pieces for Jennie, putting them on her tray, and also served two plates for her and Ryan. She opened the fridge, holding up a bottle of wine, and Ryan nodded agreement and she poured two glasses, as well.

The meal was a typical one for Erin. Erin ate while at the same time watching Jennie get as much food on the floor and high chair as she did into her mouth. After dinner Ryan made no attempt to leave so she included him in their bathtime and bedtime rituals. "Good night, my love," she murmured sweetly, before gently covering her daughter. She closed the door and returned to the living room, where Ryan was seated on the couch.

She went to the fridge and refilled their glasses of wine before joining him.

"I don't know what to say to you. She's a happy,

healthy, wonderful little girl and part of me is grateful and the other part of me will never forgive you for keeping her from me if she's mine."

It was honest and it was fair and she couldn't argue against his feelings. "I'm sorry."

"Why? How could you do something like this?"

She wished he would yell at her. Yelling would be better than hearing the pain come through his confused, calm voice.

"Do you know what Jennie means?" It wasn't the immediate answer to his question but the best explanation she had. "It means 'God is gracious' and ever since I found out I was pregnant that has been my only thought. Jennie is my miracle, the baby I desperately wanted and never thought I would have. Since the moment I found out I was pregnant I have been terrified of losing her."

"You thought I would take her away?"

"The last time I saw you you made it clear that I was the last woman in the world you would want to be the mother of your child."

"And that gave you the right to possibly keep me from my child?"

She did her best not to rise to his accusations. "It took away any sense of trust I had in you."

"So now we're even, except this time the consequences are considerably higher. Can you organize the paternity test?"

"Yes."

"I want answers, Erin."

Ryan stood in the hospital's large garden, waiting. It was the last day in June and the annual graduation ceremony for the finishing residents. The sun was hot but a breeze off the water dampened its effects.

As a member of the staff who was closely involved in resident education he had been asked to speak at the commencement, but his mind was distracted from his requested purpose. He looked through the crowd, waiting for Erin to arrive. Finally he spotted them. Erin was walking through the crowd, beautiful in a sleeveless midlength turquoise lace dress that was tied with a simple black ribbon belt. In her arms she held Jennie, who was wearing a vibrant red summer dress and was happily looking around the crowd. He had never seen Erin look more beautiful.

At his request Erin had sent him a photo of Jennie and since then he hadn't been able to keep his eyes off it. It would take time to do the paternity test and get the results back, and until then all he had were his gut instincts. Those instincts were telling him Jennie was his child. Her hair was darker than Erin's, more like his. She had Erin's nose and mouth but her eyes reminded him of his. Her smile was definitely her own. He couldn't imagine that a child so wonderful could ever be a part of Kevin Dufour.

When he wasn't thinking of Jennie he was thinking of Erin. He had heard her explanation and her apology, but that didn't change the anger he felt over missing the first one and a half years of his probable daughter's life. He still felt as if he didn't know her. He had thought he had known her in Edinburgh, but her past with Kevin had changed his mind. Now he had competing thoughts of her inside his head.

There was his first impression of the honest, caring woman he had taken to bed. Then she had been portrayed as the other woman, the image his sister had supplied. He had worked with her enough in the past few weeks to know she was a competent, dedicated physician, and he respected her for it. And now he knew her as a mother, which brought with it the double-edged sword of watching how wonderful she was with Jennie and knowing that she had deliberately kept her from him.

He walked up to the both of them. "Congratulations."

"Thank you."

"What are your plans now that you are no longer a resident?" He thought it was a casual question but he could tell that he had set her on edge.

"I did as you asked and declined the fellowship in California. Very graciously Boston General has offered me a temporary position pending a formal hiring process."

He hadn't considered the ramifications to her career when he had insisted she not move to California. But it spoke volumes about her that the hospital had been willing to offer her a position on short notice. He hadn't been wrong about the type of physician he knew her to be.

She looked around before she resumed talking. "I talked to the laboratory and arranged the testing. You can go and give a blood sample at any time. All Jennie needs is a cheek swab that I'll do as soon as I can and then we should have the results in a few weeks."

He looked between the two, Jennie happy and content on her mother's hip, and knew what he needed to do. The two were a pair and he would never separate them for either of their sakes.

"I think we need to start again."

"I don't understand what you mean." Neither did he. What was it that he wanted from Erin?

"There was a time when both of us were very compatible and very much in sync. I think the best thing for Jennie would be if we tried to get back to a time where we trusted each other."

"I don't know if that's possible."

"It was once. Maybe it will be again if we actually take the time to get to know each other and put aside our joint pasts."

Erin wasn't prepared for Ryan's suggestion, but she couldn't fault his reasoning. There had been a time when she had trusted him, she just didn't know if it would be possible to get that back. Regardless, being given a chance to prove to him that she was a good mother before he learned for sure Jennie was his was an opportunity she wasn't going to let slip away.

"Okay, I think you're right but I have no idea where to even begin."

"What are you doing after this?"

"Jennie and I are going to the Hamptons. My parents have a house on the beach and now that I am done with residency I thought it would be the perfect time to take Jennie for a weekend away before I start my new position next week."

"I'll come with you."

"I don't know." She was hesitant. Was she ready to be alone with Ryan for that period of time? So far all their interactions in Boston had been centered around work or Jennie. The one and only time they had been alone together he had kissed her and even though it had been just once, every inch of her body remembered what she wanted from him. What would happen between them each night after Jennie went to bed?

"I do. We need this time together. When the results come back we need to have something to build on together."

He was more right than he knew so she couldn't disagree. "We are already packed and ready to go. If you don't mind driving with us, we can pick you up after the ceremony."

"Agreed." He looked down at the program he was holding. "You're speaking, as well?"

Erin smiled "Chloe and Kate nominated me to represent the chiefs. It's an honor."

"Then we'll pick up where we left off in Scotland. Hopefully this will go better than the last time we spoke in public together."

CHAPTER ELEVEN

ERIN PULLED UP to Ryan's brownstone townhouse and immediately became envious. The old brick facade and heritage trees that surrounded the yard were warm and inviting. She looked back at Jennie, who was playing happily in her car seat. This was going to be one of her homes and Erin felt emptiness at the possibility of Jennie and Ryan here together without her.

She saw Ryan lock the front door and head toward her with a small bag. He had changed into gray linen shorts and a teal-colored polo shirt. She could see glimpses of both tattoos and she knew without having to take a breath that he would smell of sweat and sunshine, just as he had the day they'd met. She wrapped her hair in her hands and lifted it from her neck to cool the heat from her body. She was happy she had changed into shorts and a loose-fitting thin cotton T-shirt.

She got out and met him at the hatch of her crossover. "Do you want to drive?"

"Sure." He took the keys from her outstretched hand. The brush of his fingers against hers was both surprisingly familiar and arousing. What had she gotten herself into?

The trip to the Hamptons was long, but not as arduous as she had worried it might have turned out to be. Jennie stayed content and they stopped frequently to let her move around and snack. She fell asleep and slept the last few hours as evening progressed into night. She and Ryan stuck to safe topics. Now that they had their careers in common there was a lot of shared experience to draw on for conversation. At times she even found herself forgetting that there should be awkwardness between them.

It was dark, the sky lit only by the stars as she directed them to her parents' beachfront house. "It's not large," she cautioned him. "My stepfather is a doctor, not the CEO of an international company."

Ryan laughed. "I know who your stepfather is, Erin. I believe he is my boss."

"True." And Erin joined his laughter.

As Ryan shut off the engine they both looked back at Jennie. Her head was tilted all the way to her shoulder and her eyes were shut, body relaxed. "I'll get her if you want to get the door," Erin suggested.

She unfastened the child belts and enjoyed the moment when the little girl relaxed back into her arms. Ryan held open the door for her and she went into the house, leaving it dark so as not to wake her. Ryan seemed to understand and he wordlessly emptied the back of her vehicle and brought in all their belongings.

The house had two bedrooms, a single bathroom and a combined living room and kitchen. Its interior was classic cape-side, with white wainscoting and wooden floors. It was furnished with comfortable light-colored furniture and accents of bright yellows and oranges. The best feature was the patio that looked out onto the beach and ocean. Most of Erin's happiest childhood memories had been made at the beach house and she had dreamed of the day when she could bring her own children here to share it.

"Where do you want her crib?" he asked. She had planned to take the master bedroom and set Jennie's portable crib in the other bedroom but she quickly realized that wasn't going to work with Ryan. His tall frame would never comfortably fit into one of the two single beds in the guest room.

"The room at the end of the hall on the left, please."

She waited until he reappeared in the hall before bringing Jennie to bed. She wasn't surprised that Ryan had had no problem assembling the complicated device and had found the sheets she had packed. She smiled at the turned-down blankets.

"I love you, my sweetheart," she murmured, as she kissed Jennie's cheek and laid her in the crib.

With a final look she left her to sleep. "She's beautiful when she sleeps," Ryan commented, still not making any move to leave the small bedroom.

Guilt swept her again. Should she tell him now that he was Jennie's father? For the first time since Scotland they'd had several hours together that had been not only pleasant but enjoyable, with no confrontations or accusations. What would happen if she told him now? Would he even believe her?

"Yes, she is," she answered simply.

He joined her in the kitchen. "Can I get you something? I had the caretaker stock the fridge for the weekend."

"I'll have whatever you're having."

She opened the fridge and discovered a bottle of

champagne tied with a red ribbon and small envelope attached. She took out the bottle and opened the card.

Congratulations, Erin.
We couldn't be more proud of you.
Mom & Stephen.

She showed Ryan the card as a means of explanation. She didn't want him to think her plans had been to drink alone in the beach house for the weekend with a small child. "We should open it," he recommended.

She handed him the bottle and got out two wine glasses. Ryan opened the bottle, the pop and emerging foam reminding her that this was indeed an occasion to be celebrated.

"I should show you the patio. It's the best part of the house." She led the way through the French doors and took her place on one of the covered wicker patio chairs, drawing her legs under her. Ryan joined her, sitting across from her, in the still of the night.

"Congratulations, Erin. I know it hasn't been the easiest journey for you and you should be proud of your accomplishment."

She was stunned by the generosity of his comments. He could easily have argued that it didn't have to be as hard as she had made it if she had only made better choices, particularly asking for his help with their daughter. Instead he didn't and she felt proud of herself, as well.

"Thank you."

"You seem to be getting along better with your parents. The last time we talked you thought they were disappointed in you."

"It's amazing what having a child does to your point of view. I realized when I had Jennie that I could never be disappointed in her, just her choices. And looking back, I made some choices that were worthy of their disappointment."

"So being a single mother didn't add to their disappointment?"

"No, I was worried when I told them, but both Mom and Stephen were wonderful. I think, like me, they had lost hope of ever having a grandchild and they see Jennie as the wonderful miracle she is."

"You call your stepfather Stephen?"

"Yes. My mother remarried when I was fourteen. She was ready and I wasn't. I loved my dad—he was my hero—and there was only ever one of him."

Through the darkness she could see Ryan's face and knew what he was thinking. They were the same thoughts she was having now. How could she deprive Jennie of a father when losing hers had been so hard for her?

She took another sip from her glass and let the cool, dry bubbles pass down her throat. "I wasn't thinking clearly, Ryan. Maybe I'm still not. When I found out I was pregnant all I could think about was not losing her."

"I know, Erin. You've apologized already and you don't need to keep doing it. I need to accept my responsibility in this situation, too."

He walked over to the patio rail and faced the ocean with his back to her. She remembered what it was like to direct most of the anger inward. It was the same way she'd felt when she'd finally left Kevin. She knew she had to give him space, but also remembered how much that anger had turned to an aching pain. So she simply stood and joined him at the rail.

"One of my favorite things about the world is the sky, no matter where you are," Ryan shared.

She stared up with him, enjoying the pitch-blackness she never saw in Boston. "That must have been comforting when you were in the military. Do you miss it?"

"At times. But it was also time to move on with my life."

"Would you have come to Boston General if you'd known I was there?" She moved her eyes from the sky to the man standing above her.

"Honestly, no, I wouldn't have."

"I offended you that badly?" Now it was her turn to be hurt.

"No, you confused me. I didn't understand how the woman I had met equated with what I had learned about your past."

"And that was enough to keep you away?"

He brushed her hair from her face, his hand resting on her cheek. "No, I stayed away because, despite everything, I was still attracted to you. I still am."

She realized she had lifted herself and was straining toward him only a moment before his head came down and his lips touched hers. She could taste the champagne on his lips as they brushed against hers. It was the softest of touches before a gentle pressure opened her to him and he deepened their kiss. If she had been capable of rational thought she would have wondered how this man, despite everything, could still cause her to feel such passion, but she couldn't think, not even when he broke away.

"This wasn't my plan." He shook his head slightly.

"I...I..." Still she didn't know what to think or say.

"When I said we should get back to the place we had been in Scotland, I didn't mean physically."

"Oh." And she was embarrassed by just how much disappointment she felt. She, too, had absolutely no plans for anything romantic or physical between them, deeming that dream well lost, but the reminder of what they had once experienced together was enough to make her feel bereft again as he pulled away.

"You should go to bed."

"Your room is the one down the other hall. I'll see you in the morning."

Erin walked quietly to the room she was sharing with Jennie, taking a moment to cover her daughter, who always managed to kick off her blankets. She looked at Jennie, the sight of their daughter giving her the strong reminder she needed—that this was not just about her and Ryan. The option for a fleeting love affair had ended in Scotland. She couldn't do anything that would jeopardize their relationship because, despite her attraction and growing romantic feelings toward him, he was Jennie's father first and foremost. Now Jennie had a father, and Erin remembered how she had treasured hers for the short time he had been in her life, Erin wasn't going to be responsible for taking that away from her daughter.

Erin awoke to the sun streaming in through the windows and the smell of the ocean in the air. She glanced at the clock and blinked. When had been the last time she had slept past eight? She immediately glanced at the crib, only to find it empty. Panic sparked inside her as she scrambled to find Jennie.

She didn't have to look far. Jennie was sitting in the center of the living room floor amid the toys Erin had packed for her, Ryan by her side. She exhaled, not even considering concealing the fear she had been feeling.

Ryan looked up at her and realized her alarm. "I'm sorry, I heard her playing in her crib and thought I would get her so that you could sleep. I didn't mean to scare you."

She was afraid and upset, but one look at Jennie and she knew she couldn't share any of those feelings. The little girl was beaming with happiness and she didn't want to upset her.

"It's okay. I guess I'm just not used to having help." She wanted to take back the words the minute she'd said them, realizing that the reason she didn't have help had been her own choice. She looked at Ryan and respected him even more for letting her comment pass.

"What are your plans for the day?" he asked.

"Not much," she confessed. "I really thought we would just go down to the beach and play in the sand and then maybe check out the farmers' market this afternoon."

"Sounds great."

She walked to the kitchen to make a cup of coffee and noticed the pot was already brewed.

"I remembered," Ryan commented, from the living room.

She poured herself a cup and took a sip of the hot, dark, full-bodied roast. It wasn't until that moment that she realized what she was wearing. In her haste to find Jennie she hadn't had time to pull on her robe so instead she was standing in the kitchen in nothing but an oversize T-shirt, her legs bare. She looked up and saw Ryan watching her and she self-consciously slipped behind the kitchen island. The kiss from last night was still very much on her mind.

He smiled at her not-so-subtle move and she heard the faint laugh coming from his lips.

"It's okay. It's nothing I haven't seen before."

She blushed and then blushed harder, remembering in just what state he had seen her.

"On your balcony in Scotland. The first night we met you weren't very shy about your choice in pajamas then, either." His explanation should have been comforting, except that she realized he had offered it because of the alternative he had guessed she was recollecting.

"If you are okay with her, I'll go get dressed."

"We're fine. Take your time."

She showered and dressed quickly, not used to having the extra time. She had packed before she'd known Ryan was coming and looked down at the meager options before her. She didn't spend too much time thinking about what was making her want to look her best. In the end she didn't have much choice, so she settled on what she had planned she would wear when she had thought it was just going to be her and Jennie, her emerald-green bikini with its matching cover-up. She blew her hair dry and then looked in the mirror, forgoing any makeup in favor of sunscreen alone.

Jennie and Ryan were still playing when she finished. She picked out Jennie's protective sun shirt and shorts and dressed her, being careful to apply sunblock to all her exposed skin.

"Ready?" Ryan asked.

"Yes."

It was nice having the extra hands as they made their way down to the beach. Between beach chairs, a blanket, toys, snacks and Jennie herself, Erin would have had her hands full. They picked a spot on the sand and immediately Jennie dumped a bucket of sand in the center of the blanket.

"Nice." Ryan laughed before picking up the little girl and swinging her round. Her shrieks of delight filled the air.

The three of them played for the next two hours and Erin couldn't remember when she had been this relaxed or seen Jennie as happy. The look on her face when Ryan dipped her feet into the ocean for the first time was amazing. They ate a picnic lunch and then headed to the market.

A different time, a different place, but as the day went on Erin realized that Ryan had been right. This was what they needed. A chance, away from everyone else and their past, to get to know each other again. She also realized what she had been missing. What it would be like to raise Jennie with two parents, a partner for all the joys and challenges that lay ahead.

They made a light salad for supper and partici-pated in the nightly bath ritual together. "It's a wonder there's any sand still on the beach!" Ryan commented, as the water drained and the entire bottom of the tub was full of sand.

Erin laughed but her attention was on Jennie. It had been a great day, a busy day, and Jennie had barely napped and showed no signs of willingness to sleep any time soon. She had a bad feeling about where this was headed. Sure enough, the simple act of putting her in her pajamas was the last straw and Jennie began to cry. The cry progressed to earsplitting wails as Erin struggled in vain to soothe her.

It was impossible as the little girl rubbed her head back and forth into Erin's neck and shoulder, large, wet tears streaming down her face.

"What's wrong with her?" Ryan asked, Jennie's complete meltdown a new experience for him, as well.

"She's overtired," Erin answered very quietly, begging Jennie to stop.

The more Jennie cried the more distressed they both became. Erin walked up and down the short hallway, whispering reassurances to her daughter, but nothing worked. It wasn't Jennie's first meltdown and normally Erin would have been more relaxed and let it run its course, but not in front of Ryan. She needed to prove she was a good mother and what kind of mother couldn't soothe her little girl?

More tears, only this time Erin's as Jennie's wailing continued. She put her down, but she only cried harder, her arms reaching up for her mother.

"Here, let me take her." Ryan's words broke through the cries.

She wanted to say no, that she could do it, but she couldn't and she wasn't in a state to argue that she had control of the situation. She passed Jennie to him and her wails increased for a minute before there was silence, a few more cries, and more silence. Erin wiped away her own tears and saw Ryan gently rubbing Jennie's back, her little face pressed against his chest as he walked the halls with her.

A few minutes later she was out cold, her body limp in Ryan's arms. Erin walked with him to their bedroom, watching as he laid her in the crib and covered her. "Good night, my sweetheart." She bent down to kiss the still-wet cheek softly.

They carefully closed the door and retreated, the house now eerily quiet in the aftermath of the meltdown. She took a seat on the couch, moving one of the orange pillows to hold it protectively in front of her.

"I'm sorry," she said, her nerves totally shot both from Jennie's crying and her inability to soothe her in front of Ryan. What must he be thinking of her mothering skills?

"Why are you sorry?" He sat beside her on the couch.

"I couldn't comfort her."

"That's okay."

"No, it's not. I'm her mother, I'm supposed to be able to comfort her."

"Erin—" he started, but she interrupted him.

"I don't want you to think I'm a bad mother." She moved her hand to her mouth the moment the words escaped. It was another example of her inability to keep her thoughts to herself in front of him.

"No one is perfect all the time, not you, not Jennie."

"I'm so afraid you are going to take her away from me." Now that she had started there was no stopping her and her own tears resurfaced.

He reached forward, taking away the pillow she held between them, turning his whole body toward her. He looked more confused than ever. "Why would I take her away?"

"Because you don't think I'm a good person, because maybe you won't think I'm a good enough mother. I wanted this weekend to go well, to prove to you I was a good mother to our daughter."

"That's the first time you've ever called her our daughter." Ryan's voice was soft.

She had, and there was no going back. Just spending the day with Ryan as a family, she'd realized that Jennie wasn't just hers, she was theirs, together. She also no longer just wanted Jennie as her family, she wanted it to include Ryan.

"She has your eyes."

"I know," he admitted.

She looked at him, feeling more vulnerable than she had when they'd first met on that hillside in Scotland. "What are we going to do?"

"What do you want?"

"I want to do what's best for Jennie."

"And what about you?"

"I'm not important."

"To me you are."

His words could not have been more perfect. As her feelings for Ryan had resurfaced one of her fears had been that she would be the consolation prize that came with his daughter. She needed him to tell her otherwise, to prove to her otherwise.

"Kiss me," she said quietly.

"I can't." She looked up at him and she started to pull away but he grabbed both her hands, keeping her facing him.

"I can't just kiss you. I want you too badly just to kiss you."

She understood everything he was saying so instead she leaned in and kissed him. Everything about the taste of his lips, the feel of his skin and the smell of him was familiar, so much so that it instantaneously sparked a fire inside her. The first time they had been together she'd thought she had wanted him, but she had been wrong then, because nothing compared to the desperate need she felt now.

He broke away and lifted her from the couch and into his arms. She didn't ask where they were headed as Ryan carried her to the master bedroom. He pulled off his shirt before coming down on her on the bed, his lips finding hers and his tongue exploring and tasting her. She wove her hands into his short hair, holding him to her. She never wanted the kiss to end but at the same time she wanted more.

She felt him rise slightly from her, his arm a study in flexed muscular perfection. The casual beach shorts and jersey halter top she had changed into after the beach gave him no bother as he quickly stripped her naked and then did the same with his own clothes. The bedroom window was open and she could smell and feel the night's ocean air against her skin. Between the slight coolness of the air and her anticipation she felt as if her whole body was trembling in want of him, every hair in every pore poised for his next move.

He didn't leave her waiting for long and soon there was nothing cool about the feel of his completely naked hard muscular body hotly pressed against her. He paused, looking into her eyes, and she felt she could drown in the depths of the blue. He wanted her, too. She arched her back, pressing herself even more against him, feeling every inch of him and his want for her.

His hand swept up her side and over her tattoo before his hand cupped her breast, his thumb stroking her nipple. She didn't have to wait long before he caressed the swollen tip with his mouth.

The more he touched her the more she wanted him and she could feel her body readying for him as she unconsciously spread herself more and more open for him.

"You're even more beautiful than I remembered," he murmured, his breath hot against her breast.

"I need you." And truer words were never spoken. She needed him to make love to her, she needed him to be a father to their daughter and she needed him to love her because she knew she was in love with him.

He broke away from her, reaching into his shaving kit to bring out a small foil wrapper. She didn't miss the look of irony on his face as he sheathed himself. He kneeled between her legs, his hand stroking upward from her ankle to the top of her thigh. Without thinking, she wrapped both legs around him moments before he pushed into her.

It had been over two years since she'd had this feeling. The last time she had been touched so intimately had been with Ryan and she had never wanted any other man. She found herself matching his every movement. Their rocking back and forth echoed the waves of the ocean heard through the open window. As she reached ever nearer to her climax she wanted even more from him and she moved her hands from their strong hold on his back to touch his hands. He immediately took hold, lacing his fingers through hers. Now with each movement she felt truly complete. As Ryan pushed deeper each movement moved her closer to the edge, his virile length hitting hard against her core, her breasts pressed hard against his chest, her hands in his being pressed into the mattress as each mini-peak was met with the sound of the waves crashing on the beach.

Then she could hold on no longer. She moved both her legs behind his back, locking her ankles, and with one final stroke she pushed herself hard against him as his mouth came down on hers, stifling both their cries of ecstasy.

They stayed like that for a long time before he finally pulled away from her, only briefly to discard the condom, before he pulled her against him and the sheet over both of them, their sweat-covered bodies cooling quickly in the night air.

"I think that is the only thing that hasn't changed between us," Ryan murmured against the back of her neck.

"Mmm…" she moaned, still in a satiated fog.

"The last time we were together was the most passionate night I had ever had, until now."

He had more of her attention now, as she thought back to the revelation she'd had right before they'd made love. She loved Ryan. She was in love with Ryan and she desperately needed him to love her, too. She waited, but her hopes of hearing those words were dashed as she recognized the gentle repetition of his breath signaling he was asleep.

* * *

The next few days were almost perfect. They spent their days as a family, going to the beach, exploring the public gardens, and after Jennie went to bed their nights exploring each other. Neither Ryan nor Erin did anything to ruin the budding relationship between them. They never spoke of their past, his sister, and Ryan didn't ask her any more questions about Jennie's possible paternity.

They celebrated the Fourth of July sitting together on the beachfront patio, watching the fireworks with Jennie, who barely managed to keep her eyes open in Ryan's arms.

The next day it was time to return to reality and Erin felt uneasiness build. They had been perfect together in Scotland. Perfect together again here in the Hamptons as a family. But what would happen when they had to face the realities of their lives together in Boston? What would happen when the paternity test definitively proved Ryan to be Jennie's father? Would he want to be a family? Could she continue in their relationship just waiting and hoping he fell in love with her?

Eventually they would also have to face their past. She knew he loved his sister and she had no idea how Sabrina would take the news of Erin's involvement in her brother's life. She had wanted to explain to him the truth about her past with Sabrina and Kevin, but was afraid to ruin the ideal of their family time together by bringing up such an unsavory subject. Was their relationship strong enough to overcome his family's disapproval, and what would happen if it wasn't?

CHAPTER TWELVE

THREE WEEKS AFTER their return Ryan felt sure about what he needed to do. Without discussion he had practically been living with Erin and Jennie and he had never been happier with his life. Every day he felt even closer to Erin and Jennie. He had done the bloodwork more to confirm paternity. He wanted the world to know that Jennie was his daughter.

The heat from the late July afternoon hit him as he opened his car door and walked along the stone path toward Sabrina's front door. Her house was a suburban family home in Cambridge only a few blocks from their parents' and perfect for her growing family. The neighborhood was filled with children running and playing outside and he thought about how much he wanted that for Jennie.

Ryan rang the doorbell and waited for an answer.

Sabrina answered the door and the similarity between Sabrina and Jennie struck him instantly. All of his features he saw in Jennie he also saw in Sabrina. She was dressed casually in capri pants, a loose-fitting T-shirt and with a beaded necklace his nephew, Simon, was struggling to grab and put in his mouth. "Well, this is a surprise!" Sabrina exclaimed, as she reached out and gave him a one-armed hug. "What's the occasion?"

"Can't I just stop by and see my little sister and nephew?" he asked her casually, knowing there was much more behind his visit, and that Sabrina knew that, too.

"You can, but you don't," she teased.

She was right so he didn't disagree. "Can I come in?"

"Of course." She walked with him to the heart of her home, the kitchen, and he took a seat at one of the barstools that lined her granite-covered island. "So are you going to tell me what is wrong?"

"How do you know something is wrong?"

"Because my very important doctor big brother does not just drop by on a weekday in the middle of the afternoon."

"I need to talk to you about something and I'm not sure you are going to like what I have to say."

"Then just say it. I'm not as fragile as you think I am, Ryan."

He was taken aback at her comment and took a moment to truly look at her. She was right. She didn't look fragile. She actually looked nothing like his memory of the depressed, broken woman she had been. Instead, she looked relaxed and at peace and he began to wonder if he had been making decisions to protect her when she didn't need his protection after all.

"I need to talk to you about Erin Dufour." He watched her carefully and she didn't appear anything but surprised.

"That wasn't what I was expecting to hear." She

placed Simon in his baby swing and came around to sit on the barstool opposite him.

"I met her at Boston General. She goes by her maiden name, Madden, now."

"I know," she replied simply.

"You know?" He couldn't hide his shock.

"I met her a few months ago when I had Simon. She didn't recognize me with all the swelling from my pregnancy and my new last name but I recognized her."

"You never said anything." He still couldn't believe what he was hearing.

"You never asked. Why are we talking about Erin?"

"I had a brief relationship with her two years ago before I knew who she was." He looked at his sister carefully, trying to read her response. "When I realized she was Kevin's ex-wife I broke it off."

"Why would you do that?" Sabrina appeared genuinely confused and he felt frustrated at having to explain his motivation.

"Because of what she did to you. The pain she caused you."

"She saved my life. She saved Simon's life."

"What?" This conversation was reaching surreal proportions and his sister's revelations were doing nothing to ease the turmoil inside him.

"When I was pregnant with Simon and started feeling unwell she was the only person who really took me seriously when I said something was wrong. When the others tried to send me home she refused and she ordered the testing that diagnosed my preeclampsia."

"So you forgave her because she took care of you in your pregnancy?"

"There was nothing to forgive."

"What about her affair with Kevin?" He hated having to remind Sabrina of it, hated having to remind himself of Erin's marriage.

"It saved me from a serious mistake. When Kevin first broke off our relationship I was devastated. I wasn't ready to face the fact that the man I loved, whom I had built all my dreams around, had really cheated on me with another woman, so instead I placed all the blame on Erin. It wasn't until after she had married Kevin that I had the courage to confront her. She had no idea who I was, never mind that she had been the other woman. That was when I realized that that man I spent the past four years with had been a liar and a cheat. I felt used, and foolish, and ashamed, and those feelings were the catalyst for my depression."

He wanted to talk more about Erin, but this was the most Sabrina had ever shared with him about her depression and he couldn't dismiss her admission.

"I thought you still blamed Erin. I didn't realize you felt differently. Why didn't you say something back then? I still blame myself for not being there to help you."

"You were away saving the world and I didn't want to bother you with my problems. My feelings didn't seem as important as the wars that you were helping to fight and the lives you were saving."

"I wish you had." For all of their sakes, how he wished he had known.

"Is that why we are talking about Erin?"

"I've been fighting my feelings for her for the past two years, thinking I was betraying you."

"Oh, Ryan." Sabrina was gently shaking her head from side to side.

"She has a daughter, Jennie. She's a year and a half and I'm sure she's mine."

"Oh, my God! When did you find out about her? Why didn't Erin tell you about her?"

"Because before she had Jennie the last time we saw each other I accused her of being an immoral other woman who seduces and traps other women's men." Even to his own ears it sounded horrible and Erin's reaction in not telling him when she had learned of the pregnancy became more clear to him.

"You didn't!"

"Not in those exact words, but the point was made."

"I understand, then," Sabrina commented.

"You agree with her keeping Jennie a secret from me?" Now it was his turn to feel betrayed.

"I understand how on the heels of her divorce from a man who spent their entire relationship violating her trust, she wasn't keen to give you the benefit of the doubt. So what are you going to do?"

"I don't know. I still don't understand why she never told me the truth about her and Kevin."

"Maybe because it's humiliating and embarrassing to admit that you were in love with a man who not only didn't love you but also had no respect for you as a woman?"

He let Sabrina's words sink through him, but she didn't stop there. "Or maybe because it's even worse after going through that to put your trust in a new man, only to find out he thinks the worst of you, too."

"Okay, I get the point." He felt totally unworthy of having Erin in his life.

"So what are you going to do?"

"Tell her I love her and ask her to marry me." Something he regretted not doing sooner. If anything, his conversation with Sabrina had highlighted how lucky he was to still have Erin in his life. Jennie really was a miracle. If it hadn't been for her they wouldn't have found their way back to one another.

"Oh, Ry, you haven't even told her you love her yet?"

"No." He didn't need Sabrina to highlight how foolish he had been.

"Watch Simon. I'll be right back."

He looked over at his nephew and couldn't help but think of everything he had missed with Jennie. Over the past weeks Erin had shared with him her baby albums and videos but it hadn't been the same. Erin hadn't cheated him—he had cheated himself out of Jennie's first year of life.

"Here." She handed him a square velvet box.

"What's this?"

"It's Grandma's engagement ring. Mom gave up hope years ago that you would ever settle down and marry so she gave it to me. I think Erin should have it."

He opened the box to discover the platinum ring that was handcrafted with intricate trellis-like embellishments that led to a central circular diamond that was surrounded by a circle of smaller diamonds. "It's perfect. Are you sure?"

"Yes. I can't think of a woman I would want more as a sister and you need to secure her place in our family as soon as possible. Simon wants to meet his cousin and I want to meet my niece!"

"Thank you, for everything." He stood and hugged his sister, more grateful than she would ever know.

He left Sabrina's finally feeling as if he had the answers. Even after their weekend in the Hamptons he hadn't been able to put together who Erin was completely. He didn't understand how the woman he knew could ever have been the other woman, but now everything made sense. His only regret was not recognizing sooner that Erin could never deliberately hurt anyone. Erin was the same woman he'd fallen for in Scotland, the woman he'd fallen in love with in the Hamptons and the mother of his child. If he was lucky, she would agree to be his wife.

He looked at the ring box and wondered how he was going to make it through the weekend. Erin and Jennie had gone away for her friend Kate's wedding and it would be another four days before he could tell her he loved her.

Long weekends were notorious for the emergency department. Alcohol and an above-average sense of fearlessness typically led to at least a 20 percent increase in volume. Ryan was happy to be busy. His evening shift was taking his mind off waiting for Erin and Jennie to return home.

The emergency medical services dispatch radio sounded. They were ten minutes away with a motor vehicle accident trauma.

"Activate the trauma team," he told the unit clerk, and she keyed in the single code that paged the eight-person team to the trauma bay.

He arrived at the trauma bay and looked around to

make sure all the required equipment was there before donning a protective gown and goggles. Three nurses, a respiratory therapist and one of the emergency medicine residents gathered with him. One of the orthopedic and general surgery residents soon followed.

He could hear the sirens as they approached and could tell the ambulance was racing toward them. It arrived less than a minute later, driving through the bay and coming to an abrupt stop outside the doors. He went through the automatic glass doors and helped the team unload the stretcher, getting a good look at the patient.

He recognized the paramedic, who began to give report. "Restrained middle-aged male involved in a frontal collision. Lost consciousness at the scene and was intubated for airway protection. Obvious open femur fracture."

Ryan glanced down to the man's thigh and saw the protruding bone.

The team moved quickly into the trauma room, and each person specialized in their particular role began their assessment. He gave them three minutes before he intervened. "What do you want to do?" he asked his resident.

"Stabilize, transfuse for blood loss and get full-body imaging to ensure that we are not being distracted by the femur and missing something worse."

"I agree."

He stood in the doorway for the next thirty minutes, being unobtrusive but also making sure the patient was receiving optimal care.

"Why haven't you booked the femur for the operating room?" he heard a voice yell down the hall. It was a voice he had no desire to hear. He looked down the hall to see Kevin Dufour yelling at the trauma team orthopedic resident and now making his way toward them.

"I want this patient in the operating room now," he yelled at the remaining residents and nursing staff. The team paused and looked at Ryan.

"Stick with the plan. Dr. Dufour, can I speak to you for a moment?"

"I want that patient in the operating room now," Kevin seethed.

Ryan did his best to remain calm, which was the opposite of what he really wanted to do. "The patient is still to be stabilized and still needs to have his imaging survey completed to ensure there are no more serious injuries before you spend three hours fixing his femur."

"His femur is his most serious injury, isn't that obvious?"

"No, it's not, which is why we have ordered a CT of his head, chest, abdomen and pelvis."

"I'm in charge here, and I want him transferred to the operating room."

"No, you are not. This man is a patient of the emergency department and under my care and will remain so until I choose otherwise."

"We'll see about that."

Ryan paid no attention to Dufour's exit and returned to his patient.

Twenty minutes later he received verbal report from the radiologist. The victim had an extradural hemorrhage in his brain, requiring immediate evacuation in order to help prevent permanent neurological injury. He called the neurosurgeon on call and made arrangements for transfer.

"Dr. Callum," the unit clerk called to him. "Dr. Williamson is on the phone."

"Sir," he answered, his respect for his superiors bred from his military training.

"Ryan, I'd like to see you in my office. Is there another physician who can watch your patients?"

"Yes, sir, but I would prefer not to leave right now. We are getting slammed and have already had two major traumas this evening."

"Are there any major traumas not managed at present?"

"No."

"Then I'll see you in my office now. This won't take long and you will still be in the building."

Ryan didn't have time to respond before the other man hung up. He walked up the three flights to the administrative offices, knowing what he would find. Dr. Williamson's receptionist showed him into the office, where Kevin was sitting, looking overly smug.

"You brought this on yourself." He snickered as Ryan took the place beside him.

Ryan balled his hand into a fist and then forced himself to relax. A few minutes later Dr. Williamson entered, looking unimpressed at both men.

"Gentlemen, I can't tell you how much it does not impress me to have to come in on a long weekend to deal with this complaint.

"Dr. Callum, Dr. Dufour has filed a complaint alleging you endangered a patient by refusing to transfer care following a motor vehicle trauma." He paused and looked directly at Kevin. "However, I am well aware that you have more trauma experience and are a better physician than Dr. Dufour will ever be so I thought it would be best to remind him of that in your presence. I trust you two can figure things out from here. Good evening."

Ryan tried hard not to smile as Dr. Williamson left the room.

"You may think you won but that had nothing to do with you. I should have known he wouldn't have been able to be professional."

"Because?" Ryan was waiting, waiting for him to say something about Erin.

"Because he thinks I fathered and abandoned his precious little bastard grandchild. Well, the joke is on him. His perfect little stepdaughter got herself knocked up again, but this time it had nothing to do with me."

"How do you know?"

"Because I had a vasectomy right after the first time she played that card to make sure it never happened again."

"So you are the reason Erin thought she was infertile?" He looked at Kevin and wondered if he had any idea how much pain he had caused the two most important women in Ryan's life, and realized he didn't care. Seconds later Kevin was on the floor, holding his rapidly swelling face with a look of sheer confusion.

Ryan looked over to the door that had just opened and saw Dr. Williamson standing in the entry. "I forgot my briefcase. You should have that looked at, Kevin." And he walked across the room, retrieved the forgotten briefcase and walked out with no further words spoken.

CHAPTER THIRTEEN

ERIN WALKED THROUGH the hospital's front entrance, eager to find Ryan. She knew that he had gotten the same call she had last night, confirming he was Jennie's father. Even though she'd known what the test was going to show she still felt hopeful that it would prove to be the turning point between them.

Her pager went off and she recognized the number of the maternal fetal medicine unit. She had continued to follow Chloe in her pregnancy and had arranged an urgent ultrasound for her that morning. If it was normal, they wouldn't be calling.

"This is Dr. Madden," she announced as her call was picked up.

"Please hold for Dr. Young."

Dr. Young was the perinatologist who was following Chloe in conjunction with Erin. "Erin, I just finished scanning Chloe Darcy. She's just past twenty-six weeks in her pregnancy but the baby has started showing signs of acute heart failure. There is also reverse flow in the umbilical cord. I think you need to get her delivered."

"Thank you. I'm in the building and will be right there."

Erin felt a panic she hadn't felt since her own pregnancy. She couldn't let anything happen to Chloe's baby. Not when she had already gone through so much. She knew that the finding in the umbilical cord meant that a stillbirth could happen at any moment and she had to act quickly.

She ran to the ultrasound unit and directly to Chloe's room. She could tell from the panic on Chloe's face that she had already been told the devastating news. She had to stay professional and do her job. "Chloe, when did you last have anything to eat or drink?"

Chloe knew the reason Erin was asking. She needed another surgery, and urgently. "Last evening," she answered. "The baby's in heart failure," Chloe declared, looking at Erin, obviously hoping she would say something different.

"Yes," Erin confirmed. "I'm sorry, Chloe, but we need to get you delivered."

"I'm not ready. The baby's not ready. I'm only twenty-six and a half weeks.'

"There's no other option, Chloe. The heart failure and the reverse blood flow in the umbilical cord shows that the baby is at high risk for stillbirth at any moment. Dr. Young is reviewing the images and she is on phone to the neonatal intensive care unit now, letting them know what to expect with the baby." She didn't want to scare Chloe any more than she was already scared but she needed her absolute cooperation and time was of the essence.

"Erin, what's going to happen?"

For the first time since entering the room Erin slowed herself and sat down next to Chloe.

"Right now the baby weighs about two and a half pounds, but some of that is swelling from the extra fluid that has built up in the baby's tissues. Following birth, the baby will be intubated for respiratory support and also given some medication down a tube and into its lungs to help the lungs mature and make breathing easier. We can use the umbilical cord to establish intravenous and arterial access so that we can both monitor the baby and provide medication and nutrition in a more direct fashion. There is at least an eighty percent chance of survival and a fifty percent chance of no major complications."

"I haven't exactly been doing great in the luck department this year, Erin."

"Chloe, we need to focus on the positive. We diagnosed the baby before anything really horrible happened and we are going to get you delivered right away."

"A Caesarean section?" Chloe asked.

"Yes. It's the fastest way, and the baby is still breech right now, making a vaginal delivery a poor option."

"Okay," Chloe agreed, and Erin felt a little relief, knowing Chloe was accepting of the plan.

"They are preparing the obstetrics operating room across from the nursery. We need to walk to the unit now and get you admitted so we can deliver this baby as soon as possible."

"Okay."

Erin reached over and grabbed the paper drape, wiping the jelly from Chloe's still-exposed abdomen. She helped her sit up and then walked with her as

quickly but as calmly as possible toward the obstet-
rical unit.

"Chloe, when you get on the unit it is going to be
chaotic. Everyone is going to be coming at you, asking you questions, getting you changed, poking and
prodding you to get you ready. I have to make a call
and get changed into my scrubs. Just remember that
you and this baby are going to be okay. Do you have
any questions about the plan or the Caesarean?"

"No."

"Chloe, do you want me to call Tate?" Over the
previous weeks Chloe had confided in Erin about her
relationship with Tate. Erin would never normally interfere in a patient's personal life, but Chloe was her
friend and she knew that she would regret not having
the father of her baby at her delivery. Erin had.

"Yes."

Once they stepped onto the unit the predicted chaos
ensued. Erin squeezed Chloe's hand hard before letting go. She went to change and then quickly made
phone calls to Tate and then the blood bank. Chloe's
pregnancy had been complicated by blood antibodies
she had created after she had received emergency un-
matched blood products with her ectopic pregnancy.
Now it was even harder to find blood to transfuse her
with if she needed it.

She felt her whole body shaking as she watched
Chloe being sat up for her spinal anesthetic. The last
time she had operated on her she hadn't had time to
think about the fact that her friend's life had been in
her hands. At this moment she thought she preferred
that. She watched as they laid her down. It was time.

She waited until Chloe's abdomen had been painted

with antiseptic and then covered her with surgical drapes. The room continued to fill as the neonatal intensive care team arrived. She found herself looking at the door, praying Tate would get here in time. She couldn't wait for him. Then he arrived and took the spot next to Chloe, where he belonged.

"Chloe, can you feel anything?" Erin asked, as she pinched her stomach hard with a pair of surgical forceps.

"No," Chloe answered.

"Patient is Chloe Darcy. She is having an emergency Caesarean section. She has no allergies. There are two units of blood in the room, and she received a gram of cefazolin at nine thirty-two. Does anyone have any concerns?" the circulating nurse asked, as she completed the presurgical safety pause.

"No," Erin answered, when in her head she had a thousand concerns. Would Chloe's baby be okay? What would she do if Chloe hemorrhaged again?

"You can proceed," the anesthetist confirmed.

She held her hand out for the scalpel and followed the line she had made months earlier. The room quieted and she focused on the technical aspect of her job and not her feelings for Chloe. Within two minutes she had made the uterine incision.

"Uterine incision," the scrub nurse notified the neonatal team.

"Chloe, you are going to feel some pressure on your abdomen as we help get the baby out. Tate, if you want to stand up you can watch your baby being born. The baby is breech, so you are going to see legs and bum first," Erin counseled both parents.

She cut the last layer of the thick muscle as gently as possible so as not to cut the baby. Clear fluid drained into the drapes and onto the floor. Two little feet protruded immediately and pushed against her hand and she found herself smiling, reassured by the little one's spirit. She went through breech maneuvers, being as gentle as possible with the delicate newborn. Once the baby was out she showed Tate that they had a son as the little one let out a small cry that was the best sound Erin could have asked for. She looked briefly at Tate, his eyes glassy as he looked down at Chloe, and Erin smiled, honored to be included in their moment. She handed the baby to her assistant, who took the baby over to the resuscitation team before she continued with her job.

Her sense of reassurance didn't stay with her long as Chloe started to bleed heavily from the uterine incision, the uterus too soft to close off all the blood vessels that had fed it while Chloe had been pregnant.

"Tate, I think I'm going to be sick," Erin heard Chloe mumble.

Erin looked at the blood-pressure monitor and saw that Chloe's pressure had dropped.

"Open and hang the blood," Erin ordered, as she tried to clamp the corners of the incision while massaging the uterus, begging it silently to firm up.

Her actions were in vain as the blood kept coming. She looked at the anesthetist and he understood that they were in trouble with no words spoken.

"We need another four units of packed cells and two of fresh frozen plasma crossed and in the room. Open the postpartum hemorrhage tray and have a hysterectomy tray standing by, please," Erin commanded.

"It's going to take at least an hour to cross her for more blood," the anesthetist responded.

"Then let's get on it," Erin responded, frustrated but knowing it was the truth.

"I'm going to put her out," the anesthetist declared.

"Agreed."

Erin injected the uterus directly with medication, with no effect. She was running out of options. It had been thirty minutes since the baby had been born and they were only getting further behind.

She looked at the hysterectomy tray. She had asked for it to be opened, thinking that if she opened it she would never have to use it. Now it was looking more and more likely that she would have to take out her friend's uterus to save her life. The fragile little two-pound boy that Chloe had just delivered would be her only child and he might not even survive.

She resolved to try one more option then she was going to have to move on, no matter how much she disliked the other option.

"Can I get the B-lynch, please?" She saw the nurse's brows rise beneath her mask as she put the hysterectomy clamp back on the table and instead handed her the elongated suture.

With care Erin sutured a tension suture through and around the uterus until it was physically forced to contract. She watched for two minutes and saw the bleeding was better. She closed the uterine incision and watched again. It was now dry.

"Dry?" she asked her resident, who looked more shocked than she did.

"Dry."

The anesthetist stood up and looked, too, his nod a subtle agreement with her assessment.

She watched and waited for another ten minutes, but there were no signs of further bleeding so she began to close the incision and in twenty minutes Chloe was being wheeled into Recovery. The baby was in serious but stable condition in the neonatal intensive care unit but was already showing good signs.

For the first time since she had been paged, other than the brief moment at delivery, Erin thought of Ryan and Jennie. She hadn't heard from him since he had gotten the results and that both surprised and bothered her. He had already accepted that Jennie was his daughter so she didn't understand why he was holding back now. She glanced at the clock—it was two in the afternoon. She dialed his cell phone and waited—no answer. She tried his pager, only to get the same response. She wanted to find him but she couldn't, not for the next couple of hours until she was sure Chloe was stable.

Her pager went off an hour later and she didn't recognize the number. Hoping it was Ryan, she dialed.

"Dr. Madden, this is Dr. Williamson's assistant, Beverly. Dr. Williamson was hoping you could stop by his office this afternoon."

It was an unusual request. She and Stephen had never interacted personally at work, and he certainly had never had Beverly page her while she was working. Was she in trouble professionally? She checked back in with Chloe before heading to the administrative offices.

"You can go right in, dear," Beverly directed.

Erin still stopped to knock at the door before letting

herself in. Stephen was behind his desk, going through a pile of paperwork on his desk. "Take a seat, Erin."

"Okay." She did as she was told.

"I thought you would want to be the first to know Kevin handed in his resignation this morning."

Of all the things she had prepared herself to hear, that was not one of them.

"Why?" she asked, utterly surprised. Kevin had spent months, years, trying to force her out of Boston General. It made no sense that he would leave now.

"I believe it may have something to do with the black eye he received last night and a lack of support from hospital administration."

"What happened?" Erin was still in shock, and was that a twinkle in Stephen's eyes?

"Officially he walked into a door. Unofficially Ryan Callum from the emergency department gave him what he deserved."

"Ryan hit him?"

"No, he walked into a door. But I have to say I am very fond of Dr. Callum. I hope we will be seeing more of him."

She didn't know how, but Stephen knew about their involvement and she was surprised at how much his approval meant to her.

"Thanks for letting me know." She smiled and excused herself from their meeting.

Erin unlocked the front door of her apartment, anxious to see Jennie. Seeing Chloe's son today had only made her feel more grateful for her healthy child. She walked directly to the living room but Jennie wasn't there. Instead, the entire space was filled with long-stemmed red roses and Ryan. He was dressed in a gray pinstripe suit with a white shirt and matte red tie that matched the single rose he wore on his lapel.

She inhaled sharply, only to have her senses overtaken by the scent of the fresh-cut flowers.

"What is all this?" she asked in confusion.

"What you deserve. I know you like to focus on the meanings of things, your tattoo, Jennie's name, so I thought I would tell you what I need to tell you in every way I possibly could."

"With roses?" she asked hesitantly, her hopes growing by the second.

"With red roses."

"Ryan, do you know what red roses mean?" Oh, how she needed him to say it.

"They mean passionate love, which is how I feel about you."

It wasn't enough that he felt passionate toward her; she knew that from their lovemaking. She needed to know he loved her. "You love me?"

"Very much so, and I'm desperately hoping you love me, too."

"I do," she confessed, her words giving her a sense of freedom.

"Ah, that part I was hoping we would save for later, but if you insist." He reached into his pocket and pulled out the most stunning ring she had ever seen. "Erin Madden, would you do me the great honor of becoming my wife?"

"Yes." And she watched in absolute awe as he slipped the ring on her finger.

"You aren't just doing this because Jennie is your daughter and you want us to be a family?"

"I'm doing this because I love you and there is no other woman in the world I would want to be the mother of my children."

"We just have Jennie." She hoped that would be enough. She remembered the look on Tate's face when he'd seen his son.

"I need to tell you something and I hope it will give you more joy than heartache."

"Okay," she answered, wondering what else there could possibly be.

"I had a conversation with Kevin yesterday."

"A conversation?" she asked, with one eyebrow raised.

"It started as a conversation. He told me he had a vasectomy right after you two were married—that was why you couldn't have more children after your miscarriage."

She felt anger and joy at the same time. Anger for everything Kevin had put her through and joy at the possibilities that had just opened up for her. "We can have more children?" she asked him, as though she didn't know the answer to her own question.

"Yes, we can."

EPILOGUE

"Push—one, two, three, four, five, six, seven, eight, nine and ten. Take a breath."

She exhaled, her breath hot against her damp skin.

She felt the cool cloth being pressed against her forehead and the plastic of the straw against her lips. She took a quick sip of water, trying her best to relax every muscle in her body and not think about what was coming next.

"Okay," Erin managed, and she took the offered hand and squeezed it hard. An incredible pressure overwhelmed her as she tried to focus her efforts.

"You're doing great," Ryan murmured quietly.

As the contraction passed she looked around the room, knowing that any minute her life was going to change. The lights of the delivery room were low and aside from Dr. Thomas and the delivery nurse it was just her and Ryan.

She pushed again, and again with the next contraction. "I can't," she cried out, completely exhausted.

"Yes, you can. You've done it before and you can do it again," Ryan encouraged.

"That was different. Last time I had an epidural."

She tried to argue, but had to stop when another contraction brought on an unbearable urge to push.

"And this time you have me. I know how strong you are and I know you can do this."

She opened her eyes, which had been closed from the pain, and looked at her husband. He was right. Last time she had felt alone despite her mother's presence. Now her life was completely different. Her pregnancy had been a complete time of joy, her fear of losing her baby not a dark cloud lingering over this pregnancy. Each milestone was new again as she got to reexperience it as if it was the first time through Ryan's eyes. She had a husband who loved her and was 100 percent devoted to her, and together they had a happy, healthy four-year-old daughter, who was with her mother in the waiting room, eager to find out if she had a new brother or sister.

"All right," she agreed, as she reached deep inside herself to find strength left she hadn't known she had.

She pushed harder, her focus on meeting their child. And then in an instant her cries were joined by their baby's. She opened her eyes just as she felt their baby being laid on her chest and she reached up to hold the baby against her.

"We have a son," Ryan murmured, bending down to their level. "Thank you for our son. I love you, Erin."

Tears of happiness streamed down her face. It was the moment she had always wanted and finally had.

Two weeks later, their home was filled with laughter and celebration. A baby "sprinkle" Chloe had named it when Erin had tried to dissuade her from hosting a baby shower. But she couldn't disagree with Chloe's argument that she had never had this with her first baby and their family deserved a proper welcome.

"I think he wants his momma," Ryan said, handing her their son. The nine-pound expression of their love snuggled into her arms immediately, recognizing her scent. Already Ian was the spitting image of his father, from his dark hair to the shape of his eyes, there was no doubting whose son he was.

"Did you have trouble picking his name?" Kate asked, her one-year-old daughter, Darcie, bouncing happily on her lap. Darcie, named after Chloe, even had the sense to look like her namesake, the surprising swath of red hair she had been born with sealing her name fate. As neither Kate nor her husband, Matt, had red hair, they had taken it as a divine sign.

"I've delivered enough babies to know what not to pick. Fortunately, Ian did not look like a Dynamite or a Twister so he was lucky there." She laughed.

"Come on," Chloe teased. "Think of the luck he would have had later in life with women with a name like Danger."

"True, it was a tough choice. But we knew we wanted a Scottish name and when we found Ian and learned it had the same meaning as Jennie's name we knew it was perfect. They both mean 'God is gracious.' Ian Madden Callum. My maiden name in honor of my father."

Squeals of delight erupted loudly and all three women turned to look as Jennie ran across the living room, her pants mysteriously gone, with Chloe's three-year-old son, Spencer, chasing her. Spencer, who had been born premature, was still a little on the small side but made up for it completely with his robust personality. He was completely fearless and spent most of his time scaring the life out of Chloe and Tate.

"She does that these days. Most of the time it's funny, except when we're in public," Erin explained, still smiling.

"I still can't believe that it all worked out. If you had asked me five years ago where I would be now, I would never have guessed this," Erin commented.

"I know. It's amazing, isn't it?" Kate agreed.

"It's hard to believe that at one time they all wanted to hit each other," Chloe commented, nodding her head toward the group of men who stood in the kitchen, conversing but also keeping a close eye on the commotion in the connecting family room.

"In Matt's defense he was insanely jealous of Tate." Kate laughed, now able to make light of the complicated path to love she and Matt had taken.

"And Tate didn't make things any easier on him, or Ryan, for that matter," Chloe agreed, knowing her husband and his protective nature.

"But it's all been worth it," Erin agreed, thinking back to the turmoil each of the women had endured on their road to love. "If we hadn't gone through all of that then we wouldn't have all of this."

She looked at Ian, then Ryan, and then at Jennie, who was carefree and happily playing in the family room, and knew she deserved this. They all did.

* * * * *

A DECEMBER
TO REMEMBER

SUE MACKAY

This one's for Daphne Priest and Diane Passau –
two women I've known most of my life and with
whom I shared many experiences as we grew up.

Thanks for the catch-up lunch and
may we share many more.

Hugs, Sue.

CHAPTER ONE

'PHA THAT LUANG,' the jumbo driver said over his shoulder, pointing to a stunning white temple behind high gates with two guards standing to attention outside. On elegantly crafted pillars gold gleamed in the bright sunlight. 'Stupa.'

'Wow, it's beautiful,' Ellie Thompson whispered. She even hadn't noticed they'd driven into the centre of Vientiane, her brain being half–shut down with sleep deprivation. *Wake up and smell the roses. You're in Laos*, she admonished herself. But she was shattered. *Too bad. New start to life, remember?* Probably no roses in Laos. Definitely no ex.

Right. Forget tiredness. Forget the humiliation of everyone from the CEO right down to the laundry junior at Wellington Hospital knowing her husband had left her for her sister. Forget the pain and anger. Start enjoying every day for what it could bring. There'd be no nasty surprises for the next four weeks while in Laos. She could relax.

Holding up her phone, Ellie leaned over the side to click away continuously until the temple was out of sight. Slumping back against the hard seat, she thought longingly of the air-conditioned taxis that had been waiting outside the border crossing at Nong Khai railway station. With the sweat trickling down between her shoulder blades adding to her unkempt appearance, this window-less mode of transport open to the air, dust and insects kind of said she'd had a brain fade when she'd chosen the jumbo over a taxi. But taxis were old hat, jumbos were not. Except right now a shower and bed were looking more and more tempting, and sightseeing a distant second.

Leaning forward, she asked the driver, 'How far?'

'Not long.' He shrugged.

Guess that could mean anything from five minutes to an hour. Shuffling her backside to try to get comfortable, she watched the spectacular sights they passed, nothing like New Zealand at all. Vientiane might be small and compact but there were people everywhere. Locals moved slowly with an air of having all day to accomplish whatever it was they had to do, while jostling tourists were snapping photos of everything from temples to bugs crawling on the pavement as if their lives depended on it.

After a twelve-hour flight from Wellington to Bangkok, followed by a thirteen-hour turned into sixteen-hour train trip to Laos, Ellie's exhaustion overshadowed the excitement only days ago she'd struggled to keep under control. Yep, she'd had a few days after she'd finished at the hospital for good when she'd begun to look forward to her trip instead of constantly looking over her shoulder to see who was talking about her. That excitement was still there; it just needed a kick in the backside to come out of hiding.

This was her first visit to Indochina and her driver was taking her to the amputee centre and hospital where she'd signed on until the second week of December. Ellie pinched herself. This was real. She'd finally taken the first step towards moving beyond the mess that had become her life and recharging the batteries so she could make some decisions about her future. 'Where to from here?' had been the question nagging her relentlessly for months. Laos was only a stopgap. But it was a start. Then there was the six-month stint to come in Auckland. It was the gap of nearly four weeks between jobs that worried her. Those weeks included Christmas and had her stomach twisting in knots. She was not going to her parents' place to play happy families when her sister would be there.

As the jumbo bumped down a road that had lost most of its seal the yawns were rolling out of her. Damn, but the air was thick with heat. Her make-up was barely sticking to her face and where her sunglasses touched her cheeks they slid up and down, no doubt making a right royal mess. So not the look she wanted to present to her new colleagues, but trying to fix the problem with more make-up would only exacerbate her untidy appearance. Nor did she carry an iron in her handbag to tidy up the rumpled look sported by her cotton trousers and sleeveless T-shirt. Today a fashion statement she was not. Hopefully everyone would see past that and accept her for her doctoring skills, if nothing else. That was all that was required of her anyway, besides being all she had to give these days.

Taking that train instead of flying from Bangkok hadn't been her wisest decision but back home it had sounded wonderful when the travel agent showed her the photos—highly enhanced pictures, she now realised. Face it, even riding all the way here on an elephant would've been tempting compared to living in the shadow of her ex and the woman he now lived with. Caitlin. Her sister. Her ex-sister. Her supposedly close and loving sister. Pain lanced her. The really awful thing was she still missed Caitlin, missed their closeness, the talks— Huh, the talks that obviously hadn't mentioned anything about both of them loving the same man. *Her* husband.

Sounding bitter, Ellie. Damn right she was bitter. Freddy had slept with Caitlin—while still married to *her*. She shook her head. The self-pity was back in New Zealand, as was the humiliation from having people knowing what happened. Putting up with everyone's apparent sympathy when most of those so-called concerned friends enjoyed keeping the hospital gossip mill rolling along had been gross.

But no more. Her contract was at an end, and nothing the CEO had said or offered had tempted her in the slightest to stay on. From now on she'd look the world in the eye, and make plans for Ellie Thompson. Taking back her maiden name had only been the first step. She liked her brand-new passport with its first stamps for a journey she was taking alone, in a place no one knew her or her history. It was a sign of things to come.

She patted her stomach. *Down, butterflies, down.*

Then they turned the corner and at the end of the street a muddy river flowed past and she leaned forward again.

'Is that the Mekong?' When the driver didn't answer she raised her voice and enunciated clearly, 'The river? The Mekong?'

He turned to nod and smile his toothless smile. 'Yes. Mekong.'

The mighty Mekong. She'd always wanted to see the

famous river and now it was less than a kilometre away. 'Wow,' she repeated. She knew where she'd be going for her first walk in this delightful place. Another yawn stretched her mouth. That would have to be after she'd slept round the clock.

'I show you.' A sharp turn and they were heading straight for the river. Their stop was abrupt, with Ellie putting her hands out to prevent slamming against the seat in front of her.

'Out, out.' Her new friend smiled. 'See Mekong.'

He was so enthusiastic she couldn't find it in her to say she really wanted to get to her destination. Anyway, wasn't she supposed to be grabbing this adventure with both hands? Climbing down, she went to stand on the edge of the river beside the driver. It looked like running mud, nothing like the clear waters of New Zealand rivers. But it *was* the Mekong. 'It's real. I'm here right by the river my dad used to talk about.' Except he'd seen it in Vietnam. 'Hard to imagine all the countries this water flows through.'

The driver stared at her blankly. Her English obviously beyond his comprehension. Or too fast. She tried again, a lot slower this time, and was rewarded with a glower at the mention of Vietnam.

'Go now.'

Okay, lesson learned. Avoid mentioning the neighbours. After a few quick photos she climbed back into the jumbo, fingers crossed they were nearly at the clinic.

The next thing Ellie knew she was jerking forward and sliding to the edge of her seat.

'Here centre,' her driver told her. He must've braked hard.

She'd fallen asleep with all those amazing sights

going by? Idiot. Looking around, she noted the rutted dirt road they'd stopped on. Beyond was a long, low building made of concrete blocks, painted drab grey. A few trees that she didn't recognise grew in the sparsely grassed front yard. Nothing like home—which was exactly what she wanted, needed.

Out of the jumbo she stretched her back, then rubbed her neck where a sharp ache had set in. No doubt her head had been bobbing up and down like one of those toy dog things some people put in the back window of their cars. Great. Heat pounded at her while dust settled over her feet. What was a bit more grime? It'd wash off easily—as she hoped the past year would now she'd arrived in Laos, a place so far from her previous life it had to be good for her.

'Come.' The driver hoisted her bag and headed towards a wide door at the top of a concrete step, where a group of men and women sat looking as if they'd been there all day and would be there a lot longer. It had to be the main entrance.

She followed him, pausing to nod at the lethargic folk whose soft chatter had stopped as she approached. When she smiled and said, 'Hello,' they all smiled back, making her feel unbelievably good.

Inside it was not a lot cooler, and as she handed the man his fare and a huge tip she was greeted by a kind-looking woman who had to be about twenty years older than her. She came up and gripped Ellie in a tight hug. 'Sandra Winter? Welcome to the amputee centre.'

As Ellie tried to pull out of this lovely welcome that wasn't for her the woman continued, 'We've been looking forward to your arrival all week. The doctor you're replacing had to leave early. Oh, I'm Louise Warner, one of the permanent staff here. I'm the anaesthetist while my husband, Aaron, is a general surgeon. He's gone to the market. You'll meet him later, along with the rest of the staff.'

Ellie smiled, trying to keep her exhaustion at bay for just a little longer. 'I'm not Sandra Winter. I'm—'

'You're not?' Louise looked beyond her. 'That explains the jumbo.' Louise returned her gaze to Ellie, a huge query in her eyes. 'I'm sorry. It's just that we were expecting someone and I saw you and made a mistake.'

Ellie let her bag drop to the floor and held out her hand. 'I am Ellie Thompson, your replacement doctor. Did you not receive an email from headquarters explaining there'd been a change? Sandra has had a family crisis and couldn't come.'

Louise slowly took her proffered hand, but instead of shaking it wrapped her fingers around Ellie's. 'No email, no message at all. Nothing.'

Yeah, she was getting the picture. 'It was a spur-of-the-moment thing. I used to work with Sandra and when I heard how she couldn't come I put my hand up. My contract with Wellington Hospital literally ran out the same week. It was manic for a few days.' Hard to believe everything she'd got done to be ready in that time. Getting a passport and visas had had her running around town like a demented flea. She'd booked flights, bought appropriate clothes for the climate and job and had dinner with Renee and two friends. No wonder her head was spinning.

Louise still held her hand. 'Forgive me for not knowing and thinking you were someone else. I am very grateful you could come over at such short notice. It can't have been easy.'

No, but it had already begun to act like a balm to the wounds left by her husband and sister. 'Believe me, I'm the grateful one here.'

'We'll debate that later. I'd better text Noi. He went to the airport to meet Sandra.' She gave Ellie another quick hug.

When was the last time she'd been hugged so much? She wouldn't count the tight grasp the head of A and E had given her at her farewell. A fish had more warmth, whereas this woman exuded the sort of kindness that would make anyone feel comfortable.

'I'm very glad to be here.' *Where's my bed? And the shower?* All of a sudden her eyes felt heavy and gritty, her head full of candy floss and her legs were struggling to hold her upright.

'The children are busting to meet you. And the staff.' Louise finished her text and set off in the direction of a door, leaving Ellie no choice but to follow.

Of course she wanted to meet the kids she'd be working with, but right this minute? 'How many children are here at the moment?'

'Fourteen. But that number fluctuates almost daily depending on new casualties. Then there are the families who can't leave their children here, or can't get to see them at all so that we go out to their villages for follow-up care. I'm only talking about the amputees. The hospital annex sees to a lot of other casualties, too.' Louise sighed. 'It's hard. For the patients and their families. And us. In here.'

They entered what appeared to be a classroom. Ellie must've looked surprised because Louise explained, 'We have teachers working with the children who stay on after their surgeries. Some are with us for months so we try to keep the education going during their stay.'

Chairs scraped on the wooden floor as kids stood up, some not easily, and the reason quickly became apparent. Three had lost a leg or a foot. Looking closer, Ellie noted other major injuries on all the children.

Her heart rolled. What was tiredness compared to everything these youngsters were coping with? She dug deep, found a big smile and tried to eyeball each and every kid in front of her. 'Hi, everyone. I am Ellie.' She stepped up to the first boy. 'What's your name?'

'Ng.' The lad put out his left hand, his right one not there.

Ellie wound her fingers around the small hand and squeezed gently. 'Hello, Ng. How old are you?' Then she nearly slapped her forehead. These kids wouldn't understand English, would they?

'Six.'

Six and he'd lost an arm. *And* he understood her language. A well of tears threatened, which was so unprofessional. Do that and Louise would be putting her back on that train. Gulping hard, she turned to the next child. But seriously? She really had nothing to complain about.

The next half hour sped by with Ellie sitting and chatting with each child. Not all of them understood her words but they must've picked up on her empathy and her teasing because soon they all crowded around touching her, pointing at themselves and laughing a lot. Over the next few days she'd get to know them better as she changed dressings and helped with rehab, but this first meeting was unbelievable. She filed away each name and face so that she'd never have to ask them again.

They deserved her utmost respect and she'd make sure they got it.

'Ellie? Ellie Baldwin, is that really you?' The male voice coming from across the room was filled with surprise and pleasure.

She snapped her head up and stared into a familiar pair of grey eyes she hadn't seen in four years. Mind you, they'd been angry grey then, like deep, wild ocean grey. 'Luca?' Her heart pounded loud in her ears. 'Luca, I don't believe this.'

'It's me, El.' No one else dared call her that. Ever.

As she stepped forward Louise was prattling an explanation about why she was here, but Ellie cut her out and concentrated on her old friend and housemate. Concentrated hard to make sure she wasn't hallucinating. Checking this truly was Luca Chirsky, even when she knew it was the man she'd shared notes and rosters with at med school, and more than a few beers at the pub or in the house they'd lived in with Renee and another trainee doctor. Time hadn't altered his good looks. Though he did appear more muscular than she remembered, which only enhanced the package. Bet the ladies still plagued him. Some plagues were okay, he'd once joked.

Finally she said, 'I haven't seen you in forever.' Wow, this was a fantastic bonus to her trip. A surprise. She shivered. A *good* surprise, she told herself. 'Who'd have believed we'd meet up here of all places?'

Then she was being swung up in strong arms and spun in a circle. 'It's been a while, hasn't it?' Those eyes were twinkling at her as they used to before she'd gone off to marry Freddy. This was Luca. He had never hesitated with telling her what he thought of her fiancé, none of it good. The thrill of seeing him again dipped.

If only there were some way of keeping her marriage bust-up from Luca.

Not a chance. 'Didn't you say your name was Thompson?' Louise asked from somewhere beside them. 'I'm not going deaf as well as forgetful, am I?'

Luca almost dropped Ellie to her feet. His finger lifted her chin so he could eyeball her. 'You've gone back to Thompson, eh?' Then he deliberately looked at her left hand, which was still gripping his arm, her ring finger bare of a wedding band, and then back to lock his gaze on hers. 'So you're single again.' He didn't need to say, 'I warned you.' It was there in the slow burn of his eyes, changing his pleasure at seeing her to caution.

Ice-like fingers of disappointment skittered across her arms. So much for being excited to see Luca. She'd had a momentary brain fade. *Having a few of them today.* After all this time without any contact between them he'd gone for the jugular straight up. Guess that put their friendship where it belonged—in the past. She didn't understand why. They'd been so close nothing should've affected their friendship. The last person on the planet she'd expected to find here was Luca, and he knew too much about her for these weeks to now be a quiet time. She could do without playing catch-up, or the shake of his head every time he said her surname. Luca would cloud her thinking and bring back memories of where she'd planned on being by now if she hadn't gone and got married. Plans she'd sat up late at night discussing endlessly with him until she'd started dating Freddy.

Even now Luca's head moved from side to side as he said, 'Seems you're right, Louise. Ellie Thompson she is.'

Fatigue combined with annoyance and a sense of

let-down to come out as anger. 'Are Mrs Chirsky and your child here? Or are they back in New Zealand awaiting your return?'

The expression on his face instantly became unreadable as he took a step back from her. 'Don't go there, Ellie,' he warned.

So he could give her a hard time and she should remain all sweetness and light. Too bad she'd forgotten how to do that since that fateful morning she'd found Freddy in bed with more than a pillow. 'Or what?' she snapped. Last time they'd talked he'd been gearing up for his wedding. More like girding up. There'd been a pregnancy involved that he definitely hadn't been happy about. Nor would he talk to her about it, or anything going on in his life then. He'd clammed up tighter than a rock oyster. Kind of said where their friendship had got to.

Louise tapped her arm. 'Come on, I'll show you to your room so you can unpack and take a shower.'

It was the worried look Louise kept flicking between her and Luca that dampened down Ellie's temper; nothing that Luca had said. 'I'm sorry. I must sound very ungrateful. I'd really like to see where I'm staying.' She didn't want Louise thinking her and Luca couldn't work together, because they could. It would just be a matter of remaining professional and ignoring the past. Easy as.

Luca picked up her bag before she could make a move. 'I'll take that.'

Louise scowled. 'Maybe you could catch up with Ellie later when she's had some sleep.'

To lighten the atmosphere that she'd created just by being here, Ellie forced a laugh. 'Trust me, there won't be any talking about anything past, present or future for the next twenty-four hours. I'm all but comatose on my feet. The sooner I can lie down, the better. I got no sleep at all on the train from Bangkok. The carriage was too noisy and stuffy.'

Luca draped an arm over her shoulders. 'That's what planes are for, El. They're comfortable and fast, and the cabin crew even feeds you.' Back to being less antagonistic, then. His use of El was a clue.

'Remind me of that later when I come up with some other hare-brained scheme for getting home.' She'd left booking flights as she had no idea what she might want to do next, where she might go to fill in the weeks between this job and the position she was taking up early in January. Following Louise, Luca's arm still on her shoulders and feeling heavy, yet strong and familiar, she sucked in on her confusion. Maybe she did need familiar right now. Maybe her old friend could help her by going back over that time when she'd made the monumental error of thinking she loved Freddy more than her future and wanted to spend the rest of her life with him. Now she wanted to reroute her life and, if she stopped being so defensive, talking to Luca might turn out to be the fix she needed. If he didn't rub her nose in what had happened, they should be able to get along just fine. Surely their past friendship counted for something?

Then heat prickled Ellie's skin. Damn, but she needed a shower. She probably smelled worse than roadkill that had been left in the sun for days. Except this heat felt different from what she'd been experiencing all morning.

She shrugged away from Luca's arm and straightened up the sags in her body. 'I'm looking forward to catching up.' She smiled at Luca. The heat intensified when he smiled back. Most unusual. Had to be excitement over seeing him again, despite the shaky start. 'But not today.'

Might as well go for friendly; after all they used to be very good at it. There'd been a time, when they were sharing that house, that there was little they didn't know about each other. At one point just before they'd finished their first year as junior doctors she'd wondered if they might've had a fling. They'd seemed attracted to each other in a way they'd never been before, and then she'd met Freddy and that had been that. Eventually she'd moved to Wellington and lost contact with Luca and the others she'd lived with for so long, until the beginning of the year when she'd caught up with Renee and now shared an apartment with her. Ellie had presumed Luca had married and become a father. Seemed she'd been wrong.

Thankfully today she could categorically state she felt no attraction for Luca at all. Not a drop. That heat had been something out of the blue. Hell, today she was struggling with the friendship thing after the way he'd looked at her with that 'I told you so' in his sharp eyes. It made her want to grind her teeth and kick him in the shin. It reminded her how he used to be so positive about diagnoses when they were junior doctors. That was 'the look' he'd become known for. Unfortunately he was more often right than wrong about everything.

Just like his prediction about her ex. Except not even Luca had got it as bad or humiliating as the demise of her marriage had turned out to be.

CHAPTER TWO

'KNOCK ME OVER,' Luca muttered as he stood back for Ellie and Louise to enter the small room that would be El's home for the next month. Ellie Thompson had popped up out of nowhere in full splendour, if a little bedraggled around the edges. All that thick, dark blonde hair still long and gleaming, while her eyes watched everything and everyone, though now there was a wariness he'd never seen before. 'Your smile's missing.' Did he really say that out loud?

Ellie lifted those eyes to him and he saw her weariness. 'It's probably back in the third carriage of the overnight train I was on.'

Somehow Luca didn't believe her exhaustion was all to do with her trip. It appeared ingrained in her bones and muscles as well as deep in those hazel eyes, even in her soul. So not the Ellie he used to know and had had a lot of fun with. What had Baldwin done to her? Played around behind her back? That had always been on the cards. The guy had never been able to keep his pants zipped, even when he'd first started dating Ellie. It had broken Luca's heart when Ellie had told him the guy loved her and was over being the playboy since he'd asked her to marry him. The old 'leopard and its spots' story. But she hadn't wanted to hear what he could've told her. Then his own problems had exploded in his face and he'd been too caught up dealing with Gaylene's lies and conniving to notice Ellie's departure.

Placing her bag on the desk, he turned for the door. 'We'll catch up when you've had forty winks.'

'Make that a thousand and forty.'

'You okay, El? Like, really deep down okay?' he asked, worry latching on to him. They might've been out of touch but she used to be his closest friend. He'd never replaced her and would still do anything for her—if only she ever asked.

Her eyes were slits as that hazel shade glittered at him. 'Never been better,' she growled. 'Now, can you leave me to settle in?'

'On my way. Or do you want me to show you where the showers are?'

'I'll do that.' Louise stepped between them. Putting a hand on his arm, she pushed lightly. 'Go check up on little Hoppy.' Then her phone rang and she stepped away. After listening for a few seconds she said, 'Hang on. Sorry, Ellie, I'll be a couple of minutes. Aaron left the shopping list in the kitchen.'

Ellie's shoulders slumped as she watched Louise bustle away. 'All I want is a shower and some sleep.'

Luca's heart rolled over for her so he reached out for her hand and gently tugged her close. 'Come on, grab your toiletries and that towel and I'll show you where to go.'

She did as he said, silently. What had that man done? Or was this truly just jet lag and a sleepless night on the train making her like this? 'El, while you're showering

I'll make you a sandwich and grab a bottle of water. You must be starving.'

'You still call me El.' Now there was a glimmer of a smile touching her lips. 'I'm fractionally shorter and nowhere near as beautiful as the model you wanted to compare me with. I'm fatter too.'

'The hell you are. You're thinner than I've ever seen you.' And he didn't like it.

The smile fell away, and she shivered. 'I needed to lose weight.'

'I'll have to start calling you stick insect.' He grinned to show he was teasing, something he'd never had to do before when they'd spent a lot of time together. But he needed to know what was going on. Something had happened to her. He'd swear it.

'I've been called worse.' Distress blinked out at him.

He opened his mouth without thinking about what he'd say. 'Who by?' When she winced he draped an arm over her shoulders to hold her in against him as they walked along the path to the ablutions block. 'What did that scumbag do to you?' he asked next, struggling to hold onto a rare anger.

Just like that, crabby Ellie returned. Her back straightened as she yanked her shoulders free of his arm. The face she turned on his was red and tight, her eyes sparking like a live wire. A dangerous live wire. 'You haven't told me if your wife's living over here with you.'

She fought dirty, he'd give her that. Her being Ellie, that meant she was hiding something. Stepping farther away from her, he waved along the path. 'Third door down are the showers. I'll get one of the kids to put that sandwich and water in your room.' He spun away to stride towards the clinic, where he could bury himself in patients' problems and not worry about what might've happened to Ellie. Strange, but for a long time he hadn't thought about what Gaylene had tried to do to him all those years ago, certainly not since he'd arrived here. It wasn't as though Ellie and Gaylene went hand in hand, but the friendship he'd had with El had gone belly up at that time.

'Luca.' A soft hand touched his biceps. 'Luca, stop, please.'

He turned midstride to face Ellie, and instantly his anger dissipated. It wasn't her fault that he'd been made a fool of way back then. 'I'm sorry.'

'Me, too.' Ellie huffed a long sigh. 'I got such a shock seeing you across the room, and I don't seem to have returned to normal since. I don't want to fight with you. We were never very good at that, and starting now doesn't make a lot of sense.'

'I guess four years is a long time, with many things having gone down for each of us. Let's go back to when we were happy being pals and downing beers as if it was going out of fashion on our days off.' He'd like that more than anything right about now. A cold beer—with his pal. They had a lot of catching up to do. And not just the bad stuff.

Ellie nodded slowly. 'That'd be great. A friend is what I really need more than anything.'

Don't ask. 'Done.' He followed through on his previous thought. 'Get some shut-eye and tonight we'll go to a bar in town for a reunion beer or two. Then you can catch up on some more sleep before you start to get to know your way around here. How does that sound?' He held his breath.

At last. A full-blown Ellie smile came his way, like

warm hands around his heart. 'Perfect.' She started to move past him.

Luca suddenly felt the need to tell her. To get it out of the way, because it would hang between them like an unsolved puzzle if he avoided the issue, and he didn't want that. 'I never married her.'

She nearly lost her balance, and when she raised her face to him her eyes were wide. But she kept quiet, waiting for him to finish his story.

As if that could be told in thirty seconds, but he supposed he could give her the bones of it. 'She terminated the baby. Said she'd met someone else and didn't want to take my child into that relationship.' If it had been his child. She hadn't exactly been monogamous with him. He would've insisted on a DNA test being done but he'd been trying to trust her and accept what had happened.

He'd always been supercareful about using condoms during every liaison. But no child of his would ever grow up without his father at his side, and that edict had taken him straight into Gaylene's hands—until she'd found a richer man. Luca's hands fisted on his hips, as they always did when he thought about that selfish woman. The only good thing she had done was remind him exactly why he had no intention of ever, ever getting married or having children.

'You always said you weren't going to marry or have children. I was surprised when I heard about the circumstances of your wedding, but so many people get caught out by an unplanned pregnancy.' Ellie leaned against him. 'I should've phoned then.'

But by then he'd told her what he thought of her marrying Baldwin. He got it. She'd still been angry with him. 'We were both tied up with our careers and finishing exams, not to mention other things. There was a lot going on.' *I wouldn't have told you anyway. Like I've never told you about my father and my grandfather and how they let down those nearest and dearest big time. How my father took his would-be father-in-law's propensity for deserting his wife and children to a whole new level.* Some things were best kept in the family.

Ellie nodded. 'Our friendship was under a fair bit of strain, if I remember rightly.'

'You do.' But he wouldn't raise the subject that had come between them again. Not today anyhow. 'Go shower and head to bed. Your eyeballs are hanging halfway down your face. I'll warn everyone to be quiet around your room.'

'Nice. How come I didn't scare the kids, then? I must look very ugly.' Her smile slipped as a yawn gripped her.

'They're a lot tougher than you'd guess.' Luca felt his usual sadness for these beautiful and gentle people who dealt with so much, then he glanced at Ellie and brightened. 'But they're also very like kids anywhere in the world when you buy treats or play cricket with them.' Things he was always indulging in.

He felt his heart lurch as Ellie stepped through into the ablutions block and shut the door. El. His dearest friend. Damn, but he'd missed her, and he was only just realising how much. No one quite poked the borax at him the way she had whenever he'd got too serious about something she'd deemed to be ridiculous. She was usually spot on too. But now something was definitely not right. He'd never seen her so beaten, as though all the things she held dear and near were gone. Somehow, sometime, over the coming weeks he'd find out, and see if he couldn't help her to get her spark back.

* * *

Ellie woke to knocking on her door. *Where am I?* She looked around at the children's drawings covering the walls and it all came back in a hurry. Vientiane. The amputee centre. She stretched her toes to the end of the bed and raised her arms above her head. She'd slept like the dead and now felt good all over, ready to start her job in this country that was new to her.

Knock, knock.

'Who is it?'

'Chi. Luca said you have to get up. I've got you more water.'

Luca. So that hadn't been a dream. She'd be excited about catching up with him if she didn't know he'd want all the details about her failed marriage. He wasn't going to get them but he'd persist for days; she just knew it. Then again, he had told her why he wasn't married. What a witch that woman had turned out to be. Terminating their baby with no regard for its father. That was beyond her comprehension. But then she'd never faced a similar situation. Freddy had made certain she didn't get pregnant.

'Ellie?'

'Sorry, come in.' Ellie shuffled upright and leaned back against the wall as Chi entered.

'Luca said you're going out at seven o'clock.' The girl spoke precisely and slowly as if searching for the right words.

Damn, she'd forgotten Luca's suggestion of a beer in town. Taking the proffered bottle of water from Chi, she snapped the lid open and said, 'Thank you, Chi.'

The girl beamed as Ellie poured the cool liquid her parched throat.

'What time is it?' she paused long enough to ask.

'Half past six. Are you still tired?'

'A little bit, but eight hours is more than enough for now. I wouldn't have slept tonight if you hadn't woken me.' As Chi sat down on the chair in the corner Ellie asked, 'Where did you learn to speak such good English?' The girl looked so cute in her oversize shirt and too-small trousers.

'Here. The doctors and nurses teach me.' Pride filled her face, lightened her eyes.

'How long have you been in the centre?' To have learned to speak English to a level she could be understood without too much difficulty she must've been around the medical staff a long time.

'I was this high when I came with my brother.' Chi held her hand less than a metre above the floor. Ellie guessed she was now closer to one hundred and twenty centimetres. 'Long time ago. My brother was this high.' Half a metre off the floor.

'Is your brother still here, too?'

Chi blinked, the pride gone, replaced with stoic sadness. 'He died. The bomb cut off his leg and the blood ran out.'

Ellie shuddered. Reality sucked, and was very confronting. Flying fragments of metal did a lot of damage, and were often lethal. It had been a spur-of-the-moment decision to come here. When she'd heard about Sandra's family crisis she'd thought about the weeks looming with nothing to keep her busy before she took up her next job and put her hand up. Helping people in these circumstances was so different from working in an emergency department back home, where life was easier and a lot of things like medical care taken for granted. Here

people, many only young children, were still being injured, maimed or killed by bombs that had been left
lying around or shallow buried decades ago.

'Louise and Aaron adopted me. My mother and father are gone, too.'

How much reality should a child have to deal with?
Leaping out of bed, she scooped the girl into a hug. 'I'm
so happy to know you, Chi.'

'Knew I couldn't trust a female to get my message
across without stopping to yak the day away.' Luca stood
in the doorway, his trademark grin including both her
and Chi in that comment.

With sudden clarity Ellie understood how much she'd
missed that grin and the man behind it. Missed their conversations about everything from how to put a dislocated
shoulder back into its socket to which brand of beer was
the best. They'd argued, and laughed, and fought over
whose turn it was to clean the house. They'd cheered
each other on in exams while secretly hoping they did
better than the other.

She ran to throw her arms around him. 'I'm glad I've
found you again.'

'I'm glad, too, because tomorrow's your turn to do
the washing.' He laughed against the top of her head.

His hands were spread across her back, his warmth
seeping into her bones and thawing some of the chill that
had taken up residence on the morning she came home
from work to find Freddy and Caitlin in her marital
bed, doing what only she should've been doing with her
husband. She breathed deep, drawing in the scent that
was Luca, her closest friend ever, and relaxed. Friends
were safer than husbands and sisters, the damage they
wrought less destructive.

'I have missed you so much.' *I just hadn't realised it.* How dumb was that? Who forgot someone important in their lives because they'd fallen out about a man? Not any man, but Freddy. Luca had been right about him, but she wasn't going to acknowledge that. She couldn't bear to see the 'I told you so' sign flick on in his eyes again. Not yet anyway. Even if she could laugh because he'd won that argument there was too much pain behind it for her to be ready to make light of what had happened. That day would probably never come. 'We should never have stopped texting or emailing even when we were in different cities, no matter what we thought about what the other was doing.'

Luca swung her around in a circle, her feet nearly taking out the bed and then the chair with Chi sitting on it. 'I do solemnly swear never to stop annoying the hell out of my best buddy, Ellie, ever again.'

'Look out.' Chi leaped on top of the chair out of the way of Ellie's legs. 'Ellie makes you crazy, Luca.'

Ellie was put back on her feet and then Luca grabbed Chi and swung her in a circle. 'You're right, she does. I'd forgotten how to be crazy until today.'

Chi giggled and squirmed to be put down. 'Ellie, can I be your friend, too? I want to be crazy.'

'Absolutely. We'll be the three crazies.' Ellie reached for the girl and hugged her tight, trying hard not to let the lurking tears spill. What a day. What a damned amazing day. She'd found Luca, gained a new friend and was starting to feel a little bit like her old self. A teeny-weeny bit, but that was a start.

'Okay, crazies, time Ellie got ready to go out. Chi, I'm sorry but you're too young to go to a bar, but I'm sure we'll find somewhere else to take you while Ellie's here.' Luca cleared his throat and when Ellie looked up she'd swear there was moisture at the corners of his eyes, too.

It was all too much to cope with. Seeing Luca get all emotional wasn't helping her stay in control. 'Go on, shoo, both of you. I'm going to take another shower and get spruced up.'

'It's a bar in Vientiane, no need for glad rags.' Luca grinned. Then slapped his forehead. 'Oh, I forgot. Lady El won't be seen anywhere in less than the best outfit.'

She picked up her pillow and threw it at him. 'Get out of here.'

She hadn't arrived in the best-looking outfit, even if she'd started out looking swanky back in Bangkok after a shower at the airport. But hey, in the interest of her self-esteem she wasn't going out in a sack, either. Though maybe here where the temperatures were so hot and the humidity high and everything definitely casual she could let go some of the debilitating need to be perfect. After all, there was no one here that she desperately had to please. Not even her friend. Luca had always accepted her for who she was, even if he did tease the hell out of her at times.

Suddenly she realised she was only dressed in a T-shirt and knickers; her bra lay on top of her discarded trousers. This might be Luca, but she had some pride. Glancing at him, she was dismayed to see his gaze was cruising down her body, hesitating on her breasts. She couldn't read the look in his eyes, but it was different from how he'd ever looked at her before.

Ellie shivered—with heat and apprehension. What was going on? 'Get out of here. I'll see you shortly.' She needed a shower, a very cold one.

* * *

'Like your dress,' Luca told her an hour later as she perched her backside on top of a high stool and leaned her elbow on the bar. 'When did you start wearing red?' His eyes held the same expression they had back in her room.

She chose to ignore it. 'Since I found the most amazing saleswoman in a very exclusive boutique.' It was true. That lady was very skilled at her job and her shop was Ellie's favourite, though lately there hadn't been any call for beautiful dresses.

The one she'd slipped into tonight was a simple sheath that was casual yet elegant. Her new look, she decided there and then. No more going for the tailored, exquisite clothes her husband had demanded she wear even to cook dinner. She'd miss the amazing clothes because she had loved them but hated the criticism rained down on her for not looking perfect enough. But, hey, she wasn't in that place anymore. She was with Luca in Vientiane. Ellie grinned. A real, deep all-or-nothing grin. Life was looking up. Strange glances from Luca or not.

'What's up? You look as if you won the lottery,' Luca pushed a glass of Beer Lao towards her.

The condensation on the glass made her mouth water and that was before she'd tasted the contents. 'As good as, I reckon. I'm starting to unwind and enjoy myself.'

'Things haven't been so great for you recently?' There was a guarded look in his eyes as though he was afraid of overstepping the mark. Something they'd never had to worry about in the past.

A deep gulp of beer and then, 'You were right. Freddy was an a-hole. I left him and now I'm trying to decide what it is I really want from my life.'

'I'm sorry to hear that.'

No gloating, thank goodness, or she'd have tipped her beer over his head. And that would've been such a waste. It was delicious. 'You know what? I'm not sorry.' It had only just occurred to her but, no, she was not sorry that episode of her life was over. Now all she had to do was pack it away completely. If that was possible considering her sister's role in it. Hopefully, being so far removed from the complications of her family, she might find some inner peace. Though she might never learn to trust anyone after what had been done to her.

'Then, find that smile again.' Luca placed his hand on top of hers on the counter. 'You look better when your eyes light up with pleasure.'

Turning her hand over to clasp her fingers around his, she said, 'Seeing you makes me feel good. I couldn't believe it when you said my name.'

'*You* were surprised? I got a helluva shock considering you weren't the doctor we were expecting. How was that for coincidence? Or was it our stars aligning or some such babble?'

'You've been here too long.' As laughter bubbled up Ellie's throat something strange was going on with her hand. The one covered by Luca's. She could feel heat and a zinging sensation that had nothing to do with the weather and all to do with— No way. She jerked her hand free, folded her arms across her chest and rubbed her arms vigorously.

'Ellie? You're going weird on me.' Luca locked his eyes on her.

Looking into those grey eyes, she searched for recognition of what had just happened but found nothing.

Seemed her imagination was running riot. 'I'm fine,' she croaked.

'Phew. For a moment there I thought you were changing on me.' His gaze was intense, as if he was checking her out.

Zing. She felt it again. This time it was as if someone were lightly dancing down her spine. Tearing her eyes away from Luca, she snatched up her glass and drained the beer in one long gulp. The glass banged back on the counter and she stared around the bar, looking at everything and everyone but Luca.

'I'll get you another.' His hand scooped up her glass. The fingers that wrapped around the moist receptacle were long and strong, and tanned. Not that she understood why she was noticing.

Ellie's mouth dried, despite all the fluid she'd just swallowed. *They're only fingers. Luca's, what's more.* She shivered, as though it were cold, except the temperature was beyond high and her skin was on fire. What had just happened? She had to get herself under control. Getting wired over Luca was so not a good idea, let alone sensible. And despite her mistakes she was usually sensible. Or had that attribute flown out of the door and floated away on the Mekong just across the road?

Guess it had been so long since she'd been close to any man that her body had reacted without thought. But this was Luca. *Down, girl, down.* He was the last man on earth she should be having feelings about that had nothing to do with friendship and all to do with sex.

CHAPTER THREE

Luca aimed for relaxed, trying to ignore that something big was bugging Ellie. The defining strength of their friendship had taken a battering years back and he wasn't prepared to push. Not yet anyway. He'd hate to lose her now he'd just found her again. Not that he'd been looking. He'd kind of shut off most things from his previous life, except the mantra he'd always lived by—Chirsky men were bad husbands and fathers.

'I should head back to the compound,' Ellie muttered.

What happened to spending the evening together? 'Let's have another beer and then we'll eat.' Not waiting for her to answer, he waved at the barman busy with another order and indicated their empty glasses. He didn't want to walk even a few metres down the bar because Ellie looked as if she was about to bolt, and that was the last thing he wanted.

He went with, 'It's unbelievable. I was coming into that room to meet some doctor I'd never heard of and there you were, looking like my Ellie.'

She blanched. Then slowly she slipped off the stool, standing straight—and bewildered. 'I really should go.' There was a wobble in her voice.

Luca placed a hand firmly on her shoulder. 'Sit down.

The heat and travel hits you hard at first, but you need to stay awake till a reasonable hour to get your body clock back on track. The sooner the better.' He doubted those were the reasons for her looking as if she'd been run down by a train, but he played along. 'When I first arrived it took me ages to settle into a routine.'

'How long have you been here?' She still looked ready to flee.

'Nine months, three to go.'

Leaning her elbow on the counter, she propped her chin in her hand. 'Then what?'

'Maybe a spell in Cambodia.' Or Vietnam, or even Australia at a major hospital. He hadn't made any decisions about a whole load of things that involved his future since he'd come over here. He was avoiding them, because it was easier that way.

Her eyes widened and at last she gave him a smile. There were long gaps between those and he was already learning to appreciate them. She asked, 'Since when did you want to give up your goal of being head of the busiest A and E department in New Zealand?'

The problem with changing the subject so Ellie would relax was that he ended up in the hot seat. About to start telling her about the clinic's pet pangolin instead, he paused. They used to tell each other just about everything. Shouldn't he start renewing their friendship by doing what they'd always done? 'Gaylene doing her little number on me was a shock.' *That's an understatement, El, in case you don't realise.* 'I thought I'd made myself invulnerable, invincible, so that no one would catch me out. How wrong could a guy be? Maybe I'd become arrogant. I don't know.' He glanced across at Ellie and smiled despite himself. 'Okay, I was.' Hopefully that had changed. He'd sure as hell been taken down a peg or three, though not for anything to do with his medical work.

'I can understand wanting to protect your feelings but you're sounding as if you don't ever want to let anyone near, into your heart.' She eased her butt back onto the stool.

Luca felt some of the tension in his belly lighten. At least she didn't look quite so ready to run for the door anymore, but did she have to go straight to the centre of his problem? So easily? Maybe he hadn't missed her as much as he'd thought. But of course he had. Strange how he hadn't known that until he'd found her again. Should've done something about looking her up years ago, but he couldn't stand Baldwin. Not at all. 'I've never made any bones about the fact I do not want a family— no wife, no children.' Okay, *want* was the wrong word. He wouldn't risk having a wife and family. That was closer to the truth.

'That was an excuse for bonking every moving female while you were young, but not forever, surely?' She was laughing at him, soft and friendly-like but laughing nonetheless.

'Wrong,' he snapped. Telling her what made him who he'd become was a mistake after all. But then he'd known that, had always kept certain things to himself, even from this woman.

'Hey.' Her hand covered his. 'I didn't mean to upset you. You've got to admit you spent a lot of time chasing females back then.'

'I didn't have to chase anyone.' Yep, maybe he still was a little bit arrogant. A sigh huffed across his lips. 'You want to hear my story or not?'

The surprise in her eyes told him she hadn't expected him to continue his tale. *Well, Ellie, nor did I.* But now he'd started he didn't want to stop. He wanted her to know what drove him and how he'd arrived here. The idea of opening his heart to her appealed, when it had never done so in the past. Never. Which should be a warning.

So he stalled. 'Let's order some food. Want me to choose? Anything you won't like?'

'As I have no idea what the locals eat, you go ahead. I can't think of anything I won't enjoy. Tell you what, though, they brew great beer.'

'Their food's just as good.' He beckoned to the waitress and rattled off a few dishes he thought would be a good introduction to Lao food. Then he drank deeply from his glass and wiped the back of his hand over his mouth. 'My father left before we were born.' Ellie had met Angelique, his twin, when they were sharing that house in Auckland. Ange would often drop in for a night, sleeping on the floor in the corner of the lounge. 'Growing up knowing he'd never wanted to meet us, to be a part of our lives, that he didn't love us...' He paused, looked directly at Ellie. 'It was horrible. I used to look at men who were about the age I thought my father might be and wonder if they were our dad.'

Ellie ran her fingers down his arm. 'That's horrid. Did you never try to track him down through phone directories or electoral rolls when you were older?'

'Mum refused to tell us his name or where he came from, not even what he did for a living. Nothing. It was as though he'd never existed.'

'Her way of coping, maybe?'

'Possibly, but as kids we didn't understand that. Hell,

as an adult I still find it hard to accept.' He wasn't admitting to the equally awful thought that maybe his mother hadn't known who their father was because she'd slept with more than one man at the time they were conceived. As Gaylene had done with him, but they hadn't been a couple until she'd learned she was pregnant.

As far as his mum was concerned, he wouldn't judge her. His mother's life hadn't been easy growing up. Her father had been a bully and a thug to both her and her mother, and was not the kind of man a daughter could rely on for love and safety.

Understanding was blinking out at him from those hazel eyes less than a metre away. 'So when Gaylene declared you were the father of her baby you stepped up because no child of yours would not know their father.'

'Got it in one. Not that Gaylene knew my story, but she sure went for the jugular. In her eyes it didn't hurt that I was destined to become that head of department I'd planned on and would be earning a fat salary when I got there.' He tasted the sourness in his mouth. Thought he was long past letting what she'd done hurt him, huh? Thank goodness he hadn't loved her. That would've really turned him beyond bitter.

'You'd have married someone you didn't love for your child? Wouldn't it have been better for everyone to have remained single but fully involved with that child?' Ellie made everything seem so simple. Was that how she looked at life? A memory rose of her spitting words in his face, defending Baldwin when he'd tried to make her see reality. *He's a real man, of course he's played the field, but now he's settling down—with me*, she'd insisted.

Now she was here, without a wedding ring on her finger, and a change of name. Not so simple, eh?

'Didn't matter in the end,' he sighed. It hadn't been as straightforward as Ellie made it sound. Certainly not when Gaylene had been pressuring him so hard. He hadn't wanted to appear not to be taking his responsibilities seriously but at the same time it hadn't been easy to accept he was going to be a father when he'd spent his adult life doing his damnedest not to become one. 'I would never put any child through what Angelique and I had to deal with. Never.' Which was why he wasn't going to have children. Not only hadn't he known his father, his grandfather had been the worst example of a parent. He'd often wondered if having bad male role models on both sides of his family meant he'd be a terrible father, had inherited some chromosome that made men bad. He wasn't going to find out because if he was like them then it would be too late for any offspring he procreated.

'Oh, Luca, I never knew.' She locked those eyes on his. 'Not that I was meant to. I get that, too. But for the record I think you'd be a wonderful father. Just in case…' Her words trailed off.

Had the bile rising in his throat been that obvious? 'Thanks for the vote of confidence. It's good to know someone believes in me so blindly.'

'Ouch. You're not playing fair. I know you, have seen you working with children when they're in pain and terrified, still remember you cuddling Angelique's wee boy only hours after he was born. You have the right instincts, believe me.' This time she sipped her beer.

He'd like nothing more than to believe her, but that would be a huge leap of faith, right off the edge of the planet, in fact. He settled with, 'Wee Johnny is now at school and whipping up merry hell with his teachers. He wants to be an All Black without having to go through the usual channels.' Johnny was a great kid, so bright and busy and full of beans. He missed him.

'Is he? Got a photo?' Ellie seemed keen to get away from the uncomfortable conversation they'd been having.

He tugged his phone from the back pocket of his pants and tapped the icons. 'There. Isn't he a handsome dude?'

Snatching the phone from his grasp, Ellie stared at the picture. 'Just like his uncle.'

'I'm handsome?'

'I meant cheeky and obviously up to mischief.' She swiped the screen, moving on to more photos of his nephew. And Angelique. 'Oh. Your sister looks so much like your mother now.'

As in sad and bitter? 'Yes, the spitting image.' In every way. 'I tried to make up for Johnny not having a father, but for her I can't be anything but a brother.' Not even a good one now. Anger welled up. 'How could she have done the same thing as Mum? She knew what it was like not having a dad around the place. Hated it, and swore she'd never let her kids go unloved.'

'Hey.' Ellie's hand was back on his arm, warm and soft.

Almost sexy—if she wasn't a friend and that wasn't a friendly gesture. What was going on? Luca blinked. 'What?'

'Angelique's not as strong as you. Never was. Remember when you used to insist she should be studying at university for a career and she wanted to work in a café? She liked what she was doing, and you couldn't change who she was.'

'Yeah, I've finally worked that out.' *Focus, man. On the conversation and nothing else.* He had to be out of sorts because of Ellie's sudden reappearance in his life. He'd missed her. A lot. Yeah, that was all that odd sensation around her touch was about.

She hadn't finished. 'But, Luca, you support her, stand by her and look out for her son. That's huge.' Ellie sounded so sure, it was scary.

'Wrong. I'm over here, not at home, aren't I?' Guilt ramped up, but Angelique had told him to get out of her life and stop interfering with how she raised her son just about the time his carefully planned career was getting on top of him. It had begun to seem a hollow victory when there was no one to share it with. He'd started questioning everything he'd believed in. Except not being a parent. That was non-negotiable. No exceptions.

Hot spices wafted through the air and four small plates of mouth-watering food appeared on the counter in front of them. Perfect timing. This talking with Ellie was getting too deep and uncomfortable.

She was licking her lips and sniffing the air like a dog on the scent. He did what he always did when the going got tough—he grinned. Amazing how that helped all the tension fall away. However temporary, it felt good to be with her knowing she wouldn't try to rip him off or take something from him he didn't want to give. Good friends were rare and priceless. And El was the best. So why did he feel he had to keep reminding himself of that? It was as though something had changed between them that he couldn't fathom. Luca shrugged. He had four weeks to work it out before she headed home again.

The woman distracting him said, 'Tell me more about the clinic.'

A reprieve, then. 'It's heartbreaking seeing what these children deal with, and yet uplifting because of their sunny natures and how they take it all in their little strides.'

'I was really moved today when the kids gathered around me, all chatter and laughter when they'd never met me.' The sticky rice and peanut sauce were delicious. Ellie forked up more and watched Luca do the same. He'd told her more about his past tonight than in all the previous years she'd known him. He'd surprised her, but then today had been full of surprises on all fronts.

Thinking back, she saw where she'd missed little clues about his past. Whenever talk had got around to families he'd been reticent, and she couldn't remember what he'd said about his father except he hadn't been around. Not once had he said that the man had never been there, was basically unknown. Hell, she might've got her marriage all wrong but her family had always been there for her when she was growing up. It was different nowadays, though. Awkward and sometimes downright hostile with Caitlin still coming and going in her parents' lives as though she'd done nothing wrong. But Luca had missed out on a lot, hadn't had that loving childhood she'd had, so why wasn't he wanting to have his own family and make up for that? Had he ever fallen in love? Come close, even? Sad, but she suspected not.

'Are you listening to me?' Luca elbowed her, causing rice to drop off her fork.

'Heard every word.' *I hope, or I'll be asking questions about what he's just told me tomorrow and then he'll give me stick.* 'The clinic is full to bursting at the moment.'

His grey eyes squinted at her. 'I said there are four spare beds.'

'You did not.' She laughed, and even to her that sounded strained. She changed the subject and determined to concentrate on everything he said. 'Who's Baxter?' She'd heard the kids talking about him when she was getting ready to come out with Luca.

'The clinic's pet pangolin.' She must've looked bewildered because he explained further. 'An anteater. They normally live in the trees. Apparently this one turned up one day with one leg half severed off. It was before my time. Aaron operated and now it slopes around minus a leg.'

'So Baxter knew where to go for an amputation.' This time her laughter was genuine.

Luca smiled back. 'The kids adopted him and he's stayed, sometimes foraging for ants farther afield, but he never goes very far. You'll see him soon enough.'

He pushed their empty plates aside. 'Feel up to a stroll beside the Mekong?'

Not really. She'd like nothing more than to fall into bed and get some more sleep. Glancing at her watch, she saw it was only just after eight thirty. And here she'd thought they'd been in the bar for hours. It was too early to go back to her room, especially after having slept most of the day. An evening stroll with Luca would be the next best thing. Maybe even better, and she could walk off the effects of all that beer. What had she been thinking having so much? Hadn't been thinking at all, that was what. Standing up, she slung her bag over her shoulder. 'Sure.'

Outside the air had cooled all of about two degrees. Ellie shook her head. 'To think I was looking forward to the warmth after a particularly cold spring back home.'

Luca caught her hand in his and swung their arms between them. 'I still haven't got used to the heat. Especially at night when I'm desperately tired and sleep's evasive.'

Ellie gently squeezed his hand, enjoying the strength of those firm fingers. This felt good. Being with someone who knew her and wouldn't make up things about her, wouldn't be sniggering behind her back, wouldn't be breaking any vows.

Neither of them talked as they strolled along a path lined with bars and nightclubs. Despite the noise from those buildings the sound of the river seeped into Ellie's mind, a steady pouring of an unbelievable amount of water carrying debris and fish along its path. Where had that branch come from? A few kilometres farther north? Or from another country? China, even? 'Amazing.'

'What is?'

'The river and all the countries it runs through.' Ellie turned towards Luca and missed her footing on the uneven surface.

He caught her waist, held her as she regained her balance. 'Careful. Can't have you breaking your ankle before you've even started working with us.'

'That would make me very unpopular.' Those hands were definitely showing their strength. And their heat. She could feel each finger distinctly from the others. A different kind of warmth than what the climate was producing caressed her feverish skin. Tipping her head back, she met Luca's stunned look. Carefully taking a backwards step, she extricated herself from his hold and dropped her gaze. And instantly felt she'd lost something. Something important. But this was Luca. Not some hot guy she'd want to go to bed with.

Really? Luca wasn't hot? Yes, he was, but she'd never thought of him like that. That would be too— Too strange? Or too hot to handle? She peeked up at him, found him staring out at the river now, an inscrutable look on his face. When had he got so good at those? Not back when she'd last knew him, for sure. Back then he used to make jokes to divert unwanted interest. These days she also had a few of her own special expressions that hadn't been around in those days.

'I think it's time for me to get back to my room,' she muttered and began to turn around.

'No problem.'

Even his voice sounded different: deeper, huskier. Reading way too much into everything? Eek, was she on the rebound from Freddy? The thought slammed into her brain, almost paralysing her. Was that what this was about? Reacting strangely to Luca because she felt safe with him? Could trust him? He'd never hurt her, physically or mentally. No, but she could get hurt by her own stupidity. Because she was being stupid. She mightn't have seen or spoken to Luca for years but she knew him—as a friend, and he was perfect like that. She didn't need or want to have anything else with him. Surely tomorrow she'd wake up refreshed and over whatever was ailing her.

'Ellie, are you all right?' His concern sounded genuine.

Had he not felt anything? Did that mean she could relax? No. Not until she'd stopped these silly sensations tripping her up every time Luca touched her. If she didn't, four weeks working with him were going to be tricky. Luca had always touched his friends whenever he wanted to share something with them or comfort them. 'I think I'm so tired I have no idea which way's up.' Which was completely true. 'I shouldn't have had those beers.'

'They might help you drop off to sleep quickly.' He waved over a hovering taxi. 'Come on, Sleeping Beauty. Time for your bed.'

Huh? Sleeping Beauty? More like droopy sad sack.

Luca handed Ellie out of the taxi and paid the driver. 'I wish they wouldn't turn all the outside lights off,' he growled as they headed up the path to the staff sleeping quarters.

'I'd have trouble finding my room if you weren't with me,' Ellie agreed.

'You'll soon know your way around. It's not a complex setting. The hospital is at the back with long wings off three sides. Ours is on the right and houses staff quarters, wards and our small operating theatre, with the tourist centre at the very end.'

'Tourists?' In a medical centre?

'The museum room. There're photos of bombs in the ground and the craters caused when they explode. Pictures of wounded children and their families hang everywhere. There's a real bomb that's had the detonator removed in the centre of the main viewing room, which is very dramatic and has tourists putting their hands in their pockets for money to fix more kids. Not that we'd stop even if the funds were rock bottom.'

'Is the foundation struggling?' Ellie asked, thinking that she could easily hand back the money she was being paid for her month here. She felt sure she was going to be the winner of her time spent with these wonderful people. Money didn't compare to exchanging hugs with a thirteen-year-old with only one arm who was determined to become a teacher when he grew up, as one lad had told her in her first five minutes here.

'Struggling's probably a bit strong, but there's never a well of cash. The foundation relies heavily on donations. One benefactor in the States has set up an investment fund that pays handsome dividends, and without that I'd say we'd be in big trouble.' Luca spoke with authority, as though he'd dug deep to learn all he could about the organisation helping these kids. No surprises there.

'You are getting quite a kick out of working in such a different environment from what you were used to, aren't you?'

'More than I'd expected,' Luca acknowledged. 'At first I worried I'd been stupid to sign up for twelve months, but it didn't take long to realise that I was enjoying practising medicine outside my usual comfort levels. There's as much drama here as in an A and E department, as you'll soon learn. But more than that, I'm in on the follow-up care, and over here that means getting to know the whole family—if there is a family, that is.' His voice went from excited to sad within a few words.

Ellie wrapped an arm around his waist. 'Reality sucks, doesn't it?'

'It can.' Then he said with what she thought was a smile in his voice, 'Then there are the success stories, like Chi who wants to become a doctor to help her people. She's going to Australia with Louise and Aaron when they decide to return home, which they're saying will be within two years.'

'What happens when they go? Are there replacements queuing to get in?'

He shrugged. 'Who knows?'

Was Luca considering it? 'Would you put your hand up?'

'The idea has crossed my mind.'

'You don't want to return home? You don't miss Auckland?' Now that they'd reconnected she didn't want to lose him again, but that didn't mean she'd be moving over here full time so as to spend more time with him.

Going back to the city where she'd done her internship and had loads of good times with Luca and her housemates had been an obvious choice when the temporary position at Auckland Hospital became available. She'd be housesitting for the specialist she was covering for and couldn't move into the house until he and his family headed away to America for his sabbatical.

A part of her still wanted the house-and-kids package— with a hot man, of course. But that meant learning to trust again, and she wasn't brimming with confidence of that happening. Especially since it wasn't only her husband who'd cheated on her but her sister, as well. Sometimes she thought Caitlin's treachery was worse. They'd been so close. *Not close enough to see she loved your husband.* True. Caitlin and Freddy were apparently talking about getting married when the divorce was settled. They had a wait on their hands because with New Zealand law that couldn't happen for more than another year.

Luca twisted out of her hold, reminding her he was with her. He'd remained silent for so long her mind had taken a trip into things she didn't need to be thinking about right now. Had her question about missing home hit a chord? Should she press the point? Once she would've. But there were years between then and now. She went for the easy option. 'You've gone quiet on me.'

'I don't have a home to miss. Angelique and Johnny have their own lives to lead that apparently don't include me. Auckland is my hometown, always will be, but it'll be there whenever I choose to return.'

'Hell, Luca.' That sounded incredibly sad and bleak. Where was the man who was always happy and making jokes, always acting as though he didn't have a worry in the world? Had he been leading a double life? But then she hadn't known about his father, or lack of one, until tonight, either. She stopped to look up at him, only just seeing his facial expressions in the star-studded darkness. The sadness for him grew into something else, roiling through her so that she wanted to reach out and touch him deeply, to show he wasn't alone, that she cared. 'I will never let you out of my life again.'

His jaw moved as he swallowed. He was staring at her, his eyes unblinking. When he spoke his voice was low and loaded with emotion. 'Thank goodness for that. It's been too long, El.'

Way too long, and the worst thing was that she hadn't even noticed until today. Reaching out to him, she was going to hug him, as she used to whenever they'd celebrated an exam pass or lost a patient or felt a little lonely. But then Luca's arms were tugging her in against his body, his head dipping so that his mouth found hers. With his lips on hers, his tongue slipped inside her mouth.

Ellie breathed deep, drew in Luca, a mix of beer and chilli and hot male. Of safety and—hot male. Surrendering to the need clawing through her, she focused on kissing him back and hoping she was wiping away that sadness that had been rolling off him in waves.

Then as suddenly as it started, the kiss ended. Luca abruptly dropped his arms and stumbled backwards. 'Ellie, I'm so sorry. I don't know what came over me. Look, that door to our right is your room. I'll see you tomorrow.' And he was gone, racing back the way they'd come, out onto the road and still he didn't slow down.

'Thanks very much, Luca. You're sorry? Talk about taking a knife and cutting into me. You're sorry for a mind-blowing kiss that I reckon you were enjoying as much as I was?'

But she was talking to the night. Luca was way beyond hearing her. Staring around the dark grounds, she could only sigh with relief that the lights were out. Doubtful anyone had seen them kissing. But her heart wasn't letting her off that easily. It pounded hard and fast while her hands shook and her skin tightened with need. Luca. What had they done? Whatever it was, she wasn't sorry. But she should be. She'd been kissing the man when only minutes before she'd acknowledged she never wanted to let him out of her life again. *Way to go, Ellie. No one kisses a friend like that, with that intensity and emotion.* It was sexy; very, very sexy. And her body was suffering withdrawal already. Which meant the future of their friendship was now in jeopardy.

CHAPTER FOUR

LUCA STUMBLED ALONG the road, not bothering to look where he was going. What had he been thinking when he'd kissed Ellie? He hadn't been thinking. That was the problem. Not with his brain anyhow. Ellie, of all people. He'd kissed her, his best friend, damn it.

And wanted to do it again.

No, I don't.

Yes, he did. Now. Sooner than later.

Oaths rent the air blue. What had he done to their friendship? As if that was going to move ahead after that particular little fiasco. Damn it. Ellie was—El. His long-lost friend. So lost he'd have been able to get in touch with her simply by going online and looking up her phone number. Or ringing the A and E department at Wellington Hospital. But he hadn't done it. He'd been smarting over her telling him to butt out of her life if he wasn't prepared to accept her decision to marry the man who was now her ex. Being right felt hollow. He regretted walking away. Not even being preoccupied with his own problem in a short skirt was an excuse. He'd let Ellie down.

Ellie didn't ring you, either.

Didn't make it right. But nor was kissing her right.

It had to be way up there with the dumbest things he'd ever done in his whole goddamned life. Worse, they had to work together for four whole weeks. That could prove uncomfortable. Or interesting.

Come up with some good news, will you?

Nope, couldn't think of any at this moment.

His pace slowed and he jammed his fists on his hips, tipped his head back to stare up at the sky.

No answers up there.

He resumed walking at a slower pace, breathing deep, letting the heavy, warm air calm him. There were no answers at all. He'd spent an evening talking with Ellie, sometimes about subjects they'd never touched on before, like about his sorry past. He'd got tied up in the fun of seeing her again and spilled his guts. Then he'd goddamned kissed her.

He needed his head read—only problem there it was such a shambles no one would be able to make anything out of it.

It was some kiss, though.

Shut up.

Go on. Admit it. When did a kiss ever give you an achy feeling in your heart?

There was the answer he was looking for. He hadn't realised just how much he'd missed Ellie, and now his heart was happy. As in how one friend would feel about another after four years' absence and everything that had happened in that time. For Ellie that had been a failed marriage for reasons he had yet to find out, and for him the loss of a child he'd never wanted but hated the opportunity being stolen from him. But Gaylene had only started this sense of not belonging anywhere. Angelique with her outrageous demands that he stay out of her and Johnny's lives had exacerbated his need to question everything he'd thought *his* life was about. Including being the head of a large A and E department.

No wonder his emotions were all over the show. That kiss had come out of nowhere, blindsiding him. Now all he had to do was move on and forget it ever happened.

Yep, that should work. Easy as.

Ellie woke slowly the next morning, her head feeling as though fog had slipped in to fill it while she'd been comatose. Guess the good news was that she'd slept at all. After Luca's knee-knocking, bone-rattling kiss she'd figured she'd never sleep again.

Luca had been late getting in last night. She'd heard him bumping into furniture in the next-door bedroom that she knew was his. Had he gone back to town and found a bar to try to drown out that kiss? Or didn't he care that he'd kissed her and stirred up all sorts of emotions she so wasn't ready to deal with?

Knock, knock.

'Who is it?' *Please don't be Luca.* Not yet while she was still in her satin shorts and cotton top.

'It's Chi. You've got to get up. Breakfast's nearly ready.'

Phew. Sometimes she did get what she asked for. 'Come in, Chi.'

The girl opened the door cautiously and peered around the room before stepping inside and closing the door again. 'Morning, Ellie. You've had a big sleep.'

If only that were true. A certain someone and his kiss had kept her awake staring into the dark for hours until eventually exhaustion had won out and dragged her under for a brief spell. 'I don't know where the kitchen is yet. Do you want to show me around after I get dressed?'

Chi nodded solemnly. 'We have breakfast early before everyone begins working. Then the tourists start visiting at nine.'

'Right. I'm heading for the shower. Two minutes, okay?' She snatched some clothes from her bag that had yet to be unpacked.

Chi was still in Ellie's room when she returned from a fast and cold shower. The bed had been made, every corner tucked in neatly, the pillow perfectly straight and the cover smoothed so as not one wrinkle showed.

'Thank you so much, but you don't have to look after me. I'm sure there are lots of other people here who need you more than me.'

'I like you.'

Tears blocked Ellie's throat. A hug was called for. It was the only way she could show her feelings right now with words backing up behind the lump in her throat, unable to squeeze past. For everything this child must've suffered it all came down to simple observations and reactions. Give and take. Hugs. 'I like you, too,' she finally managed to get out, then focused on getting ready for the day. She slapped on some make-up. Even here she'd try to look her best.

Not for Luca by any chance? *No way.*

'You've got a text.' Chi nodded at her phone on the desk.

Probably Mum or Dad. Despite the rift between her and Caitlin that overlapped into her relationship with her parents they would still want to know how she was settling in. Then another thought snapped into her head. What if it was from Luca?

'Come on, Chi, show me where to go.'

If it was from Luca he could wait until she'd worked out how to handle today after what went down last night.

She couldn't resist. Snatching up the phone as she headed out, she pressed Messages and gasped. It was from her sister, Caitlin. There was nothing she wanted to hear from her. Her finger hovered over the delete button. What if something had happened to Mum or Dad? That would be a good enough reason for Caitlin to text. But wouldn't she ring if that was the case?

She sighed. The message read, Just checking to see you arrived safe and sound.

Why don't you ask Mum? I sent them a message on the way in from the train station.

Ellie shoved the phone into her shorts pocket and followed Chi. What was Caitlin up to now? They didn't do texts or any form of communicating. That had finished the day she'd learned the truth about her sister and her husband. It had been a stunning birthday present; one she'd never forget. But sometimes when she wasn't thinking clearly she did admit to missing Caitlin. They'd been closer than grapes in a bunch, told each other everything. Everything? As in 'I'm sleeping with your husband, Ellie,' everything?

'In here.' Chi took her hand to tug her into a long narrow room that housed the kitchen and a very long trestle table.

'You must be Ellie.' A man in his late forties and of average height crossed the room, his hand extended in greeting. 'I'm Aaron. Sorry for the confusion yesterday about who you were. I've been in touch with headquarters and they admitted the oversight was entirely their fault.'

Ellie shook his hand in return. 'It doesn't matter. I'm here, you've got the bases covered. That's what's important.'

'True. We'll try to break you in quietly today. But there's no telling what will come in the doors at any given moment.' Aaron's smile was completely guileless and relaxed Ellie enough to put her sister aside for a more appropriate time when she was on her own.

Her nose twitched as the smell of something hot and delicious reached her. 'What do we eat for breakfast?'

'*Chew makork*. Eggs, carrots and sticky rice,' Chi told her.

Different. 'Bring it on.'

It was simple and delicious. There were other vegetables with the carrots, and a chilli sauce made her skin heat and her mouth water. For her the food was all part of the adventure.

Unfortunately so was the grim awakening as to why she was here that arrived as everyone was finishing breakfast.

Aaron, who'd headed away to check on a patient he'd operated on yesterday, now stood in the doorway. 'Incoming patients. Two of them. All hands on deck. Ellie, that includes you. We'll show you the ropes as we go along.'

Gulp. She hadn't seen the hospital or the small theatre yet. 'I'm ready.' *Fake it till you make it.* It wasn't as though she didn't know what to do, but she'd have liked a few minutes to learn where everything was kept.

Louise must've seen her hesitation because she said, 'You'll be fine.'

Love it when people who know next to nothing about you except what was in your CV say that. Ellie shook her head and prepared to face whatever had arrived in the little building at the end of the garden. 'Where's Luca this morning?'

His absence had surprised her. Was he avoiding her? That would be plain silly considering they had to spend a lot of time together over the next few weeks. Better to front up to last night and move on.

'He went out early to visit a family in a village who don't have the wherewithal to get in here for check-ups and dressing changes. It happens a lot and we try to accommodate everyone.'

Maybe he hadn't gone to get away from her. Ellie wasn't sure how she felt about Luca this morning. Good, bad or indifferent? Certainly not indifferent. Or bad. Okay, so her feelings were good. As in friends good? Or more? As in used to be friends, now might be something else? Lovers? Well, there wasn't anything else. She wasn't going down the full-blown relationship of being married and contemplating kids track for a long time—if at all. Her skin prickled with the humiliation of her last attempt at that. Then there was the pain she'd known as all her dreams had shrivelled up into a dry heap.

'In here.' Louise turned into a large room busy with people dashing back and forth and someone crying out in agony.

The sight had Ellie drawing on all her strength not to gasp out loud. The young patient being carried across the room hadn't had the benefit of an ambulance crew and a relatively soft ride. The child had been piggybacked in by a small man, the blood from where a foot should've been dripping a trail right across the hospital room. At least someone had managed to tie a makeshift tourniquet around his lower thigh so that the blood flow had been minimised, though not completely stopped.

'Where's the other patient?' she asked, trying not to convey her horror as she and Louise lifted the unconscious boy off the man's back and placed him on a bed. 'Aaron said patients, plural.'

'In front of us. The boy's father. He has an injury to his buttocks.' Louise nodded at a gaping wound that Ellie hadn't noticed as she'd been too busy focusing on the child. 'You can take him over to that bed for an assessment and report back to Aaron. Noi will interpret for you.'

'I haven't met Noi yet,' Ellie said over her shoulder as she approached her patient.

Louise beckoned a young man over and made the introductions. 'Noi learned English at school. He wants to be a doctor and is spending time with us until he can get into medical school here in Vientiane.'

'Sabaai dii.' She'd learned the greeting that morning over sticky rice and carrots. 'Lovely to meet you.' Ellie shook Noi's hand.

The way Noi said *sabaai dii* was definitely an improvement on her botched attempt.

She smiled. 'I need practice.'

Noi nodded. 'You'll soon learn. Let's help the father.'

Ellie could not imagine how the man they were easing onto the bed had carried his son on his back with the wound she was now seeing. He'd have been in agony, even without the constant pummelling he'd received from his load, yet he hadn't said a word or groaned out loud. Turning to Noi, she said, 'Can you explain to our patient what I'm going to do? Also ask if he has any other injuries.'

While Noi spoke rapidly in Laotian she cut away what was left of the man's trousers, careful to be as discreet as possible, and hearing the tremor in the father's voice as he replied to Noi.

Noi told her, 'The father heard the explosion and found his son on the side of the road with his foot missing. When he stepped around him to lift him away from the danger another, smaller explosion happened. That's when he was hurt.'

Lucky for him there were no other injuries. This one was bad enough and going to cause him a lot of pain and anguish until it mended.

Crossing to where Louise and Aaron were working on the boy, she reported, 'That wound on the buttocks is the only injury. Muscle damage is severe and will require deep suturing. I need to administer pain relief before cleaning the wound and stitching.'

Aaron replied, 'Louise will get what you require from the drugs cabinet. Later this morning when we're done with these patients I'll show you everything and give you the codes for that and other locked rooms.'

'We'll be in surgery shortly with this lad, trying to save his lower leg,' Louise told her. 'Can you intubate him while I get what you require?'

'Of course.' She swapped places with Louise, and suctioned the lad's airway clear of fluids prior to inserting the tube. Next she attached the mask and began running oxygen, keeping an eagle eye on the boy's breathing. 'Don't the locals know to stay clear of the bombs? Or am I being simplistic?'

Aaron was having difficulty getting a needle into a vein in the thin forearm but eventually managed to get it into a vein on the back of the boy's hand, giving access for saline and drugs. 'At last.' He looked up at Ellie. 'You're seeing things as someone coming from a safe and relatively comfortable society does, as we've all done when we first arrived. These people are extremely poor. Scrap metal fetches on the market what's to them a lot of money. If a child can sell a piece he's helping feed his family. It's a no-brainer for them. It's also why a lot of children are missing limbs. Or worse. Welcome to Laos.'

Ellie surprised herself by finding a smile. 'I'm glad to be here. Truly.' Helping people and animals when they were in need had always been a big deal to her, and was the reason she'd gone into medicine. At first she'd been aiming to become a vet, but as she'd got older she'd swapped frogs and guinea pigs for humans. The idea of going to vet school had been quickly vanquished when her favourite dog had to be put down after being run over by a truck. No way could she ever deliberately put down any living creature, even if it was for the best. She just didn't have what it took.

Louise returned and handed her a kidney dish containing vials and syringes. 'Here you go. Once you've finished there can you move over to the day clinic and help with the day patients? I'm sorry we haven't had time to show you the ropes, but Luca assures us you're very good at your job.'

Luca had? Guess he'd talked with these two about her yesterday while she'd been in dreamland. He was four years out of touch, but she'd take the compliment anyway. Those had been lacking lately, and it felt good to have someone still believing in her without qualification. 'Not a problem.'

'Thanks.' Louise began heading for Theatre, then

paused. 'If Luca's not back when you're ready, ask Noi to introduce you to everyone.'

'Here I go, then,' Ellie whispered as she vigorously scrubbed her hands under a tap. 'The first day of a new venture. The first day after Luca kissed me.' And apparently he was due back any time soon. How would they look each other in the eye? The knowledge of their responses to that kiss had to come between them. So how to move beyond it without making a hash of things? If they didn't, the rest of her days here would be uncomfortable and difficult for both of them.

Ellie, focus on the job and stop worrying about the tomorrows.

If only it were that easy.

It could be. Face it, why did everything have to be complicated? What would be wrong about having a few kisses with Luca? Seeing where they led? Chances were they'd get over each other quickly and return to a relationship they were comfortable with. Not one where they didn't see each other or talk together for years, please. She was done with that. Done with losing the people in her life that were precious to her. Getting one person back was amazing, and she needed to tread carefully or risk losing him again.

So how did one go about retracting a kiss?

A memory of the heat that had zapped between them at his touch told her. It was impossible. As in it was too late. She was fried. The chances of looking at Luca without wondering what it would be like to feel his body against hers, inside her, were remote. This rebound thing had a lot to answer for. Who'd have thought it? The only explanation she could come up with on the spot was that she knew Luca well and would be safe with him while she tried to find her feet in the dating game. But she hadn't been contemplating getting into that murky pool for some time to come.

Luca leaned a shoulder against the door frame of the outpatients' clinic. A yawn rolled up and out, stretching his mouth and making him aware of the grit in his eyes. Damn, he was tired. Sleep had been impossible last night. Every time he'd closed his eyes his mind had filled with images of Ellie.

Ellie blinking at him in astonishment as he'd crossed the room to hug her for the first time in years.

Ellie in that curve-hugging shift dress that emphasised her figure and did nothing to curb the desire tugging at his manhood.

Ellie looking glum when she mentioned her broken marriage. Not that she'd said a lot. But there'd definitely been sadness and despair in those hazel pools that seemed to draw him in deeper every time he locked gazes with her. Like a vortex, swirling faster and faster. He had yet to hit the centre, but it was coming. He could feel it in his muscles—each and every one of them, damn it.

Watching her now as she talked to Noi, obviously getting him to explain to their patient what she had to do to help him, Luca felt that peculiar clenching of his heart again. A sensation he'd only felt once before— yesterday when he'd been with Ellie.

So much for heading out early to avoid her until he'd got his thoughts and emotions into some semblance of order. Only minutes back at the clinic and he was in trouble. Wondering where these feelings would lead him. Hoping nothing was about to come between him and Ellie again. He'd do anything for that not to happen.

So he wouldn't be kissing her again?

Damn right he wouldn't.

Dragging air deep into his lungs, he crossed to help with her patient. 'Hey, need a hand?'

Startled eyes locked on him. 'Luca. When did you get back?'

'Minutes ago.' There were green flecks in her eyes he hadn't noticed before. Could eyes change like that? Or had he just opened his wider? Begun to see things that had always been before him? 'What's the story here?' He tried to shut down the runaway heat speeding through his veins. 'Apart from those buttocks, I mean.'

'Nothing else. This man's been lucky.' Ellie's mouth twisted. 'I mean luckier than his son, and luckier than he might've been. It's unbelievable what's happened to them.'

Touching a finger to the back of her hand, Luca nodded. 'It's okay. I know what you mean. It takes time to get past the horror of bombs blowing up and hurting innocent people. This is for real, and we are so not used to it. You'll never get comfortable with it to the point you stop thinking and wondering why it has to happen at all, but you will come to accept that it does and we're here to help.'

Her teeth nibbled at her bottom lip as she stared down at the wound she was about to repair. 'Thanks. I needed to hear that. Here I was thinking I'd seen it all in the emergency department. Stabbings, shootings, high-speed car crashes. Awful scenarios, but this—' she waved a hand through the air '—children, adults, bombs, severed limbs. It's grotesque.'

'Yes, it is. Now, do you want me to assist while you put this man back together?' One of the nurses could do that but he was hoping with everything he had she'd say yes. He wanted to work with her. Maybe then reality would return, banishing this stupid need thickening his blood every time he so much as looked at Ellie. Time spent doing a medical procedure together would bring back memories of their training days in A and E and hopefully follow on with more reminders of what their relationship was about.

'That would be great,' she answered. 'I've given him painkillers, enough that hopefully he'll be drowsy while I stitch him back together.' Ellie proceeded to outline how she intended going about fixing her patient's wound. 'What happens when we've patched him up? Does he stay here?'

Luca shook his head. 'He will be transferred to Mahosot Hospital. We don't keep adult patients in our ward.'

The man turned his head to stare at Luca. He asked in Laotian, 'My boy. Where is he? Is he safe?'

When Luca interpreted Ellie told him, 'Aaron has him in Theatre. He's lost his foot and ankle. You'll know what to tell him about how Aaron will help his boy.'

Nodding, Luca explained to the father how the doctors would clean the stump and stop the blood flow. He kept it brief and simple. There'd be time later for the family to come to terms with the extent of the surgery going on in Theatre. Then he focused on assisting Ellie.

They worked well together, each anticipating the other's requirements without a word being spoken. And yes, the memories flooded in, unnerving him. A whiff of the past when they worked well together gave a hint of what the future could hold if they went down that track.

Nearly thirty minutes later Ellie tied off the last stitch and reached for a swab to clean the last of the blood on the surrounding skin. 'The risk of infection will be high, especially if this man goes back to his village in the next few days. What's the next step in his treatment?'

'Don't expect him to stay in hospital. There'll be pressing issues back home he'll want to attend to, like earning enough money for food,' Luca told her.

'The people I saw sitting on the front step yesterday when I arrived. They were parents of our patients?' She added, 'I thought *they* were the patients.'

'They'd mostly be mums and dads.'

'What about our man's son? Will he go home, too?' Again horror was reflected in her eyes.

A gnawing need to hold her tight against him and to shield her from all this grew larger and larger, and he had to swallow hard to hold back. 'Hopefully, with Noi's help, we can persuade the family to leave the boy with us until his wound heals. Sometimes a relative will move in to be with their family member, but that depends on if they can afford someone to be away from home for so long.'

'I've lived a very sheltered life.' Ellie lifted sad eyes to him.

'You're not regretting coming here?' He hoped not. Otherwise her month would stretch out interminably for her. But he also didn't want her stressed by what she was dealing with. Not everyone could cope with it, and Ellie seemed to already be under pressure from something else.

'Not at all. It's an eye-opener and I think I needed that. I've been getting too self-absorbed lately.'

Guess a marriage breakup might do that. 'Come

on, we'll grab a coffee while we can. Day clinic starts shortly. I'll be showing you the ropes.'

And working my tail off to forget that damned kiss.

'What do you do for a social life here?' Ellie asked, her eyes not quite meeting his.

'Drink beer with long-lost friends,' he answered flippantly.

'That exciting, eh?'

'Yeah, very exciting.'

'Luca, about last night—'

He shouldn't have said *very exciting*. She was getting the wrong idea. 'Last night was a mistake, okay? I'm putting it down to the shock and surprise of us catching up when we least expected it. Nothing more than that.'

'Fine.' Her gaze dropped, focused somewhere below his chin. 'That's good. I'll do that, too.'

Yeah, except it didn't feel good. Not at all.

CHAPTER FIVE

IN OUTPATIENTS, ELLIE ruffled a toddler's hair while squatting down beside the wee tot to check out a healing wound on the girl's arm. Luca's mouth dried. Ellie was beautiful. More beautiful than ever, even with that wariness that never seemed to completely go away. How could he not have kept in touch? Even knowing that the man she'd chosen to marry was wrong for her, especially knowing that, he should never have let other things get in the way of their friendship.

But he had. Now she was back, in his life, on his turf. And he was having these weird and wonderful reactions to her. Weird and wonderful? Or weird and weirder?

Beside him Noi said, 'The children already love her.'

'She certainly has a way with them,' Luca acknowledged. Not something he'd particularly noticed before. But then why would he? He hadn't been in the habit of taking notes of her attributes.

As Ellie carefully lifted the toddler's shirt she spoke softly and got no resistance to her gentle prods around the child's rib cage.

Luca sighed. 'She'd make a wonderful mother.'

He hadn't realised he'd spoken out loud until Noi asked, 'Ellie doesn't have children already?'

'In the Western world it's not uncommon for women to have children later in life than they do here.' Did Ellie want children of her own? He couldn't remember ever discussing that with her, but then they'd been so busy getting on with becoming doctors they hadn't been looking that far ahead. Until she'd met Baldwin, that was.

Noi shook his head, but refrained from comment. Probably didn't understand the differences between their cultures. 'I'll see you in the ward.'

'Luca, there you are,' a little boy squealed and ran across the room to him.

Ellie jerked around, a startled look on her face. 'Luca.' She gave him a brief nod and returned to her patient.

As he reached for the boy flinging himself at him he winced. Ellie hadn't been falling over herself to be friendly since yesterday when they'd talked about their kiss. While he should be grateful she wasn't pushing for a follow-up kiss, a part of him wished otherwise. He'd like nothing more than to repeat it, to taste her sweetness again, to feel his body fire up in anticipation of something more. No, not that. That desire had kept him awake again last night. Keep this up and he'd be a walking zombie by the time her month was up.

'Luca, say hello,' the boy demanded.

'Hi, Pak. How's that arm?' he asked, watching Ellie and tucking the boy against his chest.

'It's better now. The concrete can come off.'

'No, it can't. You've got another week before I remove it.'

A smile was hovering at the corners of Ellie's mouth, as though afraid to come out fully. 'Concrete, eh?'

'It's what the kids call their casts. Concrete sleeves,'

he explained as Pak wriggled in his arms. 'You want to get down already?' he asked in Laotian.

'Yes.'

'I like that you speak the lingo.' Ellie stood up, admiration lightening those big eyes and lifting her mouth into a full, delicious smile.

Delicious smile? He was deranged. Had to be. Why else was he wanting to kiss that mouth? Again? When he knew absolutely that it would be wrong, would lead to all sorts of complications? 'Not very well.'

The smile faltered, disappeared. 'You've made a start.' She turned away, picked up a stethoscope and knelt down to the toddler, who seemed rooted to the floor as she stared at Ellie. Had she fallen for her, too?

Fallen for her? *No damned way. I have not.* This was getting stranger and stranger. Luca mentally slapped his head. Put Pak down. Strode back the way he'd come, heading for the ward and the children who needed him to check their stumps, needed encouragement to start walking again, or using arms that were shorter than they used to be. Away from Ellie and those eyes that drew him in.

So he was running away? Acting like a coward now? What else was he supposed to do?

Face up to her. Get past that kiss.

Luca didn't miss a step as he spun around and headed back to the outpatients' room, right up to where Ellie was straightening up again. Reaching for her, he drew her close and lowered his head.

Just before his mouth claimed hers he muttered, 'This has got to stop. We need to move past whatever's causing us to act out of character.' Then he kissed her. Long and hard, tasting her, letting her taste him. Feeling the moment when the tension left her body and she melted in against him. Feeling those lush breasts pressed against the hard wall of his chest. Sensing her heightened awareness of him.

His growing need strained against his trousers, about to push against the softness of her belly.

Luca tore his mouth away, dropped his hands to his sides, glared into Ellie's startled eyes, and growled, 'There, we've got that out of the way. Now we can work together without any distractions.'

And he walked away. If he could call his rapid shuffle a walk.

How had he come up with all that stuff? No distractions? He'd just made a monumental error and ramped up the distraction meter to such a level it was off the Richter scale. And he'd thought he couldn't get any more stupid. Went to show how wrong a guy could be when diverted by a beautiful woman. So much for bravery. He had not intended on kissing Ellie when he returned to her.

So why had he gone back?

He seriously had no idea. Other than not wanting to be thought of as a coward. Which only went to show what an idiot he really was. Kissing Ellie again had not dampened down his ardour. Hell no. Now he wanted more. More kisses, more touching, more of everything.

Good one, Chirsky, good one.

Idiot.

Ellie's fingers were soft on her lips, tracing where Luca's mouth had touched hers. *Stunned* didn't begin to describe how she felt. When Luca had charged back into the room with a determined expression darkening his face she'd had no idea what it was about. There'd been a moment when she'd wondered if he was angry at her for some misdemeanour, except she hadn't been here long enough to stuff up anything. But then he'd hauled her into his arms and kissed her—thoroughly. Not angrily.

She'd kissed him back equally enthusiastically. It had been a kiss to defy all kisses. It shouldn't have happened. But it had, and now Ellie had to work out a way forward. In Luca's eyes that kiss should end all speculation and leave them free to get back to being who they were to each other. Friends without benefits.

'Ellie?' Louise stood before her, that worried look of two days ago back in her kind eyes. 'Are you all right?'

I've just been kissed by my best friend. How am I supposed to feel? 'I'm fine.' Uh-oh, had Louise seen her and Luca in that embrace? 'I was checking out Took.' *Before I was interrupted.* 'She's got a chest infection.' *I was checking out Luca, too, but that doesn't count. Not much. I think his chest is okay. Nah, it's hard and muscular and I want to run my tongue the length of it. Much more than okay.*

'That's Took's second infection in three weeks. I don't think there's a lot of clean water at home for keeping the wound site under her arm sterile.' Louise was studying Ellie with a very wise expression on her face. 'When you're done here, would you like me to show you how the outpatients is run instead of you working with Luca in the amputation clinic?'

Ellie knew Louise had been looking forward to a morning off to go into town. Tempting as her offer was, Ellie couldn't accept. She was here to help, not hinder the running of the clinic and the staff's downtime. 'Not at all. I've been looking forward to meeting some of those other patients.'

'As long as you're sure.'

'Louise—' Ellie grimaced '—I'm sorry. Luca and I used to be very close friends and then life got in the way. It's the best thing that could've happened, finding him working here. Truly.' On a long, slow breath she added, 'I've missed him a lot and I think he feels the same. Things have just got out of whack, but we'll settle down. You'll see. I do not want to upset anything going on here. I came to help, not disrupt.'

Finally she got a big smile from Louise. 'Any time you feel like a glass of wine and a girl talk you know where to find me.'

'You're a champ. Now I need to get some antibiotics for Took.'

'I'll walk down to the drug cupboard with you. Aaron wants some mild painkillers for his patient.'

One of the many notches in Ellie's tummy loosened. 'I heard the markets are only open in the mornings. Is that right?'

'That's what the brochures say but I've never found them closed before late afternoon yet. Aaron and I usually go there at least one afternoon a week and carry on to a bar and restaurant. Want to join us this afternoon after everyone's wrapped up here? Luca's coming,' she added quickly.

'I'd love to.' She wasn't going to let that kiss spoil her getting out and seeing the sights and enjoying shopping in the local places. Doing that with people who already knew their way around would be more fun, too. She wasn't into getting lost and trying to find her way around. Didn't have the patience, for a start. 'There's something about markets I adore.'

'You're a softie. I can see you buying from every stall.'

'Could be a long day,' she agreed. 'It will be fun.'

Hopefully Luca would see things in the same light and not get het up about her joining them. Otherwise he could be the one to miss out. She wasn't going to stay back in her room. And the added bonus was more time spent with Luca. She had an itch to quieten.

'Hey, Ellie, come meet Ash,' Luca called out the moment she walked into the clinic. He was all professional and outwardly friendly. Almost as if that kiss hadn't happened. Or was on hold?

He'd got himself all together quick enough. Guess that meant he wasn't as rattled as she'd been. Still was. But then Luca had had plenty of experience at hiding what he didn't want anyone else to know about him. She tried to follow his example and focused on the boy. 'Hi, Ash. Why do we call you that?'

Luca explained, 'Because his name is longer than the alphabet and equally unpronounceable for Westerners. It starts with A so he's called Ash.' Luca was squatting beside a boy who couldn't be more than four, and had only one leg.

'Makes a lot of sense—not.'

When Luca looked up at her she found smiling at him wasn't too difficult. There were no recriminations peeking out, no annoyance with her for succumbing to his kiss. So she could even begin to think he might have been right—they'd needed to get that second kiss out of the way to move on. Really? Make that a no, but she'd do her best not to show how much she wanted to follow up on it.

Kneeling beside Ash, she turned to concentrate on the boy's stump. 'This happened recently? Two or three weeks ago?'

Luca nodded. 'Three. We're still getting the hang of using crutches, aren't we, Ash?'

The boy nodded slowly, his huge dark eyes sombre as he studied her, still staying close to Luca. As if he trusted his doctor for everything. That was wonderful.

The boy was so young, younger than most she'd seen around here so far. 'Does Ash stay here all the time or is he a day patient?'

Luca locked his gaze on her and that was when she saw the apprehension in the backs of his eyes. So he wasn't being blasé about her or their kiss, just working on keeping it in perspective. But he answered the question she'd voiced, not the one spinning around her skull about where they went from that moment back in the treatment room. 'Ash is living with us for now. His mum and dad visit whenever they can get in from their village, which is up in the hills north of here.'

In other words not very often. Ellie's heart squeezed for this brave little guy, and she put her own concerns aside. 'How many brothers and sisters have you got, Ash?'

Ash stared at her for a moment, before turning to Luca for an interpretation. 'Four' was the answer.

'I can see why you've learned some of the language,' Ellie told Luca. 'These kids need you to understand them, don't they?' It had to be hideous finding themselves with such awful injuries in a clinic surrounded by people speaking strange words. Yet Luca chattered to Ash as though he was totally au fait with the boy's language. She asked, 'How do you say I like you?'

Luca nodded in understanding and slowly enunciated a phase that was almost incomprehensible.

Ellie grinned at Ash and tried to repeat the phrase. 'Don't think I'm making any sense to him at all.' She laughed.

'Try again after me.'

Same sound, same result, except Ash was starting to smile at her. A slow awakening that lifted his sad face and lightened those eyes to a dark brown, the blackness dissipating.

When Luca told him what she'd been trying to say his little smile grew and he nodded at her before putting his tiny hand on her arm.

That felt like the best thing to happen to her. After Luca's amazing kiss, that was. A quick glance at Luca and she found him watching her so intently her cheeks began heating up.

'Ash likes you, too.' His words were a caress, making her think there was more to what he said. Luca liked her, too?

Right, let's get this show on the road and stop mooning over Luca. 'Can I help him with his crutches?'

'Sure. We've just had a new pair made, which in clinic speak means an old pair cut down to Ash's size. The ones he's been using were way too big for him and he kept tripping, which caused awful pain.' Luca was all doctor mode now.

'So he's not going to be keen to get moving on these newer ones.'

'You got it.' Luca ruffled the boy's hair in that casual yet caring manner he did so well. Had he ever thought about having his own family? A warmth trickled through her at the thought of Luca surrounded by his own children.

'Is there an adult pair somewhere?' she asked and grinned when Luca's eyes widened in understanding.

'Why have I never thought of that? Over in that walk-in cupboard.' He nodded in the direction of two doors butted up together. 'Have you ever had to use crutches yourself?'

'Nope. But that's the point. I can make mistakes, too.'

'This I have to watch.' Luca chuckled as she headed for the cupboard.

Trying the crutches out for size, she quickly had a pair and started back to Ash, swinging between the wooden implements that had seen better days a long time ago. It wasn't as easy as she'd thought it would be, but that was fine. She didn't want to be perfect in front of the boy. She'd rather fall over and laugh. Though she didn't want Ash falling. For him it would be too painful. 'Let's go.' She nodded at him.

Ash stared at her, not making any move to get off the chair. Two big tears slid down his cheeks and he shook his head from side to side.

Ah, hell. Tears would be her undoing any time. She'd rather wrap him up in a blanket and read him a story than make him do this. But, 'Come on. You'll be good.'

Luca held out the small crutches and said something in Laotian. Whatever it was his voice was soothing and encouraging, and slowly Ash stood up on his good leg and took the crutches being held out to him.

Go you, Luca. 'We'll do this together,' Ellie said and, standing on one foot, moved her crutches forward and waited.

Luca interpreted.

Ash bit into his bottom lip and his face crunched up in concentration.

Ellie held her breath.

So did Luca.

Ash lifted the crutches and put them farther in front of him.

'Go you. Now we hop.' Ellie demonstrated, making sure she didn't go too far forward.

Luca interpreted.

Ash hopped. The crutches wobbled dangerously.

Ellie held her breath as Luca held his hands beneath Ash's arms without actually touching him, ready to catch him if the crutches went from under him.

Panic flared in Ash's eyes as he swayed and grappled for balance. When he was standing straight again he looked down at the crutches as though they were to blame for his predicament.

'That's good, Ash.' Ellie kept her tone light and encouraging. 'Now we'll do it again.' And again, and again.

Slowly they progressed across the room, and with every step Ash's confidence grew. The fear softened from his face as determination crept into his eyes, tightened his mouth. He was going to make these crutches work no matter what.

'Don't get too cocky,' Ellie warned. A fall onto the floor would set him back again.

'Take a break,' Luca told her, and then repeated the same thing to Ash in Laotian.

Or she supposed that was what he was saying. 'I'll stop if Ash does.'

Ash said nothing, just turned and began crossing the room back to where they'd started.

Ellie hurried to catch up, nearly tripping over her own feet. Ash looked at her and almost laughed. Almost but not quite. His mouth widened, his eyes lit up and his chest lifted, then everything stopped and he went back to solemn. Guess he didn't do laughing since the devastation that had brought him to the clinic's attention. Life for these kids would become very hard when they grew up and had to struggle to compete for work in an environment not flush with jobs and cash even for the uninjured.

She wasn't going to let that distract them from having fun while he learned to get around. This was only the first step of learning to be mobile again. 'You little ratbag.' She grinned. 'It's a game now, is it?' She held back on racing him. He was not ready for that yet. But it wouldn't be long before he was running around on those sticks as though born with them. Ellie reckoned that soon the staff would be wishing he'd sit down and keep still for a while. 'I am so glad I came here.'

Luca grinned. 'Glad you see it that way. I get such a kick from helping these guys.'

'You're a natural with children.'

He looked shocked. 'I am?'

'Definitely.' And what was more, she really liked that. How come she'd never noticed it before?

'Luca,' Sharon, a nurse, called across the room. 'There's been an accident outside the clinic and the victim's been brought in here. His heart's stopped so there's no time to wait for an ambulance to take him next door.'

Luca said, 'Coming. Get Carol to take over with Ash. Ellie, can you join me?'

'Be right there.' She helped Ash put down his crutches and sit on his seat again. His legs were shaking from the strain of learning to balance and hop, but his eyes were wide with excitement.

'I'm here.' Carol sank down on the chair beside the

boy. 'We'll do some exercises and rubbing on your muscles now, Ash.' Carol was a physiotherapist and had a love-hate relationship with the children for the pain and relief she brought them.

Ellie dashed to the small resus unit, where an elderly man lay on the bed. Luca was already leaning over him performing CPR while a nurse gave oxygen as required.

'There's a defib in Theatre,' Luca told her.

Ellie raced to get it and, returning, opened the kit and began attaching the pads. 'Stand back, everyone.' After checking everyone was out of the way she pressed the start button and held her breath as the mechanical voice recited the procedure that was underway. The patient's body arched off the bed, dropped back. Instantly the cardiac monitor began beeping instead of the flat tone it had been giving.

'Hoorah.' A muted cheer went up.

Luca stepped back and wiped the sweat from his brow with the back of his hand. 'Strike one to us. Might as well sort out those wounds while he's here. I wonder which came first—the accident or the cardiac arrest?' he said as he began examining the man thoroughly.

Ellie shook her head in amazement as she tossed her gloves into a bin half an hour later and watched their patient being wheeled through the building to the hospital annex. 'That's one lucky man. Who gets catapulted through the front windscreen, lands on a pole in a ditch and only gets concussion with lacerations and bruising?'

'You're forgetting the heart attack that probably caused him to drive off the road in the first place.' Luca rubbed his eyes with his fingertips.

'He chose the right spot for his accident,' Ellie said as she watched Luca. There were shadows under his eyes. 'Are you having trouble sleeping?' she asked before she engaged her brain in gear. What if he said he'd lain awake last night thinking about that first kiss? She wouldn't know how to handle that. It was bad enough having to work with him and pretend they hadn't kissed a second time, and that the entire staff probably knew about it because little children knew no boundaries when it came to being discreet.

'It was hotter than usual last night,' Luca muttered without looking at her.

'Really?' A little devil was making her question things best left alone. The same devil that had her wanting more of Luca's kisses. 'I didn't notice.'

'You've only been here a few days. All the night temperatures will be hot to you.' Luca's gloves headed in the same direction as hers. 'Coffee?' he asked, then looked shocked for asking.

The devil replied, 'Sure. Why not? Unless we're needed in the clinic again.' She should be wishing they were. But she wasn't.

'We're due a break.'

Ellie followed Luca to the kitchen. 'What's next on the list of things to do?'

As Luca stirred a load of sugar into his coffee he said, 'This afternoon I'm visiting two villages where we have kids still adjusting to their prostheses. You're coming with me.'

'Great. Seeing where these families live will be interesting.'

'It's a damned eye-opener is what it is. Don't go expecting a pretty picture, Ellie, otherwise you'll get a rude shock.' His voice was laced with anger. At her?

Taken aback, she snapped, 'I said interesting, not exciting or fun.'

'Good. Then, we'll head out after lunch.'

'I'll let Louise know. She's expecting us to join her for the market and a meal afterwards.'

'No need. She knows where we're going, and that we'll catch up with her and Aaron at the market.' His tone hadn't lightened.

'What's your problem? If you'd prefer I didn't come with you then just say so. I won't be offended.' *I might be hurt a wee bit, but I'll get over it.* If he didn't want to be shut in a vehicle with her for the afternoon then he didn't, but he could at least tell her. Didn't need to go all grumpy on her.

'You need to see these people in their own villages. It will help you understand better how much they have to give up when they visit their children, why they often send another child to be with the injured one.'

'Will it help me to accept that these kids have to dig for metal in order to have food at the end of the day?' she growled back. Two could get wound up and snap at each other.

Luca's shoulders lifted as he drew a deep breath. 'Unfortunately yes, but it won't help you condone it. Nothing, no one, would. Those bombs are so destructive. But hunger is worse—or so the villagers think. As they're the ones living with it, who am I to argue?'

Instantly her mood softened. Whatever was going on between her and Luca, her job was about these children and their families, and her time here was about her job. Somehow she'd get through the time spent in close proximity to Luca without going off her head yearning for another kiss. Fingers crossed.

CHAPTER SIX

'WE'RE GOING TO see Lai first.' Luca drove slowly around a group of schoolchildren on bikes. 'She's a fourteen-year-old who had the misfortune to fall into a crater and land on large pieces of shrapnel, piercing her abdomen and perforating her bowel.'

'Unbelievable.' Ellie grimaced. 'Did Lai work or go to school before this happened?'

'She worked the family stall at a nearby market selling vegetables that the village grew. Now someone else does that job and she tries to look after some of the gardens, but she's weak and suffers a lot of pain and inflammation that we haven't been able to control very successfully.' Luca had a box in the back of the vehicle for vegetables he'd buy from Lai to take back to their kitchen. Any little amount helped the village a lot.

'They're a tough people, aren't they?'

He nodded. 'They are. Here we go.' He pulled into a yard where hens were fossicking for any unfortunate worm or beetle. 'That's Lai over in the shade.' The girl looked as though she were dozing but sat upright the moment he stepped out of the four-wheel drive. 'Hi, Lai.'

'Dr Luca. I didn't know you were coming today. Who's that?' She nodded at Ellie.

'This is Dr Thompson. She works at the clinic with me.' He kept the words simple because he didn't understand the language as well as Ellie had given him credit for.

But Lai must've understood. 'Has she come to see me?'

'Yes.'

'She's pretty.'

At least that was what Luca thought Lai said. And if it was he had to agree. Ellie was pretty, downright beautiful really, with her high cheekbones and sparkling hazel eyes that sometimes were more green than brown—like today. Then there was all that dark blonde hair she'd tied in a high ponytail to keep it off her neck. As it swung with her movements it made him itch to let the hair free and run his hands over and through it, to feel if it was as silken as it looked. 'Lai says you're pretty,' he told El. He'd always known that but never got in a stew over her looks. Now they did things to his libido that shouldn't be happening.

'What does she want from me?' Ellie smiled towards the girl. 'Hello, Lai. My name is Ellie.'

Luca translated roughly, and earned Ellie the biggest smile he'd ever seen the girl give anyone. El did that everywhere she went. All the children at the clinic adored her already, their little faces lighting up the moment she stepped into their room. She was so good with them. Like today with Ash and those crutches no one had been able to get him back to using since his last tumble. Now the kid was almost racing on them.

Already Ellie was squatting down, holding Lai's hand and talking softly. It didn't seem to matter that Lai didn't understand her words; she certainly understood that compassion and care radiating from Ellie's face.

'You're like old friends,' he mock growled. 'Yakety-yak.'

Ellie squinted up at him. 'You can join in. It's what friends do.'

Was that a poke at him? Because of that kiss? 'I'll get the medical bag.' Anything to give him a break from those eyes that saw too damned much. He shouldn't have brought her out here today. It had been the perfect opportunity to get away alone for a couple of hours while he relived that kiss and put it to bed in his mind. Put it to bed? He knew exactly what he wanted to put to bed and with whom. Making love to Ellie shouldn't even enter his mind, but it had from around the instant he'd started kissing her the other evening. And it sure as hell didn't seem in any hurry to go away again.

His knuckles were white where he clenched the bag's carry strap. How was he supposed to get through the coming weeks if this was how he felt after only days? Look at her. Chatting with Lai as if she knew the language and making the girl laugh. Now there was a first. Lai didn't laugh, ever.

But hey, he understood perfectly. Ellie made him smile more often than he had lately, so bogged down in what to do next with his career that he'd become unable to find his usual cheery persona. She made him feel other things, too, like excitement for being with her, for being alive. Like this need to hold her and make love with her. His friend, best friend back in the days they lived and worked together. Never had he felt a twinge of desire for her, and yet now his whole body pulsed with a throbbing need that would not go away. Damn it.

He slammed the door shut, the bang echoing through the village. Ellie raised questioning eyes in his direction and stood up. 'You okay?'

'Why wouldn't I be?' Hell, he was turning into an old grump. A smiling old grump. 'I need to take Lai's temperature and check her wounds.'

'Want me to do it?'

No, I want you to take a hike, give me some space and stop looking so damned desirable in that thin-strapped top that barely reaches your waist and those short shorts. 'Come with us into Lai's family home.' He should've insisted she dress in a shirt with sleeves down to her wrists and baggy trousers that didn't outline her butt so well.

The tiny lopsided dwelling was spotless, an amazing feat considering the dust swirling around outside. Lai's mother was cooking rice and something he couldn't make out by smell or sight. She gave him a shy smile and shifted a stool out from under the table for him.

'Your temperature is normal today,' he told Lai. That was a first. Hopefully that indicated the start of Lai's return to full health.

'The wound looks clear of infection, too,' Ellie said a moment later.

Luca asked to see Lai's pills and gave her some more antibiotics to take if redness returned at the wound site. Then he negotiated to buy some vegetables from her mother and soon he and Ellie were back on the road.

A few minutes along the road and Ellie started laughing.

'What?' he asked. 'Have you got heatstroke?'

She only laughed louder. 'I'm trying to put Luca the

A and E specialist and Luca the Laos clinic doctor together. It's not easy.'

'Thanks a bunch. I don't think I'm a bad doctor. I do an all right job anywhere I'm needed.' Didn't he?

Her hand suddenly covered his on the steering wheel. 'Relax. I wasn't having a poke at you. You're an amazing doctor.'

A different heat from that of the climate seeped into his blood, warmed him deep inside. 'Thanks.' For the compliment? Or the touch? He hoped she forgot her hand was there for a little while.

'I'm still getting used to seeing you working here where the urgency is less—except when new patients turn up bleeding all over the show. I only remember you on full alert, going from patient to patient, giving each of them your undivided attention, and yelling orders to the nurses. Here you're calmer, work at a pace that suits the children and still get to see twice as many patients as everyone else.'

Quite a speech. His chest swelled with pride. 'Coming here has been good for me. But I want to return to emergency medicine some time in the near future.' When had he made that decision? Only a couple of days ago he'd been wondering whether to take up a twelve-month contract in Cambodia. Was Ellie's presence changing everything for him? 'Would you give up what you do back home and spend a year doing something similar?'

She withdrew her hand.

Damn.

Ellie nibbled her bottom lip for a moment. 'I don't think so. But it's early days. Ask me again at the end of my month here.'

One month. It could be a very long time, or it could

speed by. With Ellie he had times when the minutes seemed to whizz past, and then when he was busting to kiss her again and had to work with her instead the minutes felt like hours. Now he had to sit in a car with her so close his skin was constantly aware of her. He should've hosed her off before they left to remove that tantalising scent she wore.

She hadn't finished telling him about what she was doing next. 'I've already got a six-month contract back home starting after Christmas. Any ideas of working offshore will have to wait.'

'Christmas. Being here I'd sort of forgotten about it. You'll be spending the day with your family?'

'I don't think so.' There was a sharp edge in her voice.

'Why not?' She had always tried to get home if she wasn't rostered to work on the twenty-fifth.

'I'll be in Auckland.' A definite 'don't ask' echoed between them.

But this was his friend; he needed to know. 'There are planes.'

'I don't want to be in the same city as Freddy, all right?'

Didn't make sense to him. It wasn't as though Freddy would be sitting down to Christmas dinner with her parents. 'We used to talk about things that were bugging us.'

'We did.' She stared straight ahead.

Okay. He'd fall into line and stop pushing her. He didn't want her wrath, nor did he want to upset her, and it seemed that was where he might be headed, though for the life of him he didn't understand why. 'You're going to love the market. Hope you've brought lots of cash.'

'They don't use EFTPOS?' She looked relieved that he'd changed the subject.

What had that been about? He hoped she'd tell him sometime before she headed back home.

'Buy this one.' Luca passed her a hat from a stall table to try on. 'The kids will fall over laughing if you wear that around the place.'

Ellie took the cotton creation with fabric elephants and bears swinging from the brim. 'The kids or you?' She chuckled. She put down the sane and sensible sunhat she'd just tried and plopped Luca's suggestion on her head.

The woman behind the counter grinned and pointed to a mirror. 'You like? You buy?' The hope in her voice would've had Ellie buying the hat if nothing else would.

'Go on, and this one.' She handed over the sensible one, and picked up two more brightly coloured caps. 'And these.'

'You've only got one head,' Luca quipped.

'They're not exactly expensive,' she retorted, happily handing over some American dollars.

'You're supposed to barter.' Luca shook his head at her. That smile that had started as he followed her around Talaat Sao, the morning market that ran all day, just got bigger and bigger. So he was enjoying her company. On the trip to the villages she'd begun to believe he couldn't wait for her to be gone.

'Next time.' Not. She hated bartering. Wasn't any good at it because she felt it was cheating someone out of their money.

Luca only laughed. 'I'll do it for you.'

Aaron called from farther along. 'Luca, here are some shirts that might be what you're looking for.'

While Luca headed that way Ellie waited for her

change and the hats to be folded neatly and placed in a plastic bag. *'Kowp jai,'* she said, and smiled at the woman's surprise at her butchered thank-you.

The woman nodded and grinned. *'Kowp jai.'*

That sounded nothing like what Ellie had said, but, hey, she'd tried. Turning in the direction Luca had gone, she scanned the heads of the crowd pushing through the narrow walkways between overladen stalls and couldn't see him or Aaron. Luca's height had him shoulders above most people and he was nowhere to be seen. Making her way to where she thought Aaron had called from, she found dozens of shirts hanging for sale but no sight of the two men. Or Louise. Where were they? How would she find them? If she went outside she could end up on the wrong side and not know where to go next.

She stared around, ignoring the bumps from people trying to move through the crowd. *Think, Ellie. Getting freaked out is stupid. It's not a massive market. They won't have gone far.* Looking at the next stall, she saw there were more shirts for sale, as there were at all the stalls along this line. She began walking quickly, suddenly wanting nothing more than to see Luca.

If she didn't find them along here she'd return to the stall where she'd got her hats and wait for them to find her.

'Ellie, come and tell Luca he should buy that shirt,' Louise called from behind her.

Spinning around, she saw the three people she'd been searching for crammed into a back corner of a stall she'd walked straight past. 'You think he'll listen to me?' She gave a lopsided smile and hoped her racing heart settled fast. How silly to get all worked up over not being able to see these guys for all of five minutes.

'Depends what you've got to say.' Luca looked at her across the tiny space. 'Hey.' He shrugged out of the shirt. 'I'll take it.' Then he crossed to her and gripped her hands, bag of hats included. 'Breathe deep. You're okay. You're not in that underground cave now.' His fingers tightened around her hands, his thumbs rubbing her wrists. 'You're fine. Promise.'

See? Her friend understood her, knew why she'd got worked up over nothing. 'I looked around and couldn't find you. I didn't know where to go, where we'd come in.'

'Ellie? You okay?' Louise looked at her with concern.

She let go a sigh. 'Yes, sorry. Years back a group of us went to some caves and when we were all deep inside the guides turned the lights off for a short time so we could see the glow worms. I got a bit lost and panicked. Ever since I get a wee bit stressed in crowds if I'm not sure where I am.'

Luca kissed her fingers before dropping her hands. 'My fault. Knowing how you were that day, I shouldn't have left you at that stall on your own.'

'No, Luca, it's not your fault. I'm a big girl. I should've watched where you went and kept an eye on you until I had my shopping sorted.' She liked that he had recognised her panic instantly and had come to her. That was special, and she felt cared for.

'Should we head out for that drink, then?' Aaron asked.

'No way. I haven't seen half the market yet. And I know Louise is looking for some earrings to send home to her niece.' She wasn't preventing everyone doing what they'd come here for. Anyway, her panic had gone, she was with Luca and all was well in her world.

'Trinkets and jewellery next, then.' Louise nodded her approval.

By the time they all sat down to beer and wine at a local bar Ellie was pleased with her shopping. 'Those earrings are lovely.' She sipped her drink.

'Which ones?' Luca drawled. 'I thought the stall holder was going to faint with excitement the number you two bought.'

'Says the guy who bought five shirts,' Louise said.

'I can't wait to visit the craft galleries,' Ellie enthused. 'Handwoven fabrics and embroidery will get me every time.' And might put a bit of a dent in her bank account, especially if her baggage allowance was exceeded going home. But, hey, what was money for if not sharing around? She knew she was a sucker for the shy smiles on the faces of the women selling their wares.

'He knows you well.' Louise nodded at Luca when he leaned on the bar waiting for the barman's attention so he could order a snack.

'He does.' Better than anyone else, Ellie realised with a start. Not even her ex had known her as well. Whose fault had that been? Hers for not offering up titbits about herself, or Freddy's for not thinking to ask? 'It's kind of good having someone aware of who I am.' It was something she hadn't had for a while.

'And it helps that that someone has a nice butt,' Louise said, grinning in the direction of Luca.

Aaron's eyes rolled.

'What are you trying to do here?' Ellie asked, while trying not to gape at what was truly a very nice butt. She was a butt girl after all.

Louise shrugged through a soft smile. 'Nothing.'

Now *her* eyes were rolling. 'Of course.' Where had

this longing for something more with Luca come from? Kisses were great, but what would making love with him be like? Shock rippled through her, bringing a sweat to her arms, between her breasts, her thighs. Sex with Luca? Yeah, that too-good-looking-to-be-true man. Was it even possible to go from best friends to lovers? Her skin heated further at the thought.

I really do *want to find out, want to match my body to his and feel him inside me.*

The glass shook in her hand, but she dared not set it down for fear of knocking it over.

Sex with Luca and there'd be problems. Keep him as a friend, and they'd always get along no matter how many arguments they had over the dumbest of things. In her experience friends were more forgiving than husbands. Take Luca as a lover and everything expanded, became filled with tension and the potential for hurt feelings that no one recovered from. She trusted Luca as a friend. It might not be the same if he became her lover. There was more to lose.

A dose of reality was needed about now to stop her head spinning. She checked her phone in a pathetic hope that she was needed back at the clinic. Nothing doing. She reached for her glass and forced her mind to follow the conversation Luca and Aaron were now having about deep-sea fishing in the South Pacific. She hadn't known Luca had tried it. Hadn't known he enjoyed fishing, even.

Next they headed to a restaurant filled with loud tourists, and followed that up with a nightcap at a nightclub so that she could apparently see more of the city.

'Can't have you going home without seeing every side of Vientiane.' Aaron grinned. 'Hope you're into dancing.'

'There's no music.' She stated the obvious, staring at Luca and fighting the sense she was slipping into a deep hole with no way out. She couldn't dance with Luca. That would mean touching him, feeling those muscles moving under her hand.

Luca chimed in. 'There will be. Very loud, too. The band's taking a break.' He leaned close and asked, 'What do you want to drink?'

As she breathed in his scent her mouth dried while her skin heated. 'W-water,' she managed, wanting to grab him to prevent him moving away. She turned her head, her nose brushing across his cheek. 'Luca?' she whispered.

'Ye-es?' He remained perfectly still.

What? Luca what? Her mind was blank, totally absorbed in all things Luca and unable to come up with a single word.

Finally he stepped away. 'Two waters,' he said to the barman before pulling a stool close to hers and parking that very nice butt down.

Her lungs struggled with the whole in-out thing. Air seemed lodged somewhere between her nose and her chest. Was she ill? Could that be what this was all about?

You're kidding. You've got the hots for Luca. That's what it's about, nothing more, nothing less.

Right. Now what? She stared around the club, finally focusing on Louise and Aaron on the dance floor. 'They're a lovely couple.'

Luca's gaze followed hers. 'I wonder sometimes if they don't get enough privacy. Living on the compound all the time means there are always others around.'

'I wouldn't cope with that. I like my own space, and if I was with someone I'd want him to myself some of the day.' Yet she and Freddy hadn't spent hours together at home. One or other of them was usually working long hours or he'd be playing golf or she'd be at the movies. It hadn't bothered her then. Over the past couple of days her marriage had started to look a little different from what she'd believed it to be. Had she been an unknowing part of its breakdown? There were usually two sides to everything.

As that blinding truth struck her, Luca took the glass from her hand. 'Let's dance.' Before she could say no he was leading her onto the floor to join other couples dancing to the fast tempo. Luca held on to her hand and began to move in time to the music.

Ellie found a smile for him. 'You always were a smooth dude on the dance floor.'

His face cracked into a wide smile. 'You bet.' And he grabbed her to spin them around in a wide circle, scattering half the other people nearby. 'Glad you remembered.'

There wasn't a lot she'd forgotten, just things she hadn't known about until this week. What else hadn't he spoken about? She wanted to know it all, felt the need to understand more about him. Why was he here and not in that A and E department? That had nothing to do with Gaylene's betrayal, surely? Why didn't she know what he wanted to do next in his life? That might be because he'd lost his child. Something that big would change her focus, too.

The music changed, much slower this time, and Ellie found herself being tucked against Luca's body, one of his hands around her waist, the other holding hers against his chest, as they stepped in unison to the rhythm. Their hips touched, her breasts moved over his chest as she danced, and she breathed him in. She forgot all the questions she'd wanted to ask. Forgot all the reasons why she shouldn't be dancing like this with Luca. Knew only his heat, his scent, his hard body against hers.

She didn't want to go back to her tiny, stuffy room. Could stay here in Luca's arms all night. Being held so tenderly almost broke her heart. She hadn't known such tenderness before. Yet there was strength in his hands and body, in his face too. His beloved face. How had she forgotten the warmth in his eyes? In his heart, his hands?

She'd never really noticed it. That was how. Luca had been a friend. Now he was more than that. And somehow she had to ignore the desire unfurling deep inside her body, not let it take over and rule her besotted brain. But she'd wait for one more song before she shifted out of his hold. Just one more.

No one told the band that she didn't want to step away from Luca and minutes later they were dancing all over the show at a fast pace.

Ellie's mood lifted as she jived and shook in time to some of her all-time favourite songs, Luca moving right along with her.

'Time we headed home,' Aaron interrupted. 'Unless you want to grab a cab later.'

Luca raised an eyebrow at Ellie.

Yes, she'd love nothing more than to continue dancing the night away, but she really had to remember she and Luca were no more than friends. That to take this any further might help her heart for a while but it would only get broken all over again when Luca had had enough. Or finally made up his mind where he was going next because that wouldn't be in the same direction as she was headed. Unfortunately. Because she was beginning to see a future that involved Luca, despite knowing it was impossible. 'We're coming with you.'

'We are?' Luca stretched that eyebrow higher.

'I am.' She shrugged. 'Sorry, but— Well, I'm sorry.'

He draped an arm over her shoulders. 'Not a problem, El. Glad one of us is thinking straight.'

Couldn't he look a little bit disappointed?

CHAPTER SEVEN

A WEEK AFTER that night dancing at the club Ellie was still vacillating between relief she'd insisted she came back from the nightclub with the others and wishing she'd given into the relentless need to learn more about Luca and that incredible body.

'Ellie, come and play.' A young boy stood in front of her, swinging a cricket bat from side to side.

How incongruous was that? Cricket in Laos seemed unlikely yet someone previously working here had introduced the game to the kids and apparently they couldn't get enough of it. Given the falls and knocks the kids received, the staff had to limit the number of games. She put her laptop aside and stood up, stretching her calves when they protested at the sudden change in position. 'Sure. Who else is playing?'

'Everyone,' she was told. 'They're waiting over the road.'

Over on the vacant land where houses used to stand before they burned to the ground in a dreadful misadventure years ago. 'Right, have you got the ball and the wickets?'

'Yes, Ellie, we have.' This little guy enjoyed practising his English. He wanted to be a truck driver one day and take tourists everywhere. 'Dr Luca got them.'

Of course Luca would be playing. If the kids were involved, then so was Luca. They could have a team each. This was the first time she'd joined in, but she'd seen a game the other day and had admired the kids for their determination and strength. Some swung crutches, another waved an arm that had been cut off at the elbow. All of them carried scars on some part of their body. All of them were laughing and chatting like monkeys in a tree. She loved the lot of them.

Noi called out from the clinic front door, 'You want a wicket keeper?' He'd never admit it but she'd heard he loved cricket as much as the youngsters. He also kept the children in line, gently admonishing them when they got carried away with heaving the ball at the wicket and their pal holding the bat. Even tennis balls could hurt when hitting the wrong spot on a small body.

'You bet,' Luca yelled back.

'I'm first batting,' said the boy who'd asked her to join them.

'I'm throwing the ball,' said another.

'Shouldn't we have teams?' she asked no one in particular.

'I want to be in Dr Luca's,' someone yelled.

'Me, too.'

A girl said shyly, 'I'm playing with Ellie.'

'You know what? I've got a plan. Noi, can you bring some crutches out here? Our size.' She tugged the belt off her shorts and handed it to Luca. 'Strap my leg up so I'm the same as these guys.'

Luca's eyes widened. 'You're kidding, right? That's going to be very uncomfortable.'

'Like it is for the kids all the time,' Ellie parried. 'You can tie one arm to your chest so that you can't use it.'

'You're nuts,' but Luca took her belt and tied up her leg.

She tried not to notice when his fingers touched her skin. Tried really hard. Then he pulled his shirt off and somehow managed to make one arm useless by twisting the shirt around his neck and tying it over his arm. She had to focus on the ground so as to avoid staring at the view created when he'd removed that shirt.

'Completely bonkers,' he told her with the first spontaneous smile she'd received from him all week.

What was bonkers? Oh. Her idea that all the staff out here were now partaking in by incapacitating themselves in some way. Not her longing for Luca. So much for putting the brakes on her highly fired-up hormones the other night. She'd been uptight ever since, and he'd been reacting the same way whenever he was around her. It might've been for the best if they had made love and got it out of the way.

'Bet no one back home has seen a cricket game quite like this.' Ellie laughed half an hour later as she lay sprawled on the ground after tripping over her crutch for the third time. 'Running for the ball and making catches is incredibly difficult but a whole heap of fun.'

'It was a great idea.' Luca nodded as he tried to get his breathing under control after chasing a ball right across the field. 'The kids are loving this more than ever.'

'So are you.' He looked the most relaxed she'd seen him for days.

He nodded. 'You know what I like best about working here?' He didn't wait for her to answer. 'We're not only doctors but physiotherapists, psychologists and friends to these kids. It's the whole package.'

'Changing your thinking about returning to emergency medicine?' It would be a shame. He was so good at it, but then again he was proving to be good at this. He was starting to become involved with people in a way he'd never done before. It suddenly struck Ellie with blinding clarity why Luca had chosen emergency medicine over all other specialties—he could treat people and send them home or to a specialist, but he didn't have to know who they were outside the emergency department. No learning about their family or their job, or whether they liked sports or were couch potatoes. He worked in the immediate picture with no tomorrows.

Ellie sat up and looked at this man she'd thought she knew. Back then she hadn't even started getting behind his facade. He'd fooled her as much as everyone else. Kind of undermined their friendship. When she'd thought they shared most things about themselves Luca had been holding back big time. She should be annoyed, angry even, but no. She was liking him more and more each day. This revelation only made her more determined to get to know Luca better, properly, and not only in the physical way. In fact that could take a hike for a while so that they could spend time together talking and enjoying getting out and about in Vientiane. *As if your hormones are going to settle down while you do that.* No harm in trying.

'You're staring.'

'Yes, I am.' *And liking what I see.*

A loud cry cut off whatever Luca had been about to say. A girl had tripped over her crutch and landed flat on her face. Ellie scrambled upright and raced across on her one leg and the crutch to drop down beside her. 'Lulu, let me see.' She gently removed the girl's hands from her face.

Blood spurted from Lulu's nose, and tears streamed down her cheeks. 'Hurts, Ellie.'

'I know.' Kissing Lulu's cheek, she gently felt the nose, then the rest of her face.

Luca knelt down opposite Ellie. 'What's the damage?'

'Everything seems fine,' Ellie told him, then said to Lulu, 'You've flattened your nose a bit, but it's going to be all right.'

'I don't want to play anymore.'

'Fair enough. Can I look at your back?' Lulu had three wounds zigzagging from her right shoulder to her left hip, caused by an explosion outside her school that had thrown her sky-high then dumped her on top of a wooden fence.

When Lulu nodded, Ellie carefully lifted her shirt. Phew. The stitches had held. Not that Ellie really expected otherwise, but she liked to be sure. 'I'll take you back over the road and get you a drink.'

Luca told her, 'I'll carry on with the cricket a bit longer.'

'See you later.' She began undoing the belt that held her leg bent, grimacing as pins and needles stabbed her muscles when the blood began circulating again.

'Want to go into town for a meal tonight?' He seemed to be holding his breath as he waited for her reply.

'Love to.' They could start on that talking stuff and getting to know each other better. Did that mean she'd tell him what Freddy and Caitlin had done to her? No. She wasn't going there, wasn't ready. She'd become quite adept at ignoring the truth and pretending she didn't have a sister or ex-husband—except in the middle of the night or when she was tired and not controlling her thought processes as well as she might. She wasn't any better than Luca at putting it all out there.

Lulu was crying steadily now.

'Hey, come on, poppet. Let's get you cleaned up.' She took the girl's hand and headed for the building.

Luca watched Ellie and Lulu all the way to the clinic and in through the doors that seemed to gobble them up. Ellie was a marvel, strapping her leg to be like the kids. She'd run—if using one leg and a crutch could be called running—back and forth after the ball whenever it was hit in her direction. No wonder the kids adored her. She was so natural with them. Aaron had hinted at trying to get her to take a twelve-month posting but she hadn't been very receptive.

Slap. The tennis ball bounced off his thigh. Luca looked around to find the culprit and met a pair of laughing eyes. 'Ng, you little tiger.' Reaching for the ball, he threw it at the wickets and missed by a mile, which only made the kids laugh and chase after it.

'You were daydreaming,' Ng said as he ran to the other end of the wicket. 'I got a run,' he shouted at his friends.

If the kids were noticing how distracted he'd become he needed to do something about it. Like what?

Take Ellie to bed.

Or have a long, cold shower every thirty minutes.

Or— He had no idea. Ellie had climbed into his skull and wasn't about to be evicted. And, he huffed, he'd damned well gone and suggested they go into town tonight. Again. They'd been doing quite a bit of eating out but usually one or two of the other staff members went with them. So there was his answer. Ask around to see who else wanted to join them.

'Catch it, Luca,' someone screamed at him.

Hell. He was meant to be playing cricket. He scanned the air between him and the wicket, saw a black shadow dropping towards the ground only a couple of metres away. Lunging at it, his fingers found the ball, curved it into the palm of his hand. When he held it up for everyone to see there were shouts of jubilation and a grizzle from Ng.

'I'm on your team.'

So why am I fielding? Luca wanted to ask. But basically if a person wasn't batting or bowling they were trying to catch the ball. No one really won, but then they didn't lose, either. 'Want to bowl next?' he asked, knowing Ng would never turn down that opportunity.

Glancing at his watch, Luca sighed. Still hours to go before he and Ellie headed into town. Hours when he'd be busy rubbing sore muscles on some of these kids caused by falls and skids in the field. It never failed to amaze him how eager they were to get into the fray, knowing they might hurt themselves. Tough little blighters, each and every one of them.

When he returned home he'd miss them all, even those he hadn't yet met. Returned home? Okay, he meant when he left Laos. Didn't he? Going back to NZ was on the cards but much further down the track. Emergency medicine still held its thrall and when he returned to that he wanted to be at the top of his game, but right now he was getting so much pleasure out of knowing his patients better than a BP reading and a diagnosis. Who'd have believed it? Not him—

Mr Avoid-All-Relationships-That-Involve-Exposing-His-Weaknesses. He liked having the kids hanging around demanding his attention. Who'd have thought it? Not him.

'Your turn.' One of the older girls stood in front of him, holding out the bat. 'But you can't hit the ball too hard.'

He grinned. 'Want to bet?'

Later, when everyone traipsed into the kitchen for food and water Ellie was there with Lulu, who looked decidedly happier now. Again Ellie had worked her magic.

She was so good with children. Where had she learned that? Or was it inherent? She'd be a brilliant mother, seemed to have all the right instincts.

As kids shouted and teased and bumped around him he heard Ellie's laughter. Raising his eyes, he met her amused gaze.

'Look at you.' She grinned. 'Not much more than a kid yourself, the way you've got chocolate icing on your chin.'

Luca ran his tongue around his lips and tried to find the icing dollop she'd mentioned. His tongue wasn't long enough. But when he looked back at Ellie she was obviously fascinated with it. Snapping his mouth shut, he turned away, trying to deny the heat zipping through his veins.

'Who's first for a massage?' he asked above the din.

Everyone got even busier eating and talking. Not one kid looked in his direction.

'Lulu's had hers,' Ellie told the kids. 'Pogo, bring that cake and come with me.'

Pogo, named for the way she usually bounced everywhere, reluctantly picked up another piece of cake and limped out of the door behind Ellie.

'Ng,' Luca said. 'Come on. The sooner we do this, the sooner you can do something more fun.'

'Can we sing?' Ng asked hopefully.

Another thing Ellie had started. Singing while massages were going on.

'Great idea. Come on, everyone. Bring that cake and follow us. We'll do this together.'

Soon the clinic was filled with the less than tuneful sounds of simple English songs Ellie had taught the children being yelled and sung and whispered. Even the other staff members helping were adding their voices. Ellie's voice was there, in tune and strong, the words clear and her face alive with joy. At that moment he'd swear she was the happiest he'd seen her since she'd arrived. Such simple pleasure had a lot going for it, and Ellie was soaking it up. He'd forgotten how much she enjoyed singing, and how she'd been an avid karaoke fan.

'The amputee clinic works a kind of magic on you, doesn't it?' Luca said as they wandered through the city centre later that night.

'It's the children who do that. They're so upbeat at times I want to bottle whatever it is that makes them that way and take it home. They're amazing.' Ellie stooped to stare into a shop window. 'Look at that. The weaving is beautiful. I'm going to have to get a piece before I go home.'

'What would you do with it?'

She lifted her shoulders, dropped them. 'No idea. It doesn't matter. A piece of handwoven fabric will make a wonderful memory of Vientiane.'

He had stored some of those lately. All with Ellie in them, all able to go with him wherever he went. 'Along with the zillion photos you've taken.'

She never seemed to go anywhere without her camera or phone. There were probably as many pictures of the children on her phone as in her camera. 'It's going to take me months to sort through those, and pick the best for an album.'

'Do people still do that?' He was happy leaving the few he occasionally remembered to take on a stick, which meant one day he'd probably lose them. But then photography wasn't one of his passions.

'I guess it's too easy not to get photos printed these days, but I like flicking through the pages of an album. Turning on my laptop and clicking on different folders doesn't give me the same satisfaction.' Ellie continued walking along the street. 'Got loads of you, too. Wait till I show Renee the cricket-doctor shots. She won't believe it's you.'

'Renee? You two are still in touch?' She'd been one of their housemates way back.

'I've been renting a room in her apartment since I found myself single again. She's just as bossy as she used to be.'

'And you still take no notice, I bet.'

'Something like that.' Ellie looked around. 'Where shall we eat tonight?'

'How about the restaurant tucked behind that hedge?' It was more upmarket then anywhere they'd eaten before.

Ellie's eyes widened and she turned them on him. 'Are we treating ourselves?'

'No. I'm treating you.' Out of the blue had come the need to take her somewhere better than a rice and sauce kind of place. Somewhere special with the napkins and wine and waitresses who made a career of their job. He wanted to spoil Ellie. And himself. It'd been a very long time since he'd gone upmarket for just about anything. There hadn't been the inclination because he hadn't had anyone he wanted to share that with. Taking Ellie's elbow, he led her across the road, dodging jumbos and cars, and into the outdoor area of the restaurant.

So much for a quick meal and a couple of beers, then returning to the clinic. So much for not spending too much time with Ellie and getting himself all out of sorts.

When he'd ordered a bottle of wine and they'd perused the menu and given their orders, Luca leaned back in his chair and stretched his legs under the table. 'Are you going to do any tripping around after you finish with the clinic?'

'I'd like to, but I haven't made any plans yet. Have you gone further afield than Vientiane and its surrounds?'

'No. I've been a real stay-at-home kind of guy, always finding things to do with the kids.' Travel hadn't been big on his list of things to do once he'd qualified as a doctor, and now that he was in Indochina nothing had changed. 'I'm probably wasting a golden opportunity.'

'I hear Luang Prabang is wonderful.'

'Some of the nurses who were here in June came back raving about it. You should go. It's only about an hour's flying time from here.'

Their wine arrived and Ellie sipped, her expression thoughtful.

'Something wrong with the wine? I can order another one.' He raised his glass to his lips to taste it.

Ellie's eyes locked on him. 'Come with me.'

'What?' he spluttered into his glass.

'Let's go to Luang Prabang together. It'd be a whole lot more fun going with you. I don't fancy joining tours to see everything and then not having anyone to say do you remember to.' Her eyes were imploring him to agree.

He didn't want to disappoint her. Not at all. Besides it was way past time to get out there and see the country. 'You're on.' He could take a few days. Mid-December wasn't any busier or quieter than the rest of the year and Aaron had been nagging him to take a break.

'That's fabulous.' Her smile was worth everything. Warm and exciting, it wove through him, lifting the tension hovering in his body forever, making him want to laugh out loud.

Instead, he put down his glass and reached for her hands. With her fingers linked between his, he said, 'Thank you for giving me the kick in the backside I've been needing. It's too easy staying here pretending I'm too busy to take time out for myself.'

'I'm glad you're coming with me.' Her smile widened. 'We'll have to go after I've finished my contract.'

'That's not a problem. I'll warn Aaron tomorrow and then we can go online to make some bookings.' Flights, hotel rooms—as in plural. They wouldn't be sharing a room, a bed. The tension returned. He had to be sick in the head. Or looking out for his heart. He didn't do long-term relationships. He had his father's genes but he'd learned something growing up. Best to know his faults and act accordingly, which meant love 'em and leave 'em. He was not loving and leaving Ellie. Leaving might turn out to be impossible for starters. As for loving her? Best not to go there. He didn't want to wake up one morning to find he had a complete family around him, knowing he would one day walk out and break their hearts as he went. Yeah, he'd seen it all, knew the hurt it had caused his mum and sister, and himself, and could say he never wanted to do that to anyone. Especially not to Ellie. But what he hadn't figured into the equation was how much he could love her, and how deep it cut not to act on that.

To think he'd agreed to go away with her. Two nights would be like two months in her company and unable to follow through on the longing he felt for her.

Ellie leaned back to allow the waitress room to put her plate down. 'Yum.' She sniffed the air and grinned. 'I wonder if I can take a local chef home to Auckland with me.'

'Are you looking forward to living in Auckland again?' he asked before forking prawns and rice into his mouth.

Her grin faded. And he felt chilled. He should never have asked. If he'd spoiled the night he only had himself to blame.

'It's going to be different. Last time you were there, as well as the other two in the house. I knew everyone training with us, whereas now I don't really know anyone up there. I'm sure I'll bump into people I used to know eventually. I do like Auckland and the job should be good.' She pushed rice around her plate. 'And it's at the other end of the North Island to where Freddy's living.'

'You'll miss him?' Was she still in love with the man?

'Not at all.' Her eyes met his and she said, 'Promise.' Finally she managed to get some rice into her mouth. When she had swallowed she added, 'I'll be able to relax. I won't be bumping into him at work or downtown. I never seemed to be able to get completely away from him. Not that either of us wanted time together, but at the hospital if we were even on the same floor people would be watching us, waiting to see if we yelled at each other—which we didn't. Not in public anyway, and then it was me doing the yelling. Not Freddy.' The spark of excitement had gone out of her eyes.

'That must've been hell. Having people watching you all the time, I mean.' Ellie tended to be a private person except with close friends and family.

'It was. So yes, Auckland's looking good. And who knows? I might decide to stay there permanently if I get another position when this next one runs out.' Sounded as if she was trying to convince herself.

If Ellie was in Auckland he'd be very tempted to return home. Where was the contract for Cambodia? He needed to sign it now before he gave in to temptation.

Temptation was staring him in the face right that moment. Ellie licking sticky rice from her fingers, then her tongue caught up a grain from the corner of her mouth. And his groin tightened exponentially. Goddamn. They were only halfway through dinner. How could he eat a thing now?

By picking up your fork and putting food in your mouth. Close your mouth—you're looking like a thirteen-year-old in lust with your teacher. Chew the damned prawn, and don't dribble.

He shuffled his butt on the chair, aiming to make everything more comfortable, and only succeeding in making his erection more apparent—thankfully only to himself. He was that teenaged boy all over again. The difference being Ellie was his age and not ten years older and wiser. They were both grown-ups and there was nothing to stop them having sex together. Nothing.

Except friendship and the future.

'More wine?' Ellie asked, holding the empty bottle up.

'Sure.' Might as well overindulge. The evening was already going pear-shaped fast. He nodded at the waitress across the room and leaned back, easing his legs further under the table in an attempt to shift the pressure between his legs. Pear-shaped? He nearly laughed. Not at all.

'Am I missing something here?' Ellie asked. 'You seem to be having a private joke.'

Oh, damn. Forgot she never missed a damned thing. 'You want dessert?'

Those hazel eyes locked on to his, the flecks now green and brown. Her tongue was back to its antics, tracking first along her bottom lip and then over the top one. 'Dessert? As in?'

'As in fresh fruit salad or apple pudding.'

Her tongue disappeared. Her gaze didn't. 'Right. Not as in hopping into bed and finding out exactly where we're headed?'

The shock that ricocheted through his body, crashed into his brain, was reflected back at him from those piercing eyes. He'd swear she hadn't meant to say that. Not at all.

The wine arrived. Perfect timing, or not. Their glasses were suddenly full once more. In need of a huge gulp, Luca reached for his, slopped wine over the edge and onto his hand. He was quick to reach for his napkin to wipe his hand, not needing Ellie to lift his hand anywhere near her mouth and that tongue—if she was that way inclined, and right now he had no idea what she was thinking.

Her cheeks were pink, her gaze had shifted to a spot

in the middle of the table and her glass shook when she raised it to those lips that seemed to have stolen his sanity and left him with the biggest hard-on he could remember.

Luca tugged his wallet from his back pocket and peeled out some notes, tossed them on the table, snatched up the wine bottle and got to his feet. Reaching for Ellie's hand, he said, 'Let's go.'

Her hand was warm in his. 'Where to?'

Good point. The chances of no one noticing them sharing a room back at the clinic were next to none. 'We'll find a hotel room.'

'Sounds sleazy.' She giggled. 'But I think I might like sleazy.'

'Why is every hotel full tonight of all nights?' Luca growled as his frustration increased forty minutes later. It was all very well that there was some big festival on, but they only wanted one bed, one room. Hell, they'd give it back in a few hours.

Ellie leaned her head against his shoulder. 'Guess we'll have to run the gauntlet at home, then.'

'Taxi,' Luca yelled at a vehicle moving off from the other side of the road. 'Wait.'

He was taking Ellie to bed tonight. Nothing would stop this incessant need clawing through his body except making love with El. Nothing. He knew common sense and logic had taken a hike, knew that tomorrow he might regret this, but he had to have Ellie, had to know her better than he ever had before. Ellie was his friend, his sidekick, his—

Say it and you're doomed. Lost forever, to live a life of purgatory, always wondering and missing out, never to be even Ellie's friend. For tonight he had to live in the moment. Not look to the future, not think back on his past. Tonight was about tonight, about him and Ellie and the sexual tension that had been simmering between them from her first day in Laos.

He held open the taxi's door. 'Let's go.'

CHAPTER EIGHT

Beside Ellie in the taxi Luca leaned forward and swore. 'Looks as if every light in the whole damned place is on.'

Ellie stared out of the side window as they drove up to the clinic. 'What's going on? The children's ward is lit up like Christmas.' She was reaching for her door handle even before the driver stopped. Her heart thudded in her chest, this time with concern for the children, not with lust and need for Luca. How quickly things changed. Though she was still hot for him her need had taken a sideways step, waiting for that moment until they found out what was happening and could hopefully get back to their evening.

They ran inside, heading straight to the ward. 'What's with all this water?' Ellie gasped.

There were people everywhere, mopping, sweeping waves of water through the ward, removing sodden bedding. The children were helping as best they could and getting blissfully soaked as they did.

'Burst water main in the wall,' the physiotherapist told them as she squeezed a mop into a bucket. 'Not sure what happened but there was a big bang and the wall literally blew out, forcing concrete blocks outward. Pogo's bed took the full force and she's in Theatre now with a stoved-in chest from where one block slammed into her corner first.'

Ellie looked around, spied Noi and went to ask, 'Are either Luca or I needed in Theatre?'

Noi shook his head. 'No, Aaron and Louise have got it under control. One of the hospital doctors is there with them. Aaron said if you got back while they were operating you could help in here.'

Luca stood beside her. 'No problem. Any other kids need medical attention?'

'No. They're soaked and their beds are useless but no one else was hurt.'

Relieved at that, Ellie tossed her bag onto a shelf and grabbed a mop. Turning, she bumped into Luca, felt that hard body aligned with hers. Unfortunately this was not how, only minutes ago, she'd envisaged having him against her. 'I'm sorry.'

His finger on her chin lifted her head. 'Me, too. Very sorry.'

'We might get finished cleaning up before daybreak.' How pathetic. She was almost pleading with him to take her to his room. But her disappointment was so enormous, so debilitating she wasn't thinking straight, was putting her own needs before those of the children. She should be ashamed. She was, and she wasn't. But she knew the children would win out. They had to, and she really didn't mind. But why tonight? Why couldn't that blasted pipe have burst tomorrow? Or yesterday? Or not at all?

Luca's finger brushed her bottom lip, sending sparks right down to her centre. 'We'll be lucky to get this dried out and ready for the kids before the end of the week.' His disappointment gleamed out at her from those steely eyes.

'I know.' When she'd finally decided to go for it with him and to hell with the consequences they'd been stopped in their tracks. Was it a portent? And if it was should she heed it? At this moment she could not find it in her to say yes. She wanted Luca. 'If only there'd been one hotel with a bed to spare.'

Luca's chuckle was flat. 'If only.'

'Right. Let's get cracking. We're needed and that's got to be good, even if I wish I was somewhere else.' Ellie slopped through water to the far side of the ward where everyone was tackling the flood. 'It seems the more you're all mopping up, the more that comes out of the wall.'

Noi shook his head. 'The plumber only found the mains tap outside to turn off five minutes ago, and then it was rusted open. The water should stop any second.'

'Where are the children going to sleep until this room is habitable again?' Luca asked.

'The hospital is making room for them,' Noi answered. 'They'll be placed in various rooms with other patients.'

'I hope Pogo's going to be all right.' Ellie shivered despite the warm temperature. 'She's already had enough to deal with for a little girl.'

'A crushed rib cage is no picnic,' Luca agreed as he swept water towards the open doors that led outside. 'She was due to go home on Friday.'

Ellie squeezed her mop through the wringer on the bucket and dropped it back in the water to soak up more. Just went to show that you never knew what was around the corner. One minute Pogo was getting ready to go home, the next she was in Theatre undergoing major surgery.

One minute I was on my way to bed with Luca, the next I'm mopping a floor in the children's ward.

Kind of told her she should grab every opportunity that came along—the ones she wanted anyway. And she definitely wanted Luca. Even as she swept up water she watched him. The muscles in his arms flexed as he lifted a sodden mattress off a bed. Her mouth dried. Ironic given the amount of water around the place. She smiled. Luca did that to her.

'I'll take your bucket to empty.' Noi swung it away and placed an empty one in front of her. 'Sorry your night was interrupted.'

Ellie gaped at him. Did he know? 'It doesn't matter, Noi. Not that this is your fault.'

'I know, but you and Luca seem to be getting on better than your first day.' He flicked looks between her and Luca.

He didn't know where they'd been headed. Relief lifted her spirits. 'That's because we've always been such good friends. I know we lost each other for a while but that friendship was strong, and still is.'

Noi turned his full attention on her. 'Friendship is good. Love is better. You know what I mean.' He wasn't asking, he was telling her.

'Aren't you meant to be emptying that bucket?' *I don't love Luca. Not like that. Not as the man I'd want to marry and have a family with.*

Noi didn't move, his gaze still fixed on her. 'He's different now. Happier and more playful with the kids since you arrived. As if you've made him come alive.'

For a man from a totally different culture from hers

he seemed to understand a lot about this. Too much. 'I didn't know he'd been unhappy.' Luca was always happy, though she'd come to realise these past weeks that had often been a front.

'So were you when you got here. Not now,' Noi said, the seriousness in his voice drumming his words into her.

Of course she'd been unhappy, in fact downright upset, distressed and incapable of moving forward. But to have got past that in such a short time? Not likely. The pain and anger was too much to evaporate so quickly. She bent to push the mop through the water, sent a wave heading across the room. 'Let's get this job finished so we can help the kids settle into their new beds.'

Noi nodded and strolled away, totally unfazed by the storm of emotions he'd started rolling through her.

What a night. She had enjoyed having dinner with Luca in a special restaurant, and appreciated the change from their usual haunts with other staff. Just sitting with him talking about things only they knew about had been relaxing. There'd been no sting in anything he'd said to her, and she hadn't felt the need to defend herself about anything. He accepted her for who she was. It was something she did not want to risk losing again.

Which meant no sex. That would put the risk factor right up there. She had no idea what the morning after would be like. Would she be able to walk away and believe they had had their moment and could return to normal? Or would she wake up and know she'd made a mistake? Realise that it had been too soon after her failed marriage and that she was probably using him to get back on her feet? Rebound sex. Rebound love.

Ellie gasped. Love? No, not that.

'You okay?' the man distracting her from the clean-up asked as he placed a bucket between them.

'Why wouldn't I be?' she growled. Rebound or not, loving Luca was not on. She couldn't love him because— Because she couldn't. It wouldn't feel right to love her best friend. Why not? He was a man, sexy as they came, kind and caring, knew her well, too well at times. There'd be no surprises. That wasn't an issue. She'd had a surprise with Freddy and look where that had got her. Single and here, debating about her feelings for Luca.

'You're pushing water in the wrong direction.' Luca grinned. 'I like it when you're muddled.'

'I don't.' *I can't love him. Not like that. Do I want to set up house with Luca? Be with him day in, day out? Have his babies? Does my heart race whenever I'm near him? My heart races—with desire. Set up house with Luca? I doubt it.* As for babies, she didn't want Luca's or anyone's. She wasn't ready. So, not love, then.

Her head shot up and she stared at him. Really stared, seeing his face, those beautiful grey eyes, that nose that had been broken when he was a kid and bent slightly to the left, that stubborn chin. She hoped not anyway. She'd loved Freddy and this felt different. *Yeah, and look where that got you.*

Noi nudged her. 'Here's your bucket.'

When she dragged her eyes sideways she found Noi nodding slowly. 'Like I said,' he added with a quick glance at Luca.

Ellie turned to run out of the room, and noticed all the people busy trying to clean up the mess and knew she wasn't going anywhere. She had to remain here, doing her share. As much as she wanted to escape and find solitude while she absorbed this new information her mind had thrown up, she couldn't. Leaving when she was needed wasn't in her psyche. So she pushed the mop harder than ever and became totally focused on water and the floor, working twice as hard as anyone else. But every time she looked up she got an eyeful of a wet and gorgeous Luca happily cleaning up the ward, teasing the kids, laughing when they tipped water over him once.

And she'd compared him to Freddy? No way. Her ex would've said to call him when everything was back to order; he wouldn't have picked up a mop. He was a surgeon, not a cleaner.

Gulp. Ellie dropped her gaze to the job in hand. Maybe she'd never really, deeply, loved Freddy at all. So what were these feelings for Luca? Friendship or love?

There was a holiday atmosphere in the clinic the next morning. The kids were hyper after their exciting night, acting as though the whole incident had been put on for their benefit.

Luca scratched his unshaven chin as he tried to eyeball every kid at the long table. 'You still have to have massages and go to school,' he told them over breakfast.

'Good luck with that,' Ellie quipped as she dumped her plate in the sink.

He needed a lot of luck with quite a few things at the moment. Like sorting out what was going on between him and Ellie. Last night they'd come so close to changing their relationship forever. So close. He was still trying to work out how he felt about that.

Sure, he'd wanted to make love with her. No question. He still did. His body had throbbed half the night with the need to touch her, to caress that soft skin, to be inside her. But this morning, in the harsh light of day, his brain had started throwing up some serious thoughts. Like, even with Ellie he had to remember his gene pool and the likelihood he'd be a bad husband and father. Like that Ellie hadn't had time to get over Freddy yet, and that *he'd* probably take the brunt of that when she came to her senses.

'I'm going to see Pogo,' Ellie announced, as though needing to make it clear she was working. Trying to combat leftover emotions from last night?

Had she had a change of heart? Finally decided last night's disaster in the clinic had been a good thing, that it had run interference before she'd had time to think everything through fully? In some ways he could agree. But a huge part of him mourned not having had that opportunity to make love with Ellie. Something in the dark recesses of his mind seemed to be saying she might be the best thing for him, might be the one woman he could risk his heart to. She certainly was nothing like Gaylene, wouldn't deny him his child—even one he thought he didn't want. Whatever it was, he shut it down immediately. Shoved to his feet and stomped across to the sink to rinse his cup and plate.

But his gaze fixed on Ellie as she left the dining hall: her head high, her shoulders tense, her hands clenched at her sides. Exhaustion after the eventful night? Or something deeper? Him? Them and what they hadn't managed to do?

He knew the feeling all too well. Throw in confusion and a need that seemed to be growing every day and he was toast.

'Can we play cricket today?' one of the boys called to him.

'Yes, of course.' That should fill in a few hours.

'Luca.' Ellie stood in front of him an hour later as he was instructing a boy on caring for his wound where he'd lost two fingers.

'Hey, Pogo's not doing so well, I hear.'

Her mouth turned down. 'No, poor wee girl. I've been sitting with her after changing bandages and adjusting her meds. Her parents are with her now.'

'They'll be gutted. Only two days ago they were saying how excited they were Pogo was going home.'

'We need to talk.' Ellie's eyes were wide as she looked at him.

His heart sank. He didn't want this conversation, would prefer to carry on as though last night hadn't nearly happened. 'About last night?'

Her smile was wobbly. 'Sort of. We are going to Luang Prabang, remember?'

How could he forget? Two nights away with Ellie and knowing now that they really shouldn't have sex if they wanted to remain friends. Oh, yeah, he remembered all right. 'Are we still on?' he asked, aware that she must say yes. *Please.*

'I hope so. We need to make bookings—for flights and a hotel.' Her cheeks turned a delicious shade of pink.

He nearly reached out to run a finger down one of those cheeks, only just in time thinking better of it. That would be an intimate gesture and he wasn't sure where he stood today. With her—or with his own thoughts. 'Want me to do them? I've got time now.'

She nodded. 'That'd be great. Do you know anyone here who could recommend accommodation?'

'Aaron and Louise went up there six months ago. I'll check with them. Two rooms, right?'

The pink deepened as she nodded. 'I guess that would be sensible.'

The last thing he felt like being was sensible. He'd done sensible all his life and lately he found it was getting tedious. But this was Ellie he was thinking of breaking the rules with and she could get hurt. That was the last thing he wanted to happen. 'What are you doing after Luang Prabang?' She'd be a free agent then. Her contract at the clinic was due to finish soon and her new one back home didn't start until the New Year. There was plenty of time for her to indulge in travelling around Indochina if she wanted. Or even stop off in Australia, as she'd mentioned one day when they were talking about one of their old housemates who'd moved to Perth.

'I'm going home.'

That was not the answer he was expecting. His surprise must've shown because she explained.

'I keep thinking there are loose ends back there that I need to deal with. I have to pack my gear and move out of Renee's apartment. Spend some time with Mum and Dad before Christmas.' A troubled look came into her eyes at the mention of her parents. Or was that Christmas?

'Seems to me you're making excuses for not staying over here longer. None of those things are going to fill in the nearly four weeks until you start work in Auckland. You don't even have to find a house up there—you've got one fully furnished for the duration.' Did she want to get as far away from him as possible?

'I could go for a coffee break right now.'

Luca took her elbow. To hell with being careful and wary. His friend appeared lost today and he'd step up to the mark for her no matter what it cost him. 'Come on. Coffee out under the tree.' Where hopefully no one would disturb them.

'I'm struggling with not knowing what I want to do,' Ellie told him ten minutes later as she sat down on the grass, not at all concerned about the ants that might bite her.

'The Ellie I remember always knew what she wanted to do about everything.'

'Right up until my marriage fell apart. Then I focused on dealing with that and the shame that followed me around. I was determined to get away from Wellington and the hospital, and here I am.' Her hands were tight around her mug.

'With the first six months of next year sorted. That can't be too bad, can it?' There were things she wasn't telling him, he just knew it, but was reluctant to ask for fear she'd walk back inside.

'Then what do I do? Work in an emergency department? Buy a house, and if so where? Even travel doesn't excite me, and I've always thought I'd do that when I had time. Pathetic.' Her sigh was long and filled with despair.

The urge to wrap her in a hug was huge but Luca sensed she wasn't ready. 'You're not pathetic, so stop feeling sorry for yourself. You've been knocked sideways by your ex, and lost sight of those plans you had with him. Of course you're confused about where you're headed.'

'I'm over here with so many places to visit, and beyond going to Luang Prabang with you I can't find the enthusiasm.' She sipped the coffee, staring at her feet.

'Give yourself time.' She was enthused about going away with him for two nights? His heart melted at the thought. He wasn't on the 'get rid of' list, then. 'They say it takes a couple of years to get over a breakup.'

'I wonder if *they* know what they're talking about.' She wrinkled her nose.

'Want to look at where you could go to after our jaunt north? Hanoi's not far from Luang Prabang.'

'You think I could do that on my own?'

'Asks the woman who did a solo parachute jump because she was dared? I reckon there's nothing in this world you can't do if you want to.'

Finally Ellie lifted her head and gave him the full benefit of a big smile, one that reached her eyes. 'Thank you for that. It was my turn to need a kick in the backside. You book Luang Prabang and I'll make a decision about where I'm going after that.' She placed her hand on his thigh for balance as she stood up. 'Watch this space.'

They were back to being friends, easy with each other. 'Thank goodness,' he muttered even as disappointment rippled through him. He wanted more. He knew that now. Last night hadn't been about just one night at all. But was he prepared to risk it?

No. He could get hurt, but, worse, he'd definitely hurt El somewhere along the way. No doubt about it.

CHAPTER NINE

ELLIE'S CONTRACT WAS UP, and she and Luca were in Luang Prabang. Over the weeks she'd survived the temptation of Luca by keeping frantically busy with the children. Now they were visiting the bear sanctuary on a day trip out from the town, which had been a priority for her. 'I want to set them free,' she muttered to Luca as she clicked her camera nonstop getting photos of the black bears behind the wire fences set in the lush vegetation near the Kuang Sii waterfalls.

'I know what you mean. It seems cruel to keep them enclosed but they'll be killed if they're not protected. Catch twenty-two, I guess.'

'What I don't get is why anyone would want to hunt them in the first place. They're so beautiful.'

'As we've both said often, this is a very different world from the one we're used to.' Luca was holding his camera to his eye. 'Look at me. And smile, woman. I'm not pulling your teeth out.'

'Have you got one of the bears in the photo?' she asked.

'The bear's smiling. Now will you?'

It wasn't hard; despite the ever-present tension in her stomach brought on by all things Luca, she was having fun. Not even thinking about what she might be missing out on sleeping in separate rooms at the hotel could wipe her smile away. They'd been on the go since arriving yesterday.

'At last,' Luca growled and clicked a photo. And another, and another until she shifted away. 'I could sell them on the internet.'

'Good luck.' She laughed. 'The guide's beckoning— guess it's time to head back.'

'A cold beer would go down a treat.' Luca smacked his lips. 'This humidity's getting to me.'

'They sell it at the stalls where the van's parked.' She wouldn't mind one, either. She slipped her arm through his. 'Let's check them out before we go. Bye-bye, bears.'

'You're dribbling, and I haven't got anything to wipe your slobber up with.'

With beers in hand they clambered into the van to join the three Australian guys sharing the trip. Ellie stretched her legs towards the door and leaned back in her seat to enjoy the terrain they'd pass through. 'Next stop, Elephantville.'

The weather turned wet about the time they climbed off the elephant they'd ridden through the jungle. Rushing under the shelter, where there were bananas to feed the animals, Ellie felt the sweat trickle down her back. 'The rain doesn't stop the humidity, does it?'

Luca shoved his camera into a plastic bag and put it inside his day bag. 'Give it time.'

Suddenly the rain became torrential, pounding the tin roof of the shelter and making conversation next to impossible.

Ellie leaned close to Luca to yell, 'Wonder how long this will last.'

'Who knows?' he yelled back, then jerked his head back.

'Luca?' He hadn't shaved that morning and a dark stubble highlighted his strong jawline—and sent waves of something suspiciously like desire rolling through her. What would he do if she ran a finger over his chin?

'Let's go. The driver's waving us over to the van.' He raced away, stomping through puddles, getting soaked from all directions.

Not that there was any choice. Ellie braced herself for the drenching she was about to get and chased after him, wondering at his abrupt mood swing.

'The skies are angry.' The driver laughed as he slammed his door. 'We have muddy ride back.'

Ellie felt a prickle of apprehension. The road hadn't been that great when it was dry. Her hand slid sideways, onto Luca's thigh. His fingers laced around hers and he squeezed gently.

'We'll be fine. This guy will be used to driving in these conditions. They're not uncommon up here in the hills, from what the man at the hotel said this morning.'

'I guess.' The apprehension backed off but she didn't withdraw her hand, enjoying the way Luca's forefinger rubbed across her knuckles. *Please don't pull away. Not yet.* Heat sparked along the veins of her arm. Eek, if having her hand held by Luca did this to her, what would making love be like? She suspected like nothing she'd ever experienced.

On the ride up out of the valley the van slipped and slid on the mud and water pouring down the road. The sound of the wheels spinning filled the van. Ellie wondered if they'd have been better waiting until the deluge slowed, but when she'd voiced that opinion the driver replied, 'Might not stop for days.'

Her grip tightened around Luca's hand. Her jaw ached as her teeth clenched. Leaning against him, she found some comfort even though there was nothing he could do if this trip went badly. Luca's jaw was jutting out, his eyes not wavering from the road ahead. The van was quiet, everyone probably holding their breath as she was.

Then suddenly they popped over the crest of the hill and the van tilted forward as they headed down. The relief was palpable, until everyone realised going down had its own set of problems. The driver braked repeatedly to slow the van but they skidded more often than on the way up.

When the van slid towards the edge of the road Ellie thought she must be breaking the bones in Luca's fingers, her grip was so tight. She tasted blood on her lip where her teeth pushed down. The air stuck in her lungs, her ribs tight under the pressure. 'Oh, no. We're going over the edge. We're going to crash.'

Up front the driver was shouting something incomprehensible as he spun the steering wheel left, then right.

And the van slid closer to the top of the ravine.

A scream filled Ellie's throat, but when she opened her mouth nothing came out.

Luca's hand was strong around hers. His body tense beside her. 'Jeez.' Then he let her go to grab at the latch that was the internal handle on the sliding door. His muscles stood out as he strained to tug the door back on its rollers. His lips pressed together until there was no colour in them. And still he pulled, frantically trying to open the door.

Nothing happened.

The back of the van lurched forward with a thud. The wheels were over the edge.

Ellie's heart stopped.

This was it. The van would drop like a boulder to the bottom of the ravine. *We're going to die.* Ellie jerked in her seat, staring around, frantic for a way out.

Slam. The noise was horrendous. Air whooshed inside.

'Come on,' Luca yelled as he grabbed her arm. 'Jump.'

The door was open. That had been the slamming sound.

'Jump, Ellie. Now.'

She didn't get a chance. Even as she strained against the steepening angle of the van Luca snatched at her, wrapped his arms around her and fell out backwards.

Thump. They landed heavily on the side of the bank. Pain tore through Ellie's side where her hip had connected with something solid and unforgiving. The air whooshed out of her lungs. Her head snapped back, crashed against the ground. Luca's arms were no longer holding her. She cried out, 'Luca?' Then she gasped in air, tried again. 'Luca, where are you?' He had better be all right. She couldn't imagine what she'd do if anything had happened to him.

'El, I'm here. Are you okay?'

She'd never heard such a beautiful sound. 'Yes, I think so. Are you?'

Her relief was snatched away by a loud bang and the noise of metal being torn and bent. The van had come to a halt wrapped around a tree.

'The driver, the Aussies. Luca—' The words dried

up on her tongue. They didn't have a chance of surviving that crash.

A familiar, warm hand gripped her shoulder. 'We'll get help.' That hand was shaky. 'Are you sure you're all right?'

Pain thudded through her hip but when she shifted her leg nothing felt broken. She nodded. 'Thanks to you.' Twisting her head, she kissed the back of Luca's hand. 'What about you?'

'A few bruises but think I got lucky.'

'You're not lying? Not going all macho on me?' When Luca shook his head Ellie began pushing herself up to the road, sliding in the mud as she made hard work of the short distance. Her body was shaking as if she had the DTs. Shock did that, she knew. She concentrated hard, thought about the situation. 'What are the chances of another vehicle coming along in this weather?'

Luca was right behind her. 'That tourist bus was due to leave right after us. Though how a bus will manage on that road when the van was struggling, I don't know.'

Ellie shuddered. A busload of people going over the edge didn't bear thinking about. 'Wait. I hear something.' She strained to listen through the torrential rain.

'Not a bus but a four-wheel drive, I'm thinking.' Luca stepped into the middle of the road, slip-sliding in the mud and waving wildly. 'Hell, not one but three of them. We just got lucky, El.'

Guess luck was relative. Guilt assailed her. They *were* lucky. There were four people still in that mangled van down the bank. The only luck for them was she and Luca were doctors, doctors with nothing but their bare hands and the knowledge in their heads. If they were still in need of medical intervention.

'You're not going down there,' Luca informed her moments later in a do-not-argue-with-me tone. 'It's too dangerous.'

'Right, I'm to stand up here watching you risking your life? I don't think so.' She turned to find people from the vehicles now parked to the side of the road approaching with ropes.

'El,' Luca growled. 'Two of these men are going down with me. If we can get anyone out of the van, the others will pull them up here for you to attend to.' Again his hand was on her shoulder, his fingers gently squeezing. 'There won't be an ambulance turning up. It's up to all of us to get these people stabilised and to a hospital.' His voice was calm, encouraging, not like that of someone who'd barely escaped with his life minutes earlier.

Shame at her outburst had her apologising. The last thing Luca needed right now was a hysterical female on his shaky hands. 'Sorry. You're right. Again. But, Luca, please be careful.' She couldn't lose him now. Even as a friend he was too precious to her. She'd lost enough people this past year for various reasons.

'Promise.'

Standing around waiting, peering over the edge and sucking a deep breath every time one of the men slipped, which was often, nearly drove her nuts. She only let the breath go when she knew for sure that man was all right. When Luca slid down a steep, muddy patch too fast her heart slammed her ribs. 'You promised you'd be careful,' she whispered. 'I should've asked you to promise that you'd be safe and not get hurt.'

'Over here,' a male voice called through the gloom from halfway down the slope.

Luca and another guy veered off to the right, and very

soon were crouched beside a small bush where what Ellie finally recognised as feet were sticking out from.

Soon Ellie's first patient had been hauled up to the road and she had something to keep her mind off Luca. The guy was caked in mud and muck, soaked through from the rain, and still managed to crack a joke. 'Didn't read this bit on the tourist brochure. Must've caught the wrong ride.'

Hot tears filled Ellie's eyes and she had to blink rapidly to dispel them. 'You and the rest of us. You want to tell me where you're hurt so I can check you out?'

'I don't need to be hurting for you to do that, babe. Been eyeing you up all morning.'

'I'm a doctor,' she told him. His face was pale underneath the mud that was slowly washing off in the rain. 'Let's get you into one of the vehicles. Don't see why we need to be getting any more drenched than we already are.'

A man she hadn't noticed standing nearby put a hand under the Aussie guy's elbow. 'Here, lean against me.'

The Aussie was limping and he held the other arm tight against his chest. 'Thanks, mate. Think my arm's broken.'

After slitting the sleeve up with a pocketknife the other man handed her, Ellie noted a large swelling over the tibia that suggested her patient was right. 'I'll create a makeshift sling so that you don't move or jar your arm until you're in hospital.' When and where that was she had no idea. 'What else? You were limping.'

'Everything seems to be working. Think my thigh hit something hard when I was thrown out of the van. Probably only bruised, though it hurts like a bitch.'

Yeah, Ellie could commiserate. Nor was her hip

happy, protesting every time she bumped against the door or moved sharply. 'Let's take a look.'

More vehicles stopped, more people slid down the bank to help extricate the driver and the other two passengers. Luca finally returned to the road and helped Ellie do whatever she could for the injured men. One by one they were taken away in various vehicles, heading for proper medical care. The driver remained unconscious throughout the whole ordeal of being pulled free of his stoved-in van and hauled up the bank. With no oxygen or monitors of any description Ellie and Luca did their best to make him comfortable before seeing him off in a truck that had just turned up.

'I'll give you two a lift into Luang Prabang,' one of the first men to stop told them. 'You look knackered.'

That would be an understatement, Ellie admitted to herself. Sore, soaked through, muddy and still shaking, she desperately wanted a hot shower.

Luca held her hand all the way back to their hotel. Tightly. They were both shivering from cold and fright. Though the temperature was as hot and the air as muggy as ever, Ellie couldn't believe the chills tightening her skin. Her saturated clothes clung to her, pulling at her skin every time she moved.

At the hotel entrance she tugged off her canvas shoes before going inside, but she still left a trail of footprints and water as she crossed to the stairs leading up to where their rooms were situated. Luca still held her hand, his shoes swinging from the fingers of his other one.

They hardly uttered a word all the way, and even when Ellie tried again and again to shove the key into the lock, Luca said nothing. He merely took the key from her shaking hand and tried three times before he succeeded.

He followed her into her room, dropped his shoes on the mat and headed for the bathroom. 'You need out of those clothes and under the shower, like now.'

'So do you.' She was already unbuckling the belt on her trousers, then pushing them down her legs, the wet fabric clinging to her skin.

The sound of running water came from the bathroom. 'Give that a few seconds to warm up.' Luca stood in front of her.

Ellie stopped struggling with her T-shirt and stared up at this wonderful man who'd just been through hell with her. For all the moisture she carried in her clothing and her hair, her mouth was dry. 'That was way too close.'

His eyes widened in agreement as he reached for the hem of her shirt and started to lift it up over her breasts and then her head. 'Yes, it was.'

She shuddered. And slipped her arms up so as he could get her shirt off. Her hands joined behind his neck, pulling his head closer to hers. 'We're alive.'

'Yep.' His lips brushed hers. 'And wet and shivering.' He scooped her up into his arms and headed for the bathroom and all that glorious warm steam that was now beginning to fill the tiny room. One arm was around her back with his hand on her lace-covered breast, the other arm under her knees with his fingers splayed across the top of one knee. Heat filled her, banishing the chills, even where Luca's wet shirt clung to her rib cage. Need poured through her, need to prove she was alive and well, need for Luca.

Setting her down in the shower box, he began unzipping his shorts. 'Move over.'

She didn't need a second invitation. Scuttling sideways, she reached for him, pulled him into the shower even before he'd finished undressing. Gently wiping the mud off his cheeks, his neck, his arms, she felt him unclasp her bra at her back.

Luca pushed her thong down, his hands taking it past her thighs, over her knees and down to her ankles, where he lifted one foot then the other to free the thin scrap of lace. Upright again, those strong hands she adored touching her gripped her buttocks. 'We're alive, El. And I'm going to prove how much.' Then he lifted her so she could wrap her legs around his waist.

Her mouth sought his, her tongue instantly inside the hot cavern of his mouth. Hot. Heat. Real. This was real, making the blood pound through her veins, in her ears, deafening yet wonderful as the regular thumping beat the rhythm of life. *We're alive.*

Pushing her breasts hard against his chest, she rubbed back and forth, absorbing the exquisite sensations blasting her as she felt Luca's skin sliding against hers. Feeling each individual finger where he touched her backside, knowing the sensation of his palms on her soft skin. Feeling, feeling, feeling. Nothing, no one, had ever felt so wonderful, so full of promise.

Now she wanted all of him; needed to feel his length slide inside her, fill her. Then, and only then, would she truly believe they had survived. His erection was pulsing between her legs, against her opening. Ellie began to slide down over him, drawing his manhood into her, gasping with wonder at the strength and length of him. 'Luca,' she cried. She was more than ready. As the tension coiling in her stomach, at the apex of her legs, everywhere, began tightening farther, Luca tensed, then thrust upward, hard, driving into her, again and again, proving he was here, alive and well, and with her.

As the tension gripping her exploded into an orgasm Ellie screamed, 'Luca. Luca.'

'El, oh, yes. That's it. That's good.' He rode her hard and deep, and when he came his eyes snapped open to lock with hers. Eyes full of understanding and longing and bewilderment—and gratitude. For being here, and not down that ravine? For sharing this with her?

'El' was all he said as he held her tight against his body, his hands lightly rubbing her buttocks, shivering through the end of his release. 'El.' The tiniest word meaning so, so much.

They dried each other off, taking their time to discover the other's body. 'You are beautiful,' Luca whispered as he carefully ran the corner of his towel beneath her breast. The small, heavy globe filled his hand to perfection. Her nipple peaked even as he stared at it and he lowered his mouth to savour her. One swipe with his tongue and that peak tightened further. So did his penis. *Down, boy.* This time they were going for long and slow and getting to know each other better.

Something like hope filtered through the postcoital haze blurring his mind. Never had he known such excitement with a woman, so much release and relief and care, so—different and special. Almost loving. Had he been driven by the need to acknowledge he'd survived a horrific crash? Or something more? Something to do with Ellie herself? Had she always been his future? Had he been blind to what was right under his nose?

His gut clenched into a tight knot. Ellie was soon leaving Laos, bound for Perth and then home. Which was a good thing; it had to be. They didn't, and couldn't, have a future other than their rekindled friendship. That was the only way he could ever continue with her in his life. The other—becoming lovers beyond today—was unthinkable, would break every rule he'd made for himself. Would open him up to his vulnerabilities. He wasn't prepared to do that. Not even for Ellie, not even to have her by his side forever. Because she was a 'forever' kind of girl. He suspected that was why she hurt so much about Freddy leaving her. The commitment she'd made to him and their marriage had been broken.

Forget her failed marriage. Right now his body was humming with after-sex lethargy and the need to repeat the whole thing. As soon as possible. His body was going in the opposite direction to his mind, and he couldn't stop it. His body, that was. Why did he say making love when with Ellie? Every other time in his life he'd had sex. When he'd driven into her, pumped his soul into her, he'd known he was safe in every way. Hell, he'd felt complete for the first time in his adult life, maybe since the day he was born. As if he'd found home, which was plain untrue. Home was where the heart was, or something like that, according to a saying out there. But his heart wasn't up for grabs. Not even Ellie was going to snag it. Though these past few weeks it'd been getting harder and harder to deny he wanted and needed her in his life on a regular basis. As in a partner. A life partner. His heart.

'Luca.' Her soft voice skidded across his skin. 'You still with me?' She dropped his towel and ran her palms over his chest, her thumbs lightly flicking his nipples and sending sparks flying out to every corner of his body. Those warm, tender palms cruised lower, over his abs, and lower.

The breath caught in his lungs.

Her hand wrapped around him. Slid down, up, down.

His brain went on strike. The time for thinking was over. His body took up the challenge. He had to have El. Again. Now. The need to taste her, to feel her hot moistness surround his desire was rampaging along his veins, through his muscles, weakening his ability to stay upright—even when his hands were fondling those beautiful breasts.

'El, I need you.' Snatching her up into his arms, he carried her the short distance to the small double bed filling the tiny room and laid her down. Had he really said that?

It's true. I did and I do.

Hopefully Ellie hadn't heard, or if she had then she'd pass it off as something he'd said in the heat of the moment. Which it was. If his brain had been in good working order he'd never have uttered those words.

Truth will out.

Yeah, so they said. He lowered himself beside Ellie and reached for her. His fingers caressed a trail from her lips to her throat to her breasts to her belly button and beyond. El.

CHAPTER TEN

'I'M STARVING.' ELLIE STRETCHED the full length of the ridiculously small bed to ease all the kinks out of her muscles. Pain erupted in her hip. 'Ow!' she cried out. 'Why didn't I feel that when we were making out?'

'Because I'm a bigger distraction?' Luca raised up onto an elbow and lifted the sheet to study her hip. 'That's a piece of work. More colours than the rainbow.' His lips were softer than a moth as they brushed over the tender surface of her beleaguered hip.

She did an exaggerated eye roll. 'Oh, please. Your ego needs controlling.'

He grinned. 'I know.' Then he turned all serious. 'Sorry I threw you onto a rock on the way out of that van.'

There was a lot behind those flippant words. He had saved them from a worse fate. Instead of freaking out in that tumbling metal box that was their transport he'd done something about the situation, done his absolute best to save them. He was her hero. She thought of the driver. 'I wonder how Palchon is. If he's regained consciousness.' *If he's alive.*

'We could go find out on our way to Luang Prabang's airport this morning.'

'I'd like that.' Ellie sat up, groaned as pain again reminded her of her hip. 'My upcoming flight to Perth is looking less exciting. Can you get me some painkillers in Vientiane, and something to help me sleep?' Not that she'd been thrilled about leaving Laos anyway. *Be honest.* It was Luca she didn't want to leave. But that shutdown look that had just appeared on his face told her more than anything that he did not want to carry this on any further. What they'd had together in this small hotel room was all they were going to have.

Her heart shattered. She loved Luca. She'd loved him as a friend, and now as a lover. But most of all she loved him as a man, for all the pieces that made him who he was. For his tenderness, for the way he had always listened to her grizzles and cheered her up when the world came tumbling down on top of her, the mess of dirty clothes he never put in the wash for days on end, his skill as a doctor. She loved him completely.

Ironic really, when she'd come to Laos to sort herself out and instead got herself caught up in love with Luca, when he'd made it plain he did not reciprocate her feelings. She'd be going home flattened and filled with despair. Home would now be in Auckland, a city filled with memories of Luca.

Unless this was love on the rebound, and then she could hope that eventually, hopefully in the not too distant future, she'd get over Luca. It was debatable whether they could ever go back to be best friends again. So whichever way this turned out, she'd lost someone else important to her. The sooner the year finished, the better. She was going to dance and drink and sing the new year in like never before, welcome it with open arms, then get on with her new job and creating the career that'd take her through the next twenty years without falter.

'I'll head back to my room to shower and pack my toothbrush.' Luca stood up from the bed in full naked glory.

'Sure.' He was beautiful. Had he always looked like this beneath his snappy shirt and fitting trousers? She'd seen him in running shorts and T-shirts, in track pants, in jeans, everything a normal well-dressed man would wear, and she'd had no idea what he was covering up. Blind? Or had she been that unaware of her feelings for him? Went to show this love thing was new, not something that had been lurking in the back of her head.

'If we're going to have breakfast and visit the hospital we need to get a shake along, Ellie.' He wrapped a towel around his waist.

'Sure,' she repeated, still drinking in the sight of toned muscles and long, strong limbs. How could she have missed those? 'See you in thirty,' she muttered through a salivating mouth.

'Make that twenty. We don't want to miss the flight back to Vientiane. Who knows when we'd get another one? We were lucky getting this one.'

And tomorrow she was heading to Australia. Tossing back the sheet, she leaped up, ignoring the protest from her hip. Funny how that hadn't been a problem while making love with Luca. 'Twenty it is.' An exciting thought snagged her, Miss the flight and have more time in bed with Luca. But looking at his face showed that wasn't going to happen.

Slamming the bathroom door shut, she jerked the taps on and stepped under the cold water. Gasping, she crossed her arms over her breasts and gritted her teeth until the water warmed up. She tried to put aside thoughts of Luca and her new-found love and concentrate on the mundane, like getting clean, dressed, her make-up on and the few items she'd brought here back in her bag. Forget everything else for now. There were many hours in the air when she'd have nothing else to do but think. Or sleep if Luca got those sleeping pills for her.

According to the American doctor at the local hospital their van driver had regained consciousness but he wouldn't be going anywhere in a hurry. Both femurs were broken from where he'd impacted with the dashboard, and ribs had been fractured, presumably by the steering wheel as he was thrown forward.

'What happens?' Luca asked. 'Does he stay in hospital until he's back on his feet? Or will he be sent home within a day or two?'

'I'll keep him here as long as possible, but—' the man shrugged '—it won't be nearly long enough.'

'I'd like to help out financially,' Luca said quietly. 'How do I go about that?'

As Ellie listened to Luca and the other doctor discussing how to give the man's family money to see them through the next few weeks she looked around at the basic hospital emergency room. Nothing like what she'd trained in: not a lot of equipment or any up-to-date beds. There was little privacy for the patients, and families sat on the floor by their loved ones. Yet everyone seemed grateful for any attention they received. Also not like home where some patients and their families felt no compunction over telling medical staff what they expected of them.

'Right, let's go. That plane won't wait.'

That plane was delayed for nearly an hour. Sitting on a cold, hard seat, Ellie watched Luca pace up and down the departure lounge. It was as if he was busting to get back to the clinic. He sure as hell didn't have anything to say to her. He'd gone from caring, loving and sexy to cool, focused and resolute. She'd been cut off.

Beside her a baby kicked her tiny legs and made gurgling noises. Ellie turned her attention to the cutest little girl she'd ever seen and made cooing sounds. Swathed in pink clothes and blanket, the baby had to be sweltering but Mum seemed unperturbed.

'She's gorgeous,' Ellie said.

While it was obvious the mother didn't understand the words she'd picked up on Ellie's tone and smiled broadly. Nodding her head, she spoke rapidly in a language Ellie hadn't heard before. Not Laotian, for sure.

'Can I?' Ellie held her hands out, fully expecting to be rebuffed.

But the woman happily handed her precious child over, adjusting the blanket around the baby's face when Ellie settled her in her arms.

More kicks and gurgles came her way from the warm little bundle. 'What's her name?' she asked without thinking.

The mum stared at her, a question in her big brown eyes.

Ellie tapped her own chest. 'Ellie.' Then she lightly touched the baby's arm. 'Name?'

The woman said, 'Ellee?' Or something that vaguely sounded like her name. Then she tapped her chest and said, 'Sui.' Nodding at the baby, she added, 'Bubba.'

Bubba as in baby, or was that her name? Something in

a foreign language that Ellie couldn't decipher? 'Bubba.' She copied the mother and grinned down at the baby.

What would it feel like to be holding her own baby like this? Her heart slowed, squeezed gently. It would be wonderful, precious. And not something that was about to happen in the foreseeable future. She didn't seem to do so well choosing the men she fell in love with. One hadn't wanted a family with her despite reassuring her in the beginning he did, and Luca didn't want a relationship with her at all, when he'd be brilliant as a dad. He didn't want a family of his own at all. Maybe she should abandon any hope for a husband and her own children. That could save a lot of heartbreak in the future. Except her heart had begun to ache for those things. With Luca.

The PA system announced their flight was ready for boarding. Ellie looked around for Luca. She stilled as she found those intense grey eyes fixed on her, flicking between her and the baby. What? Had she done something wrong? Was it not the done thing to hold another woman's baby for a few minutes? To enjoy feeling the tiny girl squirming and kicking? Whatever Luca thought, it had been a magical moment she was glad she'd taken.

Another look at Luca and she saw it—the longing fighting to get out. Luca wanted children. She'd swear it. But as she locked her gaze on his he shut her out. The blinkers were back in place and he was giving nothing away. Instead, he tipped his head in the direction of the door leading out onto the tarmac and mouthed, 'Ready?'

Handing Bubba back to her mother, Ellie said, 'Thank you for letting me hold her.' Then she put her hands, palms together, in front of her chest, nodded and said, 'Goodbye.'

The woman rewarded her with a huge smile.

A smile that Ellie wore in her heart on the hour's flight back to Vientiane. Luca might be withdrawing but she wouldn't let that dampen the feelings holding that baby had evoked. No way.

If only Luca would admit to feeling the same. About babies. About her and him.

Luca knew he was behaving badly but he didn't know how else to keep Ellie at arm's length. He was afraid that if he let her close he'd haul her into his arms and never let her leave his side.

That night in Luang Prabang should never have happened, yet he couldn't find it in himself to wish it hadn't. Making love to Ellie had been off the wall. Like nothing he'd ever experienced before. That sense of finding himself had increased when they'd gone to bed for their second intimate connection.

With Ellie he thought he probably could face his demons and even keep them at bay. But reality sucked. Beneath the surface lurked those genes he'd inherited from his father and his mother's father. More than ever he did not want to hurt anyone when that person could be Ellie. She'd had her share of pain. She didn't need him giving her a relapse. Which was why when they'd finally got back to Vientiane yesterday he'd made himself busy at the hospital until long after Ellie had headed to her room for the night.

'You can smile.' Ellie leaned against his arm. 'Everyone else is.'

Aaron and Louise were having fun, drinking copious quantities of wine and cracking mediocre jokes. They were at a restaurant and bar, enjoying the evening despite the fact they were losing Ellie in a few hours. 'Seeing

Ellie off in style' was how Louise had put it on the way into town nearly two hours earlier.

It was the nature of the clinic, people coming and going with monotonous regularity. Not many stayed for a year like him, while Louise and Aaron set the record for how long they'd been here.

'I guess our misadventure has caught up with me,' Luca murmured as his nostrils filled with that particular scent he now recognised as Ellie's. Floral without being too sweet, reminding him of the spring air back home. Reminding him of what he could not have.

'Great,' Ellie snapped, tipping her head away from him.

Hiding? Then he thought about what he'd said and shook his head. 'That wasn't a criticism of you or us or how the night unfolded. I am tired, but, more than that, I'm trying to deal with having found my best friend only to be losing her again.'

'Come on, you two. Let's all dance together one last time.' Aaron stood up and reached for Ellie's hand, but Louise took one look at Ellie and then him and dragged Aaron away, leaving them to this conversation that sucked and had no possible outcome that would please either of them.

'You haven't lost me,' Ellie argued, now back to facing him. 'We've changed the nature of our relationship but we're not breaking up.' Was that hope in her eyes?

'I've lost my friend,' he reiterated. He was being cruel to be kind. He couldn't give her anything but friendship and she appeared to want more. Lots more.

The colour drained from her cheeks as she gasped. Hurt glittered out at him from those eyes that followed him into sleep every night. 'No. You can't do that to me.'

I can't save your heart? Give me a break here. I'm thinking of you, looking out for you. 'Ellie, go home and start that new job, find an apartment or a house to make yours, give yourself time to get over your marriage and then start dating again. One mistake doesn't mean you can't find happiness again.' *Only, it won't be with me.*

Ellie lifted her glass, drained it of water and banged it back on the table. 'I don't want to lose anyone else. I just got you back.'

'We made a mistake.' At least he'd had the good sense not to realise that until after he'd learned what it was like to make love with Ellie. He'd never forget, even if he was now spoiled forever.

'I'll tell you what a mistake is.' She held one finger up in front of him. 'Marrying a man I believed loved me enough to want to be there when I got old and grey and used a walking stick.' A second finger went up. 'Trusting Caitlin not to sleep with my husband.'

Shock stunned him. 'Your sister slept with Freddy?' He'd always believed the worst of Baldwin, but this? Luca couldn't get his head around the idea of the guy going with his wife's sister. That went way beyond bad. No wonder there was always wariness and despair lurking in Ellie's eyes. She and her sister had been close.

Ellie hadn't finished. A third finger rose, and her whole hand shook. 'Freddy loves Caitlin. Caitlin loves Freddy. They want to get married as soon as the divorce goes through.'

Luca wrapped both his hands around the one wavering in front of his face. 'El, don't torture yourself. They're the bad guys here, not you.' How did she get up every morning? When did she plaster her smiles on? Seconds before bumping into the kids waiting for her to appear outside her room at the clinic? Who did she trust these days?

Him. It struck him with blinding certainty. Ellie trusted him. *Wrong, girl, absolutely wrong.* Which was why he was fighting the churning need to take her in his arms and kiss her better, never to let her go again. To forget everything he'd been trying to tell himself moments earlier.

'I need a friend, Luca. You.' She swallowed. 'But there's more to what I'm feeling. I've always loved you as a friend.'

Don't say it. Don't. Please. It was going to hurt them both, and then he'd hurt her some more. But he couldn't look away, couldn't find the right words—if they existed—to stop her from laying out everything between them.

'My feelings for you aren't like they used to be, and yesterday kind of underlined that. Making love with you was beautiful.' She paused, staring into his eyes. Searching for what? Waiting for what? Finally, on a long, sad sigh, she continued, 'You know what I'm afraid of, Luca? That for me this is rebound love, and that I'll wake up one day and wish my friend back and my lover gone. The pain would be enormous, but I'm prepared to risk it. Because I believe you—we—are worth it. Because I'm not so sure that this isn't the real deal and what I felt for Freddy was the lesser.' Her head dropped. 'Which doesn't put me in a good light at all.'

'We all make mistakes.' Though not always as big as what this sounded like—on both sides of the marriage. 'You've got to learn to let go, El, drop all that hurt caused by Freddy and Caitlin, and then you'll see our relationship for what it is. Friendship. Nothing more. Or less.'

'You make it sound so easy.' Acid burned in her words; pain flattened her mouth.

Luca stood up, pulling Ellie up with him. He needed fresh air, to walk, to stare at the stars. To explain to El that she was so wrong about them, had got everything completely back to front. Because of what Freddy and Caitlin had done she was searching for someone to make her feel better. Sounding more and more as if her rebound theory was correct. 'Come for a walk.'

'There's not a lot of time before I have to head to the airport.' Suddenly she sounded reluctant, as if she knew she'd gone too far.

'This won't take long.' At least it wouldn't if he could get the words out. He was afraid. Because the moment he said what had to be said he'd lose Ellie again, this time probably permanently. When he reached for her hand she stepped sideways and folded her arms as though she was cold and not avoiding him. But he knew different.

If he waited a while longer there'd be no time, and he owed her an explanation. Dread lined his stomach, making it heavy and tight. 'In Luang Prabang, that was glad-to-be-alive sex. We'd both had a huge shock, were grateful to get off that hillside in one piece, and naturally we celebrated in the most obvious way. It was great sex, the best I've ever had, but, Ellie, you must see that there's no future in it. We're friends, I care a lot for you, but nothing's changed. I still won't get married or have kids.' If he said it all fast enough it started to sound right. 'Those are the things you ultimately want in your life. Not yet. I get that it's far too soon. But I'm *never* going there.'

He was breathing fast, as if he'd run a marathon or something. His heart beat hard and erratically. As for what was going on in his head, the kaleidoscope of emotions and need mocking his words—he wasn't going there, couldn't go there. He'd hate to find he'd got this all wrong.

Ellie rounded on him, stabbed a finger at his chest. 'Aren't you going too far with your assertions that I want to marry you?'

He held his hands up. 'Just laying it all out right from the get-go. I come from a line of lousy commitment-phobes. I'm trying to save you here.'

'Pathetic.' Her hands banged onto her hips, and she winced. Must've hurt the bruised one. 'You're blaming the men in your life for your avoidance issues when deep down you want to love and be loved. You want a family of your own, but you're too damned afraid to reach out and try for that.'

'You don't know what you're talking about.'

'Really? Then, why have you only ever dated the kind of women that won't want the whole nine yards?' Ellie turned away, turned back, her face softening as she gazed at him. 'You've proved yourself time and time again, Luca. You did everything you could for your nephew. You haven't given up on him despite his mother kicking you out of his life. I've seen you with young patients, never letting them down, always ready to stay hours longer than required to make sure they're coping.'

'That's not the same.' Why couldn't she understand he wasn't doing this for the hell of it? That, yeah, he'd like to make happy families—with her, what was more—if only there was a spitting chance in hell of it working. 'Even Angelique proved we've got bad genes by doing to Johnny what Mum did to us—refusing to acknowledge his father.'

Ellie shook her head at him and began to walk back towards the restaurant. Her time was almost up and she had to get to the airport. Luca's heart was breaking. This time was different from when they last went their separate ways. Then she'd been going to Freddy, and he'd had Gaylene on his back. He'd always believed that one day they'd get back in touch. Tonight he knew this was the end for them. 'Ellie,' he called softly. 'I'm sorry.'

She had to have supersensitive hearing because she came back to him and placed her hands gently on his cheeks. 'So am I, Luca. So am I. Do me one favour? Let go of some of that control you hold over your emotions. Start taking some risks with your heart. Stop blaming everyone else.' Reaching up on her toes, she kissed him, not with the passion of yesterday, not lightly as she used to as a friend, but as a woman who loved him and knew she'd lost him before they'd even started.

CHAPTER ELEVEN

ELLIE STARED AROUND the apartment she'd been sharing with Renee since the day she'd moved out of her marital home. 'I'm going to miss this, you, even Wellington,' she told Renee. 'But not the hospital.' Though now, after Luca, it almost seemed easier to stay here in the same city as her ex and Caitlin. At least here she had Renee and a handful of casual friends she enjoyed evenings with at five-star restaurants or going to shows.

She had this awful feeling that wherever she went her heart was going to take time to put all the pieces back together. All she could hope for was that some day way ahead she'd stop feeling this debilitating pain. Hell, she'd thought Freddy and Caitlin had hurt her. She'd had no idea.

Renee gave her a tired smile. Three gruelling nights with an extremely ill two-year-old requiring two emergency operations had done that to her. 'You can change your mind any time you like. Save me the hassle of finding another roomie.'

It was tempting. Running away didn't come naturally. 'I've signed a contract.'

'Six months isn't exactly long-term.' Renee never minded firing the shots directly at her target, which was why Ellie liked her so much. No bull dust. 'I'll keep your room for you that long.'

'Stop it. I might do a Luca next and go overseas, though not to Asia.' Australia or the UK appealed more at the moment.

'I still can't get my head around Luca ditching his super career and going over there for a year. Back when we were all sharing that house he drove the rest of us bonkers with his plans for running the biggest and greatest A and E department in the country.'

'That Luca's gone. Or missing in dispatches at the moment.' Whether he'd ever return to those goals she had no idea. 'He's not easy in his new skin, but I now wonder how comfortable he was in his old one.'

'Backstory. I wonder what his is. He never talked about his family, did he? Even when we'd been on the turps and talking a load of nonsense about ourselves.' Renee looked pensive. 'Does that mean there are some nasty skeletons in his cupboard?'

'Luca definitely thinks so. Certainly lets them rule how he lives his life.' Anger rose suddenly, unexpectedly, nearly choking Ellie. He let his unknown father dominate him. He'd pushed her away because of a man he hadn't met. *Thanks a bundle, Luca.* He didn't deserve her. Yeah, way to go. Her anger deflated as quickly as it had come, replaced by sadness—and despair. 'He does have issues, but until he decides to talk them through they're not going anywhere.'

'And you? You've come home broken-hearted.' Renee handed her a mug of milky coffee even though she hadn't asked for one. 'Are you going to be okay?'

'I'm an old hand at this. At least in Auckland I won't have to put up with knowing nods and snide remarks about my model sister and how awful it must be trying to keep up with her fashion sense and stunning figure.' Ouch. *More than bitter, Ellie.*

Renee growled, 'Stop it. It's over now.' She was repeating Luca's words. 'Even if you stayed on in Wellington I think you'd find no one cares anymore. In fact I've lost count of the number of people asking me how you're getting on and when you're coming back.'

'So they can talk about me again.'

'Ellie, give it a rest. I thought you were moving on from all this, then you return from Laos all in a pickle again. If Luca's upset you, that's one thing, but to carry on about Freddy and Caitlin still is another. It's been nearly a year. Don't you think it's time to accept they are serious about their relationship? Even if they did go about it all wrong and hurt you so badly.'

'There would never have been a right way to go about it,' she snapped, and banged her mug down. Time to throw her bags in her car and get out of here. It was a long drive to Auckland, and she intended on dropping in on her parents first.

'So you'd rather have continued being married to a man who was no longer in love with you just so you could feel righteous. What about your feelings for Luca? Are you going to walk away from them? Not fight for him, show him how much you love him?'

Ellie's mouth fell open. What? 'Have you gone crazy?'

'Probably.' Renee's stance softened and she pushed the mug of untouched coffee back towards Ellie. 'But you know me, never one to keep my mouth zipped.'

'I thought I liked that about you.'

'Changed your mind?' Renee smiled. 'When was the last time you saw Caitlin? Talked to her?'

Months ago when she'd been in a shop trying on leather jackets Caitlin had strolled in with a friend to look through the racks of clothes on sale. Ellie had tugged out of the jacket she'd been admiring in the full-length mirror, left it on the counter and stormed outside, ignoring Caitlin's pleas to stop and talk. 'The last time I said a word to her was January. When I demanded she get out of my bed, out of my house and away from my husband.' That had been the day she'd learned that the house no longer appealed to her and her husband wasn't really hers in anything but name. She'd ditched the name by the end of the day.

'Go see her.'

Ellie gasped. 'Next you'll be telling me to forgive her.'

Renee shrugged. 'If that's what it takes.'

'To do what?' This conversation was getting out of hand, but she couldn't help herself wanting to know where her friend was headed with it.

'What happened with Luca?' Renee asked.

'He sent me packing, said we had no future together.'

'And you came away. Didn't fight for him. Oh, Ellie, you need to sort your stuff out. Starting with Caitlin and Freddy.'

Ellie couldn't get Renee's words out of her head as she drove north. It hadn't helped that Mum and Dad had asked her to give her sister a call sometime. Everyone made her feel as if she were the guilty party. That she'd gone off and had an affair behind her husband's back with someone close to him instead of how it had really gone down.

You need to sort your stuff out. Renee might be back there in Wellington but her damned criticisms were in the car, going to Auckland with her.

Luca had told her to drop the ball of pain directing her life. *It's not pain.* She slapped the steering wheel with her palm. *It's anger.*

Actually it was red-hot, belly-tightening rage. The people she loved most in the world hurt her. Freddy. Caitlin. And now Luca. They did it so effortlessly. They picked her up, then tossed her aside as they chose.

Only one reason for that. She let them.

She needed windscreen wipers for her eyes. The road ahead was a blur. Lifting her foot from the accelerator, she aimed for the side of the road and parked on a narrow grass verge.

Every time she had pangs of longing to see her sister, to talk with her, she turned them into a ball of hate and hurt, put the blame squarely on Caitlin. Shoved the past aside: the nights when they'd sat in bed together talking about the guys they'd dated, the drones they'd dumped, the bullies at school or the teachers they'd hated. The clothes they'd shared—mostly Caitlin's because she had such great style, with the added bonus of being in on bargains at the right places because of her modelling career.

The tears became a torrent. 'Do you miss me, Caitlin? Like I miss you? What did I do wrong that you had to fall in love with my husband?'

Tap, tap. Ellie looked up to find a traffic cop standing beside her door. Flicking the ignition one notch, she pressed the button to open her window. 'Yes, Officer?'

'Is there a problem, ma'am?'

Quite a few actually. 'No. Am I parked illegally?'

'No, but it's not the safest place to pull over if you

didn't have to.' The woman was staring at her, no doubt taking in her tear-stained scarlet cheeks. Her mascara was probably everywhere but on her lashes by now.

Ellie stared around, saw she had stopped only metres from a sharp corner. 'I was in a hurry to stop, I wasn't thinking clearly.' Would the cop stop her from driving on, or hurry her away from here?

'Can I see your licence?' When Ellie widened her eyes the cop explained, 'Routine. I have to ask every time I stop a driver.'

Ellie handed the licence over. While she waited for the cop to go check her details on the car's computer she blew her nose, finger combed her messy hair and tried to wipe away the black smudges of mascara staining her upper cheeks.

'Thank you, Doctor.' The licence appeared through the window.

'That was quick,' Ellie commented.

'I've just had a call. There's been an accident two kilometres further up this road. Truck versus car. An ambulance has been called but it will take a long while to arrive. Could you help in the meantime? I'll take you with me.' Her thumb jerked in the direction of the blue-and-yellow-striped car with the lights still flashing.

'Of course.' Ellie was already closing the window and grabbing her handbag to hide in the boot. Vehicular accidents were the thing at the moment—for her at least.

The speedy trip had Ellie's heart racing and her mouth smiling. 'I should've been a traffic cop.'

Rose—she'd given her name as they set out on this crazy ride—laughed. 'I'm not supposed to admit this, but I love the high-speed moments.' Then her smile switched off. 'Until I get to the accident and have to see all that gore. I couldn't do your job for all the money in the world.'

'So we're both doing what we enjoy, though I still hate the sight of mangled bodies. Usually I get them when they've been straightened out on a stretcher, not shoved awkwardly into a car well or around a steering wheel.'

Rose weaved around the stationary traffic already forming a long queue. 'Look at that. This isn't going to be pretty.'

Ellie had already taken in the car squashed under the front of a stock truck. 'How can anyone survive that?' she asked as she pushed out of the car. 'The car roof is flattened down on top of the occupants.'

Making her way directly to the accident site, she looked around to see if anyone had been pulled from the wreckage, saw only a brawny man standing with another traffic cop answering questions and rubbing his arms continuously.

'Hey, you can't go there,' someone called out.

'I'm a doctor.'

'She's with me,' Rose added from directly behind her.

'You don't have to come any closer,' Ellie told her. 'You go do the traffic thing and I'll see what I can do for the driver of this car.'

Two men stood up from the driver's side, allowing her access. 'We've found two men in the front. No one in the back,' one of them told her.

The driver's head was tipped back at an odd angle and his eyes were wide-open. Not good. Ellie felt sure he was deceased but she went through the motions in case. The carotid vein had no pulse. Nor was there any at his wrist. Leaning close, she listened for any sound of breathing.

Nothing. Gently closing his eyelids, she looked across to the other seat at a young man also not moving.

Then his lip quivered. Just the smallest of movements, but movement nonetheless. Thankful she'd seen it, Ellie reached over to find his carotid and sighed with relief when she felt the thready beat of his pulse. How long that would last considering how much blood there was seeping from under his shoulder was a moot point. 'This man's alive,' she called as she gently probed his chest to ascertain if his ribs were broken. A punctured lung would not help his chances of survival. Nothing to indicate a rib forced into the lung cavity, but she'd go warily as only an X-ray would confirm that. 'Can we get his door open?'

'We've tried but it's stuck,' she was told.

'Then, we need to move this man out so I can get to his passenger.' Standing up, she eyeballed the two men who'd been here when she'd arrived. 'He's gone, I'm afraid, so this won't be pleasant for either of you, but the other man needs help. Fast.'

'There's a tarpaulin on the truck we can wrap him in,' a policeman said. 'Let's get this guy out of here so you can work some magic.'

Magic. She hoped her imaginary urn was full of that, because it really looked as if the passenger was going to need it all and then some. She said, 'Rose mentioned an ambulance was on its way but this man needs to get to hospital fast.'

'I told them back at base to get the rescue helicopter out here, but it still takes time for the crew to scramble and get airborne.'

'Yes, but at least they'll get him to where he needs to be faster than if he goes by road.'

'Exactly.'

Ellie steadied herself. This was so different from the accident in Laos where everyone had relied on the help of passers-by. There this man wouldn't have had a chance; here he might. 'I don't want to shift him out of that space without a neck brace and a backboard. We really need the car opened up.'

'That's our cue.' A large man dressed in a fireman's uniform stood beside the car, holding a set of Jaws of Life in one hand. 'We've got a first-aid bag with your brace. And a board.'

'Our man's chances have just gone up a notch.' Ellie wished the words back the moment they left her mouth. Talk about tempting fate. She crawled inside the mangled wreck and tried not to listen to the screeching metal as it was slowly and carefully removed by the firemen, and instead concentrated on finding the source of all that blood.

One of the firemen leaned in from the new gap in the car's exterior. 'Tell me what you require from the kit and I'll hand it through.'

Once again she was doing the emergency medicine she'd trained for in very different circumstances from what she was used to. Her admiration for ambulance crews and firemen rose higher than ever.

After an interminable time when Ellie despaired of that flying machine ever arriving it was suddenly all over. She stood with hands on her waist watching the helicopter lift off the road with her patient. 'That's that, then.'

Beside her, Rose shook her head. 'Now the fun really starts. We've got to get this lot moving again.' She nodded towards the traffic, many with their motors already running. 'I wonder how far out the coroner's vehicle is. The sooner we get that other man taken away, the sooner we can investigate the scene and open the road completely.'

Sadness rolled through Ellie. A man had died here today because, according to the truck driver, he'd come round the corner halfway across the median line. Because of that there were going to be people whose lives would never be the same again. People that the police had yet to go and break the sad news to. 'It's so heart-breaking.' The speed at which lives could be taken, or others altered, was shocking. Everyone should hug their loved ones every day.

'I'll get someone to take you back to your car,' Rose said.

Ellie looked around, saw the impatient drivers desperate to get going, the firemen pulling what remained of the car free of the truck, the police working hard to sort everything out, and felt humble. 'You know what? I'll walk. It was only a couple of kilometres.'

'What if that had been Luca?' Ellie asked herself as she strode along the grass verge. They'd argued and were in disagreement over where their relationship should go from here on in, but he was fit and healthy back in Laos. She could talk to him just by picking up her phone. She could even hop on a flight and be able to see him, touch him, in less than twenty-four hours. She could tell him she loved him. But the family and friends of that young man had lost those opportunities forever.

Why she was thinking like this now, today, she had no idea. It wasn't as though death was new to her. She'd seen it in the department far too often. Probably the fact that she was already feeling despondent over Luca had made this worse. He'd been the first face to pop into her mind when she'd seen that crash site.

Her phone vibrated in her back pocket. It was her mother texting.

Are you safe? Caitlin's worried, says there's been a fatal accident near Levin.

Ellie pressed the phone icon. 'Hey, Mum, I'm fine. Got caught up in the traffic jam but should be on my way any moment.' Not a lie, just stretching the truth. She didn't want to say she'd been attending to the victims, didn't want to hear her mother's questions.

Her car was around the next corner.

'Mum, I've got to get going. I'll call you when I get to Auckland if it's not too late.' Which it probably would be now. She might have to look at other options. 'Love you.'

Flicking her automatic key lock, she slipped into her car. The last thing she felt like was driving for the next eight hours. A shower would be good. She could stop halfway at Taupo, hole up in a motel for the night.

She tapped her phone. Caitlin had told Mum. Caitlin. Should she let it all go? Forgive Caitlin? No way. How could she do that? The betrayal had been huge.

But so was the void in her heart. Damn it, but she missed her sister. Caitlin had told Mum she was worried about her today.

Another worrying thought struck Ellie. Was her anger and grief over her failed marriage going to hold her back from achieving more with her career, with finding love again?

You love Luca.

Yeah, she did, but could she trust herself with that

love? There was that rebound theory spinning around her skull. What if she took a chance and ended up flat on her backside again in a few months' time?

That particular risk was always there. Look at her and Freddy. She'd believed that was forever. Big mistake. Or bad judgement? Or— Drawing air into her lungs, Ellie slowly let the disturbing idea enter her mind. Had she not loved Freddy as much as she'd believed? Look how soon she'd fallen for Luca. Less than a year since her world had imploded and she was in love with him. She'd been quick to believe Freddy hadn't loved her as fervently as he'd claimed in the beginning. But what if she hadn't loved Freddy as much as she was capable of? As much as she now loved Luca?

Have I always been a little bit in love with him? So what if I have? Neither of us recognised it, so nothing was lost.

Except she'd made the mistake of marrying Freddy.

Her husband—the man her sister had fallen in love with and wanted to wed as soon as it was legally possible, and whom until now Ellie had been determined to hate for that.

Ellie turned the key so that she could lower the window and let in fresh air. She wasn't ready to start driving.

Luca had hurt her with his quick denial of their relationship. He wasn't prepared to give a little on his stance, wasn't ready to take a chance with her.

Yeah, well, she hadn't been rushing in to hug her sister and say she understood. Because she didn't understand how someone that close could fall for her husband. But— Always a damned but. Caitlin did love Freddy. She got that. Had heard her parents talk about it, had learned that Caitlin and Freddy had moved in together months ago and were as happy as sparrows in a puddle.

A shiver rocked Ellie. The skin on her forearms lifted in bumps. Was she stuck in a holding pattern? Unable to forgive and move forward, unwilling to let it all go and take control of her life again? As if she was afraid of something. Hard to believe that.

But she wasn't ready for Luca, for sure. She needed to sort herself out and get back on track before she could expect him to become a part of her life. He'd been right to tell her to go home, away from him. She was not ready. She had a lot to do first—starting now.

Ellie pulled on the handbrake and let the engine idle. Staring up at the small house on the side of the hill in central Wellington, she felt her heart almost throttling her. Her hands gripped the steering wheel so tight her knuckles were white.

Could she do this?

She had to.

It was time, way past time, really.

This was the first step of her recovery.

Still she sat staring beyond her car at the quiet suburban street. Nothing like she'd ever have believed Caitlin would choose to live in. Her sister had been about fancy apartments and patios, not overgrown lawns and tumbledown houses that had been built in the 1930s.

Move your butt.

Ellie sighed. Yep, she was procrastinating because that was way easier than facing up to Caitlin. But until she did she wasn't going anywhere with her life.

Shoving her door wide, Ellie clambered out quickly, not allowing herself a change of mind. The concrete steps leading up to the front door were uneven and crumbling at the edges. The grass hadn't seen a lawnmower in months. So unlike either of the two people living in this house. Trouble in paradise? She hoped not. Sincerely hoped not.

Have I done this all wrong? Should she have had it out with them way back at the beginning?

Too late. All she could do was work on moving ahead. Who knew what was out there for her? But until she settled the past she had this strong feeling that she wouldn't be finding out.

The door swung open as she raised her knuckles to knock. 'Ellie? Really?'

Ellie's heart rolled as she stared at her sister. Caitlin looked the same, yet different. More grown up. Major life crises did that to a person. 'Can I come in?' She knew there was reluctance in her voice, felt that the moment she stepped over the threshold she'd have conceded something—but that was why she was here. To start forgiving, start getting her family back, start accepting that she and Freddy had made a mistake, that they hadn't been right for each other.

Caitlin stepped back, pulling the door wide. Tears streamed down her face while hope and caution warred in her eyes. 'You were on your way to Auckland,' she finally said in a strangled voice so unlike her usually vibrant, cheeky tone.

'I'm making a detour.' Ellie ran her tongue over her suddenly dry lips, tried to still her rolling stomach that felt as if it was about to toss her breakfast. What was she doing here? This was way too hard. She hadn't forgiven anyone. *But you want to. You want your sister back.*

Caitlin turned away abruptly, almost ran down the hall towards the kitchen. 'I'll put the coffee on.'

Ellie's feet were rooted to the floor. Should she stay? Should she go? An image of the young man she'd declared deceased snapped on in her mind. Were there people out there he hadn't apologised to for something? Had he told his girlfriend or wife or kids this morning that he loved them?

She moved forward, one shaky step at a time, to the door of the kitchen. 'I've missed you.'

That wasn't what she'd meant to say at all. She'd been going to demand an explanation for why she hadn't been told about the affair. But now that she'd uttered the words her whole body started to let go the tightness that had been there since January.

The bag in Caitlin's fingers hit the floor, spraying coffee beans in every direction. Then Caitlin was leaping at her, wrapping her arms around her, crying, 'Ellie, I'm so sorry. I didn't mean to hurt you. I love you. I've missed you every day since.' Her tears soaked into Ellie's blouse as she clung to her.

Ellie couldn't stop her own tears from streaming down her face. But nor could she find any words: her throat was blocked and her brain on strike. She so wanted to forgive Caitlin, but to verbalise that didn't come easily. Didn't come at all. Finally she lifted her head and dropped her arms to her sides. 'I'll see you on Christmas Day.'

Then she left. And started her journey all over again, this time with her heart feeling a little lighter.

Slipping a CD into the car stereo, she even hummed as she drove out of the city and along the highway past the ocean—for the second time that day. Definitely stopping the night in Taupo now. Listening to The Exponents brought other memories crowding in—all of Luca. Luca dancing. Luca laughing. Being patient with the kids at the clinic. Kissing her, making love to her. Luca. She sighed with longing clogging her senses.

What would he say if he knew she'd been to see her sister? Now she'd been to see Caitlin, would he think better of her for it? Would he work at letting go some of his hang-ups now that she'd started on hers?

Nah, of course he wouldn't. He was determined never to change, never to take a risk.

'Well, Luca, that's all fine and dandy, but I've started to turn my life around, and you can do the same, even if it doesn't bring you back to me.' She sang the words almost in tune to the song blaring from the stereo. A sad song, she realised, just as a fresh bout of tears began splashing down her face.

She'd reached Levin again, and looked around for a place to park. Strong coffee was needed. And food to stop the shakes and settle these stupid crying bursts. What was wrong with her anyway? She'd started patching things up with Caitlin, which had to be good. She might want Luca but that wasn't going to happen any time soon, if at all, and no amount of bawling her eyes out would alter that. Blowing her nose hard, she scrunched up the tissue and stepped out of the car to head for the nearest café. 'Auckland, here I come. Life, here I come.'

CHAPTER TWELVE

LUCA TOOK OVER from Aaron, suturing the wound on the right leg of their latest bomb victim while the other man drew deep breaths of air. 'It never gets any easier, does it?'

'No,' growled Aaron. 'What I wouldn't like to do to those bastards that left the bombs lying around in the first place.'

'Come on, Aaron. We've had this discussion a dozen times. You know there's nothing to do about it except what you already do.' Louise's eyes were on their patient but her words were with her husband. 'You're getting yourself all wound up again.'

Luca concentrated on his work. He'd spent many hours lying awake at night thinking about what the Laotian people had to live with but understood there was nothing he could do to remove all those bombs. The suture needle clattered into the kidney dish and he straightened his back, feeling the aches from the continuous bending over. Doctoring was what he did, had spent years learning how to do, but he hoped he'd never see another damaged limb, never perform another amputation.

'Let's wrap this up,' Aaron said.

'Could go for a plate of sticky rice and peanut sauce right about now,' Luca replied as his stomach rumbled. Dinner had been hours ago, a meal they'd barely had a mouthful of before rushing into Theatre with this teen-aged boy.

Louise shook her head at him. 'Nothing puts you off your food, does it?'

'Not much.' Except Ellie. Since she'd left after giving him a speech on how she thought he should be living his life, he hadn't been as interested in food as usual. Nor in beer, sightseeing or playing cricket with the kids. It felt as if she'd taken the sun with her. Everything—or maybe only he—was gloomy. Downright depressing some days. He'd gone and fallen in love with her. Like really, deeply in love. The sort of love he'd always known he was capable of and determined not to have.

Let go some of that control, she'd railed at him. If only Ellie knew how much self-discipline he'd lost over the weeks since he'd first seen her with Louise on the day she arrived. Try as hard as he could, he wasn't getting it back. He wasn't able to push aside his love for her, no matter how it burned him to try. He did not want to love Ellie. It broke the rod he'd used for living his whole life. Snapped it clean in two. He still didn't want to love and yet now he did.

So all he had to do was ignore it, and hope that eventually he'd be able to manage getting through an hour at a time without thinking about Ellie, without wondering where she was and what she was doing. Wondering if she missed him half as much as he did her. Hoping for her sake she didn't, and pleading with the stars for his sake she did.

What a mess he'd become.

'Let's go into town for a beer and that rice you're hankering after,' Aaron said as they pulled off their scrubs. 'Louise will stay with the boy, and Jason's here if there's any change in his condition.'

Jason. The next doctor in a long line of short-term doctors. The guy was cool, eager to help and join in all the fun with the kids, was a better bowler of the cricket ball than Ellie had been—but he wasn't El. 'Good idea.' Anything to take his mind off her for a few minutes.

But so much for that theory. Aaron plonked two bottles on the counter in a bar they used occasionally on Sethathirath Road. 'Heard from Ellie lately?'

'No. You or Louise?'

'Got an email yesterday. She was heading to Auckland today. Guess she'll be there by now. How far is it from Wellington?'

'It'll take all day. Though with Ellie at the wheel you can cut an hour off the time.' Unless she'd quietened down recently. He wouldn't know. Didn't know a lot of things about the woman he loved, when he thought about it. Which was all the damned time.

'Bit of a speedster, is she?'

'She had this fire-engine-red Mustang that she got a kick out of taking for a spin. That thing went like a scalded cat, only with a lot more revs. It was her pride and joy, and her only real indulgence. Cost her a bundle in speeding tickets, though.' *Wonder what happened to it.*

Aaron was lifting one eyebrow in his direction.

'What?' he demanded.

'You're smiling for the first time since Ellie left.'

'Of course it's not the first time.' He raised his beer to his lips. He always smiled and laughed, didn't he?

Right now he felt relaxed and happy because of those memories. Yeah, but when was the last time he'd felt remotely like this?

Aaron shook his head at him. 'I must've been looking the other way.' Then he changed the subject. 'You made up your mind where you're going after Laos?'

While it was a different topic, it still brought Luca back to Ellie. Hopping a ride down to New Zealand was at the top of his list. Seeing Ellie would be the best thing to happen to him since she'd left. Then what? He'd have to leave again. They couldn't return to a platonic friendship after that mind-blowing night in Luang Prabang. Even he knew that. So staying on in Auckland, which was the only city he wanted to work in at home, was not an option. It might be a large city but Ellie would be there and he'd never be able to forget that, always be looking for her.

He told Aaron, 'I'm liking the look of Cambodia.' Sort of. Though returning to his career as an emergency specialist seemed to be teasing him more and more every day. 'Maybe Australia.' Closer to home and more in line with his career ideas.

'If you're thinking of Cambodia why not stay here for the next twelve months? Not a lot of difference, when it comes to working with the locals, if you think about it.' Aaron had tried to convince him of this on several occasions, and was now flagrantly ignoring the Australian component of his reply.

Luca's phone vibrated in his pocket. Pulling it out, he saw he had two texts. 'Noi says our boy's doing fine.'

Aaron grunted. 'I got that, too.'

Luca's mouth dried. Ellie had texted him hours ago.

He hadn't checked his phone after they'd finished in Theatre. Hadn't thought there'd be any messages.

Visited Caitlin today. Late leaving Wellington for Auckland, stopping over in Taupo. How's everyone at the clinic? Ellie. XXX

'Wow. Ellie visited her sister.' That took guts.

'What's so odd about that?' Aaron asked.

Damn, he hadn't meant to speak out loud. 'They've been estranged all year. Like, seriously.' But Ellie had gone to see her. Had taken the gauntlet he'd thrown down to get on with sorting out her life. Good on her.

What about the challenge she set you?

What about it?

Going to run with it? Or away from it?

'That's sad, but Ellie's obviously had a change of heart.' Aaron was watching him closely. Looking for what?

'They used to be very close.' It wouldn't be easy talking to anyone who'd had an affair with her husband, but Caitlin? She hadn't said how it had gone. They might've had an even bigger bust-up, but he didn't think she'd be telling him if that was the case. 'I don't know if the girls will ever get back what they had.'

'Christmas is only one week away. That's always a good time for families to be together.'

Ellie would hate spending the day on her own. Christmas had always been a big deal for her. 'What do we do here for Christmas? Get a tree and lots of presents for the kids?' They would this year, if he had anything to do with it.

'All of that and loads of food, though it's hard to find anything like what we're used to back home. You going to be here?'

'Why wouldn't I be?' The guy knew he had less than two months to run on his contract.

Aaron stared at something across the other side of the bar. 'Thought you might want to go spend it with Ellie.'

Luca spluttered the mouthful of beer he'd just taken. 'You what?'

An eloquent shrug came his way. 'Most men I know would do almost anything to be with the woman they love for Christmas.'

Luca wanted to deny it, wanted to shout at the top of his lungs that Aaron didn't have a clue what he was talking about. But he couldn't. *Because it was true.* Which didn't lessen the urge to hurl his bottle across the room and shout at somebody. Gritting his teeth, he held on to his sanity—just. Counted to ten, again and again. When he finally believed he could speak without spitting he said, 'That obvious, huh?'

'Neon.'

'Great.' So everyone knew what had taken him four weeks to work out. Or was that ten years? Had he always loved Ellie? That little gem didn't feel wrong. Or a shock. Maybe he had. Talk about a slow learner.

'What are you going to do about it?'

Any time you want to shut up, Aaron, I'm not going to stop you. 'Nothing.'

'Fair enough.'

Huh? What sort of answer was that? 'How long did you know Louise before you realised you loved her?'

'Minutes. It was as though she hit me over the head

or something. Instant, man.' A smile lit up Aaron's eyes. 'Never regretted it for a second. Not even when she burns my bacon.'

'True love,' Luca drawled. 'No challenges, then. No problems to get over before you got together permanently?'

'Ha. A ton of them. But we weren't going to be deterred by anything. Life's too short, as that accident you were in shows. What would you have felt if Ellie hadn't made it out of that van? Think you might've spent the rest of your life regretting not telling her how you feel?'

'I think you make a better doctor than a psychologist.'

Aaron picked up their empty bottles. 'Another?'

'Sure. Why not?' Luca picked up his phone and tapped the screen, reread El's text. Short and to the point. Why had she contacted him when they'd more or less agreed to go their separate ways when she'd left Vientiane? She'd have struggled to visit Caitlin, and it wasn't something she'd have done just to prove a point so she must just be keeping in touch, treating him like the close friend he'd insisted he was.

He'd been adamant they weren't getting together and she'd got the message, loud and clear. She'd even said how she wondered if this had been a rebound thing. Sex with a man she knew well and could trust to look out for her. Yet at the same time she knew he had his limitations and would never ask her to set up house with him.

Control, she called that. Told him to let it go. Hell, if he did who knew when he'd stop unravelling? Everything he'd struggled to gain would go down the drain. Right now he was out of plans for the next year or two; let go of that control Ellie despised so much and he would be lost forever.

Ellie didn't sound lost after seeing Caitlin.

He wasn't really thinking when he began tapping in a message.

How did it go with Caitlin? Did you talk?

The moment he sent the text he wanted it back. Getting involved wasn't his greatest idea. Before he knew it he'd be wanting to be there to help Ellie through the minefield that getting back onside with Caitlin entailed. How would El handle seeing her sister with her ex? Then he saw the time. She wasn't going to read it for hours yet. It was early morning back in NZ. He had a few hours to regret his move.

We hugged. I made a date for Christmas and left.

Got that wrong. Was she lying awake worrying about her sister?

Christmas is good. Family time. Why are you awake?

Might as well ask since he'd started this.

She came straight back: Missing you.

Right then Aaron slid a beer in front of him. Perfect timing. 'Thanks.' He closed the phone and slid it into his pocket. He had no reply to that text. Not one that he was prepared to make. That would mean laying his heart on the line.

Christmas was a week away, right? Luca stretched his legs to increase his pace as he strode along the path

winding beside the Mekong. Seven days, to be exact.
Then it would be over and life could go back to normal.

Except Christmas wasn't going to be normal for Ellie,
which meant the days afterwards wouldn't be, either.
Spending time with her family would be hard, and if
Baldwin was there, which he had to presume he would
be, then, hell, Ellie was in for a terrible day.

She needed support. But who from? He was here, and
fighting the urge to give in to go home for a few days.
He coughed. Time to start being really honest with himself. It was the need to see Ellie that he was fighting.
Acknowledging he loved her hadn't taken the edge off
that need. It had made him supercautious when answering any more of her many texts. El hadn't taken a back
step when he'd told her to go home and get on with her
life without him. Oh, no.

Pulling his phone from his pocket, he went through
the past three texts. His pace slowed as he reread the
challenge she kept waving in his face.

How are the kids? Say hi to them from me. Missing
them and you.

Of course every time he mentioned Ellie to the kids
he'd be bombarded with questions about where was she,
when was she coming back and could they all text her,
too—on his phone? Kids. He'd seen the hunger in her
eyes at Luang Prabang Airport as she'd held that baby;
the hunger that had wormed into him and made him
think about having children with Ellie. Him? Having
kids? El had said he was good with children, but how
far could he take that?

Won't know if I don't try. Suddenly that idea didn't

seem so impossible. With Ellie by his side he could conquer seemingly insurmountable problems. She was his rock, believed in him—knew him too well, which was grounds for a solid relationship. Wasn't it?

The next text.

How's your nephew? Missing you.

She knew damned well he didn't have any contact with his sister's kid. Did she think he'd suddenly start emailing the lad because she thought he should? Of course she did. She was challenging him to sort his life out. As she'd started to do with hers.

Then the text that had thrown him when he'd first read it.

Saw the house I'm moving into for six months. It's stunning and has me thinking about buying my own here in Auckland. Missing you.

Two decisions in one sentence. Buying a house spoke of putting down roots, and obviously she was happy to be back in Auckland. Far enough away from her family to avoid awkward get-togethers but close enough to see them occasionally if she felt so inclined.

Luca read that one again. Missing you. She used that at the end of every message. It hit him hard in the heart every single time. Stuffing his phone back in his pocket, he stared at the brown river pouring past in its timeless way. 'Hell, El, I'm missing you fit to bust. You'll never guess how much.'

Unless he told her. Could he do that? Find the courage to commit to her?

*I want to. More than anything I want to be with Ellie
Thompson for all the years to come.*

Which meant some sharp gear changes in the head.
Did he have the guts to do that? Ellie had shown courage by visiting Caitlin. Somehow he had to find the
same within himself.

His gaze cruised the rushing water again. Water that
came from the north, through countries, towns, com-
munities, the flow barely changing from one year to the
next. The river moved on, from yesterday to tomorrow,
returning to calm after floods and storms and wars,
making allowances for small changes in direction. Like
life.

Except his was lacking something, someone. Ellie. It
spooked him to think he might've always loved her but
had been too tied up in his determination to avoid commitment that he'd pushed his feelings so deep it was a
wonder they'd come to light. He could try just jumping
in—sort of a leap of confidence in himself and Ellie.
And if it backfired? That was where the courage would
come in. He'd have to start over, but was that such a bad
thing when the alternative might be to never experience
a wonderful relationship with the woman already sitting in his heart? He'd told Ellie to let go of what Caitlin and Freddy had done, to make some decisions for
herself about herself.

Why couldn't he do the same with Gaylene? She
was a shield. He stopped walking to stare up at the sky.
Hell. Had he been hiding behind her? Using what she'd
done to him as an excuse to stay away from getting hurt
again? Because she had hurt him—badly. He mightn't
have been head over heels in love with her but he'd been
willing to try. He'd wanted some say in their child's

life. Had been devastated when she'd terminated it with no regard to his feelings. Of course he'd been hurt and angry. But that was no reason to push Ellie away. None at all.

Another left-field thought dropped into his head. Why not follow El's example and get in touch with his sister? A friendly email with no demands, just 'hi, how are you, this is what I'm doing' stuff. If he didn't try he'd never get back the family he missed.

Ellie rolled out of bed and dropped her head in her hands. Christmas morning usually made her smile with excitement. But not this one. Her stomach was roiling, making her nauseous.

Today she had to face up to Caitlin and Freddy over Christmas lunch with Mum and Dad. Play happy families. Ugh. Why had she said she'd do this?

Because if she wanted to have a life with Luca she needed to move on. Luca. All very well for him to say she should sort herself out. What had he done about doing the same with his own life? Huh?

Fumbling on the bedside table, she found her phone and checked for messages. Nothing. Not a word from Luca for days. Guess that would teach her to keep telling him she missed him. But she'd only been truthful, even when knowing he wouldn't be comfortable with it. So much for thinking he might give in and accept she wasn't going to change her mind about loving him.

'Morning.' Renee strolled into the room looking rumpled and relaxed in her cotton PJs. 'Merry Christmas.'

Ellie jumped up and hugged her friend. 'Merry Christmas to you. Thanks for lending me the bed.' She'd flown in late last night and come straight here, having turned down her mother's plea to stay with them. There was only so much time she'd be able to face spending with her sister and ex. She might be making headway but she wasn't ready for full-on happy families yet.

'It's still got your name on it.' Renee laughed. 'I've got the coffee brewing or there's bubbles waiting to be opened.'

'Think I'll start the day with coffee. Need to keep my head straight until after Christmas lunch is over.'

'You know you can come back here to join my lot if it all gets too much for you today.' Renee hugged her back.

'You're a great friend.' Her other great friend seemed to have forgotten all about her, not even sending a Christmas message in reply to the one she'd sent after falling into bed last night. Ellie tugged her bag close and pulled out the sundress she'd planned on wearing today. 'I'll grab a shower first.'

Renee was already half out the door. 'Don't take too long. I want to give you my present.'

But when Ellie made it to the kitchen Renee was in no hurry to hand her anything except a steaming mug of coffee after quickly putting her phone aside.

Instead, Renee made a great fuss of opening the exquisitely wrapped box that contained the opal earrings and bracelet Ellie had bought for her.

'They're gorgeous.' Renee grinned, slipping the bracelet over her hand. 'Beautiful.' She slowly removed one earring from the silk cushion it rested on and slipped it through her earlobe. As she plucked the second one up the doorbell buzzed. 'Someone's early for breakfast. Get that for me, will you? I'm heading for the bathroom.' Renee disappeared so fast Ellie didn't have a chance to say a word.

The buzzer sounded again.

'I'm coming,' she muttered and swung the door wide. 'Merry— Luca.' She looked behind him but no one else was there. None of Renee's family. Only Luca. Her heart rate stuttered, then sped up. Luca was *here*? In Wellington?

'Merry Luca. That's novel.' He grinned at her.

'Are you? Merry, I mean?' *Are you Luca? Or just a figment of my imagination?*

'Merry ho-ho, yes. Merry boozy, no.' Uncertainty replaced that grin. 'Are you going to invite me in, El?'

She stepped back so quickly she banged up against the wall. 'Renee thought one of her—' No, she hadn't. She'd been dilly-dallying over coffee and her present, then suddenly, when the buzzer went, she'd headed for the shower. 'Renee knew you were coming, didn't she?'

Luca nodded. 'Yes. I rang her to find out where you were staying. I wanted to surprise you, El.'

'You've certainly done that.' She led him into the kitchen, all the time trying to get her heart rate and breathing under control, but it seemed impossible. Luca was here, not in Laos. With her and not the children. 'Why?'

'Why am I here?' His eyebrows rose and he reached for her hands as she nodded once. 'I'm going with you to your family Christmas lunch.'

Her head shot up. 'You're what?'

'I'm going to be there for you, with you, supporting you. I know it's not going to be easy being with Caitlin and Baldwin.'

She should've been relaxing, getting excited. She wasn't. 'You're being a good friend.'

Luca stepped closer, finally taking her hands in his. 'No, El, I'm your partner.'

'What do you mean?' Was she being thick? The sense of missing something important nagged her. 'My partner? As in lover, kids, house partner?' *Or 'sex when he was in town' partner?*

His smile was gentle and—dare she admit it?—full of love. He said, 'I'm done with being just your best friend. I want the whole shebang. With you.' His hands were warm, strong yet soft. Enticing her closer.

Even as she held back, a glimmer of hope eased through her. Had Luca come because he loved her? It sounded like it. 'You stopped answering my texts and emails.'

'I'm not good with words, especially not in messages. But I missed you so much it started driving me nuts. I had to come see you. Nothing could've kept me away any longer.'

'Have you decided what you're doing after Laos?' What did it matter? Why was she being so cautious?

'Moving to Auckland to be near you, or with you if you'll have me.'

She gasped. 'Luca? What are you really saying?' Pulling her hands free, she folded her arms across her chest. She did not want the distraction of him holding her while she absorbed whatever he was about to tell her.

'El—' he locked his eyes on hers '—I'm saying I love you. I've missed you since you told me to get a life. You are my life. I want to share everything with you. Starting with your Christmas Day.'

Now her heart was really pumping. 'Everything?' He couldn't mean that. He'd gone to great lengths to make her understand he didn't want the same things she did.

His hands were on her wrists, unfolding her arms.
Then he was holding her hands again, his thumbs caress-
ing her. 'You, the babies, the house and cats and dogs or
pet rabbits. The whole works.'

If Luca could say all that, then it was time she opened
her heart and laid everything out there for him, too. 'I
want all those things, too, with you. I love you so much
it hurts when you're not with me. These past two weeks
have been horrible.'

His arms went around her and he gently drew her
close. 'Tell me about it.'

'I have missed you.'

He chuckled. 'Yeah, I got those messages loud and
clear.'

'You didn't reply to them.'

'I was too afraid to. Once I told you I was missing
you I'd be committed to you, and I had to be sure. I've
done a lot of soul searching, but in the end I can't deny
how much I love you and want you. Loving you is easier
than not. I promise not to let you down.'

'Luca, I never thought you would. All that was in your
head, not mine.' She gave him a little shake.

'Good answer.' He gave a lopsided smile. 'Seriously,
thank you for believing in me and giving me the boot up
the backside I needed to see what has been in front of
me for a very long time. I've done something else, too.
I emailed Ange and she replied saying to drop by while
I'm here. As in visit her in Auckland, which is where
you're going after today, right?'

Ellie nodded. 'Yes.'

'Then, so am I. I've finally worked out I've loved
you for years. Then I had to tell you face to face. So
here I am.'

Ellie reached her arms around his neck and raised up to place her mouth on his. 'Shut up for a moment.' Then she kissed him.

His arms wrapped around her, his chest hard against her breasts, his mouth open to hers. Ellie slid her tongue between his lips, tasted her man and melted further against him. Luca was here. He'd always been in her heart, but he was here in her arms, kissing her as ardently as she did him. All her Christmases had come today. All of them.

'Merry Christmas, Ellie.' Renee's voice broke through her euphoria.

Peeling her mouth off Luca's, she turned in his arms to stare at her friend. 'Best present ever.'

'That's what I thought.' Renee had the cheek to wink. 'I'm popping the champagne. What I just saw requires celebrating.'

'I agree.' Ellie grinned, finally letting all the fear and hurt and need fly. Luca loved her. What more could a girl want?

As the three of them raised their glasses Renee said, 'To Ellie and Luca.' She drained her flute and put it down. 'I'd better go and get those croissants and bagels I ordered for breakfast. My family will start arriving shortly. See you.' She waved a hand over her shoulder as she headed for her front door. There she turned around and, looking very pleased with herself, she gave Ellie a big wink. 'One hour to yourselves. Merry Christmas, my friends.'

* * * * *

Unlimited access to all your favourite Mills & Boon romances!

Start your free trial now

We Love
Romance
with MILLS & BOON

Available at
weloveromance.com

JOIN THE
MILLS & BOON
BOOKCLUB

* **FREE** delivery direct to your door

* **EXCLUSIVE** offers every month

* **EXCITING** rewards programme

50% OF
YOUR FIRS
PARCEL

Join today at
Millsandboon.co.uk/Bookclub

MILLS & BOON
MEDICAL
Pulse-Racing Passion

Set your pulse racing with dedicated, delectable doctors in the high-pressure world of medicine, where emotions run high and passion, comfort and love are the best medicine.

t Medical stories published every month, find them all at:

millsandboon.co.uk

LET'S TALK
Romance

For exclusive extracts, competitions
and special offers, find us online:

☐ facebook.com/millsandboon
☐ @MillsandBoon
☐ @MillsandBoonUK

Get in touch on 01413 063232

For all the latest titles coming soon, visit
millsandboon.co.uk/nextmonth

MILLS & BOON
A ROMANCE FOR EVERY READER

- **FREE** delivery direct to your door

- **EXCLUSIVE** offers every month

- **SAVE** up to 25% on pre-paid subscriptions

SUBSCRIBE AND SAVE

millsandboon.co.uk/Subscribe

MILLS & BOON

THE HEART OF ROMANCE

A ROMANCE FOR EVERY READER

ODERN

Prepare to be swept off your feet by sophisticated, sexy and seductive heroes, in some of the world's most glamourous and romantic locations, where power and passion collide.

STORICAL

Escape with historical heroes from time gone by. Whether your passion is for wicked Regency Rakes, muscled Vikings or rugged Highlanders, awaken the romance of the past.

EDICAL

Set your pulse racing with dedicated, delectable doctors in the high-pressure world of medicine, where emotions run high and passion, comfort and love are the best medicine.

ue Love

Celebrate true love with tender stories of heartfelt romance, from the rush of falling in love to the joy a new baby can bring, and a focus on the emotional heart of a relationship.

Desire

Indulge in secrets and scandal, intense drama and plenty of sizzling hot action with powerful and passionate heroes who have it all: wealth, status, good looks…everything but the right woman.

EROES

Experience all the excitement of a gripping thriller, with an intense romance at its heart. Resourceful, true-to-life women and strong, fearless men face danger and desire - a killer combination!

To see which titles are coming soon, please visit

millsandboon.co.uk/nextmonth

MILLS & BOON
True Love
Romance from the Heart

Celebrate true love with tender stories of
heartfelt romance, from the rush of falling
in love to the joy a new baby can bring,
and a focus on the emotional
heart of a relationship.

Eight True Love stories published every month, find them

millsandboon.co.uk/TrueLove

MILLS & BOON

MODERN

Power and Passion

Prepare to be swept off your feet by
sophisticated, sexy and seductive heroes, in
some of the world's most glamourous and
romantic locations, where power and
passion collide.

t Modern stories published every month, find them all at:

millsandboon.co.uk/Modern